THE
GREAT SKY
AND THE
SILENCE

THE
GREAT SKY
AND THE
SILENCE

James S. Rand

McGRAW-HILL BOOK COMPANY

NEW YORK   ST. LOUIS   SAN FRANCISCO
DÜSSELDORF   MEXICO

1 2 3 4 5 6 7 8 9 B P B P 7 8 3 2 1 0 9 8

Library of Congress Cataloging in Publication Data

Rand, James S
The great sky and the silence.
I. Title.
PZ4.R186Gr3   [PR6068.A54]   823'.9'14   77-8341
ISBN 0-07-051175-6

This book was, and remains, for the late Mark Attenborough, a young man of great courage, strength, and loyalty, who covered many African miles when I was laid low—and who made the physical picture of *Robert Queen* easy.

—J. S. R.

Foreword

In reverse of the traditional disclaimer note, by which authors seek to protect themselves from shysters and extortion, only the names of the main characters in this book are fictional. "The Company of *Dukusa*" herein (and more than they) are squarely based on African truths of the period, and of subsequent years beyond the turn of the last century. They existed, and they did what they did!

Not, really, that that should occasion surprise or scepticism. For European overseas history in general, and its African chapters in particular, teems with men and events whose virtual overlooking passes understanding. Their names are legion: Coenraad de Buys, the Fynn brothers, John Cane, Eduardo Chiapinni, James Waugh *(Matyonja)*, Dai Leslie, Conrad Vermaak, Gerhardt Bruheim, Henry Tucker, Joao Albassini *(Jowawa)*, John Dunn *(Jantoni)*. All of them were self-made "kinglets" who won, then defended and exploited, their "kingdoms" by dint of their own strength, determination, and shrewdness.

Nor, incidentally, do these "stranger than fiction" cases of European men *and women* who grew to African fame, amongst Africans, lack ample recorded evidence in the archives.

And even today, of course, Africa is still a land of bloody treachery and genocide. As recently as September 1970, certainly, you could still buy a female slave for less than £3. At Burundi (East Africa), *"50,000 harmless peasants were massacred simply because they were Tutsi tribesmen . . ."—Daily Telegraph*, 31/5/72.

> *James S. Rand*
> *Kinsdale, County Cork, Eire*

N.B.: As in my previous novels, I prefer "Afrikander" to such contemporary forms as "Afrikaner" and "Africaner."

Contents

Book Two

Forever over never-ending grass
And have no home except the black felt tent
And the great plain and the great sky and the silence.
                              —Voortrekkers' Song

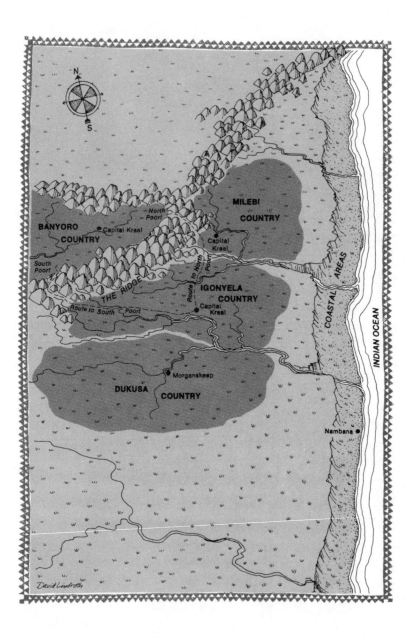

Book
ONE

Prelude to
an Indaba

He was a big man, some six feet four inches, in his middle forties. Around two hundred forty pounds. But none of his bulk ran to fat yet, nor was it likely to—because he still lived as actively as any of the *agter ryders,* white, black and colored, who served him. And the impression of strength he gave was real, not delusory as is often the case with men of great stature. His complexion was the color and grain of smoked leather, with well-formed rather than handsome features, and the kind of deeply cleft chin that suggests courage or obstinacy—qualities sometimes difficult to distinguish in the hindsight contemplation of events. He was a man of very mixed moods, which ranged from inexorable ruthlessness to boundless generosity. When he smiled or laughed a dimple puckered in each of his cheeks, giving him an air almost of boyishness. But this was deceptive. There was nothing boyish in this man. His name was Piet Haydyn de Morgan, not a conventional first name given the Welsh origins of his parents, though, like himself, they were Afrikanders born.

His African name, that by which he was known throughout Morgan country, was *Dukusa*—Great Elephant Hunter; this he had inherited, though in fact he himself had hunted the pachyderms extensively, and sometimes still did.

He was leaning on the rail of the tower that rose like a minaret from the *stoep* of *Morganskeep*. It was something he did every morning, a ritual of sorts, taking up this station at the rail of the tower. In the time of his forebears, the tower had been a vantage point of martial significance. The tower was one element in the compound known as *Morganskeep*, a stronghold built largely of stone and marble blasted from the nearby Malagena River gorge, where the first Morgan had chanced on a moderate lode of gold. It had been a long and prodigious labor, the making of *Morganskeep*, but there had been a reason for its grandeur beyond the achievement of a grandiose ambition. The place was virtually impregnable to the African tradition of burning.

Fronting the *stoep* and around the house, hibiscus, poinsettias, and bougainvillaea lent patches of color to the hard red murram of the compound, which itself was bounded by lopped white poplars laterally entwined. Within the broad area between the palisade and the stronghold's ramparts were set the cabins of the senior *ryders*, Morgan's lieutenants. Here too were the workshops and granaries. Front and back, beyond the walls of *Morganskeep*, ran a track hardened by generations of wagons and feet, which soon forked to the home kraals and to the shambas—the vegetable fields and the fruit orchards.

From time to time wagon trains trekked the long route to the coast carrying produce, hides, plant gums, and sometimes ivory—all indigenous profitable merchandise, in fact, except sugar cane. Cane demanded certain growing conditions, and this was one reason why Morgan intended, sooner or later, to secure the tract on the Malazi River, three or four days north—land well suited to the growing of sugar cane but which lay just beyond his own boundaries and just within Igonyela territory.

Morgan moved his telescope slowly across the great vista

that spread before him—until the lens finally rested on the clump of euphorbia trees that surrounded the *Kwankosinkulu*, the burial place of great Chiefs—where the first *Dukusa* lay. This daily ritual of his, of gazing out over his vast landhold, a "kingdom" that once had been a wilderness, somehow, indefinably, always helped him set into perspective whatever problems confronted him. And it also somehow reinforced his determination to hold his "kingdom" against all comers, black or white or colored, transient or political or capricious.

It was still early. Down in the compound a wandering peacock squawked discordantly, and far out across the tawny brooding panorama a soaring *korhaan* called faintly. Morgan lowered his glass and straightened up from the railing. He paused to light his first cheroot of the morning, then he started back down the stairs to eat and shave, before the business of the day, which would begin with the *Indaba*.

It would not be an important *Indaba*, but his lip curled with distaste at the thought of it. Certainly, he had no qualms at dealing out suitable punishment to the guilty, whether whipping by the *sjambok* or death by hanging. But these minor affairs of corrective trivia irked him, and they were time consuming. On the other hand Morgan would be interested to observe Robert Queen's reactions, because this would be Queen's first look at one. The *Indaba* raised the question of Morgan's one remaining doubt about Queen. Of Queen's physical prowess, experience, and skill, Morgan was now convinced. But whether the man quite understood the discipline essential to his calling was yet to be determined. It was in these judicial matters, the *Indaba*, that Morgan would have his proof. It was a proof about this relative newcomer to his group that Morgan needed—for in territorial stewardship a *ryder* in service of the *Dukusa* must often mete out swift and uncompromising retribution, a justice that was harsh as well as salutary.

5

Indaba

Morgan came through the open door onto the *stoep*. He bit off the end of a cheroot and spat the butt of it over the rail. He moved along to the cane chair and took his place among the six men already seated on the *stoep*. On Morgan's left sat Hans van Rieberk—sometimes called *Oupa*, Grandfather, though he was barely fifty, and at other times The Whip, because of his remarkable proficiency with the *sjambok* and the stock whip with which he could unerringly direct teams of up to sixteen spans of oxen. A dour, slow-spoken man embittered by experiences he had never forgotten, van Rieberk displayed a distinct indifference to women. Next to him sat Manoel Santoro. Thirty-five, the descendant of a *ryder*, Santoro was married to a colored woman and, additionally, kept three African "wives." He seemed an affable, carefree man, yet he was as deadly with the twelve-inch knife as were the best men with a Buntline Colt. Next to Santoro sat Andries Kolenbrander, thirty-three, a magnificent horseman in the Boer tradition, a big, ruddy, blond, powerful man of robust appetites and dusty manner. On Morgan's right sat Robert Queen, of English Afrikander extraction. The twenty-eight-year-old son of a hunter-trader and a schoolmistress, he possessed a

6

physique equal to that of the formidable Kolenbrander, and was taller. Queen had no wives as yet, not because he scorned or denied himself the pleasures of the flesh, but because he harbored a great ambition to which a permanent isigodhlo would have been a hindrance. As for Morgan, he had many isigodhlos, female alliances he maintained in each of the vassal kraals within his landhold, although their significance was mainly political, emblems of the prestige of Morgan's position. But he also had ten wives in the African fashion. As large a man as Queen was, Morgan was still larger—not only, of course, in the amplitude of Morgan's power, but also in the magnitude of his sheer physical dimension.

On Queen's right, leaning well back in his chair, sat Martinus van Zyl, expressionless, puffing quietly at his pipe, a strapping colored man of twenty-five, who had been sent south with his brother by old Groot Piet, just as two of Morgan's "sons" had gone north to learn the Zyl ways of it. Last and youngest of the seated men, dressed as the others were—in wide-brimmed *terais,* cotton shirts, and leather *breeks*—was Joachim van Zyl, younger brother of Martinus. Slimmer, taller than Martinus, of paler coloring with the lithe build of a long-distance runner, Joachim presented the same solemn manner that Martinus did, but he was even more inward and brooding than his brother.

Behind this row of *agter ryders* stood the three senior headmen, the Indunas—Senzana, Matshongi, and Umbaca. The first two were the sons of a moselekatse, a Zulu captain, who had come north with the first *Dukusa.* The third senior Induna was of Matabele warrior stock. These three men made up the inner cabal of *Dukusa.* They were present because they possessed intimate knowledge of the kraals and of the goings-on in the segmented tracts that constituted Morgan's "country," for each senior Induna rode for a week or more at a tour of duty that took him throughout the landhold. But it was also to provide visible evidence of their status, their life-and-death authority, that these ensigns of *Dukusa* were present at the Indaba. The presence of the senior Indunas testified to Morgan's shrewd apprehension of the powerful and subtle values of prestige that connoted the African tradition.

Before the *stoep* stood some fifty Africans, Umbaca's men, each carrying a spear and an oval shield marked with the insignia of his Induna. Drawn up in a wide semicircle, these men were the impi, from the warrior kraal outside the stronghold wall. It was these warriors who had brought in the transgressors after van Rieberk and two other *ryders* had overtaken and held them, shooting two recalcitrants as a warning, until the impi arrived.

Within the crescent formation of guards stood the seven prisoners, representative of an itinerant gang of a hundred or so mongrel Bantu who had roamed the Morgan landhold. For three days these mongrel Bantu had been allowed to graze and water their goats, had even been given a quantity of grain and mealies. But this tolerant treatment had been repaid by thievery; for the Bantu had been caught departing in the night, driving ahead of them two dozen or more prime fat-tailed sheep among the goats they had brought with them.

Using his spear, one of Umbaca's men pricked the buttocks of the leader of the seven Bantu, driving the man closer to the *stoep*. Morgan leaned forward. He gestured to the six other prisoners.

"Those are the men who urged you to take the sheep? They are the instigators? There were no others?"

It was an empty question, mere ceremony. Umbaca had already interrogated the headman with a spearpoint at his throat. But Morgan jabbed with his cigar. "Think well, dung-eater, *impisi,* for if I think you lie, I will capture six other men, but you I will hang."

The African's eyes widened with fear. "Lord, it is true!" he said shrilly. "They are the ones!"

Morgan turned his head to where Umbaca stood. "Fifty lashes for each," he briskly announced.

The Induna moved down the steps of the *stoep*. He called out an order, and the six prisoners were seized and dragged struggling toward a row of trees. Now a *ryder* moved along the row, handcuffing each prisoner's arms around a tree.

Morgan turned his head to Queen. "Well, *Uitlander*, does the newcomer think our corrective methods adequate?"

"*Drastio*," Queen said, his voice sharp. "Your methods are drastic—I'd give five to two odds all six won't survive the beating."

"So, *Uitlander*—so?" Morgan said quizzically. "And what would you have done with them?"

"Take their goats, plus, say, lay on ten stripes apiece," Queen answered firmly.

"Insufficient and pointless," Morgan said.

Kolenbrander laughed. "In the old days, in the south, they made a law against thieving. A man had to travel maybe three, four hundred miles to lodge a complaint, as they called it, leaving his house and his stock unguarded. Oh, no, we Dutch do not think much of your English government, Robbie."

"It is not my government, let me remind you. I was born here," Queen said. "I say to take the goats would have been more practical. Teach them a lesson of the belly."

Morgan shook his head. "No, useless," he said. "Their beasts are trash, not worth the fodder, and then there might have been more stealing."

The flogging had begun now. At the start, some of the victims bore up stoically enough, but then the screams came. The men on the *stoep*, and those of Umbaca, looked on impassively as the punishment was carried out. When the

9

sentence was at last executed, and the screams had tailed off to
spasmodic moans and sobs, Morgan signaled for the leader of
the offenders to approach. "Listen to me, dung-eater," Morgan said. "This time you have been lucky. Now take your
rabble and go, and do not return to the "country" of *Dukusa*.
Do you understand?"

"Lord, your word is law!" the African exclaimed.

He turned and hurriedly made his way through the hedge
of spearmen to the entrance, shouting to his people outside to
come and carry away the men who had been whipped. It
looked to Queen that his surmise had not been far wrong.
Two of the Bantu seemed to be dead.

Morgan re-lit the stub of his cigar. "And now we will
dispose of the more serious annoyance." He glanced at Queen.
"Because it comes from within, *Uitlander*—and a breach of a
law within is serious. That is how discipline and order are
threatened. Remember that, newcomer!"

A man and a woman were shoved forward. A little to one
side of them a second man stood, the husband of the woman;
he was an elder herdsman whose vocation regularly involved
patrol of the cattle kraals from sundown to sunup.

At certain ceremonial times, at the gathering of the "first
fruits," for example, a degree of promiscuity by husbands and
wives was commonly permissible. And there were other times
when a bit of discreet roving, by either husband or wife, was
more or less agreed to by the parties, the need for variety
being amicably arranged between them. But what the straying
husband had done here was well beyond the pale. A field-
worker with a notoriously roving eye, the fellow had taken up
with a woman, the association growing so bold and open that
the adulterers were eventually discovered. But it was not
without the help of the cuckolded husband that the careless
fornicators were apprehended. The husband had suspected

10

something was amiss, alerted an Induna to keep a lookout, and now the erring lovers faced the *Dukusa's* fierce justice.

The Induna stepped forward to confirm, incontestably, that he had twice seen the over-confident seducer leave the woman's hut. The prisoners, stripped to stark nakedness, stood huddled together, the woman's eyes cast down, the man's staring up at the junta on the *stoep*, his adulterer's face ashen with guilt and fear.

"You cunt-swiller, have you a woman of your own?" Morgan barked.

The African's face twitched, as if in an effort to regain the power of speech. At last he gave up and nodded dumbly.

"The man has two wives," the arresting Induna said.

Morgan turned his glance to the woman. "You, whore, wanton! You do not deny it?"

The woman was very well formed, and once she must have been pert and inviting—but now all the arrogance had been drained out of her. Speechless, she shook her head in terror.

"You have dishonored your husband's hut and polluted his kraal," Morgan said. "You will be sent back where you came from, to Shonga's kraal, and your father will repay the lobola paid for you." Turning to Martinus, Morgan said: "Send a *ryder* with her—tell him to have Shonga deal with her as he wishes, and tell him to use his whip. See that she keeps running. They should be there by sundown." Then Morgan addressed Umbaca over his shoulder: "As to the bullock, the cunt-swiller . . ." Morgan stared down reflectively at the culprit. "We will make an ox of him. Cut out his organs."

At the Induna's command, the prisoner was seized and dragged toward the row of trees. The business of the *Indaba* was over.

"And what do you think of my disposition of that case,

11

Uitlander? You count that verdict drastic also?" Morgan asked, studying Robert Queen.

Queen stroked his chin. "Lenient enough . . . for the *woman.*"

Morgan smiled. "Do you think so? Think again—think what Shonga and her father will do to her. And she will have a long run . . . all day!" Morgan snapped his fingers. "The hard-on, what of my judgment upon him?"

"*Bloody* drastic again," Queen said.

"Bloody, but not drastic," the big Afrikander replied.

Van Rieberk spat his impatience over the rail. "This *drastic* again. You are not that young, *Mynheer,* and you were born here. Time was we used to execute the whole family of a fornicator, sometimes both families. You should know that!"

"I do know it," Queen snapped at van Rieberk. "And before that the Dutch burnt 'witches.' You were for that also?" he added.

"The point is that the fellow had women of his own," Morgan interrupted. "Also, that the husband must have fidelity from a woman he has paid for—if fidelity is his wish. That is a basic law."

"Which, however, does not apply to us?" Queen said easily, uncritically.

"Not if one has paid the lobola, or the woman is a gift," Morgan said. "And so long as you stick by the rule—good specimens, no disease, and not more than seven."

Santoro laughed. "One for each night of the week! When are you going to get started, Roberto?" Santoro bent forward confidentially. "Listen. I take you to Luanga's kraal, on my territory. They got some there with tits like melons, backsides you couldn't get your arm around. Cheap also—half the lobola price."

"Do not worry," van Rieberk interposed drily, enigmatically, "the Englander does not go short of copulation."

"Just so long as you stick to the maidens, not the wives, eh, *Uitlander?*" Morgan said pointedly. "No stupidities. Our politics come before our wenching."

"Even if they did not, you would have nothing to worry about on my account," Queen said. "And besides, I do not intend any isigodhlo." He saw van Rieberk's inquiring frown change to a look of guarded approval. Queen smiled. "Oh, don't get me wrong, old-timer, I like it as much as the next man. But no wives, no hindrances. Not yet."

To the others it had no significance. But Morgan knew what Queen meant. Queen had made no bones about his intentions. He had been frank with Morgan, had told him about the ambition he had nursed since as a young boy he had listened to his father's tales of the white men who had carved out wide "kingdoms" for themselves. Nor would killing deter him. At sixteen, Queen had killed two of a band of reivers who had tried to rob his family's wagon when his father was away, an event that was seven years later followed by Queen's having to bury the bloody remnants of his father, the little that the huge wounded elephant had left for burying. Morgan knew what Queen meant, all right, and though Morgan had said little at the time, Queen opened his heart. Queen had the impression that the big Afrikander had approved.

*   *   *

A young African woman came along the *stoep* with more vessels of marula beer, and set down the clay pots in front of Santoro. Shiny-black, abundantly developed, and, save for her betshu, naked, the creature was a new house servant whom Santoro had not seen before. He regarded her with approval, and as she refilled his gourd, giggling, Santoro stroked her buttocks under the bead apron.

Van Rieberk watched this exchange with a look of disdain. He leaned out to shove the girl away. Then he glanced at the position of the sun, and tapped Kolenbrander's knee with his furled *sjambok*. "The big *spruit* by sundown, Andries—we must make Milembe's kraal by tomorrow," van Rieberk said.

Kolenbrander slowly rose. "Ja!" He glanced down at Morgan. "Lion you said, N'kosi?" Kolenbrander stretched his massive arms and yawned.

"Yes," Morgan said. "Killed two women in a week."

"I thought we'd shot out all the bad cats in his area."

"It may be that the natives have been dumping corpses again, for the hyenas. Too lazy to bury them, the filthy swine," Morgan said. "If that is the case, fine the trash twenty cows, and say that the next time it will be fifty."

"Perhaps five days, then," van Rieberk reflected. "Counting the ride each way."

"No, take a week, even longer," Morgan said. "Get that woman-killer first, and then hunt the whole tract thoroughly. Kill every cat you can find. It's a very small village and they can't afford these losses."

"Three dogs, then, to cover that tract?" Kolenbrander offered.

"Take four," Morgan said. "Blood two of the young ones."

"It might not be a lion," van Rieberk said. "Perhaps a leopard, or a pair. In that case we might lose dogs, the young ones."

"If it is leopard, use live bait—on two legs, you get me?" Morgan said briefly. "Milembe will persuade a volunteer, and the bait will give voice, all right, when the cat comes."

"*Live bait?*" Queen grinned incredulously. "Christ, I hadn't heard of that one."

"Uncommon maybe," Morgan said. "But the leopard is twice as smart as the lion. Could take a couple of weeks with a real crafty beast. I've had to do it twice myself." The *ryders* were dispersing now, but Morgan put a hand on Queen's sleeve and nodded to Santoro to also remain. "You two wait."

14

He looked at the slimmer man. "How are things on your *morgens,* Manoel?"

Santoro shrugged. "Placid, as always, no troubles. *Porque?*"

"Take Martinus with you for a few days, show him your country. I have something for you to do when you have acquainted him with it."

Santoro brightened. "So? Something special?"

Morgan nodded. "Two, three weeks . . . to the coast."

"Excellent! I look forward to it."

"I know you do," Morgan said without feeling. "I will explain tomorrow." He moved to where Queen stood against the rail.

"Also a special job for me?" Queen asked. "Business?"

"No. Talk. You have been with me over a year now. Time we got things settled. Time you made up your mind, man."

"All right," Queen said.

"Are you with me or not?" Morgan said.

"I haven't made up my mind yet," Queen said.

Morgan shrugged. "Well, you've got the rest of the day to do it. You've seen most of it now—how we run things. You know most of it, except, maybe, how to beat trouble, the politics of it." He stressed the point. "And that's the basis of it all, the politics of it."

"I know a bit about that," Queen said. "The part about we-hang-together-gentlemen-or-we-hang-separately. I know that part."

"I'm glad to hear it," Morgan said. "That's the part you never want to forget . . . as some of them did. Do not forget that it works in two colors, black and white. Now, lad, you take your supper here tonight and you and I will fix it up one way or the other."

*　　　*　　　*

Around the other side of the compound, on his way to the

15

horse corral, Santoro slowed to watch the woman who was birch-brooming the rear of the *stoep*. She had her back to him, and was bending to pick something up from the floor. It was the new housegirl. Santoro guessed she was unmarried, maybe seventeen, no more. Her full hips and shapely legs gleamed in the strong light. He felt the hardening urge in his loins and crossed to the *stoep*. He reached for the lower rail and swung himself up and over. The woman started and backed away, but Santoro shook his head, smiling reassuringly. "Come, my little seacow, don't be shy," he coaxed. But when she still hesitated, the *ryder* spoke in dialect and made his command more imperious. "Come!" he called.

She was clearly innocent, and he surmised she had been reared to preserve her virginity lest her lobola value decline. On the other hand, Santoro knew she had also been reared to respect the wishes of the white lords, to render obedience when it was required of her, for otherwise she might be returned in disgrace from the magnificence of the stronghold to her father's humble hut.

At last the servant girl came slowly forward with an uncertain smile, and Santoro slipped his hand around her bare back to circle her waist. In their exposed position, there was not much time for preliminaries; Santoro grasped her arm and led her along to a small storeroom stacked with boxes.

The *ryder* unfastened the thong of her betshu and let the apron drop to the floor. He pushed the girl down onto her back across a wickerwork case and she lay, half off the box, her thighs spread, like a sacrificial offering. Santoro moved between her legs and her back arched up to receive him. He unfastened his belt, then he changed his mind and pulled her up. Virgin she might be, but not that unaware of the ways of it. Unbidden, she went down onto her stomach and waited. He let her wait. She turned to look at him, her eyes inquiring, disappointed. "You take me?" She whispered it throatily, as if

16

sedated. Then she bent down over the case again, lifting from her tiptoes, thrusting up with her hips. The *ryder* laughed and dropped his trousers, took her hard by the buttocks, and drove savagely into her.

The interlude was pleasant enough, and Santoro was soon on his way to the corral again, with only minutes lost, scarcely anything to worry about. But Santoro never worried, in any case.

The Briefing
(Queen)

When he had finished soaping himself, Queen stepped back into the tin bath and poured the pail of water over his head.

There was always plenty of water. Aside from the *spruit*, which ran behind the palisade, there were plenty of streams and small rivers in the few miles between here and the "home" river. It was well-watered country, which was why Morgan's forebears had first put down roots here and made the region their own—sometimes with guns, but more often by the method Morgan called "politics": by trading, by hunting meat for the villages, by shrewd "marriages" into the families of chiefs and headmen, a method of penetration and control that could always be backed up by the decisive diplomacy of the stuttering guns, the Vickers-Lewises.

Three days north of Morgan's country, where the rock cairns marked the beginning of Igonyela's territory, there were forty or more rivers, some of which became formidable in the rainy season. And north of Igonyela's kraal, it was said, there were many more rivers—few of them mapped—though Queen had not yet been further north than that.

He got himself a good slug of Logan's, another luxury available at *Morganskeep,* the excellent whiskey now and then brought back by wagon, usually by Santoro, from the coast.

All right: he had to decide—Morgan had given him a day to do it.

Queen got a cheroot and began to muse, watching the smoke drift toward the fly-netted windows of the cabin. Even if he chose to stay on at *Morganskeep,* it would certainly not be for life—as, he guessed, the others would. Not that you could blame them. It was a good set-up for a man, and Morgan was generous with people who suited him. The pay, in fact, was a sight better than you could make in any comparable capacity elsewhere in Africa—and for good reason. To stay on with Morgan, you had to be a first-rate hunter, from elephant to the big cats. Morgan's standards were high, and you had to be tough, bloody tough, physically and mentally. "In this country you beat trouble by strangling it." That was *Dukusa's* unrelenting rule, and it was promptly applied in all cases, whether the trouble called for hanging a "wife" or burning a village.

It took a bit of getting used to, Morgan's rule. If you had not been reared to the absolute rule of autocracy, to the maintenance of a "kingdom" by the rigorous policies of force and discipline, a virtually martial style in all things, then Morgan's way was not your way unless you worked hard to adapt yourself to it—and overcame certain compunctions, the dictates of an egalitarian conscience, your basic humanity. In the old days, there had been many vast landholds, many great kingdoms. But the sons and the grandsons of those houses had grown soft, had failed to sustain the hard rules of a hard body, a hard mind, and hard dealing in the marketplace of men, and in time dozens of those great keeps had deteriorated and fallen into disorder and ruin. But two of the most majestic kingdoms had held themselves aloft through the disintegrating effect of the passage of generations, the relaxing of the hard rules.

These were the domains of van Zyl in the north, and Morgan farther south. It was the preservation of the old methods that preserved these kingdoms and extended them. It

19

was this that had brought Robert Queen, and his ambition, to *Morganskeep*. This and the fact that Morgan's country was remote from the impact of "civilized" government, an authority Queen found repugnant to his taste.

But north was the word that had always beckoned Queen. In the north, he was convinced, there were still new "countries" to be won. Given the necessary stake, a man might carve his own domain out of that vast, unchartered wilderness. But a stake, that came first—and here was reason to stick with Morgan—until one had what one needed to go off and do as well as he had.

Trading and ivory had provided the basis of the Morgans' fortune. But then, like men destined for wealth, they had fortuitously hit *kimberlite* in the process of blasting the river gorge for the stone of which *Morganskeep* was largely built. Some gold, too. The vein, long since exhausted, had not been a bonanza, but the "pipe" had yielded a value in diamonds that had doubled the original Morgan resources.

Queen considered the other *ryders,* wondering if they had ever harbored ambitions like his own. Oddly, Santoro and van Rieberk were very similar in one way. And their respective accouterments—the knife and the *sjambok*—seemed appropriate to their personalities. They were both good men, formidable, of the kind it is better to have on one's own side, and undoubtedly loyal. But Queen doubted that either man had possessed real ambition, the vast desire that soared in Queen's breast. Santoro and van Rieberk were frontiersmen, all right, but not of the Voortrekker, the true pioneer, stamp.

Andries Kolenbrander he had liked from the first, as rugged and dependable as any man Queen had ever met. The fellow was easier to know, less complex than the other white Afrikanders. Not unpredictable, as Morgan often was, nor brooding and taciturn, like van Rieberk, nor subtle and calculating as Santoro was.

The Zyl brothers, too, Queen held in high regard—

20

especially the younger one, Joachim. Quiet, reliable, equable young men, not yet fully stained with the brush of experience perhaps, but no greenhorns. Yet it seemed to Queen that both brothers were possessed of a certain inhibition, a tendency to defer to the others, to give way, give ground, almost instinctively to *retreat*. That was it! But it was their color, was it not? Certainly Queen had heard van Rieberk say that Santoro's mother had been a mulatto from the coast, though that might have been a bit of retaliatory slandering, but his, Manoel's, features were wholly European, whereas the African blood of the Zyls was plain enough.

At the same time, miscegenation notwithstanding, they were direct offspring of a paramount chief, as entitled to their name, by African standards at least, as any progeny of Chaka Zulu.

It had grown dark now and Queen was ready for food. He found a clean shirt, tidied up, and started out toward the palisade. From his chair on the *stoep*, Morgan watched Queen come into the yellow aura of lamplight. A good-looking man, Queen, though not in the way that Santoro was, not pretty, heavier hewn about the mouth and chin. Still under thirty, still with much to learn from experience perhaps, about the hard realities of success and survival, Morgan thought. But the fellow was clearly durable material, a man with a future, here or somewhere.

Morgan nodded to the bottles on the table that stood against the wall of the house as Queen came up onto the *stoep*.

"Beer, whiskey, or Bols?"

"Gin," Queen grinned, "to start with."

"A womanish drink, but it improves the food," Morgan said. "Pour me one too."

An African girl came along the *stoep* with a tray of nuts and some marula beer. It was the new house-servant whom Santoro had earlier aged somewhat. Before she withdrew, she managed to give Queen a smile that seemed to be meaningful

21

enough, at least it was a message both Queen and Morgan had no trouble decoding. Morgan watched Queen's glance following the girl's hips as she walked away across the *stoep*, and the thought occurred to Morgan that if Queen fell into the tradition of *Morganskeep*, it might induce the young fellow to settle here as so many *ryders* before him had done.

"Plenty of good women here in the kraals and in the villages," he said. "No need to go short, as they told you this morning."

Queen shook his head, smiling. "And as I told them, not yet. No hindrances."

"All right," Morgan shrugged. "We are not here to discuss women. I want your decision."

"You will have it," Queen said. "I am not getting any younger. You know my ideas, my ambition. They haven't changed. It has been good here, yes, but I want to find my own 'country' if I can, while this land is still young enough." Queen looked hard at Morgan. "It may be a pipe dream, but that's my dream and I'm going to follow it out. What I'm saying, man, is I must leave you. So now you have it—that's my decision."

Morgan smiled. "For an Englander, you have a very Boer outlook."

"How is that?"

"They used to say that no Boer could stand the prospect of another farm within sight of his own. If it happened, he pulled up roots and trekked."

Queen nodded. "Yes, well, it's something like that, and, well . . ." he made a gesture, "making something out of nothing, making something out of yourself."

"What will you do for a stake?" Morgan said quietly. "Wagons, guns, oxen, ammunition, and the rest of it. You figured all that?"

"I've got a year's pay coming," the younger man said.

"Two years would be more like the cost of it," Morgan said. "Why don't you work another year?"

"No, thanks." Queen shook his head. "I'll manage."

"Not going to be talked out of it, eh?" Morgan smiled. "Listen, I'm not trying to talk you out of it. You might even become an ally someday, and maybe the day will come when we are all going to need allies."

Queen grinned. "The politics of it?"

"Damn right," Morgan said, very serious now. "And don't you ever forget it. But I've got another suggestion for you. Due two months leave, aren't you?"

"Well, yes. But I don't expect to get that if I'm quitting."

The older man waved this remark aside. "North is your idea, isn't it?"

"Yes."

"Well, you're right about that. North, northwest, that's your prospect. The Banyoro country, or beyond. Rich ivory country up there, untouched, not least because of the Ridge."

"I heard about that," Queen said. "A barrier to wagons, they say."

"Yes, two, three hundred miles of it. Like the Drakensberg. But there are passes. The first van Zyl crossed once, and then swung east. The Banyoro is the high plateau land beyond the Ridge."

"How about the Banyoro?" Queen asked. "Hostile or manageable?"

The big man shrugged. "That's a chance every trekker has to take. They did some raiding once, in a small way, but that was a long time ago. Now listen," Morgan said. "Perhaps we can kill two birds here, or even three. Just now we are approaching the time of the annual First Fruits ceremony, and I should pay Igonyela a state visit anyway. Royal custom, politics, sport. Also, I have a proposition and some news for him. I suggest I ride with you as far as the Chief's kraal. Then you can go on. Prospect the Banyoro country, or wherever you want to head for. Share with me what you find out and I'll cover you in return."

"That sounds very fair, very generous," Queen said.

"Makes good economic sense," Morgan said. "And afterwards, if you find a good prospect, you can then decide whether you want to work another year with us, build up your stake even more."

"I'm very grateful, N'kosi," Queen nodded slowly. "You'll sell me a wagon and team?"

"That won't be necessary," Morgan said. "I have hunting wagons with Igonyela. You can have one of them. I also have Boer hounds there, the same as we have here."

"Thanks again," Queen said, "but I doubt I could manage the dogs as well. I'll have enough critters on my hands with the team."

"Christ, lad, you don't think I'd let you go alone, do you?" Morgan scoffed. "Got to have a *voorloper,* haven't you? Two is a minimum. But we'll talk about that later."

Queen grinned. "You're doing me proud but, sir, I don't expect all this . . ."

"It's nothing," the other man shrugged. "Time I stretched my legs again, anyway." He put his palms on the table. "We'll ride with you, then—see you started right properly."

"We?"

"Three or four or so. After all, it's an official visit to Igonyela," Morgan reminded Queen. "We'll take Joachim, also. Don't believe he's met the little fellow yet. Bit of experience for him too."

"The First Fruits business you mean?"

"Yes. You ever happened across it?"

Queen shook his head. "No. Kind of harvest festival shindig, is it? Nobody allowed to start on the new crops till the chief has eaten?"

Morgan smiled. "A shindig, all right. Goes on for days. You'll find it an experience, too—perhaps change your mind about some things. The *Ndlunkulu* girls will be there, the cream of the women from every kraal. I'll have a message sent on the drums tomorrow."

Queen laughed. "You never give up, eh, N'kosi? Peg your men down with an isigodhlo apiece and they never take off. Pussywhip them, eh?"

Morgan did not laugh at this. He drank his gin and said little more throughout the meal.

After they had eaten, Queen crossed the compound in a mood of some elation. When he reached his cabin, he paused in surprise: someone was waiting inside.

It was the new serving girl and it did not take Queen long to reckon Morgan's hand behind the gesture. A tongue-in-cheek one perhaps, but hardly to be scorned. She was clearly more delectable than the brandy and cigars that were unexpectedly produced at the end of the meal.

As for the black girl newly a woman, her enthusiasm was boundless.

The Briefing
(Santoro)

Santoro ate a spartan breakfast, in the Iberian tradition that he had inherited—an egg, a mug of maize coffee. He had finished his meager fare, lit a second cheroot of the day, his fingers drumming on the table as he looked inquiringly at Morgan.

Morgan dealt himself more ham, more eggs, more liver from the platter that lay between them. He was perfectly aware of Santoro's curiosity, but Morgan could not abide conversation competing with food, and he did not look up until Santoro had twice pointedly tapped the ash from his long cheroot.

"We need the valley tract on the Malazi . . . Igonyela's. You know why," Morgan said. "Cane sugar, rum, blue gums. The ground was made for it."

Santoro considered the statement. He knew the valley tract well enough, just beyond the northeastern beacons of Morgan's hold. But while Igonyela was easygoing, usually amenable, there was one thing he was energetically adamant about—the sanctity of his boundaries. Santoro could see only trouble ahead in this, and he frowned. "*Cristo.* We haven't got enough 'country' already, *Patrao?* This is too much greediness, and there would be much trouble." He knew he'd gone too far, quickly checked himself, and shrugged. "Of course, I know we *could* take it, even so."

"Damn right we could!" Morgan said. "Two impis could do it with the kind of firepower we have."

"What of the *Hulumeni?* They would hear of it eventually."

"Those ninnies? Of what concern are they to me? But in any case, if I told them my plan—to dam the river, raise sugar, tobacco, rum, build presses—they'd be in favor of it, much in favor. The revenues and the duty, man."

Santoro shrugged again. "All right. But sometimes the mildest ones have their blind spots, *Patrao.* With Igonyela, it is his boundaries. He might even fight for them. Why do you not make a bargain with him instead?"

"I have tried," Morgan said. "Cattle, trade goods. But you are right about one thing—Igonyela is obstinate. Stupid, too, because his own people would benefit greatly."

"So it is stalemate? We must fight for it, then? A great pity, *Patrao.*"

"But there is another way," Morgan said, "and that is why you are at my breakfast table."

Santoro waited expectantly.

"Igonyela has a weakness, a blinder spot than his boundaries," Morgan said. He took a cigar from the table and bit off the end. "The little fellow wants a white wife."

Santoro's stare of incredulity changed slowly to a grin. He slapped his knee. "*Fantastico!*"

"White, and preferably the size of a seacow," Morgan said. "A bee that has been in his bonnet since you put it there, and it has grown to the size of a hawk moth."

"*I* put it there?"

"A photograph from some French magazine you showed him, some fat circus wench. That's what brought him to the boil, and he's been starving ever since for a slice of the cake."

27

"The cake?"

"His share in what's divvied up, the privileges of power. White men take black wives, he wants it in reverse. Become an obsession with the fellow—partly plain randyness, partly prestige."

Santoro laughed. "Ridiculous . . . *unico*."

"You show your ignorance," Morgan said. "Nothing unique about white queens. There were three of them in my father's time—and not always through chance, capture, shipwreck, either."

"You are thinking of the Banyoro legend?"

"That is no legend," Morgan said heavily. "Nor was the Frenchman's daughter who married a Zulu moselekatse. Nor was Zikidawa, the Englishwoman down in the Limpopo 'country.' Nor certain others. You should go and talk to Hans, young fellow."

"You really think the Banyoro queen thing is true, then, N'kosi?" Santoro persisted.

"I've never trekked beyond the big Ridge myself. But others have, odd prospectors, diamond men," Morgan told him. "It's true, all right."

Santoro returned to the main theme. "And you think Igonyela would trade the valley tract for a white wife?"

"Damn sure he would. And if she was fat and pretty, he'd throw in his right arm, too. You think I don't know his mind, don't know what I'm talking about?" Morgan said impatiently.

"No, no." The smile faded from Santoro's face. "I was just thinking, sir. If I had realized, I might have made a deal with him myself. *Jesu* . . . 'Santoro's Valley'!" The *ryder* shook his head.

"You wouldn't have gotten far with that," Morgan said drily. "I guarantee it, man."

"Just making the joke," Santoro assured. "A seacow for a valley, eh? *Incredulo!*"

28

"A *white* seacow," Morgan corrected. "Now *get* him one—and the fatter, the better."

"You know, N'kosi, I think it could be done," Santoro said reflectively.

"Of course, it can!" Morgan nearly shouted. "I would do it myself, but I do not speak Portuguese so well," Morgan said pointedly.

"I have a good friend at Nambana, as you know. Sancho Baro, a man of considerable *posibilidades*," Santoro mused. He spread a hand expressively. "Horn, hides, diamonds too, I think, sometimes—and just occasionally sometimes also a little black ivory."

"I know," Morgan said nasally. "I was thinking of him."

Santoro shrugged. "Yes. Well, the trade is as old as history. In the north, they ship guns to the Arabs. But sometimes white women, too—Sicilians, Greeks, Slavs. But it calls for much more money than guns. That is what I was coming to. They catch the white women, then ship them through Port Said and later to the Sheiks."

"Catch?" Morgan grunted. "Like fishing?"

"It could be like that, using money bait, or kidnapping. I am not sure. But I think Sancho could arrange it."

"Yes." Morgan flipped his cigar irritably. "But that way might take *months*."

"Well," Santoro spread his hands again. "It is just possible that a woman could be had from somewhere on the coast."

"You handle it! I want to hear no more about it!" Morgan snapped. "Do it!"

Santoro tried to smile. "I appreciate the trust you have in me, *Patrao*. How do you know I shall not run off with all the money I shall need for this?"

Morgan patted the Buntline Colt against his thigh. "I'd find you, and you know it, amigo," he said affably. "Besides, you've got a year's pay due, and you'll get it, plus a bonus—when this business is done."

"Don't worry," Santoro said. "I'll do it, N'kosi."

"Leave in the morning," Morgan said. "And remember—the sooner you take care of it, the bigger your bonus."

Santoro rose and made his way across the compound toward the horse corral. He was smiling to himself. Two, three weeks leave, at least, perhaps twice as much, with a windfall at the end of it. Besides, he found the assignment intriguing. The vision of the little black man feverishly mounting the great pink sow he'd produce made the amorous *ryder* want to laugh aloud. But he didn't. For there was something in all this that Santoro did not think in the least laughable.

Across the Malagena

Queen was dressing when he heard van Rieberk's knock.

"You are leaving today for the Banyoro?" the older *ryder* said curtly.

"I am heading north anyway," Queen called out. "Is it some business of yours?"

Van Rieberk nodded as he stood in the doorway.

"Come in," Queen said. He motioned to a chair. "Tea?"

The older man shook his head, and felt in his shirt pocket for his pipe.

"What's on your mind?" Queen said directly.

But van Rieberk went on filling his pipe. "I have never crossed the Ridge myself," he said at last. "But I know that there are two passes where a wagon can make it. One is northwest, the other directly west of Igonyela."

"What is the difference . . . a week, more?"

"*Nee!* Robbery is the difference," van Rieberk said flatly. "Or death, or both. That is what I come to tell you."

It occurred to Queen that the veteran *ryder* resented this enterprise and intended to discourage Queen.

"Such dark thoughts," Queen said sardonically.

Van Rieberk ignored the sarcasm. "Due west from Igonyela

will take two or three days longer than the other way," he said. "Bushveld and *kloofs*. But you will have no trouble."

"And the shorter way?"

"Is through the southwestern strip of the Milebi. There you are always liable to have big trouble, as I said—a man on his own, even several men!"

"In these times?" Queen said sceptically. "They never heard of *Dukusa*, the Milebi? I'm not that much of a green-horn, Mynheer."

Van Rieberk bridled visibly. "That is exactly what you are, *Uitlander*. You can handle a horse and a gun. But that is all. Of the *swarts*, you know nothing. You think I don't know? By God, I know." He got angrily to his feet. "All right, fool—you find out for yourself!"

"No, wait," Queen said. "I apologize. I just thought you were, well, trying to spook me," he added awkwardly.

"I do not make jokes about such things. I leave the jokes to you and the others," van Rieberk said with a contemptuous gesture of the hand. "The Milebi killed my father and brother. I saw it happen."

"A further apology," Queen said.

For a moment the older *ryder* stared back as if making up his mind whether to continue. "It was a long time ago, before this Bejane became the Chief. It was his father then, in that time. We were hunters and traders, and we shot meat for them, for the Milebi. For two seasons it was our camp. We had a big cache of ivory, seven months' worth, and our trade goods. Three wagons. They are like snakes, these people. They are born as a snake is born, with hate and venom."

"Nothing was done? There was no . . . government action?" Queen asked, though he knew the question was superfluous.

"Those *dassies*, those rabbits . . . a thousand miles away?"

van Rieberk rasped scornfully. "*They*, to send military for two Hollanders, for *Boers?*" he stressed the word bitterly. "For a fourteen-year-old boy?"

"Still, that was a long time ago," Queen said after a pause.

"Time makes no difference." Van Rieberk shook his head. "Listen. I have seen much of this land. From the Somalis, the Kikuyu, the Masai, south to the Matabele, the Swazis, the Zulu, the Bushmen, the Hottentots. . . . Some are honorable, some are fighters, some are both, and some are neither. In this matter, I am as good a judge as any man, and I tell you that the Milebi are the scum of Africa, the crocodiles. They should be wiped from the face of the earth, and some day they will be."

This was an unusually long speech for van Rieberk, and though it was delivered without emotion, it was in deadly earnest. Queen could see this. It shaped his feeling, and what he said. "I don't question your judgment. But, as I said, that *was* a long time ago . . . in your father's time! I would have thought even the Milebi would have heard of *Dukusa*, would think twice before nailing any *ryder* of his."

The older man waved the idea away. "They have never clashed with any *Dukusa*. They are untouched, too remote from the north and the south, unaffected by any changes time has brought." Van Rieberk shrugged. "All right. I have told you what I know. Profit by it."

Queen put out his hand. "All right, Hans. I'll remember."

Queen was astonished to see the veteran's taut expression relax somewhat. The older *ryder* almost smiled as he took the younger man's hand with a strong slow enveloping grip. "*Geluk!* Good luck! Take the low road, isn't it? As your people say. I tell you that again."

Queen returned the smile, nodding. A strange one, this man, he thought, as tough as Morgan, but without the big man's tractability and humor. Queen understood the grief, what van Rieberk felt, the bitterness. Queen knew a thing or two about grief, all right.

*   *   *

The sun was well up as Robert Queen fetched his horse from the corral and cantered over to the *stoep*. He watched Joachim van Zyl join Morgan and the three African *ryders* already assembled. Each of the Africans led a pack animal loaded with a share of gear and ammunition. Except for Morgan's big black, some two hands taller than the others, all the horses were of a uniform size, Boer horses, heavier-set than the Dutch and English strains from which they were descended, tougher, able to keep up a steady tripple all day long. They were trained to stand rock-steady, even against a charging lion, supporting guns rested across their backs.

As the cortege passed through the compound toward the open veld, children called from the kraals, and further on fieldworkers paused in their work to stare and wave.

*   *   *

Just short of noon they reached the Malagena, the home river, and drew rein in the shade of a stand of euphorbias. The water was running low and brackish. Along the tree-dotted banks, the grass was greener, more nourishing than across the plain, and when they had watered the horses, the Africans hobbled them to graze for a while.

Joachim van Zyl pushed himself up into a sitting position on the grass. "Should I try for a bird or two while we are here, N'kosi? I heard some sand grouse earlier, just a bit down river," he called out to Morgan.

A few yards away the huge Afrikander moved onto his elbow and smiled. "You're a Zyl, all right, Jo." He glanced across at Queen. "Always got to be up and doing."

34

"Not a bad idea," Queen said, stretching. "Go well with the jackal stew." He tilted his hat further over his eyes and began to chew on a blade of grass as they watched the tall slim man go for a shotgun. "Never seen a croc on this river," Queen said idly to Morgan, to fill the silence.

"There were plenty once, hundreds," Morgan said. "But they're gone now, like the seacows, like the hippo."

"I never heard of crocs migrating," Queen said, picking a fresh blade.

"They didn't, *Uitlander*. Long time ago, when the skins were worth a mint, we hunted them, I mean really hunted them. Systematically, forty guns. Shot out the plover flocks first, their sentinel teeth-pickers. That allowed daylight hunting, from boats and the banks and islands. Hunted every night, too, with lanterns, dragging bait—even fished 'em with shark hooks and meat. Took wagonloads of hides, we did."

Queen nodded approvingly. "But you couldn't have wiped them all out. They'd breed up again?"

Morgan flipped a hand toward the water. "There aren't any there, are there? Herd creatures know when a place goes bad."

From downriver they heard the sudden report of a shotgun, and shortly afterwards Joachim came walking back with his long, easy stride. Five plump birds hung strung together in his hand. He held them up to show them before dropping them on the grass.

"Good enough," Queen said.

The party forded the river, and pressed on until mid-afternoon through elephant grass that finally gave way to thickets of mimosa and *umkaiya*. Now they came out into the big open country again, the tawny panorama stretching to the horizon, unrelieved save for widely scattered stands and islands of trees.

Riding farther back, alongside one of the Africans, Joachim shaded his eyes, then edged his horse forward to where Queen

35

and Morgan were moving abreast. He pointed diagonally. "Over there, N'kosi, *ingonyama*." He screwed up his eyes. "Two—no, three, I think."

The party slackened pace, and Morgan unlooped the Barr and Stroud's from his pommel. He raised the glasses to study the ground beneath the feathery shade of the triangle of acacias well across the grass. He re-hung the glasses on the saddle horn. "Yes, you're right, three vermin," he said. His lip curled slightly. "We will do what is necessary."

Joachim smiled.

Queen viewed the tableau beneath the umbrella trees with his own binoculars. He grimaced. "Aaah! Why trouble, man? Christ, aren't you sick of hunting those bastards, N'kosi?"

"Hunting?" The big man turned his head. "Who said anything about hunting. It's a duty to exterminate the mangy scum. Do you think Igonyela will object?" he added sarcastically.

"All right," Queen said. "Who'll take which of the bastards, then?"

Morgan stared out thoughtfully toward the trees. The horses were fresh enough, had recently drunk again, and the ground was flat going. "I think, Robert, we will do it the old way, the old Voortrekker way. Make some sport of it, eh?"

He turned to the younger man. "You know what I mean, Jo? You've done it before?"

"Not myself," Joachim said. "But I have seen it done once or twice."

"And you, Robert? You know the business?"

"I know it," Queen said. "But I'm not keen for it. You mean ride them down?"

"Not down. Not that close. Stay thirty yards back all the time. They'll outstrip you at first,. of course—but not for long."

Queen frowned. "They don't *all* run, you know. Some turn and charge."

36

Morgan chuckled. "That's what makes the sporting interest. You don't fancy it, *hunter?* Not important for you? Only
vermin?"

Queen shrugged. "Just seems like a mug's game to me. We
could thump them at a hundred yards—even farther. Why
waste time on it? But, all right!"

Some three or four hundred yards beyond the acacias a
straggle of sansevieria and bushthorn followed the course of a
dried-up riverbed. It was about the only real cover nearby.

"They'll go for the donga," Morgan said, gesturing toward
the ravine. "We'll let them, then we'll din them out of it and
run them down. I'll take the right flank. Joachim, you next to
me. Then you, Robbie." Morgan pivoted in his saddle and
explained to the Africans, his voice brusque, then grinned at
Queen. "What say we try it with pistols, lad?"

"Balls to that!" Queen said. "What say we get to Igonyela
still sitting upright?"

They moved their horses out toward the trees, five abreast,
fanning as they went, the third African remaining behind
with the pack horses. At two hundred yards, the small pride
began to show restiveness at the barrage of yells issuing from
the riders. The two lionesses were young, but fully grown—
and both looked pregnant. Their spouse, old, heavily maned,
big, took off first, daunted by the human voices, starting out at
a walk, but then, as the horsemen neared, breaking into a trot.
It was then that one of the females began to lope after him.

The third beast stood her ground for several moments
longer, tail switching angrily, snarling her annoyance and
threats—then she too turned and made off after the others,
toward the donga, as Morgan had predicted.

At Morgan's signal, the riders spread wider, holding to the
same relentless pace, checking the lions to a steady retreat
ahead of them. Queen could sense the tenseness in the horse
under him, and hoped it was more alertness than fear. Nine
out of ten Boer horses were superlatively well disciplined, and

there was something quietly impressive about the calm confidence in their riders that was doubtlessly conveyed to the horses themselves.

When the second lioness loped to catch up to the first two cats and into the cover of the donga, the five men cantered forward to within yards of the tangled watercourse. Now they set up a hullabaloo of shouting and occasional shooting into the brush. The mounting racket was answered by snarls and roars from the donga. It will be the big bastard first, Morgan thought. It was always the male whose nerve gave out first.

It was. The huge beast exploded from the brush, and Morgan kicked the stallion into chase. Seconds later, one of the lionesses burst from a place nearby, and Joachim went after her, his horse reacting as if a trigger had been pulled.

Queen held to his position, his horse sidling, trembling slightly. There was no sign of the third animal, nor could Queen hear more raging from the scrub. He hesitated, then alerted the Africans, and when they understood, he raced away after Joachim. The big male had veered and was heading toward the horizon on a straight run, Morgan in pursuit. But Joachim's quarry had taken another course.

The phenomenal initial acceleration of both cats had given each a substantial lead, but already the crouching horsemen were closing the gaps. Running parallel, Queen bounded after Joachim at full gallop. He heard the baritone note of Morgan's big Männlicher off to the right, then a second report. But he forced his attention on the man ahead, on Joachim, and heard the young *ryder* firing now, but not with his rifle. Incredibly, the young man had taken Morgan at his word. He was trying to destroy the lioness with his pistol! He had now drawn so close to the fleeing cat that it looked to Queen, coming up from behind at full gallop, as if the young hunter would be right into the beast if she swerved or wheeled. Queen saw Joachim shooting, heard the pistol cracks, the outstretched head of the lioness dropping as she half-somersaulted onto her side. Instantly, Joachim wheeled his horse away and came to a halt. For a moment the young man watched the big female writhing on her side, then he drew his rifle from the saddle bucket and slid from the saddle. But the echo of the final shot had scarcely faded when Queen heard shouts and looked around. The second lioness was in full cry, streaking across the grass, breaking directly for them, moving impossibly fast.

Queen vaulted from his saddle, shouting. He saw Joachim start to run back the few yards toward his horse. Queen laid the barrel of his gun across his saddle, the speeding cat ramming forward, hell-bent on her line. Queen tore back the bolt, fired just below the thrusting muzzle, and the yellow fury slewed and fell, bludgeoned off course by the thundering impact.

Without taking his eyes from her, Queen worked the bolt again. As the lioness struggled upright, he found the spot in her shoulder and fired. She dropped like a sack of wet meal. He straightened up slowly, letting go the pent breath in his lungs, and then brushed the sweat from his forehead and eyes. He ignored van Zyl, who had caught his horse and remounted now, the big cat piled within five yards of where Joachim had stood when Queen had first fired.

Morgan cantered up as the young *ryder* moved toward Queen. Joachim's face was rigidly composed, a pallor beneath his color and a strained note in his voice. "Magtig! Robert, N'kosi . . ." he managed to say.

Queen brushed the intended gratitude away with a curt wave of dismissal. "You ever commit a fucking idiocy like that again, I won't raise a bloody finger!" Queen turned and remounted.

Morgan kept his eyes on the two *ryders* as the group moved off again at a double-time pace. Following behind them, Morgan was alert to the slightest gestures that passed between

the two men, the slow and subtle process of reconciliation.
They were contrastingly different types, he reflected, the
difference between them that of an athlete, of diffident
temperament, and a man of spontaneously combustible nature
who might have done well in a prize ring. Yet, he guessed,
there was a common bond between them. It showed more
each day and probably accounted for half of Queen's ire. It
would be interesting to observe what developed.

*   *   *

About an hour before sundown, they pitched camp near the
beacons that marked the divide between *Morganskeep* country
and Igonyela's. The cairns were evenly spaced, Boer-style, at
intervals a horse could cover in twenty minutes at tripping
speed, and with the telescope two beacons were just visible on
the skyline.

Morgan settled his enormous frame beside the cooking fire.
After a time, he spoke up brightly: "This hour tomorrow,
barring unforeseen problems, we'll see the Malazi, Igonyela's
head river, from the top of that hogback. It's good country."

"Of which I hear you want a piece?" Queen could not resist
it. The close thing with the lioness rankled.

"And how do you hear?" Morgan said, but more amused
than really curious. "Yes," the big man said slowly. "I do
expect to make an agreement with the little fellow. Santoro is
arranging the substance of the business."

"Business," Joachim said unexpectedly. "Then it will just
be a trading deal, N'kosi? You will not require to take the land
by, by . . ."

"Force?" Morgan said. "Of course not!"

Such an intervention, expecially in controversial matters,
was unusual in Joachim, and Morgan glanced at the young
man curiously. "What gave you that idea, lad?"

"Oh, just I heard Hans and Manoel say you had plans . . . and that Igonyela would never agree to them," van Zyl said awkwardly.

"I heard that, too," Queen said.

"You think I am a warlord, eh, the pair of you?" The big man laughed. "*Domkopfs,* when will you learn that politics is all? This matter with Igonyela will be a lesson in African politics that will amaze you."

"But there is still one thing I do not understand, N'kosi," said Joachim, again shocking the other men with his new-found boldness. "With all the country we already have, *you* have—what is the *need* of this Malazi land, why is it so important?"

"It will give us the only things we lack—to complete our . . . *completeness,*" Morgan said. "Sugar, rum, rice—the staples for which our land is unsuitable. Then there is the dam we shall build, flooding the eastern reaches of the river to make a lake. Fish, *Jong,* but much more than fish—hippo. The hippo will return, settle permanently, breed, and we shall husband them." Morgan made an expressive gesture. "I do not need to tell you the value of the seacows. The elephant herds, in real numbers, are gone to the north and west, and we can do nothing about that. But the seacows are walking wealth. Two tons of choice fat, tender veal, hide, and small ivory to each adult beast!"

It was then that Morgan began to narrate the legend of the captured white child who would become a Banyoro matriarch, a woman who would be just shy of thirty now, by Queen's reckoning.

A small colony of bushbabies began to call from the thick foliage. The plaintive crying of the fluffy, longtailed lemurs seeking their supper of palm sap was the last thing Queen heard before he lapsed into a dream of an alabaster chieftainess borne on a litter by boy-sized coal-black men.

41

Malazi at Noon

The saffron, hunter's moon that had lit the veld and the slopes through the small hours had long since departed. But it was still early when Queen awoke. He signaled to the African nearby to get some tea brewing without waking the others, and the man swallowed the strip of biltong he had been cud-chewing and moved quietly over to the fire.

By the time the African had brought the mug of tea, full daylight was looming. Queen rose quietly, buckling his gun-belt. He moved across to the *spruit* and began to stroll along its wandering course until he found a place on a bend clear of overhanging growth where he could lie prone and sluice his face and neck.

There were still no sounds of voices coming from back over his shoulder. When he had doused himself thoroughly, he lit a cheroot and wandered on a hundred yards further, his footsteps almost noiseless in the bank grass. Rounding a patch of mimosa, Queen froze and drew back against the bush. The shape spiraled around a lower limb of the euphorbia just ahead was like two twined rope ends that had been flung into the tree and draped over the branch.

Mamba! By far the worst, the most inherently vicious, of

African snakes. Striped mambas were not necessarily fatal, as the others usually were, but all would attack without the slightest provocation, determinedly pursue a buck or a horseman for a mile at a stretch, and all were particularly vindictive during the mating season. And Queen could see now that the pair of mambas in the euphorbia were copulating.

For a second he hesitated. With the pistol you could not even be sure of getting one, and by the time you did get him, the other bastard could be into you. Queen turned and loped back across the grass.

Morgan was sitting up with a mug of tea. Queen called to the African who had made it. "The *isibamu* scattergun and some extra cartridges. Now."

Morgan yawned, fingering his chin. "Birds?"

"Mambas . . . greens," Queen said. He grabbed the shotgun and ammunition from the African. "Courting couple!" he added, turning and breaking into a run.

Morgan sank back on his elbows. "Make sure you get the female at least," he called after him.

Queen ran back the way he had come. At the mimosa bush he halted and put two shells between the fingers of his left hand in case he had to reload quickly. Then he began to edge round the scrub until he could see the white underbellies of the two green snakes. They were still at it when he gave them the left barrel at ten yards. One fell immediately, ripped away with the blast. The other, partly shielded by the branch, clung for a moment before it also dropped to the ground. The shattered one was dead, convulsing feebly in the grass. As Queen replaced the spent cartridge the second snake suddenly reared erect and came charging through the grass like a shepherd's crook come terrifyingly to life. At five yards he gave it the choke barrel and almost severed the neck, leaving the evil-looking head hanging by a strand of skin.

When the nerve tremors had ceased he pulled the mambas

43

out straight. Some grew to twelve or thirteen feet, by which standard the one under the tree was about medium size. But the one at his feet was a real daddy all right, going the limit for its kind.

Queen washed himself, then walked back towards the delectable smells of wood smoke, frying liver, and *spek*.

Morgan looked up, eyes wide in question, his mouth full of the fat bacon.

"Pair of fucking mambas. Greens," Queen said. "But one came adrift. Had to give him one on his own . . . a bastard going twelve feet."

The big man raised an eyebrow. "That's big. You were right to fetch the twelve bore."

"Filthy *duiwels!*" Joachim said vehemently. "Good shooting, Robbie," the young *ryder* added, clearly eager for the chance to praise Queen.

"Crocs and cats can be mean work," Morgan said. "But the mambas come more unexpectedly and they're harder to hit, I'll give you that."

The air was still pleasantly cool when they struck camp. But by the time they topped the ridge, near the highest of the beacons, the sun had burnt up the last lingering traces of mist. From the crest, you could just make out the thin gleam of the river at two points in the far distance, just short of the horizon. Nearer at hand, concentrations of game—impala, wildebeeste, zebra, bushbuck—were scattered over the immense panorama that spread before them, and further out Queen picked up straggles of ostriches and giraffes with his glasses.

"Pretty good, the game," Queen said.

"Still too many vermin, all kinds," Morgan said. "Needs some really serious cat-hunting. Forty, fifty hunters every day for a month to clean the killers out." He pointed. "Plenty of leopard along the Malazi."

"How far is it to the river, would you say, N'kosi?" Joachim asked. "Two, three hours?"

"What do you reckon, Professor?" Morgan said.

"Not pushing it, nearer four hours, I'd say," Queen said. "Not less."

"Yes, about that," Morgan nodded. "We'll take some scoff at the river. After that, the rivers really begin. Must be thirty or more between here and Igonyela—and more again between him and the Milebi border. They all stem from the Banyoro Ridge, they say."

"You really mean *rivers, that* many?" Queen interposed. "Not just *spirits?*"

"*Rivers.* But none to give much trouble this time of year."

"Igonyela's ancestors must have been shrewd men, N'kosi," Joachim said. "Better watered country than any I have ever heard of. Must be fertile in there, all right."

"Fat land, all right, you can count on it—and that's what has always griped the Milebi. Envy. Theirs is a very poor country by comparison."

Joachim edged his horse nearer to take the cheroot Morgan offered. He did not often smoke, but there were times when he felt he must, for form's sake.

Morgan laughed abruptly. "Bloody useless, those Milebis. The men bone idle, beneath their dignity to work. Consider themselves warriors and hunters, they do, the damn swine. The women make some effort. But they never shift their shambas or kraals, dung their fields, hedge for erosion, so the soil's worked out and crops poor." Morgan lit up a cigar for himself after rationing one out to Queen as well. "You know what Igonyela's people call them, these Milebi? The *Izinkhumbi,* the locusts," Morgan continued, "and it's right enough."

"They've got cattle, haven't they?" Queen put in.

"Inferior stock, badly nourished. As for the game, it was

good country once, but they ruined it, squandered their own meat supply like a bloody fox in a chicken run. Big-scale drives that wiped out whole herds." Morgan spat expressively. "You pick a suitable *kloof* and you dig serrated rows of big pits across the ends of the ravine, permanent twelve-foot pits. Then you circle a herd and stampede it into the *kloof!*"

"The cats must have thrived," Queen said.

The big man made a gesture of disgust. "Of course! That king of bloody lunacy always cuts several ways, spreads itself. For years the cats swarmed, but then, as the game grew fewer and fewer and moved into Igonyela's country the killers followed."

"Big trouble for them then?" Joachim reflected. "A migration of hungry cats like that."

"Oh, they were in trouble all right," Morgan said. "Losing any amount of good cattle. But we hunted them for him, like we did the crocs, by the pride, thirty, forty a day, no pissing around. Hans will tell you. We took out the numbers for them, by God, and it's another bloody thing the skinny bastard owes us for. Ah, but the Milebi mucked it all up, no end to their evil. Snared and pitted their watering holes, ran down the young of the waterbuck, the kudo, wart hog, reedbuck—with dogs—and they kept it up all year round, no let-up for calving, for breeding up again. Imbeciles, they are, the Milebi. Congenital is the word, I think. Born like it. Born mean killers. Unchangeable. It's the killing they worship. You ever see a bunch of 'em flaying a live goat, then letting him run around in his bare flesh and chopping his legs off one by one, you'll know what I mean, the dirty pig-rot!"

They reached the big brown river in the sweltering height of noon, and Joachim and Queen could see it would be formidable enough for an unburdened horseman to cross.

But Morgan seemed unimpressed. He continued into a new chapter in his hatred of the Milebi. "It was these people that

46

orphaned van Rieberk, you know," Morgan said, holding his large horse back to tell his story to the two *ryders* who flanked him on either side.

"Very drastic," he said, glancing quickly at Queen. "Ritual tribal entertainment, it was. The anus stake rite. That's how they do it—and how they did it to van Rieberk's brother and father. Bind them, hammer a stake as thick as your wrist up their assholes—until the point is lodged in the chest. Take quite a time over it, I hear."

It was this that dropped a mantle of silence over the two young *ryders,* as they drove their way across the river, a horse-length to the rear of the big Afrikander, who seemed to enjoy the spell he'd worked on them.

Inyala

They made camp that night in the lee of a *kopje,* near the source of a small *spruit.* There was little more than a trickle in the creek, but it was good water, not salty. While the beer was cooling in the *spruit,* the Africans made two cooking fires: the first for fast-frying small fish with amazambane potatoes and black udumba beans, to take the edge off the general hunger—the second for the slow simmering of big tigerfish steaks. By the time all had eaten their fill, the moon had already begun its ascent. The moonlight heralded the advent of the predators, and soon the hoarse death-scream of a zebra announced the beginning of the nightly slaughter.

Queen patted his belly contentedly. "Should sleep tight enough tonight, eh, gentlemen?" He reached for a brand from the fire, then paused for a moment before lighting up to jerk his head toward the distant sound of a sawing cough. "If we don't have any trouble with *them.*"

"Insolent bastards, the leopards!" Morgan barked.

"Should have thumped a couple of wildebeest," Queen said. "Dragged 'em out half a mile. That would have given the horses some peace."

Morgan nodded. "I should have remembered—sandwiched the meat with poison, by God."

"Speaking of sandwiches, I was thinking just now, that's how Igonyela could end up some day," Queen said irrelevantly. "The meat in the sandwich." He flipped a hand. "Oh, admittedly, one side is buttered . . . our side . . . but that's what he is. You can't get away from it. Another thing." He smiled. "I'm not suggesting it, but I'd bet you'd get the tract you want without any bride offer if your little black man thought he *couldn't* count on us."

"You think the runt doesn't know his situation?" Morgan said. "As for the other, do you think I'd suffer Bejane and his hyenas, for neighbors? The Milebi? Jesus Christ!"

"What I mean is," Queen quickly said, "if the little man should make a fuss over the valley, it wouldn't do any harm to remind him that your friendship, your mere presence, is critical to him."

"Don't try teaching me to suck eggs, *Jong*," Morgan said heavily. "But I'm glad you're beginning to grasp the rudiments of African politics. You ever achieve that ambition of yours, you won't hold onto it without politics, lad—you mark me."

"Ah, politics," Queen smiled, not without irony.

"I said you mark me, man. The two rules of survival." Morgan ticked off one finger. "If you can't annihilate your neighbor you make a buffer of him. Convince him there's a mutual threat, real or imaginary, and make common cause. The other is if you *can* annihilate your neighbor and it suits you to do it, then, by God, *do* it. That's the only kind of politics apes like Bejane understand."

"But, N'kosi, Bejane . . ." Joachim started to speak, but then broke off as Morgan held up a hand. It was the same chilling sound as before, the hunting cough of a leopard—a stratagem by which prey is panicked into disclosing its whereabouts. But it seemed closer now, and nearby a horse whinnied restively.

"We'll have a double turnabout-watch tonight," Morgan

49

said. "Don't want a horse crippled." He called to the Africans sitting around the other fire. "Matshongi, bring more beer from the *spruit* and then get the other gun-with-two-voices."

When the beer came, Morgan refilled his mug and handed on the skin bag. Then he took the shotgun that the African held out. He checked it, slid two DB buckshot cartridges into the chambers, and handed it back with two spare shells. "The *ingwe*. You heard him?"

The African nodded. "There are two, I think, N'kosi."

"Likely," Morgan said, "or more. This is *ingwe* country. Well, if that last one comes he will be here inside an hour. Take your kaross and sit with the horses. Arrange with the others to change with you when their turn comes."

Morgan finished his mug of beer and took the goatskin again. It was excellently cold now. He belched grandly—and then he spoke again. "Listen," he said with resonant authority. "Two years ago, I began to get scraps of information about a white man who had established himself with Bejane—a Portuguese half-breed from the coast. His name is Marao, but they called him *Inyala*, the crafty one. A real trouble-monger." He tossed the butt of his cheroot into the fire. "As a youth this Marao got taken in by a storekeeper and worked there some years, that's how he knows the dialects. Then one day he loaded a wagon with trade goods—presents for Bejane—cut the throats of the trader and his wife in the night, and trekked inland."

How did you learn all this, N'kosi?" Joachim asked, setting down his mug of beer. "I have never heard the others speak of it."

"Manoel! Manoel has a friend at Nambana, also a trader, with all the coastal connections. We pieced the scraps together. Igonyela's spies also confirm it.

"In any case, this Marao talks conquest, he hates all white men, fanatically.

"Bears watching, this Marao fellow. Word is he might

arrange an alliance with the Milebi. Black against white, you see. Igonyela and the Milebi together, and then put it to *Morganskeep.*"

"Oh, I doubt there's much fear of the little man being taken in by any such friendship bullshit," Queen said. "Igonyela's not that stupid from what I hear."

Morgan nodded. "Perhaps. He's convinced that the Milebi would never attack him because of *us.* But what he doesn't realize, can't believe, is that Bejane still doesn't really understand the value of real guns, still less what those Vickers-Lewises can do. He respects the noise and the novelty, but the information is that not even Marao can make Bejane understand what the big guns can do. The bloke still thinks it's a matter of numbers—you just hoist up your dead men as shields against the white men's bullets." Morgan breathed heavily, and swallowed off more beer. "So, as you may guess, I am not visiting the little man just for the First Fruits. I intend to get some things through Igonyela's head, aside from the program I have for the valley."

A sudden outbreak of noise, the mingled voicing and stomping of frightened horses, made Morgan break off. The outcry was followed by the successive reports of a shotgun, and then, the screams of a wounded leopard.

Morgan grabbed his rifle, the others following suit, as the three of them made for the horse line. Matshongi and another African *ryder* were already gathering up the halters of the terrified animals, trying to calm them. A few yards in the other direction another African stood ready to fire again.

"You did well, man," Morgan called out to him.

"It was the horses who warned us. There were two," the African said. "The other got away, but he is wounded, I think."

Queen moved the leopard's body with his foot. "*She* is wounded, this one's a tom," he said. The cat had taken the heavy-charge shot in the face and neck. "Lucky, too, leaves a good skin for you, boy." The African *ryder* bent to his knees, taking out his knife, but Queen stayed him. "No, not yet. Just let the gas out of his belly for now, and then drag him over to a place where you can see the bitch plainly when she returns. She'll be back. You just set him up as bait."

"After all that noise?" Joachim said, thinking he'd scored a point.

"I'll bet on it," Queen said, annoyed at being doubted. "Known one to stand over a dead mate two days."

"I'll take the next watch, then?" Joachim said too quickly. "Get the other one myself."

Morgan shrugged. "If you wish, *Jong.* There's no hurry, though. There's plenty out there. Give them an hour and come and have some more beer before you settle into the watch."

"That's right, Jo—get a pint of the Logan's down you first and you'll chase 'em with your bare hands," Queen said, and followed with a gentle chuckle.

The slim young man laughed a little, accepting the sarcasm. But he turned his head away.

Morgan put his big hand on the young man's shoulder. "You'd best get ready for your *ingwe, Jong*—Robbie and me, we'll try for some sleep."

Joachim nodded. "One more skin will finish my cabin mat." He reached for his Mauser, but Queen held out his own rifle.

"Here, try this one." He got out a handful of Männlicher-Schonauer shells. "She's a bit into her years now, this old girl, but you get one of those into her and that cat's not going anywhere else."

Morgan smiled. The gesture was not lost on him, and he knew that it was more than just an impulse of generosity.

"Yes, a good gun, Robbie's," he called out to the young *ryder*.

"Thank you, Robert," Joachim said. He knew no one else

52

had ever used Queen's gun, excepting Queen's father before him. Everyone at *Morganskeep* knew that—because once there was a man who tried to do it, and the beating he took was talk for a long time after.

Some hours before dawn the Männlicher sounded twice, in quick succession, but neither of the white men beside the fire bothered to shift himself. In the morning, Joachim, first with the tea, smiled and held up his thumb in the manner he had seen.

"*Geluk!* It *was* the female, Robert. A good one."

"Well, all right, laddie," Queen said drowsily. "Now you finally got yourself the best carpet in *Morganskeep*."

The Country
of Many Rivers

They had entered a rolling terrain of low hills and crossed a score of narrow rivers, Queen and van Zyl well out in front, about a half-mile ahead of the others, who followed at a leisurely tripple across the plain.

Joachim van Zyl lowered the binoculars he had at intervals been using to scan the ground ahead. "*Ingonyama,* Robert. In the donga—stalking the little bucks."

"Yes, I know," Queen said shortly.

"What did you say, Robert?"

"I know," Queen said. "Just relax, friend."

They came to the Manekewa River near noon, Morgan leading the crossing. On the far side, Morgan halted and waited for the others, holding his horse under the shade of a witch tree. He made a motion downstream when the others drew up. "We'll follow the river for a while. It's not direct, but further on, about a couple of hours, it makes a big bend. There's a swamp there, and wallows, usually holds buff and sometimes a few seacow. We'll take in a present for 'em, one or the other."

"Good politics," Queen grinned. "They say that Leslie became king of the Usuthu country through hippo and buff meat."

"Plus taking the right brides," Morgan said drily. "Chief's daughters. Don't forget that part of the politics."

"Well, Jo, sooner or later you are going to have to do your duty to Africa too," joked Queen. "Whether you like it or not."

"Don't you worry about Jo!" Morgan said heavily. "He's a Zyl. Jo knows his African pentateuch, Englander! *You're* the one learning the rules, not him. You can have all the cunt you want—even married ones, *providing* you make a deal for them. But you don't take, or steal; a woman is either a gift or you pay the lobola. You don't forget *that* politic!"

"Christ, I know that!" Queen said with unconcealed exasperation. "What are you telling me *that* for?"

"I'm *reminding* you," Morgan said with just as much heat. "Because plenty of others fouled up relationships that had taken years to achieve, and they were mostly whites who didn't believe in isigodhlos."

"For your information, Chief," Queen said sharply, "I do believe in the isigodhlo. But only when a man's good and ready." Queen pushed up the brim of his wide hat. "And I'll tell you something else, big teacher. Don't worry about the women rules—I've known them ever since I was knee high."

"Glad to hear it," Morgan said bluntly. "I'd dislike having to hold an Indaba on one of mine. But I would, and don't you forget it!"

Queen stared for a moment, then grinned. "I daresay you would at that. The bloody drastic stuff again, eh, N'kosi?"

"Bedrock politics! Igonyela is our northern frontier, buffer, and that is a bloody sight more important than the skin of any randy *domkopf*, black or white," the big Afrikander said frankly. "And the purges for breaking the women rules are bloody drastic all right, even with Igonyela."

"I know all that, too," Queen retorted. "Bloody rough on

the women, but it stops things spreading. It's all plain enough. You know what I'm really interested in—and I've never seen a woman worth more than ten head, anyway."

Morgan's expression lightened. "Well, you will this time. . . . Worth more than thirty head."

"You mean Igonyela's women are that beautiful, N'kosi?" Joachim asked, suddenly curious.

"I mean that for the First Fruits there are also the specially chosen ones, the *Ingougee* girls, from the vassal kraals the width of Igonyela's country," Morgan told him.

"What's the bargain lobola price for them, the husband-hunters?" Queen called as he moved around a *kameldoorn* tree in his path.

"One that should suit you, Shylock, if you impress their fathers," Morgan said. "Some of the women, the *etula* gift girls, are free."

"No lobola?" Joachim looked surprised. "That is surely very unusual, N'kosi."

The big man nodded. "Just these special occasions. Gifts between chiefs, headmen—but sometimes the custom is extended to us . . . by fathers who know their politics," Morgan added drily.

"Very sensible," Queen said.

For a while they lost sight of the river, and began to descend into a wide basin, a fairyland of color, forested by a variety of exotic trees. Nor was the color blaze all overhead. In the glades and avenues where the sun penetrated, the forest floor was stippled and strewn with small banks and medleys of various lilies, primroses, tulips, and tiny violets. But when the group finally emerged from the haven of the trees, onto the sun-drenched panorama of the plain, they saw only random belts of buffalo thorn to relieve the spectacular expanse.

Morgan shaded his eyes until he found the identification he

56

was looking for, the characteristic outline of teak and "cucumber" trees which almost always confirmed the presence of marshland. He pointed ahead down the long slope. "You can't see the river, but you'll see the big horseshoe of the trees. The bend is about a mile wide. Swamp in the rains, but it'll be firm enough now. You two take the south side. Go for seacow. But remember, not *in* the river. Don't want to spend a lot of time and sweat retrieving. I'll try the north side for buff in the wallows."

"On your own, in swampy stuff?" Queen said questioningly.

The big man's lips twitched. "Don't you worry about me, lad. I'll do it the old way, with a line of retreat, and I won't be walking. Now let's get it clear. It's good young meat we want, but not too much, so try for a three-quarter grown heifer, or if not, two calves."

"If we're both lucky that'll be too much meat," Queen said.

"If you find what you want," the big man said, "fire two rounds rapid, to show you've succeeded. If it's me I'll do the same." Morgan turned to the African beside him and held out his binoculars. "You heard the plan, Matshongi. Watch and wait till you hear where the shooting is, then come for the meat with the others."

Before the two horsemen ahead of him had completely disappeared, Morgan rode down the slope. Halfway across the flat he turned his horse toward a shaved-off *kopje* topped with a single stunted waterwood tree, like a holly sprig on a pudding. On the hillock, he halted against the tree. The first wallow was occupied by a square-lipped white rhino and her calf, divesting themselves of their ticks and gadflies in the brown mud. Aggressive creatures, the rhino, especially with young. Morgan knew it could be trouble whether the beast attacked or withdrew—either way he was liable to set off a

57

chain reaction among any game the meadow held further
ahead. Yet he could not afford a wide detour that would take
him right off course and into the open.

Morgan lay flat on the stallion's back, like a sack of meal, his
arms around the horse's neck, whispering to him, and the
horse meandered slowly past the wallow. To the myopic
rhino, the charade of man and horse, at thirty yards, offered
only the dim outline of a hump-backed antelope, and after a
moment the mother and calf went back to their ablutions.

Now horse and man crossed into the bend made up of
oozing patches of ground that billowed with hippo flies,
winged devils capable of biting through shirt and horsehide.
They rose from the stinking ground as Morgan drew his
neckcloth to his eyes and brushed the malignant insects away
from the stallion's neck and sides.

Slowly he threaded through the palms and fever trees and
the tall reed beds, until he heard the unmistakable throaty
grunts and the thinner murmurings of unweaned calves. He
dismounted and crept forward, keeping his gigantic frame
low. He covered the few yards to the edge of a clearing. The
parcel of buffalo ran to fifteen or so, young adults and older
beasts with calves, four of the big ones sporting in the wallow,
scuffling and rolling on their sides. The rest, well coated with
mud, were standing around the glade leisurely browsing.

He found the one he wanted, a bullock still short of his
prime. He considered the pattern of it. Even mounted, as he
intended to be, he would not have an easy shot.

Morgan backed off, slowly, carefully, but at his third or
fourth step a reedbuck whistled and crashed away somewhere
on his right. He froze, sucking in a breath.

The old bull ceased grazing. He raised his massive head,
staring straight toward where the man stood, peering intently,
then questing the air from side to side. He was obviously a

veteran, a patriarch who had many times played his part in the preservation of his kin, and the cat rakes on his flanks bore witness to past battles, past victories. Morgan watched the great scimitar horns until finally they lowered again.

By the time Morgan had fully retreated and was again mounted, he had arrived at the plan he would pursue. He gentled his horse away at an angle from the bull, and then, just before he broke cover, he drew the rifle from the saddle-bucket and extended himself forward and down so that his upper body was to one side of the great stallion. Now Morgan hooked his elbow through the loop that ended the leather thong which hung below the big animal's neck, at the same time catching his heels over the stallion's cruppers behind the saddle. His weight supported by the purchase of his heels and his arm notched through the sling the leather loop offered, Morgan eased the horse through the reeds until horse and rider emerged onto the edge of the large clearing. It was an old Boer technique, hiding the outline of your body in this fashion, a thing Morgan had learned when he was a boy, a maneuver he had had to use often enough to be very glad he had learned it well.

Now, moving steadily forward, Morgan estimated that he'd achieved firing position, and with a sudden and powerful movement he yanked himself upright and fired at the bullock. It was pandemonium, but rising above all the thrashing and snorting was the bellow of the enraged patriarch, and the big Afrikander could see the beast wheeling to charge. Morgan stood his ground and fired again, this time for the heavy neck of the staggering young bull, who dropped like so many rocks dumped from a split sack. The big bull checked his thundering advance, wavered for a moment between the appeals of revenge and the herding instinct, and then turned away to crash after the others already in flight.

59

Morgan had lit a cheroot and was fingering the cigar thoughtfully when the other *ryders* came up.

Queen brought his horse alongside and took the cheroot that the Afrikander offered. "Good shooting," Queen said as Morgan held out a match to him.

The big Afrikander smiled. "Good shooting, yes," was all he said as he held the match to Queen's cigar.

*   *   *

It was late afternoon before the party moved on again into the sweltering veld that now seemed endlessly and crushingly vacant, empty of the merest sign of life. Yet it was only an hour or so later that Joachim van Zyl rose in his stirrups and pointed, "Smoke, I think, N'kosi, smoke!"

Queen raised his glasses. Far ahead, just discernible against the lowering sky, the tell-tale spirals of cooking fires screwed into the wide sky like distant twisting palms. The Afrikander lowered the binoculars. "Right enough, lad!" he acknowledged.

Igonyela's central kraal stood on a sweep of ground which ran back gently from the river. The kraal itself was set within a hinterland of gold, brown, and green shambas. Before this large settlement lay the silver streak of the river and behind it the purple rumpled coverlet of faraway hills.

To the west, the hills pushed closer to the settlement, and at their nearest point they ended in a broad projecting defile that sloped down to the even stretch of plain and the kraal itself, where, on either side, herds of black, brown, white and piebald cattle were being driven to the enclosures of thorn and plaited fencing by a crowd of boys. You could see women moving now, carrying large earthen calabashes along the winding paths of hard-trodden red murram soil that ran back from the river.

Save for their scant bead aprons, the women were naked,

and when one of them saw the horsemen across the river, she cried out till they all turned. For a moment or two they paused to stare, and then they ran, laughing and yelling, toward the kraal to announce the arrival of *Dukusa*.

Igonyela

According to protocol, there was no immediate meeting with Igonyela. Save in time of war, or a matter of pressing urgency, any such unseemly precipitation would, by tradition, have constituted a mutual discourtesy. But all had been made ready for the momentous arrival of *Dukusa.* As soon as Morgan's party had unsaddled, the *ryders* were led to the huts specially prepared for them, whereupon a succession of deferentially smiling matrons began to serve a great variety of steaming platters.

"When do we pay our respects to the King, N'kosi?" Joachim asked as he plunged into the mass of food before him.

The Afrikander took a drink from his gourd. "I see him tonight. I'll present you two tomorrow."

"I don't know why you bother with that formality crap, Chief," Queen said, a whit disparagingly.

"It costs nothing and they like it," Morgan said sharply.

"We are in no hurry, Robert," Joachim said.

Queen shrugged. "Just thought to speed it up, get it over with," he said, and went back to his eating.

"Get *what* over with?" Morgan said, with real annoyance now. "You'll be here for a week, man, with the extent of the *Ukunyatela,* the traditional thing. And wait till the *Umewasho* and the *Umndlunkulu* girls are all assembled!" He got to his feet. "Don't worry, you'll get all the action you want pretty soon. Both kinds," Morgan said challengingly.

Queen flickered an eyelid at Joachim. "Hell, wasting time's as bad as wasting ammo, I say. Bring us back a couple of the *Umewasho* girls, Chief. That's the free gift *etula* kind, isn't it?"

Joachim turned his head away as if in embarrassment. When the big man had gone off to make his visit, Joachim got out a cheroot and smoked pensively for a while. At length, he looked closely at Queen.

"You don't believe in fooling with the customs, Robert? You think them nonsenses?"

"Oh, I'm familiar with most of the rigmaroles, Jo, whatever His Lordship may think," Queen said. "But mostly they *are* bloody nonsenses, and we don't have to go through any kowtowing bullshit here. Igonyela is beholden to us, not the other way round."

"Even so, as the N'kosi said, it costs nothing," Joachim said mildly.

Queen chuckled. "You won't catch me protocoling myself crazy, man. Come to that, Piet wouldn't, either."

"Yes, but I think the bond between them is very old," Joachim said. "Older than they are. Did you know that the N'kosi's father fought in support of the old King, and also saved his life? A spearthrust that the *Dukusa* himself doctored for a week, so van Rieberk once told me."

"No, I didn't know that," Queen said. "I knew from my father that the old *Dukusa* got all the best trading in this country—ivory, horn, hides, gums, yes, and gold. All for a few bags of umgazi beads, brass wire, solempore and red calico. Some lucky spearthrust, that . . . a king's ransom for a pint of iodine and a few stitches!"

Joachim bridled. "Oh, no, Robert, there was much more than that to it. Morgan brought medicine, crops, righted and revenged many wrongs, hunted down the thieves, the murder

63

societies, exterminated the cannibals in the hills, the bad witch doctors . . ."

"Oh, Christ, don't get me wrong," Queen recanted. "All I meant was that *those* were the golden days, eh? A man could make something of himself."

"Well," the younger *ryder* studied his cheroot for a moment. "I'm really quite content as I am with the N'kosi. A year more and I will be given the same full status as yourself and the others." He tried to explain it more graphically. "It is a good life, I think, and also, of course, I feel under, under . . ."

"Obligation?" Queen offered.

"Yes, that. Under obligation to the N'kosi."

"I agree with all that except the last part," Queen said. "But this is still what they call a land of opportunity, Jo, and a man's greatest obligation is to himself. And don't worry about Piet; he would never stand in your way if he thought you really meant it. Anyway, there's no hurry . . . think about it."

"Oh, I will indeed, Robert," the young man said. "I do a great deal of thinking, you know."

Morgan returned in obviously good humor. He put down a large calabash he was carrying and motioned to Matshongi to get more gourds. "A little of the King's special brew for you," he grinned. "Wouldn't call it very powerful, but quite pleasant—by the gallon. Give me some of the real dew, Jo."

Joachim handed across the square Logan's bottle. Morgan tossed off a dram and poured himself another with a grunt of appreciation. "Aside from the *Ukunyatela,* it would seem that our visit is very timely." He grinned more enigmatically. "I have a couple of chores for you rascals. Lion. Small kraal about thirty miles north. Some vermin turned man-eater. Shows up every two or three nights now, broke in through the roof of a hut last time. Took a woman back out over the boma."

"Christ," Queen said, with disgust, and held out a hand. Morgan passed him the bottle.

"You said two chores, N'kosi?" Joachim asked after a pause.

Morgan smiled. "Ah, well, a white rhino has turned up downriver. When it suits him, he stalks the woodcutters, morning and dusk. Charges from cover. So far he's killed two and ripped up another pretty badly."

Queen listened, and took himself a second drink.

Morgan nodded. "A strange one—born extra vicious, or driven mad. An earful of ticks, hippo flies on his balls . . ."

"Well, if they know where his regular patch is, shouldn't take too long," Queen said resignedly.

Morgan shook his head. "It might because the thing is they want to get him themselves. You may not need to do anything except cover them—in fact, that is what they want you for."

Joachim looked puzzled. "But I thought they were not hunters, except of small game?"

"That's right. But this is a kind of special business. First, it's tribal revenge—second, it's a ceremonial hunt—the *Nqina Yehlambo* ritual, the washing of the spears. Very elaborate, the cleansing hunt, washing their spears in the blood of honor, traditional ending of a period of mourning."

"And they will try to kill the mad rhino with spears?" The young *ryder* frowned dubiously. "And they are not even hunters, N'kosi?"

Morgan shrugged. "That's what they want—that's how much faith they have in our guns."

"Bloody lunatics. Bloody suicide," Queen said shortly.

For a moment there was silence. Then Morgan leaned forward. "Bloody *work* is what it is. You are hunters, the boss hunters—it will be up to you to plan it, *you* will tell *them* what you want, of course." He paused. "I have told them that we will do it," Morgan said conclusively. "If you boys aren't up to it, I will do it myself, with Matshongi."

65

There was silence again. Queen shot a glance at the Afrikander, his massive, stolid bulk. Morgan smiled grandly. "Big fuss about an old *witbooi*, isn't it? Me, I could take him out with a handgun or a slingshot."

Queen laughed sourly. "I'd like to see that, N'kosi. Oh, yes, I'd like to see that."

It was partly because of his regard for both men that Joachim felt a kind of embarrassment at the element of acrimony that now crept into the exchanges between them. He tried to dispel it.

"Well, Robert," he said, "at least they will have to reward us with much free *etula*, much pleasing company, eh, N'kosi?" the young *ryder* said lightly.

"I fancy they'll do that, all right," Morgan said, and looked hard at Queen, who stared back. "But we'll all sleep unaccompanied—eh, Professor? I want you, *Jong*, in good shape for the chores you're looking forward to."

*　　　*　　　*

Joachim woke to the chattering of female voices. There was no sign of Morgan, but Queen and Matshongi had tea brewing, and the kraal was fast coming astir. While the men took their tea, they watched the girls working on the building of an additional hut for Morgan's party. The first two layers of plaited grass mats had been fixed to the framework of poles, and now the girls were laying on the final covering. With a large wooden needle, the girls outside passed a woven grass rope through the wall of the hut to the girls inside, who then drew the stitch tight and returned it, while other girls worked on the flooring of the hut, positioning and anchoring mats.

Queen caressed the tight brown buttocks of a worker who came within reach. The girl giggled invitingly.

"Well, Jo," the older *ryder* said, "you're going to need plenty of raw eggs and steak to hold up your end around here. And lest we forget, the true beauties are yet to come."

66

The younger man grinned self-consciously.

Queen stood up and stretched to his considerable height. "All right, let's take a look around." Queen called over his shoulder to Matshongi. "Tell the N'kosi we'll be back to eat in a little while."

The kraal was bigger than any Queen had ever seen. Cattle-milking corrals divided the inner and outer bomas, and these also contained the granaries, eight-foot grain pits covered with stone and overlaid with dung. The *Inlundkulu,* or great meeting hut, faced the main entrance and fronted the clustered beehives of the royal entourage that circled the King's sleeping hut, and these isigodhlo huts, palisaded with woven reed-fencing, were further distinguished according to the wives' status. A spearman stood on either side of the harem entrance, and for a moment Queen paused to speak to one of the guards.

"What was it you asked him, Robert?" Joachim said when Queen rejoined him. They moved along again in a slow stroll.

"About the different huts," Queen told him. "One side for the senior wives, the others are for the younger ones." He grinned sardonically. "A sight more Godly than some of our towns, eh? All the stuffing they want, of course, but the wives have their own huts and the unmarrieds have got theirs."

The *ryders* reached the outer boma of the kraal and looked out across the veld. Beyond the cultivated shambas, cattle ranged wild, mostly matched longhorns, black, red, red and white, all white, osyter blues, these last more ornamented than the others, ears trimmed to fancy shapes, horns trained askew, necks hung with bead fringes, some shaved like plucked virgins.

Joachim nodded approvingly. "Good stock, Robert. As good as the N'kosi's."

"Well, originally some of the breeding bulls *came* from his father, according to Hans, but well cared for, certainly. Not surprisingly."

"You mean it's their wealth, their money?"

"More than that. Supplies pretty near everything they need. Milk, meat, leather for their karosses, betshus, even their penis stalls, sinews for thread, dung for the fires, the shambas, and not forgetting the stud fee—the lobola."

Queen got out a cheroot. "Yeah, let's go get into the steak and eggs." He winked. "Got to start building up our strength, boy. There's a heavy night ahead of us, I daresay."

Everywhere now the kraal was alive with people, their numbers swollen by those who were coming for the first fruits from hamlets and vassal kraals as far away as several days' march. The men were generally sturdy and above average height, though dwarfed by comparison with Morgan's men. Most wore plain betshus of belted hide, but a few of the younger ones curtained their leather penis-stalls with fancy aprons decorated with the short-cut tails of jackals, monkeys, sheep. In contrast to the foppery of the men, most of the women were unadorned save for their much more diminutive betshus which, in the case of the younger unmarrieds, were hung provocatively low on the hips.

Skin tints varied widely, both men and women coal-black to brown to lemon-yellow.

"Suit you, do they?" Queen muttered to Joachim.

"The women are bald enough," the young *ryder* said.

"Pudendal depilation," Queen snorted.

"Plucking it out?"

Queen nodded. "Every damned hair. Legs, armpits, fannies—object is cleanliness and beauty."

Joachim smiled. "Different places, different ideas of beauty, I suppose."

"I suppose," Queen said, "except as to basics."

"Basics?"

"Big tits and big rumps," Queen said. "Hourglass principle."

Joachim looked aside for a moment, as if deciding something. And then he faced Queen and tried to hold his eyes
with his own. "You seem so easy with things, Robert—so
self-assured."

"Oh, I've covered a few countries, you know," Queen
answered lightly. "Man and boy, as the old-timers say."

"Forgive me if I embarrass you, Robert, but I admire you,"
Joachim said suddenly, inexplicably.

Queen looked up sharply, but saw that the younger man's
expression was sincere. "For what, for God's sake?"

"You were very young when your father was killed, yet,
even so, you carried on alone, hunting and trading. Sometimes through countries from which others had not returned.
Robert, that took a helluva lot of courage, I think."

Queen squeezed his chin, accentuating the cleft in it.
"Aaah! I'd been most of those places before, with my father.
By the time I was sixteen, I'd been around, I guess. It wasn't
so risky."

"The N'kosi does not agree," Joachim said. "He also thinks
it took courage, and plenty of risks for a very young man on
his own like that—and more from men than from the big
beasts."

Queen smiled impishly. "Well, right enough. There were
times when my bowels got away from me. The whole trick is
to put a convincing face on it, brazen it out. If ever I had real
doubts, smelt hostility, I always made 'em think I was just the
scout, prospecting ahead for a big body of trekkers and
hunters. But what the hell, I'm no different from you.
Trousers go on the same way yours do, I dare say."

They had circled back to their huts now, and saw that
Morgan and the Africans were already making good progress
with platters of reedbuck liver and kidneys, eggs, *messbolletjie*
buns and fresh tea.

They ate in silence while Morgan ran his eye over them like

an inspecting sergeant. "Right then, boys—get a shave and clean shirts, I'd say. Matshongi, the feathers, and don't waste time—the king will be waiting on us now."

Queen smiled. "Political touch, Chief?"

The big Afrikander grunted impatiently. "I've had enough of your jibes, Professor." He jabbed with his cheroot. "Time will come when you'll find prestige, ceremony, counts for more than fifty *ryders*."

They moved off through the kraal towards the king's hut, Morgan in the lead, then Queen and Joachim, followed by the three African *ryders* walking abreast, each of these last now wearing a single scarlet-dyed ostrich plume—insignia of a master hunter—the procession of the six big men drawing excited murmurs from the women and envious *Aiws!* from many of the men.

Igonyela sat awaiting them, encompassed within the throne of his forebears, beneath the pruned spread of a crimson-garlanded kaffirboom tree. A small, thin, gray-haired man of jet-black coloring, wearing a royal cape of leopard skin, Igonyela's demeanor was as unimpressive as he himself was untypical of either his sleekly rotund father or his tall gangling mother.

To one side of his massive throne, a ceremonial heirloom carved from solid ebony, stood Igonyela's valet. In earlier times the holders of this high office paid with their lives for such offenses as nicking the king's cheek while shaving it or presenting him with an imperfectly polished headring. But now the valet's duties were reduced to wielding a long-shafted shield over the king's head to ward off flies. On the king's other hand stood Imbhongi, an obese professional praise-singer, a retainer whose inventive eulogies often lasted three hours at a stretch and continued well after the king himself had withdrawn. Facing the throne in a tight semicircle sat the council elders, red flamingo feathers of seniority set in their headrings. Behind this group, a throng of common people squatted, leaning on herding staves or spears.

Morgan strode purposefully through the half-circle of elders and couriers. He halted before Igonyela, who rose, hand upraised, with a smile of welcome.

"*Sakubona,* I see you, *Dukusa!*"

"*Bayede, Umtwana,* I see you, royal chief," Morgan returned the little man's smile, his resonant voice contrasting starkly with the king's piping tenor. Morgan turned and made a gesture of introduction. "My hunters. All Inkosis of *Dukusa.*"

Now Queen, spokesman of the *ryders,* took a pace forward. "*Bayede!* Greetings, *N'kosi Yakomkulu,* king of the fairest!"

For a moment Igonyela considered the strange swarthy man impassively. Then he nodded, approving the hunter's use of the dialect and the formal flattery. Igonyela moved a step forward, holding out his small hand in the manner his own father had first learned from the former *Dukusa.* In turn each man in Morgan's party stepped forward to take the King's hand as Morgan announced the man's name.

Igonyela resumed his seat. He held out his snuff box of polished horn and motioned to Queen and Joachim. "These are the Inkosis who will destroy the devil *ingonyama* at N'gama?" He pointed with his fly-whisk in the direction of the vassal hamlet terrorized by the man-eater.

Morgan snapped his fingers. "The criminal is already dead!"

Igonyela nodded approvingly. The traditional introductions over, he rose and moved toward his hut for the short interval protocol required. With a look of amusement, Queen watched the man depart.

"Well, what do you think of him, Jo—funny little bugger, what?" he whispered to the young *ryder* at his side.

71

Morgan overheard. "Listen, *Uitlander*, with what he's got under that royal betshu, he could stuff a rhino cow—so don't you worry about our little king."

Morgan seemed increasingly annoyed with Queen, with Queen's incessant sneering. Why the lad was carrying on like this, the big Afrikander did not know—but he guessed it had to do with the fellow's will to show himself a man savvy enough on his own account, to prove himself independent of Morgan's leadership. Well, if that was it, so be it. Morgan had tamed many before him—before this ambitious Afrikander.

Igonyela had returned now, and at his signal six girls came forward with khambas and calabashes of beer and wine. The sextet of women were personal servants-in-waiting of the King's household, and were already turned out in the distinctive style of tribute girls in expectation of the festivities that would presently follow. Their hair, red-tinted with ochre, was piled dramatically high. Only their ivory ear plugs and brief betshus of beads were of modest size. As for breasts and buttocks, they were generously ample. But one girl in particular, a pale-skinned thing of about seventeen, already outshone the others.

As she knelt to fill Morgan's gourd, her swelling breast brushed his knee, and he stretched out his hand to cup her chin and lift her face until she raised her long lashes and diffidently returned his look. But it was not Morgan alone who gazed at her swaying golden buttocks as she withdrew. Queen and Joachim had also noticed her immense appeal, and they too stared as she turned her back to them and retreated from the hut.

Queen inhaled approvingly. "By Christ, a ripe plum, that one. Pity the king's chosen are verboten."

"They aren't . . . to me," Morgan said reflectively, through the smoke of his cheroot. "I shall take two 'wives' from this *ukunyatela,* and I think that will be one of them."

72

"So what about the big taboo, the politics of it then?"

"Between *chiefs*, these things can be arranged, boy," the Afrikander said, not unaware of Queen's envy.

Queen sighed ironically. "The privileges of kingship, oh, my."

"If you like," Morgan shrugged. "But you may achieve them yourself some day. But witness, my friend, I shall *pay* for her." He turned aside and gestured to Matshongi. "The *igawozi*, the pale-skinned one, who served me. Find her father and bring him to me once I have spoken to the king."

For a further hour, smoking and drinking, Morgan's party watched on as Igonyela dealt out government and summary judgments. Then, when he had disposed of offenders and contentious ones, Igonyela dismissed Queen and Joachim, bidding them to take their leave with the river guide he had assigned to them.

*   *   *

Downriver from the kraal there was a place of undulating, marshy meadowland, dotted with dwarf palm and reed beds, a favorite haunt of all sorts of bird life. The ponds and lakelets abounded with eels, bream, grunter, jackpike—and sometimes the tribespeople made catchment drives, wading in all abreast until the shoals were boxed into shallow backwaters and baylets.

The two hunters were fishing, trolling for tigerfish as the African guide paddled the dugout downstream. Back upriver, in the kraal, Morgan filled the Igonyela's gourd from the square bottle he had packed among his gifts.

They had finished the small talk that etiquette demanded and now the Afrikander began to outline his suspicions of the threat from the north, the agitating for attack that had been underway since the advent of the provocateur Marao.

But Igonyela had it that no real threat existed. He strove to reassure Morgan that Bejane would never bring himself to outright attack. According to the little black man, if that had been Bejane's ambition, he would have already attempted it, Marao or no.

Morgan listened to Igonyela's obtuse reasoning, his exasperation mounting. No longer able to contain himself, he bent forward and grasped the little man's ear in the traditional manner that applied between men of equal rank, a gesture meant to mark the significance of the utterance about to be made. "Listen to me, Son of Zungelela," Morgan said. "Am I not your friend? Did I not ride to your aid many times, as the first *Dukusa* rode to the aid of your father before you?" Morgan tapped the Buntline on his thigh. "We shall need these and more, much more than these, if the jackals come, my friend. And I tell you they are near to it now, with this Marao! Mark me, my friend—invasion is not far away!"

The black man seemed confused, tortured by a reality he could not admit. A congenital procrastinator in major matters of unpleasant character, Ingonyela was clearly shaken by the vehemence of Morgan's words.

"Your words are troubles, N'kosi," Ingonyela said nervously, pulling at his lip. "But we know that your wisdom is great, as your strength is great. We will place sentries beyond the kraal, send more spies to the north. I will advise you of what we learn, and then you and I will talk more of it."

"As you wish," Morgan said. "And now, my friend and ally, let us discuss another matter, the business of the valley and the dam."

It was with relief that the black man welcomed the changed subject. He launched into the harangue of hedging and issue-dodging that routinely prefaced serious bargaining. Morgan listened to the flow of rhetoric in silence. This was mere ceremony, of course. The cards he held would prevail, he was sure, and he waited until the King had talked himself out before raising a hand.

"Five hundred head. A big price, and you know it!"

Igonyela shook his head. "It is much land, much!" He made a lateral and vertical sweep with his fly switch. "A day's march whichever way the crows might fly. Many *morgens*, as you call it."

"Yes, many *morgens* of nothing!" Morgan said. "Of cactus and dry beds that are no use to you."

Igonyela pursed his lips, uncertain of Morgan's true aims. He began a delaying speech again. This time the Afrikander cut him short. "But listen, I shall make that wasteland flourish with seacow, fish, cane, mealies, and other crops from which your people will benefit also. I give you five hundred head," Morgan repeated, with solemn emphasis. "For *nothing*, for a *wasteland*. And even that is not all."

Morgan drew an envelope from his shirt pocket. With an air of importance, he unfolded the paper and handed it to the African. It was the photograph clipped from the French magazine Santoro had once shown him. The woman, a circus performer of some kind, wore only a white tasseled strip across the nipples of her copious breasts, and another fringed band that barely covered the depression between her big cushioned thighs. She lay stretched indolently on a black rug, her milky whiteness starkly contrasting with the black background and her coiled black hair.

Igonyela was spellbound. He gasped. He gazed at the vision beckoning from the picture, his eyes frantic with longing.

Morgan waited for the right time. And then he said, "Not this one, my friend—but one like this one, just the same. Younger. Even more *konyololo*. They are of an unusual white tribe, *umtwanas*."

Igonyela did not take his eyes from the picture. When he was able to speak, it was barely a whisper.

75

"What is the lobola for such a one?"

"*Nothing*," Morgan said, with a wave of munificence. "A gift to reward my friend for his good sense in the matter of the valley."

The little man jerked bolt upright. It was done! He started to raise his arm in acknowledgment. Then he recalled his position and manners, and put out his hand instead. "*Dukusa. N'kosi Nkulu!* Now we are one people in all things."

"Not quite," the Afrikander said. "But the bond shall be strengthened further yet."

"So?" Igonyela looked puzzled.

"I shall select two wives from the *Umowasho*," Morgan told him plainly. "One I have already chosen. Then, also, two each for my captains, the white *inkosis*, and one each for the others. For mine I will pay the lobola. But the others should be gifts." Morgan raised a finger. "Remember, my brother, the *inkosis* are to rid you of the devil *ingonyama* and the killer of the woodcutters."

The monarch spread his hands grandly. "*All* shall be gifts," he said. "The fathers of the women will be honored."

Ukunyatela

Toward evening, the *ryders* returned. Matshongi escorted Joachim and Queen to where Morgan was taking his ease by the river. It was the place where the women filled their waterpots, where a trio of euphorbias made an inviting pool of dappled shade. The big man lay stretched out in a hammock woven of grass ropes, and to one side of him two other hammocks had been slung from lower branches.

Queen recognized at once the saffron girl who wielded a long-handled fly-whisk over Morgan's head. With each movement, her well-lofted breasts trembled.

"Congratulations, N'kosi," Queen said in greeting.

"I do not believe in wasting time," the Afrikander said drily. He glanced approvingly at the girl by his shoulder and yawned. "However, I was not unmindful of you fellows. You can each make two choices. What you choose, you will be delighted to learn, are to be considered gifts."

"Any more like the *meisie* here?" Queen said.

"Enough," Morgan said. He turned onto his side and felt for his cheroots. "Why don't you laddies take a swim. I might follow you down later myself."

Queen mopped at his neck. "Not a bad idea, eh, Jo?"
Joachim nodded nervously, apparently anxious over the prospects ahead.

*   *   *

The *ryders* swam for a half hour or so, and the sun was
almost behind the hills when Morgan shouted from the bank
for them to quit.

Back in the kraal, the main cattle corral had been cleared for
the festivities, and already it was filled with tribespeople, the
yellow light of the perimeter torches reflecting on their shiny
expectant faces. Igonyela sat in his throne at the head of the
corral, a pair of elephant tusks thrust into the ground on either
side of him. Next to him, there stood a second ebony throne.
He motioned Morgan to it, and then indicated the row of piled
grass mats set nearby for the others. On the King's other side,
his chief counselors squatted at the edge of the dancing arena.

Now Igonyela raised a wand of crimson-stained sheep tails.
At his signal, a troop of chanting men filed into the circle,
veterans, seniors elected for some feat or service, and this, the
Inewala ceremony, was the annual acknowledgment of their
merit. Imbhongi, the praise-singer, began an oration, but he
was soon cut short by the catcalls of the crowd, impatient now
for the violence of the *inkunzi*, the sacrificial slaughter of the
first bull.

Snorting threateningly, a jet black bull was driven to the
middle of the corral, where he was ringed by the Inewala
men. At first the crowd was hushed, but then the spectators
broke into an encouraging roar for action. The Inewala hurled
themselves against the bull. In a milling hysterical swarm,
they seized the big animal's horns, ears, legs, testicles, penis,
the heavier men leaping onto the enraged beast's back. The
bull held, bellowing and swaying, and shouldered up to his
feet again. But then he was down again and lost to sight under
the assault of struggling naked bodies. Igonyela rose and

strode forward to touch, with his wand, a horn of the
frantically straining beast, the signal for the kill. The Inewala
went to work with bludgeons, staves, *knobkerrie,* fists. Gradually, senseless under the rain of heavy blows, the bull ceased
his struggling. Grinning with exultation, the Inewala headman placed his knife at the base of the animal's ribs, made a
deep slit, and thrust in his hand. The death bellow of the bull
ended abruptly as the blade severed the windpipe. The
headman sliced the scrotum from the quivering loins and,
with a flourish, held the massive testicles aloft, the man's face
working with pride and hysteria. He laid the organs at
Igonyela's feet, and dropped to his knees in completion of the
first potency rite.

Now the bullfighters, and any of the crowd who could force
a way in, joined the free-for-all contest for the meat, tearing
great steaming hunks from flanks and quarters.

Queen nodded toward where an attendant was slicing the
testicles of the bull into raw strips narrow enough for the
monarch to swallow. Morgan winked. "Plenty more of that
kind of fruit coming yet," he said.

A woman came forward and removed the royal leopard skin
cape from Igonyela's shoulders while a second woman knelt to
take the betshu from his loins. Igonyela moved forward again,
further into the circle, his small wiry form unadorned save for
the ostrich plumes of his headdress and the elongated white
ivory penis-sheath that flashed against the contrasting black-
ness of his skin. The monarch turned slowly in a full circle so
that all might observe him, and then two men ran forward,
clasped hands, and lifted him onto the body of the dead bull.

A troop of women entered the circle, their hair high-piled in
a conical arrangement, pricked with yellow flowers.

"The *Umndlunkulu* girls, N'kosi?" Joachim whispered.

Morgan shook his head. "No. These are the chosen of the
married women."

The dance of the high-coiffed women drew to a close, and a

fresh group of women promenaded into the arena, the elite complement of nubile girls, the flowering of Igonyela's country. They were tall, taller than their menfolk, and some, with stupendous breasts sculpted down to narrow waists that swelled again to voluptuous thighs and rounded buttocks. Save for their tiny pubic aprons and waving red plumes, the badge of their maidenhood, the women were naked—not a single hair disfigured the smooth hemispheres of their remarkable bodies.

"Well?" Morgan said heavily. "You impressed, *Uitlander?*"

Queen's cheroot glowed, and he blew out a stream of smoke. "Alleluia. By Christ, you could make a grab blindfolded and you couldn't go wrong."

Morgan stretched out his legs and smiled. "The cream of the commoner crop. But the *Umowashos* come last, and they're the aristocrats—daughters of headmen and notables. Fewer in number, of course, lads—but with them rank counts to suitors as much as looks. But all in good time."

"Ah, well, I've always been a man of the people myself," Queen said with mock humility.

The women had begun to sing as they moved, and every aspect of their dancing was frankly salacious, each gesture plainly intended to arouse the senses. Rounded bellies were thrust in and out, slowly at first, then frenetically, in simulation of rising sexual pleasure, bare buttocks flaunted in sudden bending movements, as the girls sought to inflame the men and incite lobola offers worthy of their charms.

"When do we stake our claims?" Queen nodded expressively.

Morgan laughed shortly. "Gently now, lads—when in Rome, you know."

"Ballo to that!" Queen replied. "I think I'm set, Chief."

Even as Queen spoke, Igonyela rose and began to address the assembly, sometimes gesturing toward Morgan and his

80

party. The excited *Umndlunkulu* girls began to form themselves into two ranks.

Queen leaned across to Morgan again. "Talking about our
right of first choice, wasn't he? I got that much."

The big man nodded. "The rest was about the great honor
of association with *Dukusa's* chiefs, the protection we afford as
mighty allies, and so on."

Morgan got to his feet. His size was never more evident as
he stood to his great height in this assembly. "Our turn to give
thanks and renew the pledges now." The general uproar sank
to a murmur as all eyes were turned to the great Umlungu
chief. Impressively, the timbre of his voice matching his
stature, the big man spoke in praise of Igonyela's virtues, the
worthiness and valor of his warriors, the fairness of their
wives and maidens. At first it was the traditional flattery, but
then he remarked the folly of unpreparedness and the fearful
complacency abroad in the land, unpredictable disasters of
war and plague, mayhem and pestilence. And then Morgan
reminded them how, in the past, these catastrophes had been
surmounted through Igonyela's alliance with *Dukusa*. He
paused. Then abruptly he resumed, forcefully declaring
that only through continued close alliance could *Dukusa's*
friends remain assured of survival against natural calamity
and human enemies. He repeated the phrase—human
enemies—pointing meaningfully to the north, and then,
dramatically, Morgan snatched the pistol from his holster and
fired into the air.

It was an effective performance, his command of the dialect
never more skilled. And now his audience rose to a wild
chanting of passionate salutes: *"Dukusa! Dukusa, who fears no
king nor beast!"*

Grave, unsmiling, the massive Afrikander raised his thick
arm in acknowledgment, and then he lowered himself back
into the throne.

81

Throughout the big man's oration, Queen had listened with a consuming admiration that now he felt bound to admit. "No doubt about it, N'kosi, every day I learn a little something from you." Joachim nodded heartily in endorsement of the tribute.

Morgan smiled. "Business behind us now, *Jong*. Shall we play?" He fingered his chin, and regarded the women that waited in two ranks. He signaled to Matshongi, and indicated two girls, one in each rank. The African *ryder* went forward, carrying one of the skin bags that had been filled with the yield of Morgan's recent buffalo kill. To each of the women in turn, Matshongi held out a fistful of shimmering entrails. Proud at having been selected and delighted to receive the gift, the girls raised the strips of slippery offal to their lips, threw back their heads, and lowered the delicacy into their upturned mouths, licking it down with their glistening tongues sucking in the long slimy lengths until they disappeared.

Now Matshongi also handed to each of the girls Morgan's second gift, a crimson blanket. They draped themselves in the bright cloth and came forward to where their new master was seated. Both were very appealing—one, the color of sunlit corn, genuinely shy; the other, contrastingly dark, pretended to maidenly reserve but had a certain air of repressed vivacity about her.

"*Embula,* show thyself!" Morgan called to the darker girl.

"Lord!" Obediently she let the blanket fall, then slipped the beaded *betshu* from her hips and stood naked, striking an attitude before him. She was big, but excellently proportioned, and her skin was glossy as a seal fresh out of water.

The Afrikander rose, and laid his hands on her shoulders. He slid them down her back, and lifted her by her taut buttocks until her breasts were pressed against his chest. He lowered his head, pressing deep into the hollow of her neck and shoulders for a second or two, and then let her back down onto her toes. The second girl, the shy one, was still bent on one knee in the traditional attitude of obeisance. Morgan pulled her to her feet and lifted her similarly, kissing each of her breasts before setting her down again.

The selections confirmed, Morgan clapped his hands, and a captain of the king's guard came forward to escort the women away, to await *Dukusa's* summoning in due course.

"My compliments on the *meisies*, Chief," Queen said, as Morgan sat down again. "Especially since you didn't happen to pick one of my fancies."

"All right, boy," Morgan said, his voice edged with challenge, "let's see how well you can do for yourself."

"Don't worry about me," Queen snapped, pushing to his feet.

He called briskly to Matshongi. "Right, Boetie, man, bring forth the buff guts again and a couple of blankets, and follow me." Hands on hips, cheroot stuck in the corner of his mouth, Queen moved deliberately along the front rank of women. Halfway along the row, he halted before a girl whose prodigious breasts he lifted in turn, with the back of his hand, kissing the nipples as he did so. "This for sure!" When he had moved, Matshongi handed out the formal gifts of offal and blanket to the beaming virgin. Now Queen turned to the second rank and as he passed further along, half-pausing once but then proceeding again, a rising murmur of speculation went up from the crowd. He halted again, this time before a taller woman, more willowy than the first.

As before, he examined her breasts and felt her skin. He nodded to Matshongi to make the award.

When he had seated himself again, Queen leaned over toward Morgan. "I like the extremes, N'kosi," Queen said. "White as snow or black as pitch. They don't get any blacker than my two."

Morgan was unimpressed. "There are still the *Umowashos*, remember."

"Ah, yes, but a bird in the hand," Queen said.

83

Queen lit a fresh cheroot and settled back. "How about it then, Jo?" He jerked his head. "Your turn, boy."

Joachim glanced at Morgan uncertainly. "I *have* to take a woman—an order, N'kosi?"

Queen shook his head as if mildly reproving, but said nothing to add to the young man's obvious dilemma. Shyness was no crime, nor was it always permanent. "Hell no, *Jong*," he said at last. The big man waved it away with a smile. "But you could do a lot worse for yourself . . . and for us. And you'll have to come to it sometime, raising good stock, if I know the Zyls."

"It is just that I do not *know* these women, and, sometime I might meet a woman, learn to know a woman . . . ," the young *ryder* groped to find the course of his sentence, wanting to clarify the reason for his hesitancy.

"It's love we're all looking for, laddie—if the truth be told it's the same with all of us," Morgan said, his voice more gentle than Queen had ever heard it. It was not the kind of reply Queen expected, and he was touched by the big Afrikander's sensitivity to van Zyl's feelings. "But, listen, *Jong*—this wouldn't change that. It's not the same thing, boy. We also need women like we need horses, you understand— that's all *this* amounts to, and it's no big thing."

"That's right, Jo," Queen added, "it's just like going for a ride, and these are pretty fine mares." He grinned. "A fella's got to hoe the mealie patch every now and then—it comes to nothing, man."

Joachim looked away, his face working with confusion. This exchange had not escaped Igonyela, at least he could tell that the tall slim *ryder* was discomforted by the matter of the women, and the monarch was troubled to observe this. The young man, so *Dukusa* had informed him, was extremely well born, a son, in fact, of the great white chief in the north, the N'kosi van Zyl, of whose prowess Igonyela was aware.

Moreover, the boy had a certain affinity of blood with Igonyela's own kind, so how to explain his reticence in a matter that called for the opposite? Was there something wrong with the fellow? Was he not his father's son?

Igonyela threw out an arm expansively. "Why does not the young N'kosi make his choice? Are our women old and ugly, then? Without loins to bestow delight?" The little black man grinned, pleased with the pithiness of his rhetoric.

"The N'kosi is young, as you say," Morgan said.

Igonyela looked blankly—and then nodded as if in understanding. "Ah, like the young bull in his first heat, knowing not which cow to mount first? But are they not all pretty calves? Take two of them—my gift to him—a big one and a small one."

Morgan winked knowingly, trying to skirt the issue. "The young N'kosi is rightly particular, as befits the son of a king. He wishes to see the *Umowasho* maidens." Morgan shrugged his shoulders. "The son of a great chief, you understand."

"Aiw! You are right," Igonyela exclaimed. "It is better that a first wife should be of fitting rank."

"That's right," Queen called out, "Jo here is a hard man to please."

Igonyela nodded, approvingly. He gestured with his wand, and at once there was a fanfare of drums and flutes, prelude to the final ceremonial display of nubile women.

Chanting as they snaked into the arena, their regal black ostrich plumes, insignia of their high caste, swaying with their naked bodies, the *Umowasho* girls undulated as one, moving with even more abandon than had the dancing girls who preceded them. Joachim stared morosely at the animated chain of women, his eye drawn to a slender girl whose movements were rather more tentative than the others, who in fact seemed contrastingly demure. To be sure, she conformed to the generally vigorous pattern of the dance, yet there was

85

an air of aloofness that suggested she was an unwilling participant.

Morgan put a hand on Joachim's shoulder. "Well, Jo, you want to withdraw?"

The young man made a quick decision. "No, N'kosi." Joachim hesitated, searching the older man's eyes. "In fact, N'kosi, there is one there . . ." the young man said, motioning with his head.

Morgan signaled to Matshongi, who came to their side. Morgan muttered something in his ear, and then, as the dancers came full circle again, the African *ryder* stepped forward to the slender girl and the parade halted.

Matshongi delved into his bag, and breathlessly the girl swallowed a small amount of the proferred delicacy he handed her. She folded herself into the crimson blanket that, fortuitously, almost matched the bright *agapanthus* blooms in her hair.

Now Queen, Morgan, and the other *ryders* joined the chorus of congratulatory shouts from the crowd as Joachim rose to his feet.

The girl walked slowly toward him, hands clasped around her blanket, anxiously regarding the tall slim hunter from beneath her eyelids like a fawn in the moment before flight.

Suddenly a man broke from the crowd and strode forward to intercept her, his hand raised in a gesture of denial. A burly figure of fifty or so, the man wore a cape and girdle of cheetah skin, distinctions that implied rank. He addressed the girl, waving his hands about and clearly urging her to return to the others. Then he turned and began to beseech Igonyela in a manner both solicitous and insistent. Igonyela listened for a time, and then he cut him off with an impatient motion of his wand.

"What's the matter?" Joachim whispered to Queen. "Is he the father of that maid, Robert?"

86

"No, but he's making some kind of claim on her," Queen said. "Disputing the gift. I think he has already agreed lobola for her."

Igonyela motioned the tribesman to stand aside and addressed the girl directly. She answered Igonyela's questions, her statements quiet but frank. The king silenced her and turned angrily to Morgan. "It is a stupidity of the father's," he said peevishly to the Afrikander. "The girl should not have been sent out with the *Umowashos*. She has already been promised. But now her father has hopes of higher honor— with yourselves!"

"And this man, the suitor, wishes to hold to the bargain?" Morgan asked.

"Yes, he desires the woman greatly," Igonyela said.

"Who is he?"

"He is called Kilende, the headman of a kraal in the north—the village of the man-killer. He is a good and loyal servitor, but stubborn." Igonyela shrugged his thin shoulders; it seemed that no *Ukunyatela* could ever be held without some such tedious bickerings. "I will order the *etula*," he decreed suddenly, petulantly.

"No, wait; remember the North. Loyal and stubborn headmen will be wanted," the Afrikander said pointedly. "Let me speak with him."

Igonyela called to the plaintiff: "Listen to *Dukusa*. And heed him as you would heed me," he added testily.

Morgan leaned back, resting one hand on the massive arm of his chair. "Chief, what lobola did you agree for this woman?" he said equably.

"Twenty cows and two oxen," the headman raised his voice vehemently. "She is mine."

"Do not shout at me, Chief," Morgan said in a quiet voice. "How much of that price have you paid?"

"The woman is mine. . . ." The tribesman began to rant

again, his face strained with anger, but now the Afrikander's voice bored through his like a drill. *"How much have you paid?"*

The African's lip dropped. "Ten cows. The rest I pay when I take her."

"Then she is not yours yet," Morgan snapped. He reached for the bottle by his side and poured himself another dram of Logan's. But as he drank the tirade began again. Morgan put down the gourd, and shot out an arm, grabbing the spotted cape about the headman's neck. He jerked the African close, forcing him to lower his head. "Man, what is my name?" he thundered into the startled black face.

Morgan shoved the dumbfounded man powerfully away, and the man tumbled to the ground. Sweeping the crowd on either side with a look that invited their participation, Morgan paused dramatically. Then he spoke, "This man-from-the-hok, this bumpkin, this simpleton," he said in dialect, "does not know who I am. *Tell him!"*

"Dukusa! Dukusa!" the throng fairly shrieked.

"Now, man, Kilende, interferer in my affairs," Morgan declaimed, "know also that the young N'kosi is a chief of *Dukusa*. The chief who will rid you of the *ingonyama* you cannot deal with," Morgan said scathingly. "Your cattle will be returned, and ten more added—a gift from *Dukusa*." Morgan jabbed at the headman with his cheroot, emphasizing each word. *"And the N'kosi will take the woman he has chosen."*

"Lord, I will not oppose the N'kosi," the headman whimpered. And then he offered the traditional phrase in recognition of seniority: "You raise me to your armpit."

Joachim snatched at Morgan's sleeve. "N'kosi, I would prefer it if the maiden were allowed her own choice."

"The matter is over," Morgan said. He glanced at Kilende. "The palaver is over too."

"Still, I would like it," the young man persisted.

Igonyela bent inquiringly toward Morgan, who briefly

explained the young man's wish. The king stared at Joachim with disbelief. The business was resolved. What had the girl's wishes to do with it?

Morgan shrugged, then motioned to Matshongi, and the *ryder* took the girl's arm and brought her forward.

"You have heard what has been said, woman," the Afrikander said temperately. "Which of these two chiefs do you wish for husband?"

The slender girl looked mutely ahead. The silence hung like a pall. "Do not be afraid," Morgan said reassuringly. "Neither you nor your father will suffer."

She raised a hand to one of her golden breasts and then sank to her knees at van Zyl's feet. The young *ryder* reached for her wrist and raised her to her feet.

Queen poured himself a whiskey, and then another in a separate gourd. He held out the second drink to the glumly silent headman with a grin. "Here, Chief, friend, white men's wine—elephant blood!" When the African hesitated, Queen thrust the gourd at him insistently. "Drink! Are we not joined more closely with your people now? And when we come, we will kill more than your mangy lion. Come," he demanded, "let all see your good will, man."

The African drank, but there was no good will in the face he turned toward the Afrikander.

*   *   *

It was approaching midnight now. Queen was virtually alone in the corral, the rest of the Morgan party and Igonyela and his entourage having retired nearly an hour ago. He sat staring into the night, his mind racing. He finished the last of the Logan's and got unsteadily to his feet. He began walking aimlessly, and in time he stood before the dark tableau of the three euphorbias etched against the starlit sky. It was then that he heard a muffled cry and thrashing sounds, and saw,

89

there, in the deeper shadow, a man and a woman struggling on the ground, the woman scrambling to break free. Queen grabbed a handful of crinkly hair and wrenched the man to his feet, and he no sooner had the man upright than he stretched him flat with a short right hook of blinding force. For a moment the African lay as if pole-axed. Then he groaned painfully, his hands to his face.

"On your feet," Queen said evenly.

"*Unkunyatela, unkunyatela!*" The man pleaded the traditional excuse of permissible fornication during the period of high festival.

"Not this time, not with unwilling ones. My woman," Queen said. "You understand? *Dukusa* woman!"

He took a step nearer and the African began to scramble to his feet, but as he reached his knees, Queen stretched him flat again with a colossal kick between his narrow buttocks. Then he bent to the black man's ear. "You go quick, quicker than the bullet from my *isibamu,* or I cut off your parts."

But the man could not move, in any case. He lay where he was, coiled on his side, groaning.

Queen regarded the woman with a frown. "Did you invite this rudeness?" he said harshly.

"Lord." She spread her hands in an attitude of blamelessness. "They followed me." She held up five fingers. "Each wished me to kneel for him, and I ran. But that one found me."

"Woman," Queen said, "you must smell strongly of love. Now take this," he said, and slipped a bullet from his gunbelt and put it in her hand. "Any more like that, you show them this. Very strong medicine. You tell them they try to make you kneel, I will put same like this through their bellies. Red hot."

The woman looked up at Queen, only half understanding. But when he raised his hand she understood all right and moved up close to Queen, smiling, alluringly pressing her breasts into his palms. Then she lay back on the grass, her breathing husky. He knelt beside her and she worked at his belt and when she had it unfastened and had jerked his trousers away from his hips, she sat up on her haunches and slid her betshu from her hips with an urgent tug. Then she moved forward onto her knees and buried her face in the grass, offering her rounded buttocks in the attitude of submission and invitation. But Queen had another idea, inspired by a motif in the earlier ceremonies. He let his trousers all the way down, and took her by the shoulders until he had rotated her head to between his thighs. Then he raised her chin until her mouth found the quarry he wished her to discover. It was evident to him, from the teeth he felt at first, that she was new to this sort of thing, but she got the hang of it soon enough. "Better than buffalo guts," Queen said finally, trying to break her grip. But she would not stop. He had to push her away, and when he did, she made a little whimpering sound, and went down onto her face again so that her buttocks were again lofted in invitation. Queen stood up and in one sweeping powerful motion he raised the woman to her feet.

"What is your name?" he asked, taking a cheroot from his shirt pocket. In the light of the match her eyes were big and shining.

"Malende, Lord."

"And your husband's name?"

"Nodwengu."

"How much lobola did he pay for you?"

"Only seven oxen, Lord, but my father already owed him cattle."

"You are good, Malende. You make a man happy. How would you like to enter my isigodhlo?" Queen said. He could see that the proposal staggered the woman. In sequence her face first lighted, then fell.

"Lord, he would not sell me," she said resignedly.

Queen smiled. "I think he might. I think I shall convince him."

Her eyes went to the bullets in his belt. "With the strong medicine?" she said breathlessly.

Queen laughed. "Hell, no. I will repay the lobola he gave, adding a buffalo or a seacow and two skins of *ingwe.* That will be enough. And not too much, either, for a good woman like you."

The woman stared, unbelievingly. But it was dawning on her that Queen was not trifling. Her face lit with rising excitement—to enter the isigodhlo of a N'kosi of *Dukusa!*

"He has many cattle," she said urgently. "But it is true that he always hungers for more." An inspiration came to her. "Perhaps you could also give him the *Umlungu* wine when you speak with him?"

Queen chuckled. "Got a head on you too, eh, my plum? You give a man a good time and then you do some thinking for him too—what more could I want? You ever do that before, Malende?" Queen motioned to make his meaning clear. The woman shook her head and then grinned.

He watched as she donned her betshu, then he hugged her, patted her rump, and walked with her for several yards until he was sure she was safely away toward her hut. Then he wheeled and came back to where the black man had been cowering on the ground. Queen was eager for another go at him, but the African had long since fled into the darkness.

Queen sighed heavily, a portion of the night's business settled, yet more still waiting to be done. The Logan's had made him too dull-headed to remember exactly whether there were two or three girls who might still require his affections.

The Duiwels

They had not even breakfasted when Kilende and a captain of the king's guard brought the runner to them. The runner was not a young man, middle-aged and wiry, but he had jog-trotted throughout the previous day, arriving in the small hours, a performance which he himself would not have considered any great feat, descended as the man was from a race of men capable of traveling fifty miles in a day.

Kilende headed the trio to where Morgan and his lieutenants sat on grass mats taking tea. "Lord," the headman said somberly, "there have been more killings by the devil lion."

The Afrikander nodded and went on chewing. He held out his mug to the woman hovering in the background and signaled her to get more from Matshongi. "Let the runner tell it," Morgan said curtly.

The lean sinewy tribesman took a step forward. "It was two nights ago, Lord. The *duiwel* beast leapt onto the roof of a hut. He tore through the thatch and dragged forth the woman. Then Akido attacked him and was slain."

"Who is Akido, a hunter?"

Kilende shook his head. "No, we are not hunters. Just one of our young men."

93

"But with more courage than the rest—all of them," Morgan said flatly, as he speared a kidney with the point of his knife. "And why was the man alone?" Morgan inquired, without seeming interest.

Kilende shrugged uncertainly, but the runner spoke up: "Lord, he desired the woman who was taken. But he was poor, with only two cows. If Akido had killed the *duiwel*, he would have gained the woman without lobola." The runner glanced at Kilende for confirmation, and the headman nodded assent.

"This Akido," Morgan went on, "did he wound the cat before it killed him?"

"We do not know," the runner said.

"Did you look for blood, for a trail, then?"

"To what end, Lord?" the African said simply.

Morgan shook his head from side to side. He glanced at Queen but said nothing.

"You have tried pits?" Queen said, eyeing the runner. "Placed where the cat has previously broken through your boma?"

"Oh, yes, Lord, but the beast avoids them—he is bewitched," Kilende declared resignedly.

"None are bewitched," Queen said heavily. "A few, finding no resistance, become insolent. You have tried fires around the boma I suppose—big ones?"

The runner and Kilende nodded in unison. "The devil does not heed them," Kilende answered.

The runner rolled his eyes. "Because he is bewitched."

"All right, enough!" Morgan said. He nodded toward Queen and Joachim. "The N'kosis will go with you. Inform the king, then bring the dogs and wait for my men at the kraal entrance."

*   *   *

The two Africans, Kilende and the runner, rode doubled up, each behind one *ryder*. With the added load on the horses, after the first hour they had slackened almost to a walking pace, the heavy heat sieving down through an overcast of leaden thunderclouds, oppressive and enervating. Even so, the hunting dogs kept up an exuberant gait, eager for the work that they sensed awaited them. They ranged ahead of the hunting party, disinclined to heed the commands they had been reared to; the chief culprit was the leader, a big reddish hound who had twice taken off spontaneously, after first a buck and then after a hare.

Near noon the party halted by a straggle of fig trees. The runner sat apart from the rest and chewed biltong that he took from his pouch.

Despite the heat, Queen made tea as a matter of habit, and laced it with a shooter of whiskey. When he had finished, Joachim turned to him.

"Do you think we'll really need the dogs?"

Queen shrugged. "Fifty-fifty possibility. But there's a man-eater up ahead, *Jong*—make no mistake."

Joachim nodded. "But if he comes right into the kraal . . ."

"You know what a lion is like with game," Queen said. "Scraps, guts, and shit all strewn around the kill, often only the ass eaten off. Not like that with man-meat, *Jong*. No sirree. With man-meat, you find a skull, a foot, maybe a couple of fingers. Nothing left for the birds and the hyenas, no sirree. And they lick the skin off first. We don't get them in the kraal, we're going to need those dogs to smell 'em out—maybe miles away!"

They ate their fill of figs and pressed on again, riding a long while in silence. Then Queen sidled his horse over to where Joachim was holding the flank position.

"So how does the far-flung future look to you, lad?"

"The future?"

95

"That's right, Jo—spill it."

"Ah, Robert, I am not much of a talker, you see," Joachim said, his eyes averted.

"Nor am I," Queen said, "not really. Just wondered what your ambition is, is all."

"You mean for cattle, wives, an isigodhlo?" the young *ryder* said.

"That, and a bloody sight more than that! Jo, I mean do you aim to always remain a *ryder* like the others?"

Queen's tone was not contemptuous, but the younger man bridled a little, instinctively. He had a profound respect for Morgan, also for the calling of *agter ryder,* whether under the N'kosi or his own father, Groot Piet van Zyl, in the north. "What is wrong with that, then?"

"Nothing is wrong with it," Queen said. "Pays well, good life. Better than most in this land. But bigger things are possible, much bigger."

"It may be, but I think myself a lucky man already, Robert. Doubly lucky."

"Doubly?" Queen raised his eyebrows. "How do you figure that?"

"Well, I can remain with the N'kosi, or return to my own country." There was more than a touch of pride in Joachim's voice, as if the privilege of a choice was not given to many, and that was true enough, Queen thought.

"Yes, but that's only a choice of *scenery,* Jo," Queen said, not a little contentiously. "You would *still* only be a *ryder,* wouldn't you? Forever?

Joachim frowned, a bit perplexed. "What else? Am I not learning the business of it for that reason?"

Queen squeezed his chin, wondering how best to put it.

"What I mean is, my friend, Groot Piet has only one son by his first wife, his white wife?" he asked finally.

96

"That's right. *Klein Piet*. Not that he is *klein* now. On the contrary, he is a man, bigger than Groot Piet."

"And when the old man goes, young Piet will rule your country—the Zyl country, right?"

The younger man nodded in innocence. "Of course. Klein Piet is a good man, a great hunter—strong, generous."

"Maybe. But it wouldn't make any difference whatever he was. None of the rest of you *ryders* are eligible?" Queen persisted.

"Eligible?"

"Reckoned suitable. Suitable to follow the old man or have any real hand in it?"

"But Klein Piet *is* the most suitable," Joachim said, stating the simple logic of it. "He is clever, schooled in the south, and even in other countries. He has been to America and to Holland," the young man added, as if he felt a measure of reflected prestige in the fact. "Beyond doubt, Klein Piet is well fitted to govern."

"I accept that," Queen kept on, "but what I am trying to say is that he would govern anyway because his mother was white." Queen had not wanted to put it so unceremoniously, but he had to make the point before he could get on with what was in his mind. Hell, it was relevant, and it was true.

Joachim considered the blunt assertion, staring ahead. "This is also understood, Robert, by all of us," he said evenly.

"Yes, it's understood," Queen said. "And I'd probably be the same as Groot Piet, in his shoes. But there's a lot of bloody nonsense in this business of race and skin, Jo. I'm not running down my own kind, mind you. Men like Morgan, van Zyl, De Buys, and the others before and after them are as much Africans, have as much right to their countries as anyone. It's just that what I'm thinking from your standpoint, mind you, is this: there's one way you could rank equal with Klein Piet or

Morgan or any of them, Jo—and that's by partnership, full and equal partnership, with a white man."

Young van Zyl seemed unimpressed with the daring statement. He shifted in his saddle. "I have never thought beyond serving Groot Piet, or the N'kosi—and what other white man, like them, would wish to make an agreement like that except with *another* white man?"

"*I* would," Queen said. "With the right man. And you're right by me any time!"

It was out now. Take it or leave it, Queen felt better to be unburdened of the notion that had obsessed him.

"Thank you," the younger man said quietly, earnestly. "I know that you intend to trek on your own sometime, Robert—would this chat be to do with that . . . ambition?"

"Yes," Queen said, "it would, by God! This continent is still wide open. I intend to find my own country. There's no secret about it, and don't think Morgan's opposed. He'd lose a *ryder*, yes, but he might gain an ally in the end."

"Oh, I understand *that*. But there are things I do not," Joachim said. "Like you have not asked any of the others to join with you—or perhaps you have?"

"No." Queen shook his head. "As to why not, that's my business. You're the man I want."

"But why should you wish to share with *any* man?"

"Because I want to build to last! Look, I'm not an educated man—but I've studied the 'kingdoms,' *Jong*, black and white, especially those that came apart. And what I know is that two good men add up to a lot more than one good man if you're · planning to really last. And that's what I'm after, lad, a long thing, a big thing, what they call a dynasty!"

They were winding through a disorderly straggle of acacia that lay across their path when suddenly the air was rent by a sound of savage conflict. A hundred yards ahead, out across the open parkland, battle was raging close by the swollen bulk of a baobab tree. A boar, his flanks and shoulders streaming from the hooks of a leopard, stood resolutely, his back to the tree. The leopard charged again just as they emerged from the fringe of the acacia, and now the hounds were fully roused, demanding to attack, and the cat, hearing them at once, quicker to react, retreated a few paces and stared.

"Get one into him, Jo!"

Queen leaned from the saddle swearing at the churning dogs, then, as he heard Joachim's rifle fire, he gave the dogs the release. "*Loop, loop!* Go!"

Slewed with the bullet impact, the yellow cat wheeled and took off as the dogs streaked across the turf. The boar held its ground under the baobab, peering through his small dark eyes at the new danger racing toward him. He was dying on his feet, the blood fountaining from his wounds.

He tried to gird himself for the new test, but his instinct told him that it was beyond him, and he turned aside to lead his antagonists away from the baobab. For a few unsteady steps, he moved toward the fringe of the trees, then suddenly faltered and fell onto his side.

Queen dismounted and drew his pistol. Joachim rode up to where Queen stood. "You get the cat all right?"

The younger man nodded. "The first shot slowed him. My dogs made it onto him sooner than I expected."

"How were they?"

"Good."

"They bayed him?"

"Treed him. Made it easier."

Queen bit a scrap of chapped skin from his knuckle. "We'd been two or three minutes sooner the old hog here would have got away with it." Joachim detected a note of sympathy in his voice and looked closer at the wart hog. The long ragged hair on the crown of his head, like a tufty abbreviated mane, was as gray as the cracked hide of his flanks, but it was the "warts" more than his hooped tusks that gave him his grotesque appearance. He had the puffy-cheeked look of an old-time fighter who has taken a lot of punishment.

The young *ryder* pursed his lips. "The ugliest of them all, some say."

"Not to me," Queen said. "Honest. Honest-looking compared with that spotted bastard. Braver too. Know what he was doing?" He jerked his head toward the baobab. "He was fighting what the military call a rearguard action; there's a sow and family down there. The old porker was holding the bridge, and he held it for long enough. That bastard would have killed every damned one of them for sport!"

The runner had joined them from the edge of the trees and Queen motioned to the African. "You ride with the other N'kosi now." Queen got the rope from his saddle and made a loop around the boar's hams. "Drag him with us for a piece, take the hyenas further out from the burrow."

As they moved off again, the rope wound around his pommel, Queen smiled and nodded back over his shoulder. "Lesson for you there, Jo . . . African politics again . . . bears out Piet."

"What do you mean?"

"Importance of allies. Sow and the brood survive because they had an ally . . . not necessarily their daddy either . . . the old warrior. Come to that he had one too—us."

"But the boar is dead," Joachim objected.

"Makes no difference, principle still holds," Queen said. "You hadn't killed that spotted bastard he'd have hunted the sow for a week. Got the lot. First her, then the piglets. Not for food, for pleasure."

In the next two hours they came to three more rivers. The first was practically dry, but the others, though much lower than the bank striations that marked their levels at high water, were trouble enough.

100

"I have been thinking carefully about what you said earlier, Robert," the young *ryder* said as they climbed the bank of the last crossing. "I want you to know, I want to thank you now, for the great, great . . ." he sought for the English word.

"Compliment?" Queen made the suggestion with a grin.

"Yes, compliment. The honor you have paid me."

"Raised you to my armpit, eh?" Queen made a joke of it, but the younger man nodded seriously.

"That is true enough—since I am not a white," he said solemnly.

"Aaah, shit, lad—you're half van Zyl and half Zulu, and that's a bloody sight *higher* quality combination than most men can claim," Queen said with force. "And it's no compliment, boy, just practical thinking. You know the ropes, and, what's more important, I'd trust you a hundred percent."

*   *   *

It was not quite dusk when they reached the small kraal of Kilende, but already the entrance had been closed and there was some delay before the extra barrier of piled thorn brush could be drawn back enough to give the horses passage.

Night in the kraal had become a period of uneasy vigil, and most of the villagers had already retired to huts that they had sought to reinforce with interwoven switches and stakes. Only a sparse gathering of elders had assembled to greet the hunters.

The runner passed among them now, assuring the elders of their deliverance with voluble gestures. But not even his personal testimony to the great power of the white men's guns seemed to produce any great restorative effect. All seemed to have become imbued with an unshakable belief that N'gai himself had visited this scourge upon them, for their sins—and that the slaughter would continue until the god's sacrificial demands had been met.

101

Queen surveyed the resigned faces with a look of mingled pity and contempt. "Christ, Jo, the whole bloody village is about ready to pull up and flit. For some scurvy tick-ridden cat who likes black hams! Bloody unbelievable!"

He raised himself in his stirrups. "Go to your huts, and sleep without fear!" he called out. He remembered something, drew the Männlicher from its bucket, and fired one-handed into the air. "The arm of *Dukusa* is about you!"

The villagers straggled off, and when the *ryders* had unsaddled and watered the horses in the central cattle enclosure, and settled the dogs, they followed the runner to the hut that had been set aside for them. It was in the wide lane fronting the inner periphery of the boma. They stowed their gear and left for a look around. The island of the cattle corral, within the outer boundary of the kraal, was at one end of the village, its surrounding palisade reinforced with thorn brush, so that the raiding lion was thus faced with a second quite formidable barrier, and it occurred to Joachim that, ironically, though typically, the cattle were more safely ensconced than their owners. On their way back toward their hut, they saw a man with a torch heading toward a pile of brush in the midst of the aisle. Queen called to him sharply. "Not yet! And not there!" He had already noted two or three wood piles further along.

The runner stepped forward. "But Lord, it is already past time." He made a gesture indicative of the gathering darkness.

"You make fires in the wrong places," Queen said. "We will have three fires along this boundary track." He pointed to the places chosen. "Equally spaced apart. The same also on the other side of the kraal behind us," Queen jerked his thumb, "where the N'kosi van Zyl will be waiting. You understand?"

"The N'kosi knows that the fires will not last until dawn?" the runner offered woodenly.

"They will if they are *fed*," Queen said brusquely. "Tell the

102

elders I want six men, three on each side of the kraal, to watch that the fires do not burn too low. To kill your *duiwel*, we first have to see him," Queen said with slow heavy emphasis. "See to it."

Joachim moved forward. "Tell the warriors that they may remain in the huts behind the N'kosi and myself except for the short times of renewing the fires," he said reassuringly.

"Tell them also," Queen said, "that any who refuses will be hanged." He drew his finger across his throat in emphasis. "And send others to make a hole in the boma, loosen it, *there!*" He pointed. "Go now. *Get it done.*"

When the runner had moved off, Joachim touched Queen's arm. "You did not really mean that, about hanging?"

"I meant it when I said it," Queen said noncommittally.

The elders and a work detail of tribesmen appeared, and Queen went to meet them. He paced out the places where the fires were to be started, judging the spaces between so that the light they gave should link up. "Get to it, and then make the hole in the boma. Just enough for the bewitched one to notice." The tribesmen hesitated. Queen raised his voice. "You want the *duiwel* to arrive before you have done? You wish to deal with him yourselves? He gave the nearest man a shove. "Move! Stupid *domkopfs* are scared of the hole," Queen said irritably to Joachim when the group had backed away.

"It is only natural," Joachim suggested. "They think first of keeping the beast out."

"Yes, well—balls to that," Queen said. "Just a minute." The older man held out his hand. "Just give me your gun, Jo, and stop making alibis for everybody in sight." Queen got a small tin from his pocket and coated the fore sight of Joachim's rifle with a creamy substance, using a matchstick. "White phosphorous stuff, dry in a minute or two." He handed back the rifle. "Not greatly effective, but you can make out the bead a bit better in the dark." He took Joachim by the elbow.

"Come on," he said, and led the man back to the hut. He got a handful of BB cartridges from his saddlebag. "Take the scattergun too."

Joachim smiled. "No thanks, Robert—my own gun is fine, I prefer it."

"I know, but best to do it my way," Queen said. "Take my tip and lay it beside you, cocked. No more bloody argument, take the cannon along."

Queen checked the magazine of the Männlicher, then the cylinder of his pistol, and he moved into the shadowy side of the hut.

Over on the far side of the kraal, Joachim settled cross-legged in the shadows, his shoulder against the thatch of a firewatcher's hut.

Two hours dragged by uneventfully. Queen yawned, leaning against the wall of the hut, and then, adjusting his position to keep alert, he caught a sound. It was like the sigh of a sleeping man, but it prickled the hairs on Queen's neck, because he knew that sigh well enough. He was thoroughly keyed in now, straining to see the intruding form against the black mass of the boma. He did not see the shape of the thing, but he did suddenly see the fleeting glint of low-slung eyes. And then he saw the great maned face. It was the largest and most formidable mask he had seen in fourteen years of big cats. The huge killer padded forward a pace or two more, then halted. Now Queen could see the fragments of brush tangled in the ragged mass of mane, and the red-green eyes that gleamed in the night.

The lion drew back its lips, the long yellow canines visible even in this light. Queen waited for that stupendous animal roar, but no sound came. The lion moved forward another yard or two. Then halted again, pawing the turf uncertainly.

Queen considered how to distract the brute into turning, but he dared not allow any closer approach. He bore down on

104

the chest area—but even as he began the squeeze, the great cat made its decision and turned diagonally. Queen adjusted the shot, held for a fraction, and then fired for the shoulder as the lion made to move again.

The giant cat staggered, lurched, and the roar welled and echoed through the huts. But even as he ripped back the bolt, Queen knew the issue was resolved. He saw the killer go over onto its side, fired again, slamming three rounds, rapidly, into the exposed abdomen and neck.

He started toward the great carcass with a grin of satisfaction, and then he wheeled, transfixed by Joachim's shout, which in turn was overborne by a rending snarl. A second lion was in full charge. Queen dove for the turf as the great gaping mask drove at him, but the lion caught him before he made it flat, and a massive clubbing blow sent him spinning aside. As he rolled he was conscious of flame and explosion, two reports, very near, and he saw the big cat swerve for the boma and spring through the top level of the barrier.

"Robert!" Queen felt Joachim's hand on his shoulder. He managed to get to his feet, and stood there, dazed, trying to focus on the young man's face. "By Christ, Jo, I smelled the bastard's breath! He shaved my skull, the son of a bitch!"

"He hit you, all right," Joachim was saying as Queen began to take stock of himself. It was his shoulder, clawed. He gripped the young *ryder's* arm. "You must have moved bloody fast, boy." He shook his head. "Bloody fast, by heaven."

"He surprised me," Joachim said tightly. "It was right after your first shot. He came over the boma as if the roar or the shot had brought him on. I chased after him through the huts."

"That was a bloody chancy thing to do," Queen said, "and thank Christ you did it." Queen went to his pack, and when they had each taken a good pull from the square bottle, Queen tore away his dangling sleeve and yanked off his shirt. The

105

blood was welling from two gashes on his upper arm and shoulder.

"My God, you did fine, Jo," Queen said, and then added, "that big bastard didn't do so bloody bad, either."

"Just good luck, Robert, and the scattergun," Joachim allowed as he worked with Queen at dressing the wound.

They could hear voices in the hut adjacent rising to a chattering gabble. Then a man's head appeared in their doorway. Two other Africans stood behind him, their expressions disbelieving, dumbstruck. Then they turned away and ran through the kraal yelling hysterically to the men and women beginning to issue from the huts. The delirium spread, the villagers leaping and gesturing and calling out madly, and they milled toward the carcass of the lion, immense even in death. A young tribesman rushed forward, wild-eyed with hate, to plunge his spear into the tawny belly. Others moved in to follow suit, taken with the same impulse. But Queen turned them back, driving through the throng, calling out over the heads of the crowd: "Leave the *duiwel!* Do you wish to release his spirit to inhabit another?" When he had stopped them, he raised his hand for silence. "And do not rejoice too soon—there is another devil-killer yet. *Another!*" He held up two fingers. "Now go to your huts and sleep," Queen called. "The *duiwel* will not come again tonight, and tomorrow we will seek this other one." The villagers moved off in all directions, and Queen muttered to Joachim: "I don't want this bastard pin-cushioned. Ten years since I bothered skinning one of these, but I'll do *this* one. This is one fisherman's tale Morgan is going to see for himself!"

*   *   *

Queen woke up tired, his shoulder very sore. But he knew it was essential to track the second cat's blood spoor while it was still fresh enough, and the men rode out in the first

106

glimmering of daylight. The dewfall had been light, with little rain for several days, and the dogs were quick to pick up the trail.

Far ahead the peaks of an escarpment were beginning to reveal themselves in the early light, and Queen began to steel himself for the long haul. For an adult cat, even with an ass like a dripping beefsteak—as this one probably had—could easily cover twenty miles in a night. But as they climbed the steep stretch beyond the donga, they heard a cackling followed by gibbering. Queen could see the hyenas as soon as the rise flattened off. They were a few hundred yards ahead, six of them grouped in a wide circle around an island of spurge-laurel. The clump of shrub was set in a patch of marshy ground like a small everglade, where, through some oozing underlay of moisture, the grass grew in verdant contrast to the brown hinterland. The carrion hunters were at a respectful distance from the thicket, but it was clear that they were stationed there in prospect of meat. They would wait all day, if it came to that, until the thing they wanted was dead.

Queen rose in the stirrups and bellowed at the hounds. Reluctantly, the excited dogs halted, tensed, rumbling in their throats.

"Go on ahead and chase them out of it, Jo, speed 'em up while I hold the dogs here," Queen called. "Don't want 'em taking after the *impisis.*"

Queen began to move up on Joachim with the dogs, talking to them all the time. Then he gave them the word to range ahead, and they began to lope toward the thicket.

For a while, the men heard only the barking of the hounds, but then they heard the long-drawn snarl.

"It's him all right!" Queen shouted.

Joachim made a motion with his rifle. "I will go around to the other side, try to *skrik* him out."

"All right," Queen replied. "Over there, say twenty yards

107

back from the *vlei,* on the edge of the firm ground. When you're set, I'll try the same from here." Queen waited until he could see Joachim's head above the scrub, and when the men were opposite each other, they began hooting and howling. The hounds bayed in chorus to the human noise; the snarls and roars from the scrub came more often now. Despite its ferocity, the roar seemed to Queen thin, lacking the depth and timbre of an adult male.

There was no let-up in the general frenzy of sound—the dogs, the men, the wounded lion—but still nothing. Queen drew his pistol and began to fire at random into the bush.

At once he heard the crackling swish of recoiling foliage from the other side of the island and then Joachim's shout and shot. Queen galloped forward around the softer ground of the *vlei* patch until he could see Joachim turned broadside in his saddle, setting himself to fire again.

The beast, streaking for the open veld, pitched onto its face in a kind of awry somersault, a front leg broken. In a moment it was up again. But now Queen was on his feet, his rifle laid across the saddle. His bullet smashed the thigh bone of a hindquarter, and now the killer was down again, immobilized.

Joachim rode slowly along until he was in position for the angle he wanted. Then he checked his horse, aimed, and made the quietus shot. Queen stilled the dogs and Joachim dismounted to join him. Together they approached the carcass.

Queen spat malignantly. "Well, Jo, there's the bastard that almost took me off—and with the bloody ass to prove it."

The lion was smaller than the first one, though bigger than average and curiously, considering his prodigious leaping capacity, unusually plump. Joachim stared at the body. "*Alle Wereld,* Robert, look at this!" He grabbed a hind leg and exposed the lion's genitals; there, where the testicles should have hung, was only a patch of shriveled skin.

108

Queen stared. "The bastard's a *eunuch* . . . castrated!"

"Hyena perhaps, when the creature was a cub?" asked Joachim.

The older man nodded. "Something like that, or a honey badger when his mother was out killing something else's young. Those little buggers don't like cats one bit, and they always go straight for the balls."

The team mounted up, and headed back, Queen and Joachim keeping up a steady chatter all the way.

*　　　*　　　*

Women in twos and threes were working quietly in the vegetable and corn shamba outside the kraal, and as the *ryders* walked their horses towards them, Queen called out to van Zyl.

"Tell 'em, Jo! Might as well cheer the ladies."

As the hunters drew nearer, Joachim put a hand to his mouth and shouted. "The *duiwels* are dead. *Dead!*"

For a moment the staring women stood gawking uncertainly. Then they dropped their mattocks and ran yelling toward the gate. By the time the small cortege of horsemen and dogs had reached the entrance at walking pace, half the villagers had turned out to greet them with shouts of welcome and rejoicing. Unwilling to delay celebration until evening, the villagers gathered in the dancing arena and the roistering began forthwith. In just a stroke, it seemed, a distressed and dispirited community had been transformed. But the elders had not forgotten their glad obligation. That night, when the air was still, the message of the *duiwels'* destruction would go out on the drums, and would be repeated at intervals until it was acknowledged by Igonyela's drummers, until it was understood that *Dukusa's* medicine was never more powerful, his authority never more absolute.

*　　　*　　　*

An hour or so before sunset the elders approached the hunters' hut, where Queen lay stretched on his grass mat in the shade cast by the dwelling, head pillowed on a rolled kaross, Joachim dozing beside him, his back against the thatch.

"N'kosi," the head elder began, "we have come to offer you the *ukumetsha.*"

Joachim pursed his lips. He was daydreaming of Poyana, his golden woman of a few days previous. He reached across and pulled Queen's sleeve.

"Robert, it is some business of women, I think," he said captiously in English. "They think that *ryders* are always in heat," he added disgustedly.

Queen rinsed his mouth with cold tea, spat, and got to his feet, dusting himself down before the waiting Africans, their faces lit with smiles. "Well, elder, we shall accept the honor." Queen nodded gravely as if conferring a favor. "But there are things which must be understood. The N'kosi van Zyl is not a great lover of women." He made a gesture conceding the whimsy of it. "This is sometimes a way of great hunters— killers of *duiwels,*" he reminded them. "He may not choose to fully accept the *ukumetsha.* Also, your custom must be changed in one small thing to fulfill *our* custom, the order of *Dukusa.* The maidens will not choose between us, but *we* among them!"

The elders conferred, and then the spokesman turned back to the hunters with a gesture of assent. "Lords, it is understood, agreed." He made a gesture inviting them to follow toward the dancing arena.

Queen glanced quizzically at Joachim. He chuckled at the younger man's resigned expression. "Goddammit, Jo, we're not going to have our teeth pulled. You don't have to truck with 'em if you don't want to, but I doubt Poyana would expect you to refuse." His reference to the girl of the *agapanthus* blooms did nothing to lighten Joachim's expression.

Three of the six girls were not very attractive, but one had the smallish breasts, narrow waist, and disproportionately burgeoning hips of a Somali. She appraised the hunters before lowering her eyes to her fluffy white anklets.

Queen gave the younger man a nudge. "Take one. Go ahead! Christ knows you've earned first choice on this job."

"Maybe the flamingo one? She does not look so bold," the young man said.

The elders addressed the women, explaining to them the change of procedure that had been agreed. The leader of the elders turned to the hunters. "Lords, they await you." He swept the sextet of women expansively with a plump hand. "Pluck forth the sweetest."

Queen motioned Joachim forward. "The N'kosi who slew the second *duiwel* will choose first."

The young *ryder* promptly beckoned to the girl wearing the white sheepskin cuffs around her wrists and ankles. She came to his side without ceremony.

Nqina Yehlambo

Queen and Joachim sat breakfasting with Morgan, the big man choosing to finish the umanga yam he was eating before getting into the talk. "Well, lads," he said at last, "now that this Kilende business is out of the way, there remains only the nasty matter of the rhino. Of course the damn thing is complicated by this ceremonial nonsense. More than a hunt with them, as if they *could* hunt," Morgan explained. "More a rite of tribal honor and revenge. They put great value on it, but, of course, they are not hunters. It is only our being here that allows this rare opportunity for it."

"And that is why they do not wish us to kill the beast, unless they fail themselves?" Joachim asked.

"Yes, that's it."

"A load of balls," Queen said truculently. "We play their crazy games too often, N'kosi."

"Listen," Morgan said heavily with strained patience. "This *game* may cost two or three rounds. That's cheap enough. It will give them much satisfaction, and it is also good politics," he added with absolute finality. "And I have had enough of your criticism, Robbie—so stow it!"

Joachim seemed embarrassed by this outburst, but Queen appeared unimpressed—he lighted a cheroot and stretched out his long legs and took up the last of his morning tea. As for Morgan, he seemed unperturbed. His manner bright again, the big Afrikander pulled himself to his feet and belched grandly. "You go at sunrise tomorrow, gentlemen—and now I have something that should interest you." Morgan led the way out across the grass from the kraal to where Matshongi had the trek wagon installed beside a kameldoorn tree. In addition to the oxen yoked to the wagon, two others, a black and a red-and-white, were tethered to the tree. Nearby, the two black *ryders* squatted at a fire of dung and waterwood.

Queen, more than Joachim, was familiar with the sturdy canopied carts that had changed little since the Great Trek. He lacked the expertise of Van Rieberk with the short-stocked *sjambok,* but he had learned and handled the big wagon-whip since boyhood. The long whip—twelve to fifteen feet of flint butt with a thirty-foot *agterslag* lash of plaited hippo or bullock hide, tempered by a tally of antelope skin—was far more important than the *sjambok,* because there were no reins. With the long whip, and the skillful invoking of each ox's name, a gifted driver could control, direct and summon to united effort teams of eight, ten, and even sixteen oxen.

Queen reached down the long whip from the box and made the stretched hide dart out like a snake, the lash producing a report like a rifle shot. It relaxed Queen to reassure himself of his power with the long whip, and it helped to take the edge off his humiliation at the hands of Morgan. As for the iron-shod wagon, it was of very strong construction, yet it could readily be broken down into parts that would allow for portage.

The Africans began to add the tethered oxen to the long yoke, yielding a team of six oxen in all.

"Well, *Jongs,*" Morgan said. "a good buck-wagon and good beasts, I think. And good guns, and you have the tools with which countries were won."

Queen spread his hands upon his hips. "You've done me

proudly, N'kosi, Piet. Proudly." It sounded pretty inadequate and he tried to amplify it. "I intend you won't regret it—by God, I do."

"I hope not," Morgan said sententiously, "because I am not interested in goose chases and I do not stake men every day. This is an investment."

This was the second time, Queen realized, that the big man had spoken in a plural sense.

"Men?" he said, not wanting to let the occasion go by.

Joachim shifted his stance. "I am going with you, Robert. I talked with the N'kosi last night."

"Matshongi also," Morgan said.

Queen looked from one to the other. Morgan saturnine, noncommittal, Joachim smiling.

"Well, well," Queen said, and put out a hand to each man in turn.

*   *   *

It was still early morning when Queen rode through the kraal entrance, while the two hundred or so hunters chosen for the *Nqina* were gathered in the arena. Stamping their feet, shaking their spears aloft, striking menacing attitudes, the hunters sought to impress the women who stood about watching. Beneath the bravado, one could detect an undercurrent of fear and hysteria. The men were not hunters, and they knew it. To one side stood the woodcutters, their relative unconcern stemming from the fact that, once they had fulfilled their function of locating the rhino, they had no further business in the whole affair.

Queen beckoned the headmen of the woodcutters and the hunters to approach. He went through the plan slowly, methodically explaining how the woodsmen, fanned out upwind, and keeping within the forest belt in case of surprise attack, must not get too far ahead of the following spearmen.

114

Then, whoever first sighted or heard the rhino, would give the *korhaan* birdcall and all would withdraw, returning to the main body. That, and no more or less.

As for the hunters, they would follow, listening for the signal, in *silence*. When the rhino had been located, they would spread out in a crescent and approach the tract indicated by the woodcutters. As soon as the rhino saw them he would probably hesitate for a second, deciding his line, then charge directly at a single man and maintain his course until he had killed or lost his quarry. Then the beast would wheel and re-charge.

As soon as the rhino aimed his lowered head toward the lead group, the men would run for their lives, scattering, and the spearmen on either side would converge on the "tunnel" and cast their spears.

The headmen nodded their understanding and stood back, seemingly unperturbed. But Queen stepped forward and went through the plan. Then he studied them doubtfully.

"You understand?"

They nodded gravely.

"All right," Queen said. "Inform your warriors, repeat it until all know their part—then we will leave."

When the briefing was completed, the *ryders* moved out, at first leading and then following the tribesmen.

It took a half hour of cautiously working forward before Joachim's section of the enfilade heard the shrill wheedling birdcall. It came twice, and seconds later a running figure burst into the open at the far end of the glade. The woodcutter swerved toward the refuge of the forest proper as if to escape from the crescented line of spearmen. As he disappeared, Joachim ran forward toward the head of the wavering elliptical line of tribesmen. He heard the heavy pounding of earth and the crackling whoosh of sundered brush.

Suddenly, the great gray shape of the rhino thundered into

115

the open. The impetus of his charge carried him past the spearmen who had fanned out on either side of him. Halted, the ugly creature stood stock still for an instant, momentarily befuddled, his small pig-eyes squinting in the light. Then the great horn dipped and he charged like a monstrous battering ram.

Of the ragged volley of spears delivered by the more resolute tribesmen, some missed entirely, others merely flaked away cakes of dried mud from the great ribbed flanks of armored hide. Only two spears from the many volleys remained partly embedded, dangling uselessly from the enraged beast's hide. The rhino bore down on a spearman he had singled out, his head hooking upward and the yard-long horn driving home into the warrior's gut. Skewered like a gaffed fish, the tribesman was flung high and wide, screaming, into the malignant network of a thorn tree. The maddened rhino swerved away, crashed through a clump of sapling mopani, and gored a second man. Berserk, the brute wheeled again and headed back. Joachim fired twice, ineffectually, but as he did so, more spearmen rushed forward, and the rhino saw the newcomers and turned for them in mid-gallop.

Again the juggernaut focused on a single antagonist, and he had just reached the shrieking spearman when Joachim fired again. Ashen-faced, the young *ryder* sprinted toward the threshing thing on the ground. But Queen fired before Joachim was in danger, placing his load well away from the gored spearman but squarely into the rhino's heart.

The great beast went down onto his knees, but then, incredibly, he reared up again. Queen's rifle crashed once more, and this time the rhino went down and rolled flat out. Nostrils distended, burst lungs laboring, for a few moments the colossus lay spasmodically kicking one bloody-footed leg, then the convulsions slackened and the flanks ceased to heave. The great horn, dripping red, rested across the pulverized

116

heap he had mangled. His face had all the repulsiveness of an uglier age and yet there was a kind of dignity to him—and no dignity at all, Queen decided, in the carnival of violence that had contrived the rhino's death.

Trek

The sun had not completely changed from pink to gold yet, but it had dispelled the earlier chill and was beginning to warm the shoulders.

The men had made their official farewells to Igonyela and now the wagon stood outside the entrance to the kraal. The lead oxen, the red-and-white and the black, fidgeted, but were restrained, curbed from behind by their stolidly indifferent comrades of the yoke. Queen completed his inspection of the fittings and then the axles.

"All checked then? Nothing overlooked?" Morgan called to Queen.

"Not a damn thing," Queen answered in his powerful voice.

The big Afrikander sniffed. "You forgot your irons, *Jong*." He lobbed a pair to Matshongi, who sat on the box of the wagon.

Queen stuffed the handcuffs in a pocket of his bush jacket. All Morgan *ryders* normally carried them, manacles that had a variety of quick and practical uses with horses, oxen, live bait, spoke brakes, and the like beyond their traditional purpose. "I didn't forget," Queen retorted. "They're part of the sum total of unrequired deadweight I left out. I learned about dead-weight a long time ago."

"So did I," Morgan told him. "And you're right, but not about the cuffs. Sometimes they're more valuable than a gun. Take them."

"Well," Queen grinned, "maybe you're right. But I pared to the bone this time because we've got a lot more to climb than *kopjes.*" Queen swung up into the saddle and then reached down to grip the big man's hand. "Well, *Adeus*, then, Piet, as the Portuguee says—and thanks again, bossman."

The Afrikander nodded. "Go for the west *poort*, Robbie, and return the same way."

Joachim edged his horse into position and leaned down. "*Tot siens*, N'kosi—I have much to thank you for," the young *ryder* said.

"*Geluk, Jong*," Morgan said. "Keep the *Uitlander* from the women."

Queen laughed. "Keep the women from the *Uitlander*, is more like it." He called to Matshongi. "Trek, Boetie!"

The long whip cracked like sundering ice, and then again. Queen stared thoughtfully ahead. He was trekking, and already he felt himself separate from the past, from all life that had preceded this moment. His eyes and heart looked to what lay ahead, a future bright with promise.

*   *   *

It was late afternoon of the third day now and the southern extremities of the great Ridge, the immediate horizon, looked deceptively near. But it would be another full day yet before they reached the foothills.

To the northeast the escarpment stretched toward infinity like a great purple rib, and presently those of the challenging royal purple peaks which rose to eight or nine thousand feet were shrouded in white cloud. It had been a long and tedious

119

day of heat-shimmered veld, *tamboekie* and scrubland grayed with lava dust. But now, in the unpredictable African way of it, Queen's party had reached a place of great contrast to what had gone before. A spruit ran clear over white sand inset with pastel pebbles that glinted in the sun, and the bank grass was green and finely bladed.

Queen pushed back his hat. "Good water, Jo. Mountain water."

"Yes, good grazing, too."

"What I was thinking," Queen agreed. He glanced at the sun, then toward the beginnings of the Ridge. "We could go another hour or two, but we'd be lucky to find a place good as this."

"Except for one thing, perhaps. The water will draw game and the game will draw cats." Joachim nodded toward the straggle of trees and bush that marked the course of the little river.

"Still good policy," Queen said. "Give the team a good bellyfull, extra rest, they've got some bloody hard collar coming up soon."

They dismounted and Queen called to Matshongi as the wagon came closer. "Outspan, Boetie—we'll camp here." Over his shoulder Queen said, "We'll graze 'em till sundown, then bring 'em in close. Tie the dogs to the wheels for tonight and if they start showing signs, we'll take watches."

Joachim dumped his saddle, and the two *ryders* went to help with the oxen.

"Perhaps I should take the wagon tomorrow—what do you think, Robert?" Joachim suggested.

"Why not?" Queen said. "Good idea to get all the practice you can while the going's straightforward."

"Do you think we'll have trouble finding the pass?"

"Van Rieberk said 'You can't see the *poort*, but the finger-post to it is a berg with a peak that looks like a saw with broken end teeth.' Here, Jo—me and Boetie will see to the beasts, you take the scattergun, and see if you can get us some fowl for tomorrow."

By the time dusk had fallen, Matshongi had begun the outer fire, adding heavier branches to the bundled small twigs, and then deadwood lumber from the litter of past spates. When the men had eaten, Queen took the shotgun and made a turn around camp. He was not worried, but he was not willing to take chances. They were going to need full strength for what lay ahead. It would be foolish to risk losing horses or oxen to predators.

Joachim was seated at the fire when Queen returned from his stroll. He moved quickly into the thought he'd been turning over in his mind. "I tell you one thing, Robert, the white men who rose to become rulers, kings, of savage countries, men like Juwaba, De Buys, the first *Dukusa*, how did they *do* it, almost single-handed like that?"

"You should know that, a grandson of Piet van Zyl," Queen said quizzically.

"No." Joachim van Zyl shook his head. "The first Groot Piet was not alone. He came from the south with an impi of Zulu, and later they added a manyatta of Masai from the north. They were the originators of our people."

"Which is why your people have survived, as most of the others have not," Queen said.

The younger man nodded seriously. "The Zyls have ridden out many storms over time, before my time. But perhaps the English are the most knowing in some ways—the N'kosi and his father. But I have much admiration for the old Dutch," Joachim smiled. "At least half of me has."

"Damn right," Queen said. "The British never compared with them, with what the Trek-Boers did time and again, with the odds they faced. By Christ, I am for men like that, Jo—you can be proud of the Boer blood in you."

121

Queen reached for the rifle nearby, took out the bolt, and held it so that he could see down the whole length of the barrel against the background of a bright flame. He laid the rifle across the saddle back of him and felt for a cheroot. "But don't ever forget the other blood in you. Just as good, Jo."

Young van Zyl looked at his forearms, his hands. His skin, coppery, was no darker than Queen's, and yet there was a subtle difference. "They were also great fighters, I know that."

Queen raised his eyebrows at the inadequacy of it. "Magnificent," he said. "Fearless. The most humbling defeat ever suffered by any British army, that's what it says in the books. Guts and spears against cannon, Gatling guns, rockets. They carried their dead for shields against shrapnel and bullets."

Joachim smiled. "*Bayede, Bayede Zulu!*"

Queen nodded, winked. He echoed the other famous battle cry, "*Usuuthu, Usuuthu Zulu!*"

"A man might almost believe, Robert, that you think ill of your own . . ."

"Ancestry?"

"Yes, that. Of the English."

"He'd be wrong then," Queen said. "Not the people. But a barefaced dirty deal is a barefaced dirty deal in anybody's language. And that's what the English politicians gave the Trekkers, the real honest-to-God pioneers—the Africans too."

"But you want to win a country yourself—isn't that the same?"

"Not win it like that," Queen said. "*Make* one, man," he made a sweeping gesture, "out of all this nothingness. Like a farm, if you like, a bloody great king-size farm. But I don't want to spoil the land or handcuff the people. There'll be no bloody mines in our country, Jo, no slave workers."

Matshongi returned from tending the outer fire. Queen scratched his chin and looked toward the dull gleam of the water. "We'd better take watches," Queen said. "You take the first spell, Boetie." A long way distant, a lion coughed. Queen jerked his head. "I doubt you'll have any trouble from them if you keep the fire going good, but you know the *ingwes*. Would crawl right over you for a dog. Take a turn around the beasts sometimes, show them you're there."

The burly African nodded. "I will watch the dogs, also keep the big one awake."

He was a good man, Queen thought, a good *ryder*. Experienced, a fair shot, never panicked, solid.

When the others had settled down for the night, Matshongi took up his position, back propped against his saddle, just a little beyond the edge of the firelight, his kaross drawn about his shoulders. For an hour or more, he squatted without shifting. No sounds disturbed the quiet. What he was listening for was the short rasping burr, the hunting cough of *ingwe*. At length he rose and took a turn all around the camp, moving slowly, the gun across his loins, keeping outside the aura of fireglow, halting now and then. Back at his original post, he settled down again to wait.

After another hour he changed from a squatting to a sitting position, and laid the cold Damascus barrels across his lap. He heard a hyena gibber, and caught a gleam of eyes. The eyes were joined by a second pair, then another and the three sets came and went as the creatures padded about the perimeter. He brought up the gun slowly, then glanced toward the sleeping men, considering. He put the gun in his left hand, went to the fire, and got a burning brand. Then he moved around the edge of the firelight and arced the torch as far out as he could. There was a yowl of protest, to which Matshongi added an ancestral curse before returning to his position. But within a quarter hour, the eyes were back again and this time the hyenas nosed closer. He raised the gun again, waiting for the moment that would offer the best target.

123

When it came, he dropped his cheek to the wood. He fired each choke and half-choke barrel. At the echoing twin reports, Queen jerked back his blanket, and Joachim lifted onto his elbows, peering. Matshongi made a gesture of reassurance. He showed his teeth to emphasize that nothing serious had occurred. But now the horses and oxen were snorting and milling and the African wondered whether he had made a stupidity of it.

"*Impisi. Impisi,* N'kosi." He justified it. "They were too close."

Queen looked around the camp with dour disapproval. He brought his glance back to Matshongi. "Well, take that bloody daft grin off your face and go quiet the beasts, then."

"There were several *impisi,* a pack?" Joachim asked as the three men met at the fire.

Matshongi thought. "It may have been. Three were coming near," he repeated.

"Aaah, balls! Been a pack, the dogs would have howled," Queen said sceptically. "Spoiling our sleep for a couple of bloody scowses you could have chased off with a stick."

"I did so the first time," the African said. "Also, no spoiling of your sleep, N'kosi—it was time to wake you already," he went on in argument. Matshongi studied Joachim. His face twitched. "I will make tea. Then we will sleep while the N'kosi is chasing the *impisis* with a stick."

They broke camp with the morning star and were moving before full light, the tension between them not resolved yet, the first inroads of fatigue beginning to show.

The great barrier of the Ridge seemed nearer now. They had crossed a succession of dry and semi-dry watercourses, but now, in mid-morning, they had reached a steeply banked river of some consequence. Queen took his horse down a rift in the bank and across the flat into the edge of the water. It was brown, *brak*-looking, and it did not surprise him when the animal only nuzzled it before shaking away the drops. Just ten yards further out the sluggish flow rose to the stallion's belly. Queen turned and rode back. "No good!" he said to the *ryders* still on the bank. "We'll have to split up and find a drift."

Joachim was driving the wagon, and he stayed where he was on the box while Matshongi set off along the bank and Queen struck out in the opposite direction. After a time Queen fired the signal shot, and began to canter back along the river, expecting to see the others as he rounded each bend. But there was no sign of them and he had to retrace his steps the whole way. It angered him that he had to go all the way back to the wagon to find them, and it was then that Queen realized his anger was unfounded, but was nevertheless rising. He could hear Joachim call from the wagon: "Boetie has found a good place which is near—half a mile or less. We fired twice, but the wind carry must have taken it."

"Goddam, it had *better* be good!" Queen snapped. "We want to make the Ridge bottom by sundown." He glanced at Matshongi. "You Goddam sure, man?"

"I am," the African said.

"Firm bed . . . firm enough?"

Again the African nodded. "I crossed the full width, N'kosi. It is hard."

The sun was beating down heavily now, making dazzle pools on the surface of the water, and the rising dust of hooves and wheels coated their faces. Queen gazed moodily across the river toward the challenging horizon of the escarpment. The river was nothing, but it was the first check they had experienced, and the fact of it reminded him of the immensely formidable things to come. He tried to shake off this brooding. It was not like him, and he wanted no part of it. He pushed back his hat, wiped the sweat from his face, and got a cheroot. It did not occur to him to offer cigars around. It was only after

125

he had lit up and drawn several puffs that he considered his rudeness—but decided to do nothing about it.

They were nearing the place of the drift now, could see the gorge. Matshongi pointed. The gorge was not large, but it had produced a small waterfall that rose five or six feet above the level of the river. On the far side, a rocky hill rode back from the bank, its crest shaved off as if by the stroke of some supernatural scythe.

Queen walked his horse to the edge of the flat and continued in to midstream. Even midway, the water was only fetlock-deep, and beneath the skirl of pebbly silt from the horse's hooves the bed was firm. He splashed back towards the others. "You found well, Boetie."

It took several minutes to gentle the wagon down a spillway of the bank, Matshongi and Joachim dragging back on the lead beasts, and once the wagon tilted precariously. But then they were onto the flat with a short final rush. Now the two *ryders* began to splash forward abreast of the front oxen, feeling with their feet for any undue potholes, ready to sing out.

Mid-river was passed without any trouble, and the team seemed to be set fair for the shallows opposite, when suddenly, the wagon lurched and the oxen were jerked to a standstill. The jolt almost threw Queen from his seat, but he recovered himself with a curse.

One wheel was embedded in a crevice of the bed, and the wagon was now tilted at an angle. "Come back here, the both of you, get your shoulders to it," Queen shouted. "Leave the beasts to me." He got a foot against the buckboard and wedged his back against the corner of the canopy. "Now shove like hell when I shout." The two *ryders* braced themselves against the wheel. "*Now!*" The long demanding whip sang out. For a plunging, straining moment the wheel lifted a little and the wagon seemed to be coming away, but then the massive weight overcame them, and the wagon slid back again into the trough.

126

"Get up front, Jo—you too, Boetie. Keep 'em calmed down," Queen ordered. He cast around him, seeking for the answer, until his eyes lighted on a straggle of three dwarf palms a short way back along the bank. "All right, keep 'em steady for Christ's sake. Watch that boom and don't try anything—I'm going for a prop."

He got the timber axe and began to wade back across the river toward the trees. They were not much more than six inches in diameter, and he fell to powerfully. With Joachim's help, he got the prop braced under the wagon and then he climbed cautiously back up onto the box. He paused for an instant to wipe the sweat from his face, then called to the oxen. "Now . . . *trek!*" The *agterslag* thong cracked like a pistol, and this time the *voorslag* tag licked the quarter of a lead beast in earnest, recoiled with lightning swiftness and streaked out again to bite the rump of the other. At the same time, biceps bunched, the two men in the water strained their shoulders up against the lever as the oxen lunged forward, snorting and stumbling.

The wagon rose almost to upright. For just an instant it seemed to hold there, and then it crunched forward. The rawhide cut the air again, snapping through the fly-clouds about the flanks of the oxen, punctuating Queen's raging shouts as the wagon rolled forward. He could hear the cries of encouragement from over his shoulder, but Queen needed no urging, and he did not look around until he was well out onto the hard-baked strand.

When they were finally up onto the grass of the opposite bank, Queen halted the team and got down. He pulled his shirt over his head and mopped the sweat rivulets from his shoulders and chest, then threw the sodden rag into the wagon. "Beer, Boetie!" he called to Matshongi. "Get a skin down—we can all do with a bucket."

"It could have been much worse, Robert," Joachim said. "If the wagon had gone over—broken a wheel."

127

"Yeah, sure," Queen said grudgingly, almost gruffly. "Some bloody show all the same. We should have waded it first, marked a course—and from here on we will!" he said, his remarks progressively taking on the tone that was characteristic with Morgan.

Queen took the mug that Matshongi handed him, quickly drained it off, and handed it back for a refill. As Morgan might have done, he belched loudly, with satisfaction, nor was his failure to thank the African unlike the manner Queen had observed in the big Afrikander.

*   *   *

The going the next day had been easy enough. Queen, who had taken the whip himself, kept the oxen moving at a steady tripple, spurred by the gathering prospect of the Ridge.

After the evening meal, Queen walked out a short way from the stand of stunted and wind-distorted *kameldoorns* where they had pitched camp. The hefty meal and whiskey had left him a keen sense of well-being. Before him reared the great dark mass that could be the gateway to the fulfillment of his ambition. Or was it instead another barrier?

He was lost in speculation when the young *ryder* surprised him, calling "Robert" softly from the twilight behind. Van Zyl inclined his head toward the Ridge. "It'll be hard tomorrow, especially for the beasts, yes?"

"Likely," Queen said.

"At least we're this far," Joachim said.

"What do you mean?"

"If you cross by the north *poort*, you have to cross the Milebi country to come south. It was Groot Piet's order—not to take risks."

"Risks? What risks?" Queen puckered his brow. Then he nodded slowly, glanced toward the Ridge again, and slapped his knee. "Anyway, your people took their wagons over the

128

bergs, Jo, before you were born. And that's what we are going to do. Don't forget, we've got an extra ox with us, old Matshongi. By God, he's stronger than the red-and-white—eh Boetie?"

The African showed his teeth. "I will tell that one in his ear, N'kosi. I will tell that brute that if he shirks, I will take his place myself—and him we will eat. It will aid his bowels greatly."

The white *ryders* smiled. It was a fine moment, the first in a very great while.

The Poort

The dawn, it seemed to Robert Queen, took a long time coming, much longer than on the open veld. But it came at last, the first red rays stabbing down through the white halos of the tallest peaks and outlining their shoulders. Tormented by worries of every kind, Queen had not slept well, though there had been no disturbances in the night, and now he was up and washed well ahead of the others, with tea brewed, and *spek* and eggs sizzling in the pan.

He got to his feet before the others had started in on the pork. "I'll saddle up and ride along a bit, Jo. See if I can spot the peak we're looking for."

It was still too early to make out the highest contours, but the restlessness was on him and Queen wanted to get going. He rode steadily for a quarter of an hour before raising the big Barr and Stroud's slung around his neck. The heads of two of the eminences that rose from the great beetling cliffs were still wrapped in mist. But neither looked likely to conform to the picture he had filled in from van Rieberk's description.

Queen weaved his way to the top of a *kopje*. The hill was opposite an angular turn of the escarpment, and from it you could see several more miles of the face running south. Less than halfway toward the extremity of his view, his attention was taken by a berg of singular aspect. Its peak was shrouded, but when Queen had the detail sharply enough in the glasses, he could see part of the curious serrated outline that began below the hidden summit. He was on the point of congratulating himself, when he swung the binoculars to either side and saw no indication of the pass, or even of any defile. He scanned the skyline again, and the face to either side, but there was no sign of a break in the vast wall. Puzzling as this was, he could not give up the feeling that this was the peak he was looking for. He turned his horse and cantered back to camp.

"*Geluk*, Robert?" Joachim called out when he saw Queen coming in. "Any sight of the *poort?*"

Queen pushed back his hat. "Damned if I know, Jo. Not sure." He explained what he had seen. The young *ryder* listened, nodding, and then speaking: "It'd be a damn funny thing if there were two peaks as odd-chiseled as that one, even in the whole range, and another thing I've remembered—something old *Oupa* said about not seeing it until you were right onto it."

"Right you are, lad," Queen said. "Let's chance it."

When they came to the *kopje* from which Queen had made the survey, the sun had risen appreciably and more of the eccentrically jagged profile of the peak was visible. Queen handed his binoculars to the younger man. "See what I mean? Notched like a busted cog, and yet not a damned sign of a *kloof.*" He called over his shoulder to Matshongi on the wagon. "All right, Boetie, just keep her heading for the saw-tooth. Let them make their own pace."

The horsemen began to hit a good gallop now, going at a diagonal that would give the earliest view of the peak from the south side. But after several hundred yards, the great plane of the face still looked unchangingly impregnable.

Then suddenly Joachim, fifty yards ahead, turned in the

saddle with a shout and waved. "The *poort*, Robert—the *poort!*" He swung his horse out at an angle, and made directly for the mass of the Ridge. Queen caught up beside him, and together they dropped their horses into a walk.

The pass, if it was the pass, curled down the escarpment in a curve that bent around the back of the peak. At the foot, it came part-way around the mass of the berg in a dogleg bend that looked like the entrance of a roofless cavern. Aside from its screened lower reaches, the deep-grooved trail disappeared at intervals, so that you had no way of knowing if the big gaps were linked or were instead merely blunt-ended ravines.

But Joachim was jubilant. "No wonder you were puzzled, Robert! The Banyoro front door is well concealed. A man could ride the plain level with the ridge a dozen times, seeking a way, and miss it."

"Let's not count our chickens yet," Queen said. "Remember the Drift."

"Oh, no. This must be the *poort!*"

"Yeah, well, I'll be happier when we've seen around the first bend," Queen said guardedly. The bend lay a rifle shot further along the rising boulder-strewn gradient, and he pointed to it. "From here on, Jo, you're the *voortrekker*. Boetie and me will take turns on the box. Go prospect the bend—maybe the first couple to be damn sure." Queen turned and raced back to the wagon as Joachim began to make his way up the first easy gradient of the trail.

Joachim was waiting when the wagon made it to the threshold of the Pass, Queen wielding the whip and Matshongi on horseback. From here the gaunt reality of the vista came at them like a club. The towering ramparts and cathedrals reared threateningly on either side, here riding back obliquely and there looming sheer-faced over seemingly dismembered segments of the furrow that snaked upward.

Joachim nodded at the oxen. "It will be hard for the beasts, I think," he said, his manner sober now.

132

Queen grinned. "Taken a closer look now, eh, Jo? Tougher than you thought, maybe?"

"I only meant it will be slow," Joachim said, embarrassed by his concern.

"Well, time's one thing we're not short on, *Jong*," Queen shrugged. "Time, hell. It's not the steepness, lad, it's the holes and fissures that could bust a wheel!" Queen called to Matshongi. "All right, Boetie, take your *Vangstok* up front!"

The African took the stick that hooked onto the neck-chain and walked to the head of the team as Joachim moved out, and the wagon began to trundle forward over the rocky ground. Around the second bend they came onto the instep of the saw-tooth. Here, on this stretch, the oxen had to toil in earnest, and from time to time the *ryders* chockstoned the wheels to allow the animals short rests.

At noon the party halted near a hill *spruit* for a longer spell, to water and rest the beasts and to take a bit of food. They were onto the shin of the pass now and the vegetation was scantier, the *kloofs* swept and scoured of all growth save for patches of gray stunted brush that barely survived among the shaly sand and wind-honed pebbles. So far the width of the *poort* had varied considerably, in places as wide as a secondary glacier, in others too narrow to let through six horsemen abreast. The party pressed on again, Joachim still riding point to prospect the way ahead.

Presently, they made it to a broad shelf, forty yards or more wide, a shallow cavity in the shape of a D. At the far end of it, where the track narrowed again, a curious overhang loomed over the pass.

Queen walked ahead while the others stayed with the wagon. There was something unnatural about the thing. He moved over to the edge of the *poort* and flicked the stub of his cheroot down into the gorge below. The drop into the flat-bottomed barranca was immense, and Queen noticed there was no scattering of massive rubble about. But immediately below he saw one big rock-pile that differed from the character of the surrounding rocks and looked to have originated from the face of the wall well above where he stood.

He turned away and walked back to the others. When he was close enough, Queen jerked his head over his shoulder. "What do you make of the bluff, Jo?"

But it was Matshongi who answered. "*Utokolshe! Utokolshe*, the evil spirit of all heights!" he cried.

Queen shook his head, smiling. "Not this time, Boetie. Oh, I've seen the *Utokolshe's* doings before, but I'd say the first Zyl trekkers blasted that out—unless there were dynamiters before them."

Joachim turned his head and gazed along the track with interest. "Dynamite?"

"Maybe not dynamite," Queen said. "I'm not sure whether they had the stuff then. Maybe Italian powder—kind of gunpowder."

"You reckon the *poort* ended here then?"

"Yes and no. The way I figure it, in the beginning most of the ice mass got detoured and churned out the gorge, and the gorge is a sight too deep at both ends to have gotten wagons down and up. Would have taken 'em a month—they'd've had to strip every wagon to bits, carry every damn thing through on foot. But what good is guessing?" Queen concluded. "We've got to go it, however it got there."

In the next three hours of slogging, they made it up in grueling stages that punished the oxen unmercifully, and the men who drove them no less than that. Matshongi abandoned his *voorloper* position to remount and join Joachim in lending extra pull with ropes run from their saddle pommels to the wagon. Now they rested again before testing themselves against the next gradient. But Joachim refused to slack off even for brief respite that the others took. He'd gone up ahead to scout, and when he returned, his expression was grim.

134

"Trouble up there?" Queen asked.

"Around the curve—a blockage, Robert."

"Another bastarding ledge? Not enough space to pass?"

"There would have been—but—a rock-fall on the track."

"Sweet mother of God!" Queen swore.

They moved the wagon up to the barrier and then the three men took a closer look.

"I believe the three of us pushing together could move most of it, Robert," Joachim said tentatively.

Queen stared morosely at the pile. Most of the boulders did not look impossibly huge, but one massive slab reared formidably on the inner edge. "And what good would that do? There'd still be *this*," Queen said, touching the huge block, taller than himself. "Take thirty men to shift this bastard. No, we'll have to strip the wagon down—carry everything through."

"No, wait, Robert," Joachim said. He eyed the gap between the great rock and the sloping wall of the pass again—then went to his horse for his rope. Returning, he measured the space, then the beam of the wagon.

"If we remove the canopy and empty the wagon, I think it will pass, Robert, tilted onto two wheels."

Queen fingered his lip dubiously. "Worth a try right enough, would save a mint of time and sweat all right. Come on, then, outspan and tether 'em—we'll leave just one span on the boom."

By the time they had removed the hood-frame and fully unloaded, the light was fading fast. They began to edge the decapitated wagon along, Matshongi bearing against the yoke of the two oxen, Queen and Joachim bracing their backs against the side, the wagon canted at an angle.

Jerkily, its wood grating and squealing against the rock, the hooves of the inside beast scrabbling on the fringe of the incline, the wagon inched past the rock pile.

"God save the King!" Queen stood beside the beheaded

wagon, hands on hips, with a grin of satisfaction. "Jo, you're a bloody bright boy. You too, Boetie, you handled 'em fine. Well done, lads," Queen fairly shouted. They shook hands all around, and restored the wagon's canopy and load. When they were ready to roll again, Queen sent Joachim up ahead to scout a camp. Big banks of dark cloud had begun to ride over the far peaks and a distant roll of thunder sounded as he spoke. It was likely going to be a rough night, with no shelter of trees and no grazing for the beasts, only a ration of maize again, for they had kept fodder weight to a minimum.

It was nearly an hour before they managed the distance to the site Joachim had selected, and by that time the storm burst upon them with a crash. Overhead a jagged flash lit the visible extent of the pass and was followed by a shattering report, amplified and flung back at them by the looming walls of rock. It was a deluge.

For twenty minutes the hail beat down with undiminished fury, then slackened a bit. Then hail gave way to rain, and the rain came down more ferociously still, the drops bouncing from the ground like overgrown peas. The air was charged with electricity, and every so often the manes of the horses cracked audibly.

It had grown very cold, and the rain meant no fire, and the misery of it persisted until past midnight. They spent a chill cramped night waiting for dawn, and in the grayness of first light it was still cold. Behind and below, a heavy fog hung in the gorge and hid all view of the way they had come. It was a dreary vista for men who had supped on hard cold biltong and scarcely closed their eyes, and Queen stamped about in ill humor, beating his arms and hawking the stale whiskey taste from his mouth.

But when he looked the other way, the sourness of his mood began to lift. The sun, early risen, was beginning to touch the edges of the mist with pink, and the sky was very clear.

136

He turned to the others. "Jo, get the Primus. We'll just get a mouthful of tea and then pull the hell out of here. Sooner we get the beasts thawed out, the better."

The younger man glanced toward the oxen. For all their strength and stamina, they were not so hardy as the horses, who were themselves shivering. "Soon as we get them in the sun, we can rest them and give them a good *kostie* of mealies."

"Right," Queen said. "Maybe a double ration if we can see grazing from the top."

Three hours later, they came slowly, grindingly, to the head of the *poort*. Matshongi had the long whip now, and, as the party neared the crest, Queen and Joachim urged their horses to a canter to see the vista that lay ahead. But there was no dramatic panorama to be seen. Ahead the carpet of the heath stretched toward a horizon edge some several miles distant, and on either side it was bounded by peaks that rose two or three thousand feet higher still, some still snow-capped. Behind them, the lateral fangs of the saw-tooth were etched against the sky.

"Always the same, isn't it?" Queen rested his forearms across his horse's neck. "You climb a hill, round a bluff, and it's never what you think it's going to be. Was thinking we'd see the Banyoro country spread out like a map."

"Well, I think we'll see it soon, Robert—the end of this *steenveld*."

"Oh, hell, yes. Anyway this green will serve fine for the beasts." Across to their right there was a small pool fed by a *spruit*. It was bounded by reeds on one side and well-sheltered by a crescent-shaped *kopje* on the other. Queen nodded toward the place. "We'll outspan there—give 'em all a good rest."

Soon, in the noon warmth of the sun, men and beasts were eating and drinking their fill. It was pleasant here after the foulness of the night, and it was difficult not to drowse in the welcome heat.

"When do you reckon to move on, Robert?" Joachim said, shifting onto his elbow to finish his tea.

"Tomorrow," Queen said surprisingly. "Tomorrow will be soon enough."

He saw impatience flicker across the younger man's face. "Can't wait to get a glimpse of the promised land?"

"Damn right," Joachim admitted.

The touch of mimicry made the older man smile.

"Damn right *I* can't either, boy—and we will!" Queen said. "All right, just finish your tea, we'll leave Boetie rest his bones here a while, then we'll head out, man."

Presently, they were trekking again, and could see, far across the broad shoulder of the Ridge, a montane formation, like a high-pommeled saddle, rise from the flatness of the moor. But after they had been riding toward it for a time, they saw that the eminence graded up much sooner than it had seemed at first. It was the wide elongated gateway to the nearest edge of the Ridge.

They cantered forward, picking their way, and then halted abruptly, silenced by a majestic vista ahead. For forty or fifty miles, the quilted panorama spread out before them. The land was green: the dark bottleglass of the big timber and the lighter mid-green of pasturage laid over the pastel backcloth of the veld, which was veined by many *spruits* from the Ridge. These streams fed two rivers that intersticed the plain and, to the south and west, just discernible, there were blue patches Queen judged to be lakes. Only the whispering burble of a rill nearby disturbed the deep overall quiet.

"*Alle Wereld!*" Joachim drew in a breath. "What country! Robert, what—fullness!"

Queen did not answer immediately. He gazed for a long while, then finally lowered his glasses and handed them to the younger man. "That's the word, Jo—fullness," he said at last.

The young *ryder* nodded with excitement. "Game, Robert!

138

The grazing, the water! The herds need never migrate." He was scanning the slopes of the Ridge now, and the bottom-lands. The gradient of descent looked easy, nowhere compa-rable to the toiling agencies of the southern face, and clearly the plateau stood at a substantially higher elevation than Igonyela's country.

"It should not take long to go down, Robert."

"No. I figure the Banyoro by sundown tomorrow."

"You know the direction it lies in, then? The Banyoro kraal?"

"I can make a guess. To the northwest of here." Queen pointed. Joachim raised the binoculars again. He began quartering the terrain, moving systematically outwards over the plain. But then he shook his head. "I can see nothing," he said.

Queen stretched out his arm. "Follow the river till it disappears, then glass along to the end of the tree belt. I make that out to be smoke."

Joachim ranged the pattern Queen had suggested. He saw the wispy gray smudges that seemed to cap the last of the trees. Mist? Marsh gas from a swamp? But not at this hour, and when most tribes would have begun to set their stewing pots for sundown. He turned his head. "I think you are right, Robert—and if so, they have hidden themselves well."

"Wouldn't you have? The kind of warfare they were raised to, it was a big advantage to spot attackers before they spotted you."

They had made it halfway back to the wagon, moving in single file, when Joachim in front drew rein and pointed. But Queen had already snatched his rifle from its saddle bucket. One second the gorge had been empty and the next the leopard was standing on a rock near the top looking down at them, his coat bright as butter in the strong sunlight.

Queen, stationary, brought up the gun, firing just as the

leopard bunched to spring away. The yellow cat voiced a roar at the pain and fell back out of sight.

"You want to go after him—the skin, Robert?" van Zyl said. "He was well hit."

"No," Queen said curtly, and waved him to go on.

The younger man frowned. He led off again and, as they moved farther along, his eye swept the sloping wall, and then the craggy ledges opposite, until he saw the puff of dust that had not quite settled and knew why the leopard had shown like that.

Joachim slowed his pace slightly and muttered over his shoulder. "We are being watched, Robert."

"I know," Queen said. "Keep moving."

"There's men up there. Banyoro, I think."

"I know," Queen said again. "I saw three crossing a gap back there just before the cat showed. Just keep moving." He cupped his hands to his mouth and shouted up at the crags. "*Sakubona! Sakubona Banyoro!* The *ingwe* is a gift from the *Umlungu!* From *Dukusa!*"

There was no sign nor answer.

"Why didn't you tell me?" Joachim said, whispering now.

"You just might have dug in your heels—being startled, I mean."

The younger man bridled a little. "I wouldn't have."

"Maybe not. Anyway, it would have been bad politics."

"Shouldn't we go back, make contact with them?"

"Not yet. They might think we want to claim the cat and give us a greeting of arrows. Then we'd have to thump them. No, let's just let them take the word back—and the cat."

"You think they understood?"

Queen pursed his lips. He had shouted in the dialect of Igonyela and at first he was doubtful whether they would have understood. But he'd done the best he could.

When they could see the wagon again, they trotted the rest

of the way. Matshongi was waiting. He had heard the shot, and they told him briefly what had occurred and what they had seen from the brow of the Ridge.

"Do you think these stick-shooters may come in the night, N'kosi?" the burly man asked.

"Not to pepper us, not if they heard me," Queen said. "Thievery is more like it," he added laconically. "Don't want to end up with half a team. We'll bring the oxen in closer at sundown, and leave the hounds loose."

"What about leopard?" Joachim said. "They seem to be here."

"Not likely," Queen said, "nothing here to support cats."

"But the one back there?"

"Probably came up from the bottomlands—they could have been trailing him all day."

"You reckon they were a hunting party, then?"

Queen nodded. "They were hunting that cat, all right—he wasn't just taking a daylight prowl. Maybe the Chief's wife needs a new cape."

For a moment or two the group fell silent.

The sun had swung low in the west now, outlining the saddleback *kloof* across the moor with a bordering of orange. The dogs were stretched out under the wagon, and nearby, close hobbled, the oxen grazed. The moon began to rise, a honey-colored hunter's moon, almost full, that touched the crags with silver yet deepened their dark pools of shadow.

"Well, Robert," Joachim said, breaking the long silence, "we will hope that this Queen is really white, and fond of finery, of red blankets, for instance."

"Amen to that," Queen said. "But I've got something better than that in the wagon, little present I got from one of Piet's wenches."

They fell silent again, each man absorbed with his own conjecturing. After a time, Joachim's thoughts returned to the

141

golden body of Poyana, whereas Queen could think only of what lay immediately ahead. He was scarcely a poetic man, but the panorama from the Ridge had moved him deeply; he thought of the first men who had made it through that pass and seen the vastness beyond. He thought of the first men to wrest empires from this unyielding land. He would have given anything to have been among them, there with the greatness. Queen guessed he knew what it must have felt like. He guessed he knew that all right, by Christ!

*   *   *

The early morning air was keen and bracing as they set out across the grassy plain. They could have laid a course for the wagon to either side of the saddleback defile, but this was the shortest way. Moreover, it had seemed to Queen that to run either of the other routes might have given an impression of timidity. Surely, they were still being observed. He lowered his glasses. "Our friends await us, I think."

"Banyoro . . . in the gorge? You saw them?" Joachim asked quickly.

"No, but I saw birds that did," Queen said.

"We could detour the gorge, keep to the open," Joachim offered.

"What for?"

The younger man felt a tinge of heat rise to his face. "What I meant was, if they *are* hostile, we are sitting ducks in the gorge."

"You're right," Queen said. "But it would look as if we were unsure of ourselves, afraid. Bad politics. That's the last impression we want to give." He jabbed a finger, pointing ahead. "We've got a lot of business up there and the politics of it is what is going to count."

Joachim nodded shortly. "Right, then. But if they do attack us, won't you parley?"

Queen shrugged. "We've got to take some chances. But if they *won't* parley, if it turns *real* sour on us, we'll stay out of their range and pepper 'em while Boetie heads for the pass. Ah, but it won't come to that, *Jong*. All the same . . ." Queen turned in the saddle. "You hear that, Boetie?"

"I hear you, N'kosi," Matshongi said serenely. He reached down for the twelve-bore, checked it, and wedged it in the corner of the box opposite his rifle.

Queen watched the approaching crests of the saddleback. Four hundred yards short of the mouth of the gorge, maximum practical range, he held up his hand and halted. "Here's as far as you go, Boetie. If it goes wrong, you know what to do."

The two horsemen moved on again, cantering now, abreast but several yards apart. They crossed the threshold of the gorge.

They made a hundred yards, then two hundred, scanning the brownstone spurs and crags burnished by the sun. The ambush was a routine African tactic. If it happened, they were ready.

Queen felt the sweat on his neck. He slid the pistol from his thigh and rose in his stirrups. He fired two shots in the air and reared up at the slopes.

"Bayede! Bayede Banyoro!"

Along both undulating crests heads appeared like the rippling outlines of twin centipedes. Queen shouted again and waved his arms, signaling the watchers to descend.

Figures, fifty, a hundred, began to fully emerge from the crags and boulders and to move down the slopes. Many held throwing spears as well as the short bows they carried, but none as yet seemed to have notched an arrow, nor taken a barb from the hide quivers slung on their backs.

Queen's expression relaxed. "It's going to be all right, Jo—we're going to talk. Signal Boetie to come on."

Joachim turned, raised an arm. They heard the crack of Matshongi's whip as he urged the oxen to a tripple. On either side of the gorge, the bowmen halted well before the bottom of the slope and stared at the thundering wagon with differing expressions of wariness, half-suspicion, mounting interest. As the wagon came to a halt Matshongi drew himself upright, gripping the frame of the canopy on either side, displaying his formidable stature and substance, a wordless declaration of confidence, power, irresistible force.

"Usuuthu! Usuuthu Banyoro!" Matshongi shouted.

It was impressively delivered, with the panache of a Zulu headman, a salutation that conveyed the prestige of the man who bestowed it.

Queen nodded in approval. This African was worth a column of riflemen, he thought, a corps of spearmen. This African, Queen thought, could make the critical difference.

Book
TWO

Banyoro

The palaver with a trio of Banyoro headmen had been quite short. Save for their more rapid manner of speech, punctuated by its curious exclamatory clicks, the Banyoro tongue was cousin enough to the Igonyela dialect that Queen could get along. To the three headmen the name and significance of *Dukusa* was not unknown, and this was a crucial gain, Queen surmised. Queen declared that they were Inkosis, chiefs, friendly emissaries of the white king beyond the escarpment, who was the overlord of Igonyela and they would hold palaver only with the Queen of the Banyoro and her councillors.

The Banyoro captains accepted the proposition, and now, flanked by a squad of warriors on either side, the cortege of riders, bristling dogs, and wagon had begun to descend the western slopes of the great Ridge to the fertile plateau of Malendela. Whether the escort of bowmen was to be construed as a guard of honor or arrest, Queen did not know. He signaled to Joachim and Matshongi to keep a sharp eye, not that he really needed to suggest it. They were wary for the slightest change in the mood of the tribesmen, who surrounded them on all sides now.

They had reached the foothills now, and even this hem of

the escarpment offered excellent grazing, watered by the rills and *spruits* from the Ridge. It was nearing noon and, as Joachim moved up alongside Queen, the Afrikander signaled Matshongi to follow toward a clump of acacia that shaded the waters of a hurrying *spruit*. Queen nodded to the brook appraisingly. "Christ, even the water's like champagne, Jo."

They turned their horses toward the stream and then, in a blaze of motion, a semicircle of Banyoro cut them off, arrows notched. The bowmen were silent. But their expressions showed they meant business.

"Robert!" Joachim whispered. "They think we were going to run."

The youngest of the three Banyoro headmen stepped forward. Like the rest, he wore a skin kaross about his shoulders, a short betshu of hide, and a satchel that probably held tobacco, reed pipe, and food. But, like the other two captains, his head was covered by a buckskin skullcap, the mark of his rank. The man gestured angrily with his spear, motioning the *ryders* to return to the wagon. Queen leaned forward in the saddle. "Listen, Banyoro." He spoke slowly, roughly, through his teeth. "We are Inkosis of *Dukusa*. N'kosi! Your *guests, not* prisoners. You have already been told that, and *I shall not tell you again.*

"*Semana*, halt!" The Banyoro gesticulated again, emphasizing it with a tongue click of denial.

The Afrikander glared back then. Suddenly, he reared his horse onto its hind legs, prancing, screaming: "*Intsila!* Monkey dung! Out of my way lest my *injomane* eat you alive." Queen thundered it from the saddle.

The headman sprang aside, and the bowmen scattered before the menacing yellow teeth and furiously pawing hooves of the rampant advancing stallion.

Queen brought the horse back down onto its forelegs and both *ryders* moved on toward the stream at a walking pace, tensed with the sweating effort of not looking back, braced for the swish of arrows. But then instead, amazingly, a chorus of shrill laughter and catcalls broke out, the derision clearly directed at the disgraced headman and his detachment by the main body of bowmen still gathered around Matshongi.

The *ryders* dismounted, and as they led the horses to the water, Queen let out a breath of relief. "Close, eh, Jo? Shouldn't have done that—could have scuppered us all," he reproved himself severely.

"A good trick with the horse, Robert—but not good for the nerves. I could feel the barbs in my back."

"Lost my dander. Bloody stupid, what I did."

"I really thought the little bastard was going to tell them to shoot."

Queen glanced under his brows to where the young headman stood across the grass, clearly justifying himself to the other two captains.

"Kind of skunked the poor runt, didn't I?" Queen said, and allowed himself a chuckle.

Better than an hour later they had spiraled well up into the hills when Queen took up the glasses. He studied the panorama ahead in silence, then he drew in a breath and handed the binoculars off to Joachim.

"Just take a look at that, Jo!" There was a chord of great feeling in Queen's voice.

Joachim scanned the landscape ahead. He had seen dense gatherings of game in his time, but nothing like this. Blue wildebeest, kudu, roan, sable, antelope. Certainly impala, zebra, giraffe were scattered in herds and parcels over the never-ending plain. Black rhino in the pans, buffalo in the tracts near the first of the wide rivers. Swinging out again toward the middle distance, Joachim's attention was riveted.

"*Indlovu*, elephant!"

Queen smiled. "I was wondering when you'd get to them.

149

Past the *bok* of scrub near the beginning of the big timber, in the pan?"

"Yes."

"How many do you reckon?"

"Sixty or seventy that you could count."

"Yes, and there'll be plenty other herds like them," Queen said. "By, God, I knew it! Untouched elephant country. There's enough ivory here, Jo, to buy every damn thing we'll ever need—including artillery. Hides, horn, gums, too. Everything."

The younger man nodded enthusiastically, then checked. "Except for one snag, Robert. Getting it to the coast. . . . That would take weeks—and Lord knows how many trips."

"Not to the coast," Queen said. "Only to Igonyela."

"You mean build a storehouse? Then move it by big trains—the Portuguese—to the Coast?"

"Yes, but not like that. Piet will lift it from Igonyela . . . a dozen wagons, maybe more, *then* to the Coast, by Manoel and the *ryders*."

"Will Morgan *agree* to all that?"

"He already has," Queen said. "We worked it out while you were doing your courting, lad, *in case* we struck it as we have. Of course Piet gets a share, but there's something else counts a helluva lot more with him."

"Politics? The future?"

"Allies! Got a long head, has *M'zee* Piet. He wants all the allies he can set up. *Real* allies. What they call a confederacy."

"Well, it is a great plan, Robert. But what about the biggest obstacle?" Joachim jerked his head. "The Banyoro, it's they who rule the country."

"They won't stop us," Queen said with finality. "Not now. Not after what we've seen. We'll come to terms with them, one way or the other. There's ten times more country out

150

there than they need, or could rule, ten times enough for them
and us and to spare!"

"But if they oppose?"

"Oppose, hell! Politics, lad—the politics!" Queen emphasized. "We must convince them that we're the kind of allies
and neighbors they'll rejoice in, greatly benefit from—and so
they would."

"I think they will be hard to convince," Joachim said.

"We shall have to be firm, very firm," Queen insisted.

"You mean *fight* them?"

"It wouldn't be much of a fight," Queen said. "Not with
two or three dozen *ryders* and a couple of chatter guns."

"I wouldn't like that, Robert, I would greatly regret that,"
Joachim said with sincerity.

Queen shrugged. "I would regret it too."

"But it *is* their land . . . they have a right to it," Joachim
said in the tone of a man openly reviewing his conscience.

"Some of it," Queen said. "Yes. They're entitled to all they
need, more. We'd agree boundaries—as Piet and Igonyela
did—and incidentally, guarantee theirs. What do you think
would happen to these people if somebody ever found gold or
stones here?"

Joachim spoke quietly. "That is a good argument,
Robert—perhaps the best."

"Exactly," Queen said.

The Afrikander jerked his head sideways. "Mark that *bok*
well, Jo. Maybe we'll be giving these people a meat argument
to think about."

"Elephant?"

Queen nodded.

The young man smiled. "The politics and the prestige?"

"Both!" Queen fairly shouted.

They had made a good distance across the green expanse

151

when they saw the lions, a pride of nine full-grown beasts lazing in the shade of a spreading fig tree. The Banyoro did not seem to show any undue uneasiness nor deviate much from their course, though some, Queen noticed, shouted insults or spat malevolently toward the sprawling yellow killers.

Queen put two fingers in his mouth and whistled. He called to the eldest headman leading the train.

"*Hio*, Banyoro!"

When Queen had moved forward to where the headman waited, he pointed to the lions.

"You have many *ingonyama* in your country, Induna?"

The lean brown man looked puzzled, then he nodded.

"In great plenty, *Umlungu*."

"*Umlungu N'kosi*, Banyoro!" Queen stressed the term of respect sharply. "You do not find them a curse, killers of game and cattle?" he continued.

The tribesman stared, then shrugged philosophically as if the answer must be universally self-evident. "*Tchk!* We hate them."

"Then why don't you kill them then, wipe them out?" the Afrikander said contemptuously, knowing perfectly well why not.

The grizzled headman moved his shoulders. He made a gesture with his bow. "Even with many arrows, lion kill men before they die themselves. There is no wisdom in that."

Queen nodded. It wasn't hard to guess what a berserk lion would do to a group of bowmen before their poison had had time to take effect.

"Do you have use for the skins of *ingonyama*, the testicles and the fat, Induna?" Queen said with seeming indifference, well aware that many tribes believed the testicles imparted bravery and the fat cured otherwise incurable ailments.

152

The man in the skullcap crinkled his forehead at the oddness of the questions. Queen could see that he had guessed right.

"Wait here, then," Queen said in a commanding voice. "You hear the thunder of our *isibamus*." He touched the rifle butt at his knee. "Then come for the skins."

He turned in the saddle. "We'll take out two from that bunch of scunners, Jo—cat balls for the Indunas!"

They rode out across toward the fig tree at a walking pace.

"Get the big bastard, Jo," Queen said. "Get him sure while I watch the bitches."

At a hundred yards, all the pride were on their feet. At seventy, four or five had begun to slink away, headed, typically, by the patriarch, whose belly hung low from gluttony. At forty-five yards, the heir-apparent of the pride opened his jaws and roared. But to Queen's ear there was uncertainty in it. More bluster and bombast than real aggression, unlike the pitched snarling of the three lionesses remaining.

One of the lionesses had begun to move from side to side now, rage in her eyes. Queen's gun followed the movement of her shoulder blades under the supple hide. He spoke quietly out of the side of his mouth. "Blast him, Jo—the big bitch is coming."

Almost in the same instant he heard the crash of Joachim's rifle, and the thunk. But he did not shift his eyes from the female and he fired as the lioness wheeled with the report. He heard Joachim fire again, and saw that the big male was down. Queen worked the bolt and gave the tumbling lioness another round.

The other two lionesses had already begun to give ground and now, with the demoralizing uproar of gunfire, they began to lollop after the others.

153

Queen grinned. Joachim had shot well, nailing a young male as well. "All right," he said, "two sets of balls for the skullcaps. No nuts for the arrogant young one, then."

A detachment of the Banyoro were trotting across the grass to them now, led by the senior headman. Queen called to the leader. "The organs of the big one for youself, Induna."

The Banyoro showed his small teeth. "*Bayede! Bayede Dukusa!*"

The *ryders* took some whiskey while they watched the skinning and butchering of the beasts, and when they moved off again, there was a noticeable change in the demeanor of the tribesmen—save for the headman who had suffered the humiliation of the horse trick, and who went without his share of testicles.

*   *   *

It was mid-afternoon. They had begun to traverse an area of elephant grass, heading now for the distant dark mass of the forest belt. Following the line of the big timber, Queen picked out an intervening grove of uniform trees that made him pause. *Karreebooms!* The trees invariably grew near water or marshland, and the circumstance seemed to support his surmise. He handed the Barr and Stroud's to Joachim and poked out a finger. "I would bet that's the *bok* we saw from the Ridge, and I would also bet the wallow will be back of it."

Joachim studied the place for a moment, then he nodded. "It certainly fronted the tree line. You may be right, Robert."

"Damn sure I am," Queen said confidently. He drew on his cheroot and deliberated. "Maybe we should give these fellows another demonstration."

"Elephant politics?" Joachim quipped.

The Afrikander glanced toward the sun. "There's time enough."

154

"Three lions should be enough politics for one day," Joachim argued.

Queen gave the young *ryder* a hard look. "You feeling tired, Jo?"

Joachim tilted his hat and scratched the side of his head. "Well, hell, Robert, elephant is elephant," he said, his voice steady enough, yet under it the special twinge which all honest hunters admitted when it came to the most formidable of man-killers, the ones that always demanded absolute accuracy.

"You think I don't know it?" Queen said. "But I figure we'd best get all the politics we can get."

He whistled to the eldest headman, who came back across the grass to his side.

"N'kosi?"

"How long will it take to reach your kraal?"

The Banyoro considered the leisurely pace of the wagon, "Before the sun dies, N'kosi."

"Do the Banyoro value the fine meat of *indlovu?*"

"It is good meat, rich—but few have eaten it."

"Then we will take all your warriors can carry," Queen said enigmatically.

"*Indlovu?* To find *indlovu* it might require half a day, a day!"

"No," Queen said categorically. "It will require less than the time of skinning the *ingonyamas*. The *indlovu* are behind the *bok* of trees, *there!*" He pointed.

"Lord, how can you know that?" the headman said, eyes wide.

"We can smell them," Queen said laconically, impressively.

The Banyoro's eyelids narrowed again. "The scent of *indlovu* reaches you? *From there?*" He threw a quick incredulous glance over his shoulder at the *karreebooms* a mile or so distant.

Queen bent forward in the saddle. "Man, we are *real* hunters. N'kosis of *Dukusa*. How often must I tell you?"

The headman's broad nostrils dilated and he tilted his head. He gave a tongue click of complete defeat after each ineffectual sniff.

"We are wasting time," Queen said brusquely. He concluded the byplay, raising his chin and sniffing the air ostentatiously. "They may be leaving already. Bring the moving hut and your warriors halfway to the trees. Then stay there. Be sure that you remain downwind. Come only when you have heard the *isibamus* sound." He waved a hand. "Now, *loop, loop,* go!"

Joachim watched the Banyoro trotting toward the tribesmen, gesturing for them to draw close around the wagon to hear of this new mysterious development, and to receive his appropriate orders.

"Let's hope we are not going to look stupid, Robert," he said with a small laugh.

"Why should we?"

"Well, if they are gone . . ."

"What's the difference if we've figured the place right? Be enough evidence they *were* there . . . a ploughed field of it."

Queen glanced sharply at the young *ryder*, then the two of them cut through the tall grass on a trot, and when they had left it behind, Queen tested the wind. There was no perceptible current, but the drift was to the southwest so they began to make an arc to come in at the south end of the trees. At five hundred yards, they slowed to a walk. Fifty yards further on, they heard a single shrill trumpeting call, the exuberant squeal of a calf.

Queen grinned and nodded. "Some noses we got—eh, Jo?"

They tethered the horses just inside the fringe of the trees. The *karreebooms* were not closely stacked, but their branches reached out to twine hands with each other, and in the

156

interlacing avenues it was like twilight after the glare of the open. By degrees, however, the light grew stronger and the fret-work of yellow puddles more repetitive as the *ryders* approached the far perimeter of the grove. Then they dropped to their bellies and moved up to the bole of a large tree on the fringe.

Out across the pan a few beasts lay on their sides, baking their coated bodies in the sun, and more of the herd had already begun to straggle in a dawdling caravan toward the lowering sun. But there were still twelve elephants in the swamp—two bulls, several cows, the rest calves.

"*Geluk!* A day of *geluk* indeed, Robert," Joachim breathed.

Queen studied the bulls, the biggest very big, towering, his wrinkled blue-gray hide plastered with the red mud; his tusks were good enough, not phenomenal, but over a hundred pounds. Probably the patriarch, but not the leader of the herd, Queen thought; the leader would be up front waiting on the laggards.

Queen put a hand on the other man's arm and leaned close. "Take the young bull up front. I'll be covering him, too, in case he shifts out of line. But he's the boss, all right."

Joachim seemed visibly distressed. "Don't you want to take him, Robert?" It was almost a plea.

Queen paused, then he said, "No, man. Now you get on with it, *Jong*."

"All right, but not from here. Nearer."

"Watch it then, and no nearer than that rock. Farther than that, you'd be damn near upwind." Queen touched the young man's arm. "The ear slot, and even if you nail him sure, give him two more back of the shoulder."

He watched Joachim start to belly down the slope toward the small gray outcrop, freezing each time a trunk tested the steamy air. Then Queen himself began to snake out on his elbows toward a trampled busket of scrub, halfway down to the edge of the pan. Twenty yards further along Joachim had made the boulder and was sliding the rifle from his back.

Queen focused on the big one, but from the corner of his eye, he saw the young bull in the wallow roll upright onto his belly and gather his knees under him.

Now Joachim was down to it. Concentrating, thinking. *Breathe through the mouth . . . dead steady . . . suck in . . . barest fraction above midway between ear-tip and eye for the brain. . . .* He fired just after the bull had regained his feet, and Queen heard the boom and the dull slap. The big adolescent flung up his trunk and both men waited for the piercing scream but, incredibly, no sound came. The impulse from brain to vocal cords had been severed. The elephant stood rooted, then sagged forward onto his knees, and went down with a heavy squelching thud.

For just an instant a petrified silence overhung the pan, then the shrilling pandemonium of shocked cows and calves filled the air and spread the panic wave as they lumbered and floundered toward the firm ground of the plain. Still prone, Joachim fired once more. Then he got to his feet and turned with a look of tight-lipped satisfaction to where Queen still lay stretched out in shooting position.

The pounding screeching beasts were out onto the grass now, all except one. Across the wallow the old bull stood now like a statue. In the second before the first report, he had caught the man scent, and now his weaving trunk had located the place where the danger lay. His trunk reared. He towered majestically, trumpeting his declaration, and then he charged, his whole bulk slamming into Queen's vision.

Joachim checked in mid-stride and spun around. He saw the upraised trunk as he heard Queen's order. *"Run, Jo! Run for the trees!"* He whirled again, slipped, almost falling, then recovered himself and ran. Queen fired from the ground and the shot piled into the bull's neck. But the leviathan held straight to his course, pounding up the slope at twice the man's speed for the enemy he could see. If anything, the hit seemed to speed him up.

Queen came to a shooting position on his knees as the great bull drove thunderously across the grass. He fired again, and the brute pitched forward, his tusks spearing half their length into the soft ground.

Queen stayed crouched where he was. He laid a second round into the downed elephant, then rammed back the bolt and began to replace the three shells as quickly as he could. He waited, his attention fastened on the mountainous form. He still waited. At last he laid down the rifle and got the flask from his hip, drinking as he watched Joachim approach.

"I don't know what to say, Robert." Joachim spread his hands. He was pale under his color, and there was a jagged pitch of emotion in his voice. "I never dreamt . . . I thought they . . ."

Queen held out the flask. "Here!"

"It was bad—very very bad . . ."

Queen grinned bleakly. "Well, lad, I won't say it happens to the best, because it doesn't happen to the best. The best remember to stay down, doggo, until they're very bloody certain." He tasted the bile in his mouth and spat.

"Yes, yes . . ." The younger man shook his head bitterly from side to side.

"Forget it." Queen put a comforting hand on the other man's shoulder. "Let's have a look at that old *skeat*. Some bloody battler, eh?"

Joachim stared emptily at the great still body, but he made no move. He could imagine the force of the huge curled trunk, the stomping weight of the massive feet.

Queen gave him a reassuring nudge. "He's well punctured all right. . . . Took me long enough though, eh?"

The great centurion was very old, the soles of his feet

scored and cracked, his furrowed lackluster hide loose as the folds of an old man's neck. His great ears, immense butterfly wings, were tattered, his small eyes misted with rheum, and the trunk notched and segmented like a monstrous shriveled caterpillar. Yet he was a monarch, even in death.

"He was a game old bugger, only doing his job," Queen said.

They turned away and went on down the slope to where the young bull lay at the end of the pan. His tusks were shorter but creamier than the old champion's, and he was fat as a pig. His meat would be opulent, and his teeth, too, were in good condition, worth extracting.

Queen let the big pendulous lip fall back and straightened up. "Howking and butchering these beauties will take a bit, I fancy. Go back to Boetie and have him get the wagon over to the other side of the trees fast as he can."

"You're going to wait here, then?"

"Yes, I want to make sure they get the tusks out first . . . and don't make a bloody botch of it, either."

It was the young headman who made it to Queen first. Queen gave instructions, but the Banyoro shook his head. "There is only time to take enough of the meat."

"The *tusks!*" Queen said flatly. "Afterward the meat of the young bull—the old one is useless." He turned away.

"The tusks are of less importance," the African said obdurately. "First we will take the meat."

The huge *ryder* swung round. "*We* will? Who is *we?*" He took a step closer and held up the two severed tails of the elephants, universal token of ownership.

"*Who are the owners of this meat, Banyoro?*"

The headman fell back a pace. Again he felt dwarfed and frustrated by this big *Umlungu* chief, and his face worked with resentment. He could have called on the tribesmen to proceed as he had intended, but he had a growing suspicion that they might have refused. And he had a second suspicion that to do so might later produce repercussions for himself. Moreover, some of the bowmen had already moved onto the carcass of the old bull and begun to work on the jaws.

At last the headman turned, calling petulantly to others to begin the de-tusking of the young beast, masking his mortification with shrill commands and gestures.

It was late afternoon now, but there was still an hour or so of daylight, and as soon as the four tusks had been portered back through the grove to Matshongi, the tribesmen fell to on the young bull's carcass, laughing and singing in anticipation of the feasting and drinking to come, swarming over the plump gray mound of flesh like ants. The butchering squads worked systematically, in relays, slicing, hacking, tearing at the steaming meat, some gobbling tidbit mouthfuls of offal or fat as they went along, and soon the piled slabs and chunks were heaped as high as a hurdle.

Dusk was falling by the time the prime meat had been taken, and they were ready to trek again.

In the falling darkness, the pace of the wagon was slower, and Queen moved up beside the eldest headman. "How high will the moon have risen before we reach the kraal?"

The African considered for a moment, then held out his hand, palm flat.

"Your people will have gone to their mats, then?"

He nodded.

"Send runners now, then, explaining the delay and telling the women to prepare for a feast of *indlovu* meat tomorrow."

Again the headman nodded agreement, this time with a flash of teeth.

"Is the kraal away on this or the far side of the river?" Queen yawned.

The Banyoro's grin faded at the *ryder's* extraordinary perceptive powers. Certainly sections of the river could be seen

161

from the *krans* of the Ridge, but there was no indication that the kraal was situated on its bank. The headman ceased trying to fathom Queen's seeming unfathomable way of knowing things, and accepted the inexplicable with a click of resignation.

"On the other side."

"Is there a place of shallows, where the moving hut can cross?"

The Banyoro considered, but decided there was no advantage in not telling. "There is such a place, N'kosi, a short distance further down the river."

Queen nodded. "We will cross there tomorrow, then. Tonight we will stay on this side of the river." He saw suspicion in the tribesman's face, and smiled sarcastically. "You still think we may fly away in the night, Induna?"

"Lord, huts will be given you," the black man said, with a meaningful gesture.

"And we will accept them," Queen answered. "After the palaver. Does your empress queen hold *Indaba*, make palaver, in the middle of the night?"

The headman stood corrected. The *Umlungu* was right. The empress Malendela was very conscious of her dignity, and to unceremoniously lead the white men into the kraal at this time might be a rudeness, a reason for punishment.

The Banyoro were on either side of them now, intoning as they marched. Matshongi had urged the oxen to a half-tripple and Queen called back to him to slow down. "You buckle a wheel, man, and we'll leave you with it."

Joachim laughed. "I think Mattie is impatient for his mat and the river."

"For the bare rumps, you mean," Queen said, thinking, as he said it, that it was an expectation which suited him well enough too.

*   *   *

The kraal lay across the river, clearly visible in the night. Except for several figures dimly framed in the light of two torches at the entrance of the village, there was no sign of life. Several rafts were drawn up on both banks. While Joachim and Matshongi began to outspan the oxen, Queen sought out the eldest headman.

"We need wood, enough to last us till sunrise."

The Banyoro clicked his understanding. "We will send it when we have crossed ourselves."

"We shall also need herdboys tomorrow, and guards for the moving hut when we attend the *Indaba*."

"It will be done, N'kosi."

Queen raised a finger. "Be sure you make the guards understand, Induna, that in the moving hut there are *isibamus* which will spread thunder and death if touched by any strange hand. Make them understand that well, Induna," Queen said emphatically. "The dogs, too, must not be closely approached."

The Banyoro nodded. "Lord, all will be chosen well." He was quite prepared to accept that the thunderous rods of the white men were capable in themselves of belching their flame.

Malendela

Queen came out of his drowsing to the clinking of tinware. He sat up, stiff-armed, opened his eyes, closed them, then squinted again, and took the mug of tea Joachim held out.

"God bless you, *Jong*," he said thickly.

Across the river five men came through the gathering throng that were staring wonderingly at the hunter's camp from the gate of the kraal. One of them was the eldest headman and the others were, presumably, the chosen guards and herdboys. The party poled across the river on two rafts and came up the bank to the wagon.

"N'kosi," the old man said, "these are they who will guard the moving hut and watch the dog beasts and the big beasts," the grizzled Banyoro said. He waved an arm to the hobbled oxen grazing nearby.

"But first you should cross with the moving hut," the headman proposed. He pointed downstream in the direction of the drift.

Queen shook his head. "No, not yet, perhaps later. It will depend on which side we decide to hunt from, if the hunting is agreed."

"Then we will send rafts to carry you across when the *Indaba* is gathered."

"No." Queen shook his head again. "Signal us when the *Indaba* is ready and we will cross with our horses."

The tribesmen looked dubiously from the hunters to the horses and back again. "Lord, there is no need."

"Man, I pull your ears," the big hunter said, employing the phrase which stresses an important matter. "Are we Milebi, baboons, Induna? It is our custom to *ride* to an *Indaba*, a custom of *Dukusa*."

The Banyoro looked slightly disconcerted. He was not sure whether the Empress would approve of the white men's strange and dangerous beasts being close enough to do her harm.

"What does it matter if they wish us to go on foot?" Joachim said when the headman had gone.

"The prestige is what it matters," Queen said. "We don't go looking like we've only got our asses behind us." He drained off his second mug of tea.

Joachim stood, stretched, and glanced toward the river. Queen followed his look. "Just what I was thinking. Swim and a bath will clear the cobwebs and sharpen the appetite, do a world of good."

The other man turned his head again and looked doubtfully at the throng across the river. A number of Banyoro had come down to the water's edge to stare curiously, and the preponderance of them seemed to be women. "Well, I suppose we could walk upstream a way," Joachim said.

"Like bloody hell," Queen grinned.

He led the way down the slope, unhooking his belt, and stripped off at the edge. Behind him on the bank Joachim backed against the stump of a *karreeboom* and slid his leather *klapbroeks* down over his feet. Then he turned, ran the few yards, and dived out into the deeper water. He surfaced further out, and stood, waist-deep, shaking the drops from his eyes and gasping.

"Let's take a look at them while we're here!" Queen called.

They struck out across the river, swimming abreast. As they drew nearer, the children ran back up toward the kraal with shrill cries of alarm, and some of the men also backed away as if they thought the big white men were coming all the way. But most of the women stayed where they were, staring.

They were as tall as the bowmen, and some were taller. Their features were varied, lacking the relative uniformity of the men and some might have passed for various northern peoples. They were clearly the progeny of abducted women who had been chosen for their lusty bodies and the high- and large-bottomed trait of Somalis and Hottentots. Their tiny frontal aprons failed to cover the swell of their big thighs and buttocks.

The odors from Matshongi's cooking fire drew the *ryders* back to the campground. They dried their bodies, dressed, and hovered at the fire, the hunger in them great now. With the point of his knife, Queen speared a sizzling chunk of kidney from the pan, and nodded over his shoulder. "Well, Piet had it right about the little buggers, all right." Queen swallowed the mouthful and grinned salaciously. "Not much doubt about the seat of attraction for them, eh?"

Queen glanced at Matshongi with a chuckle. Matshongi crinkled his brows. "Once, the corn-haired N'kosi—Kolenbrander—told me there are yellow men in a land far away who worship geese and copulate with them."

"That's just so the birds can lay better," Queen said. "Sometimes their asses are too tight for the size of their eggs—need stretching."

The black *ryder* paused, considering the resourcefulness of it, nodding slowly.

By mid-morning there had still been no summons from the Empress Malendela. But finally a resonant drumming issued from the kraal. The children scattered. Washerwomen and water-carriers hoisted their baskets and pots onto their heads and hurried back up the bank.

166

Queen looked at Matshongi. "You read those drums, Boetie?" The African shook his head.

"Maybe it's the signal for the *Indaba*, calling the people to gather," Joachim surmised.

"Likely," Queen said. "About bloody time, too."

An elder tribesman came trotting down to the river's edge, his arms waving. He called across. "Lords! The empress awaits you. Come now."

"Tell him we understand and will come presently, Boetie," Queen said. "When we are ready." He grinned at Joachim. "Now they can stew for a spell while we have a shave and pretty ourselves up."

While they were busy with razors and soap, Matshongi took a bath in the river. When he had dried himself, he stood naked, vigorously anointing himself with nut oil until his hefty body gleamed chocolate-brown in the sun.

Queen came from the wagon carrying two packages. He put one on the grass, but broke the other with a grin.

"Here you are, Jo, brand new, from Manoel's friends on the Coast." Joachim caught the white dress shirt that Queen tossed him.

"We're going in there looking like white men, not ragged-assed doppers, *Jong*," Queen said, opening the second package.

About an hour had passed since they had been summoned. In puzzled silence, a knot of Banyoro still watched the hunters' leisurely preparation from across the river.

They could have swum the horses across easily enough from where they were, but Queen saw no necessity for sodden boots. In any event, it suited Queen to prospect the drift. The ford, an undulation of the river-bed over a gravelly stretch, proved easy going, the water barely above the horses' knees in midstream. There would be no difficulty in taking the wagon over if they so decided. Across the river they began to canter back upstream. Near the kraal entrance, Queen motioned for the other two *ryders* to fall back a pace or two, so that they passed between the half-dozen spearmen on either side of the gate in arrowhead formation. From the wide avenue that formed the inner periphery between the palisade and the web of yellow beehive huts a main aisle ran directly toward the arena in the center of the village, lined on both sides with men, women, and children.

Queen stared straight ahead. Joachim and Matshongi followed his example. All three sat bolt upright in their saddles. Toward the end of the aisle, they dismounted, tethering their horses to the structural frame poles of huts at the edge of the arena. Then they moved forward abreast, through the outer crowd and across the red hard-trodden cirque toward the close-assembled group confronting them. It was only the crunching of their boots that disturbed the silence.

Malendela sat leaning on the arm of her rough-hewn chair, beneath an aromatic *mkhuze* tree whose branches cast an aureola of cobwebbed shade. She stared intently at the approaching hunters of *Dukusa*. Immediately around her, the necklet of the assembly, her "wives," squatted woodenly like idols. There were nine emasculates all wearing a yellow-ochered skullcap crested with a tuft of green pigeon feathers and a necklace of bear and hyena teeth. Each also was marked with a scar in the form of a cross on his forehead, and wore a female betshu that displayed his lean buttocks when he stood upright. Despite their colorful finery and privileged proximity to their "husband" and ruler, they were gelded popinjays, compulsorily appointed to the position of royal menials, who had no significance at all beyond that of symbolic peacocks.

To the side of the celibate "wives" sat the councillors and the elders in two ranks. Half of them were old men who no longer had any voice in tribal matters but whose presence was in recognition of past services.

The hunters halted some ten paces from the Court of the

168

Indaba. Seated as she was in the deepest shadow of the tree, and with the strong sunlight glaring from behind the tree, the empress could only be seen indistinctly. But two things were clear enough. She was not old, and she *was* white.

Young and white, it was an anomaly that filled Joachim with a queer effect akin to awe, mystery, fable. As for Queen, it was a legend coming true and quite the strangest thing he had ever seen.

Malendela bent forward on her elbow, chin cupped in shapely hand, narrowing her eyes in appraisal and curiosity. She had acquired royal authority by pure chance, and then, ironically, because of her color, stature, and the matriarchal basis of Banyoro lore, she had been elevated to virtual deification by her abductors. Indeed, she bore herself as if she believed herself a goddess.

Queen raised his hand in greeting.

"*Sakubona,* I see you, *Inkosazana!*" he said formally.

A councillor moved forward and Queen realized with a stab of annoyance that the Banyoro were of those tribes who did not approve direct speech with their ruler, save by one of indisputably equal rank. The go-between spokesman took a further pace or two, interposing himself importantly.

"Speak through me, *Umlungu!* Why are you here and what do you seek?" Queen looked down at him coldly. "Man, *little* man, stand aside. I do not speak through your throat. That is for small chiefs and inferiors. Do you think *Dukusa* an inferior?" Queen said challengingly, forcefully.

For a moment there was silence. The councillor turned his head with a look of baffled uncertainty. Then Malendela motioned him to return to his place.

The Afrikander nodded in acknowledgment, then he addressed her directly. "We bring you a message from *Dukusa, Umtwana,* royal child—a request also. Queen squinted against the sun, but still could not see her clearly.

At last she spoke herself. "What is this message, N'kosi?" Her voice was intriguingly low, with a timbre that contrasted distinctly with the higher tones of the tribespeople.

Queen screwed up his eyes again and began to move closer, trying to see her more definitively against the barrier of gloom and sunlight, but immediately two warriors sprang from either side, their crossed stabbing spears denying further approach. But what Queen could now see was a woman with very fair complexion. She wore two graceful scarlet plumes of crane and flamingo in a narrow headband of black otter skin. White ivory discs covered the lobes of her ears. Yes, she was very fair, but only her face and neck proclaimed her whiteness, for a leopard-skin cape was draped about her shoulders, and beneath it she wore a *kanzu*, a sheath-like garment of crimson-dyed bark cloth. Queen could make out the dull glitter of silver bangles at her wrists and ankles. Still, her features remained hidden.

"*Dukusa*, King of our land beyond the Ridge, Overlord of Igonyela and other chiefs, offers you his friendship, and to make common cause against your enemies."

"Enemies?" her throaty voice sounded. "What enemies?"

"Any enemies—all enemies," Queen said sharply.

Malendela stared. Then she laughed softly. It was an agreeable sound, but there was a note of ridicule as well as amusement in it.

"No enemies threaten us, N'kosi," the empress said.

A ripple of assenting laughter ran through the rentinue of councillors, and Queen bridled at this. He let his glance travel slowly around the smirking tribesmen, his own lips shaping to a bleak smile of counter derision, staring them down until the grins faltered and faded. His voice cut through the murmuring like a whip-crack.

"Banyoro, you are mistaken! Greatly mistaken!" He

170

paused, then gestured to the east, and now his tone was caustic. "Over there, across the Ridge, are the Milebi. *They are your friends, your well-wishers?*" he said with broad sarcasm.

There was a shrill piping voice from the fringe of the crowd. "Tchk! The north pass is always guarded!" It was the bombastic young headman with whom Queen had clashed twice previously, but Malendela curtailed the upstart's intervention with a frown of annoyance.

"We do not fear the Milebi, nor could they ever take us by surprise, N'kosi," she said confidently, as if correcting an understandable and surely forgivable misapprehension.

Perhaps the sun had shifted a degree, or Queen's eyes had become accustomed to the light, but he thought he saw a smile of indulgence on the woman's face and it rankled him further. Deliberately he looked away from her and stared at the skullcapped man with the same thin humorless grin, as if the headmen were responsible for this further ineptitude. For Christ's sake, he thought, it was time this convocation of monkeys was jolted out of its complacency.

"Are *we* not here? Was it not merest chance that our presence was discovered?" Queen barked acidly.

It was a shot in the dark, but he saw that it had registered. Beside him Joachim sensed the rising tension, and put a restraining hand on Queen's arm, but the big hunter took a further pace forward and this time when the spears barred his way again, he brushed them aside and Malendela gave no sign to stay him.

"When the Milebi come, they will come by the south pass, through Igonyela's country—and without his knowledge or consent!" Queen said authoritatively. He turned back to Joachim with a shrug, as if washing his hands of imponderable stupidity.

There was a rising murmur of excited discussion. The big

171

ryder remained silent now, affecting indifference, his manner suggesting no further concern with the great disaster that threatened them, a certainty as inevitable as rain.

For several moments Malendela sat brooding.

There had been no attack in her time. But she knew well enough, from her older people, the character and rapacity of the wolves beyond the north wall. A Milebi attack could never be ruled out, especially if, as certain of her frontier spies had lately reported, the wolves were becoming desperately avid for meat, women, and plunder. But how could the white men know that? Or perhaps they possessed shrewder spies, and then she recalled perceptive powers they had been credited with by the headmen who had escorted them in.

Abruptly she raised herself upright in her chair and jabbed with the pointed index finger of her clasped hands.

"If the Milebi did think to attack us, why would *Dukusa* aid us against them—and how?"

"Because we also hate Milebi," Queen said unequivocably.

The big *ryder* took his time. He fished in his shirt pocket for a cheroot and summoned the match flame from his thumb, to many tongue clicks and looks of amazement.

"As to how. We should send messengers—Indunas—to the Milebi, to tell them we should destroy them, in their own country . . . *if you were our friends, our allies!*"

Queen glanced significantly at the other two hunters, inviting their opinion. Both nodded solemnly.

Now the ripple that ran round the body of the *Indaba* was moderately approving.

The empress spoke again, and the assembly fell into a hush. "That is big talk, lion talk, N'kosi. But *how* would you destroy such numbers as the Milebi have?"

"No, *not* lion talk! *Dukusa* talk!" Queen corrected her forcefully. "What is the meaning of *Dukusa* but *Great Elephant Killer?*"

Queen turned, running his eye over the beehives bordering the arena, then halted his survey with a grunt of satisfaction. Three vultures sat close abreast on the thatch of a hut across the compound. He eased the Buntline from his thigh, raised the long barrel upright, and brought it down, firing three times in rapid succession. One of the birds fell plumb. A second, in the act of launching, dropped limply a yard from the first quivering heap. Queen blew away the smoke drifting from the barrel of the big Colt.

"That is how, *Inkosazana!*" he said.

Malendela sat fascinated. It was the first time she had heard gunfire, witnessed the lethal effect of a bullet. She raised a hand to quell the hubbub of wondering exclamation and startled gesturings.

The Afrikander held up the pistol, dangling it on the hook of his finger.

"With guns! But not little *isibamus* like these. With the *fathers* of these! Not even the thunder-rods with which we kill *indlovu*. With big magical *isibamus* that will cut down a whole army in less time than the flight of an arrow! None of the warriors would escape such *isibamus*." He gestured toward the tethered horses. "Nor can any man outrun our *injomanes!*"

Malendela leaned back contemplatively. She glanced at the senior headman standing before his company of bowmen, and saw his repeated nods of affirmation of the white men's powers.

Again she spoke, the arrogance in her voice unmistakable. "We do not fear the Milebi. But we send thanks to your King."

Queen shrugged as if unburdening himself from the consequences of this particular stupidity. Then he spoke: "The Milebi are *nothing*. But there is *another* danger to your people beside which the Milebi are no more than a plague of flies," he said enigmatically.

173

Malendela reached out her hand and one of her "wives" hastened to offer her a platter of fruit. She waved a hand airily, and Queen caught the gleam of white teeth as she bit into a fig.

"A plague of monkeys? From the west?" She paused, anticipating the crowd laughter, then capped the witticism. "For there is nothing else there."

Queen waited for the tittering to subside. Then he raised his voice enough to reach the body of the crowd.

"No! A plague of *white* men from the *south!*" he said harshly.

The smile on Malendela's face slowly faded. Her hands tightened on the ebony arms of her chair and the scarlet plumes wavered slightly as she bent forward again.

"*White* men?"

"*White* men!" Queen repeated flatly. "Who would despoil the earth, dam the rivers, kill the game, and enslave you."

All eyes turned expectantly to Malendela. She lifted her voice, vehement and spirited.

"As with the Milebi, we should defeat them in the passes."

Queen felt an impulse of admiration. He had no doubt that if it ever came to it, they *would* fight—and *she* with them. He shook his head, leaving them to interpret his smile as pitying or derisive.

"They would come from all directions, with *injomanes* and great numbers of moving huts. Nor could you hold the passes against them, for they would bring a white army, a big army, with big *isibamus* that would destroy you and your kraal even from the distance of the Ridge."

Hisses of anger and staccato clicks of apprehension and dismay came from the cadre of elders and were echoed by the crowd. Malendela remained silent, frowning.

On a hunch, Queen turned to Matshongi: "*Ndabazulu!*" he called out with authority, "On the bones of your forefathers, tell the empress of what I speak."

174

"The N'kosi speaks truth, *Inkosazana*," the black *ryder* said gravely. His deep-drawn voice stilled the continuing mumblings. "In the south and in the countries where the rivers end, it has happened to many tribes. I have seen it myself."

Malendela considered him. Then she pointed imperiously to Queen with her wand.

"Who is this black man who speaks for white men?"

Matshongi stiffened. But it was Joachim who replied tartly, as if he felt personal umbrage at the seeming inference of treachery.

"He is the son of an Induna of Zulu, *Inkosazana*," Joachim said deliberately, with a note of hauteur that matched her own. "And more, also an Induna of *Dukusa*. And even more, *moselekatse* of Zulu do not lie!"

Still Malendela retained an air of doubt. Matshongi had in fact impressed her favorably, but she countered with equal asperity.

"Then why does he serve white men?"

"Because he is our brother and he serves himself!" Queen shouted. "And because his father served with the father of *Dukusa* and they were brothers, and together they fought against the kind of white men I have spoken of."

Malendela knitted her brows.

"How are these other white men different from you?"

"Think of them as white-skinned Milebi, whom we of *Dukusa* hate more than black-skinned Milebi," Queen said.

There was a pause. Queen felt it threatened a reversal.

"Then why have they not moved against Bejane, against Igonyela, who have not the protection of the great wall?" the empress asked shrewdly.

It was the question he had been waiting for.

"Because Igonyela—*who is our friend*—has the protection of *Dukusa*," Queen said as if explaining a categorically infallible guarantee of security. "As for Bejane." He spat and graphical-

175

ly trampled the sputum with his boot. "When they decide to, they *will* overrun that donkey. Then the locusts will consume the dung beetles."

She gripped the carved arms of her chair.

"Could *Dukusa* also aid"—the word came unwillingly, but it had to be ceded—"protect us against these other white men?"

Queen spread a hand. "That is why we are here, *Inkosazana*. Moreover, *Dukusa* is a king who himself has the protection of the white emperor's laws."

"White emperor?"

"The Great Elephant, the ruler of all white men."

He saw her look of mystification and sought for a simple analogy. "It is not easy to explain, your highness. Suppose some of your own people thought to kill, to seize the wives and cattle of one of your own Indunas."

She cupped her chin, waiting.

"You would not allow it. You would punish them, order their execution."

She nodded decisively.

"So it is with the Great Emperor, and so he would rule with any who sought to seize the country of *Dukusa*—or of *those under Dukusa's protection*." Queen gave a meaningful smile. "Not that we would need the aid of any to deal with *them*. And they would know it."

Malendela inclined her head.

"I will tell you all the ways of it, the strengths, the medicine of *Dukusa*," Queen said. "But," he glanced pointedly at the entourage of councillors, "these things are for your ears alone."

"Then we will talk more of the things you have told us later," Malendela said, not unwillingly, and Queen hoped he understood her meaning.

"Yes." Queen held up the package he had brought from the wagon. "A *bonsella*, a small gift, *Inkosazana*."

"From *Dukusa?*"

Queen shook his head. "From myself. One day *Dukusa* may visit you himself."

The empress spoke to the girl at her side, and the young woman came forward for the parcel.

Malendela took it onto her lap and unfolded it. It was a bright yellow plain gown of thin, near transparent, sendal silk, which the romantically longsighted Santoro had picked up on a coastal mission.

Malendela examined it with puzzled interest, then shook it out. She gave an intuitive tongue click. "It is a *kanzu . . .* the *kanzu* of a white woman?"

Joachim had a flash of inspiration. "More than that, *Inkosazana!* Of an *Inkosazana* of *white* women! Fitting," he said shrewdly.

The tribute was not lost upon the empress and again the *ryder* got a glimpse of white teeth.

Queen grinned broadly at the younger man's adroit retraction of his earlier seeming hostility. The big *ryder* gave a passable imitation of the Banyoro tongue-click of agreement, an effort that brought surprised glances, then laughter.

Malendela clapped her hands and called out a succession of staccato orders over her shoulder that produced a bustling of women servants in the background. A train of women entered and filed through the crowd bearing vessels of beer and palm wine on their heads or shoulders. Men appeared carrying two hewn chairs, and another brought a carved stool for Matshongi. But contrary to Queen's expectation, the chairs were set down where the hunters stood, the division between throne and forum still maintained.

The empress called out: "The *kanzu* pleases me, N'kosi! We thank you also for the other gifts!"

"Other gifts?"

"The meat of the *indlovu*, the *ingwe* skin . . ." She touched the new kaross about her shoulders.

"Oh." Queen waved the acknowledgment aside. "*Kidogos*, nothings, which already belonged to you, *Inkosazana*. You have only to ask of us any skins or meats you wish." It seemed a good moment to make a further advance, and he spread a palm. "However, perhaps we may ask something in return?"

"Women?" The simple directness of it took him by surprise. "You wish women?"

It was prosaically said, as though it was of no more significance than asking for firewood.

"No. We wish to hunt elephant, seacow, rhino, while we are here in your country. But only for their teeth," Queen stressed. "The meat would be yours."

To his satisfaction, he heard widespread murmurs of approval from all quarters.

"That is *all*?" She frowned incredulously, clearly astonished at the insignificance of it. "You wish to make necklets, ornaments, from them?"

Queen shrugged, as if he himself thought it all a fanciful nonsense.

"They please many of our people," he said condescendingly, "but there are no *indlovu, imvubu*, in the countries of the white emperor, and few of good size now in the country of *Dukusa*."

"You have killed them all?" the empress said, her teeth showing again. "*Smelt* them all out, as my headmen say you do?"

Queen simply smiled grandly.

Malendela made a sweeping gesture. "Here they are numberless as the trees. Hunt them when you wish, fill your moving hut with their teeth . . . especially the *indlovu* who trample our grain, destroy the fruiting trees . . ."

Now at last she rose to her feet, and still closely accompanied by her umbrella girl, moved out into the hard bright sunlight of the arena; Queen's eyes widened with frank

178

admiration. Beside him Joachim and Matshongi had risen to their feet and stood equally arrested.

She was striking. She was beautiful. Even amongst tall white women, she would have stood out for her height of five feet ten or more. And no less, also, for her imposing bearing, which was regal, imperious.

In the strong light her red-gold hair and blue eyes shone. And her full-lipped mouth was crimsoned as skillfully as any European woman's. But, set off as it was by the back contrast of the tribesmen, the most arresting thing about her was her milk-white skin. It was irreconcilable with the African sun, unnatural. But, yes, it was her *whiteness* they worshipped, the charismatic distinction that marked her, and so it was this that was preserved and safeguarded from the sun. Hence the constant presence of her shadow, the umbrella girl, the permanent guardian of the deity's uniqueness.

For a second, as she passed Queen, their eyes met, and the candid expression on the Afrikander's face was clearly sexual. Beside him Joachim said something, but Queen did not hear it, his eyes following the movement of Malendela's hips as she moved toward the palisade that surrounded her hut. Joachim repeated himself, nudging Queen lightly. "The Induna, Robert. He has something to tell us."

Queen stared briefly at the man in the skullcap standing before them. "Well, Induna?" Queen put his hands on his hips with a smile of satisfaction. "Your empress is not displeased with the message of *Dukusa*, I think—and your people will get all the meat they can eat, and more."

"N'kosi, you raise us to your armpits!" the elder headman said with evident sincerity. "As she has told you, there are many *imvubu*. I come to tell you that I will guide you myself."

"Thank you, Induna." Queen nodded appreciatively. "It will be downriver, I suppose?"

"Yes, but other places too. Below the watercliffs there are

179

many small herds, but further, at the Lake of *Sibangwe*, the seacows swarm like flies."

"Tomorrow, then," the Afrikander said—then checked himself. "No, wait." The growing odor of roasting meat about the kraal reminded him. "Tonight there will be a feast . . . the *indlovu* meat, and dancing?"

The Banyoro captain grinned and nodded. "Much meat, much beer . . ."

"The day after tomorrow then."

"There is one other thing, Induna. We shall want many porters for the meat, but without sore heads or bellies. No drunken *inkawus* hunt with *Dukusa's* company."

"N'kosi! I shall choose the warriors myself."

"Good. How long would you like us to hunt meat for the tribe?" Queen asked.

The short man shifted his skullcap. "The Queen has ordered new huts for you—therefore, as long as you wish."

"Very well. We will hunt the *imvubu*, the big seacows, first, for four or five days." Queen held up five fingers.

The Induna rubbed his palms. "There will be much meat."

"Yes, but afterwards we will leave them for a long rest. Let them settle back."

Joachim nodded. "Not to panic them, start a migration."

"Yes," the older hunter agreed. "But there's something else also." He turned back to the Banyoro. "Later we will hunt *indlovu*, but after the first hunting of seacows we wish you to take us to the end of your country." He pointed toward the western horizon. "That way!"

The small man looked puzzled. "N'kosi, the land is no different there from here. Even the same if you march for a moon," he said as though to exemplify the pointless exertion it would be.

"Have *you* ever marched westward for a moon, Induna?" Queen asked.

"No. But I know it is the same, for some of our older men have been that far," the Banyoro insisted. "Also, where *is* the end of our country?" His smile and shrug implied that their realm was infinite, though there was no arrogance in it, merely the implication that the question was unanswerable.

Queen tapped the African's shoulder. "The end of your country, or any tribe's country, is the furthest place from your kraal," he made a criss-cross gesture, "that you could defend, hold, and rule. *That* is the end of your country."

The older man knitted his brows. It was a thing he had never previously thought about, nor could he recollect that it had ever been discussed within the tribe.

Queen went on. "Of what use are game herds so distant that the meat would be rotten before it could be brought in? Grazing too far away to feed the cattle of a tribe?" he pointed out.

The Induna waggled his head uncertainly, shifting his feet at the complexity of such matters. "N'kosi, I will lead you," the grizzled man said firmly.

*   *   *

The festal drumming and low vibrant chanting of the dancers had begun soon after nightfall, but it was about nine o'clock when the hunters re-crossed the river from the wagon, this time by raft. There was no hurry, the feasting and drinking would continue till daybreak.

The reddish-yellow glow of evening fires was joined this night by large communal cooking fires, and when the *ryders* returned across the river to the kraal, staked torches defined the dancing arena. Everywhere there was the smell of elephant meat from the stewing pots and roasting pits. When the *ryders* approached the perimeter of the dancing circle, Atelo, the eldest of the headmen and their hunting guide, came forward to greet them. The court of councillors and

181

Malendela's "wives" were grouped about the empress, who was seated in her throne chair in the position of best vantage.

Malendela acknowledged the hunters' raised palms with a subtle doffing of her plumes. Atelo clapped his hands for food and drink as the *ryders* took their seats; others of the court called out staccato salutations. But Queen heard none of these, his eyes and ears sensible now only of Malendela. For now, except for the leopard cape that was loosely draped about her shoulders, the empress was naked.

Queen was quite utterly staggered. Her beauty made him breathless, and her seeming innocence of the effect she created made her even more incredibly sensual.

Atelo squatted nearby him, and as Queen frankly stared at the empress, a khamba girl poured him a gourd of wine. Now serving girls entered with steaming platters of meat and vegetables. As he ate, Queen gaped at Malendela, at her nakedness. She was leaning languorously forward on one elbow, her face slightly flushed with the wine and food she had taken, and now her cape slipped unheeded from one shoulder and one superlative ivory breast was fully exposed. She met Queen's frank stare with the trace of a smile, but she made no effort to adjust her kaross. Was she, he wondered, simply brazen, or could it be that she was utterly unaware of the fantastic appeal that issued from her body?

He glanced around, studying the faces of the tribesmen in the crowd and the empress's entourage. From the look of it, all regarded her as not only unattainable, but sacrosanct, and were probably accustomed to seeing her in the nude state as indeed she almost was now. For when Queen looked back at her she was naked to the waist, cape discarded altogether, back arched, breasts outthrust, smiling warmly at the cavorting dancers.

"Man, this is diabolical!" Queen whispered to Joachim. He clapped his hands on his knees and got to his feet. It was evident that he could no longer contain himself, that he was going to make some kind of approach to the empress. But suddenly his way was blocked. It was, once again, the officious, posturing young headman. He motioned imperiously for Queen to resume his seat.

The Afrikander gave a short barking laugh. There was no stopping him now. "You again, eh, *inkawu?*" Queen seized the man's wrists, swung him off his feet, whirled him around and catapulted him into the squatting crowd. The tribesmen groaned at this show of immense power.

The empress made no motion to deal with the situation. Indeed, she affected an air of indifference, her attention still fixed on the dancers, whose enthusiasm was undiminished by the incident. On the contrary, their movements seemed even more frenzied.

Queen stood before her now, his enormous frame blocking off her view of the arena. He said nothing, but she read the question in his face easily enough, and she nodded to Atelo. The headman gave an order, and the hunter's chair was carried through the group of squatting "wives" and set beside her own. He took his seat with a nod of thanks, and the empress nodded regally in return.

"Our Induna, Tsheke, does not love white men, N'kosi." She made a gesture with her wand. "Be watchful that you do not feel his spear, for he is swift as a snake."

"I thank you for the warning," Queen said, "but my small *isibamu* is even swifter than a snake."

She sat upright in her chair displaying her magnificent breasts as she signaled with her wand for more beer and wine to be brought. When the khamba girls came and were refilling their gourds, Queen bent closer to the woman. He could smell the skin oil that coated her body.

"Atelo says you will first hunt the *imvubu*, the big seacows. When will you go?" she asked suddenly.

Queen made a gesture which took in the crowd, indicating the evidence of too much drinking, dulled wits. "The day after tomorrow, I think." He nodded toward a trio of warriors staggering across the arena. "Tomorrow there will be much sleeping, I fancy, not much preparing."

"And you also will be sleeping?" The carmined lips parted. They were very red and full, a dew-filmed crescent that enhanced the whiteness of her teeth.

"I doubt I will oversleep much, *Inkosazana*."

"You do not like our wines, our beer?" she asked, her voice teasing.

When Queen made no answer, the naked empress said: "You will hunt the *imvubu* using the *injomanes*, seated on them?"

Queen smiled. "No. Only to carry us to the river places and the big Lake."

She frowned inquiringly. "Atelo said that the *injomanes* are part of your way of hunting?"

"Not always. For the cats, the antelopes, sometimes buffalo, some others, but not for seacow or elephant."

"They are not of great use, then, the *injomanes*, only for lesser beasts?"

Queen shook his head. "No, they are of much use, and in many ways, but chiefly because they carry us with speed—twice the speed of your swiftest runners." An idea struck him. "I will teach you to ride, Your Highness—to be carried on the *injomanes*," he said, as though conferring a considerable privilege.

"Aiw!" There was some doubt and apprehension in the exclamation. "The *injomane* would carry me away . . ." She waved a hand implying a flight to infinity.

Queen leaned forward, smiling reassuringly. "No, no. Once I had made you known to him, he would always obey you, only carry you where you wished."

"But they are fierce," she said, teasing or not, Queen could not tell. "They rise on their hind legs and strike men down." It was clear that Queen's rearing his horse at the young headman had been recounted to her. He wanted to touch her arm when he spoke to reassure her, but he did not.

"That is only when our *injomanes* are *told* to rise up. They would do the same for you, Your Highness."

"Ah!" she said, facing away, looking at the dancers with what he hoped was feigned absorption.

"Listen, *Inkosazana*," Queen said. "There is another thing of greater importance. It is not *fitting* that an empress should walk! An empress should ride—as do the white emperor and his empress. Also, you will find it very pleasing. I will teach you myself, and when you have learned the way of it," Queen spread his hands, "I will bring you an *injomane* of *Dukusa*—a white one!"

It was a shrewd stroke, and the naked woman nodded slowly. "I will learn the way of it, then," she said grandly.

At this, Malendela rose to her feet and her retinue of "wives" followed suit. Queen also got up. "The empress goes early to her isigodhlo? As soon as this?" He tried to make it sound casual, a passing observation.

Malendela yawned and gave a little belch as she slung her leopardskin over one rounded shoulder. "The meat of *indlovu* is heavy—and tonight I have eaten much of it."

Queen made no attempt to conceal his survey of her breasts, the soft curve of her belly, the small patch of golden hair that winked below it.

"So should an empress eat, caring for her strength and beauty," he said with unmistakable meaning.

"You will bring the *injomane*, then?" she said. Her voice was low and velvety, her manner more womanly than regal.

"One of my own," Queen said. "An *injomane* of royal blood."

185

She turned away from him then, and began to walk slowly across the arena. From behind she was nude save for her glinting ornaments at her ankles and her trailing cape, and Queen followed the sinuous movement of her wide sculpted buttocks appreciatively.

By general consent, the dancing seemed now to have given way to a period of respite. Both men and women stretched out or squatted around, eating and drinking. Queen and Joachim lit fresh cheroots; the khamba girls refilled their gourds, and Queen stiffened his wine with a shot from his flask.

Joachim turned his head, yawning, "I could sleep already. Do we have any special plans for tomorrow, Robert?"

"No, anything you fancy. Wash a shirt, grease boots, take a swim. . . . Call it a holiday—we're all due one, right enough. And I've got a little scouting around to do. . . ."

Joachim smiled. "Wouldn't be around the big hut, the one with the palisade, by chance?

"No, it wouldn't, boyo," Queen said good-humoredly. "I mean outside the kraal." He took another slug from his flask, this time neat, then offered the flask to the young *ryder*. "Here, put some tar in your soup." Queen cocked an eyebrow with mock reproval. "You don't fancy any of these *meisies*, then? Remember your duty now."

"I am remembering," Joachim said.

"Christ, there you go again. Just a matter of friendly obligation. . . . Pick yourself a handy woman."

Joachim laughed. "Hell, man, I'm full of skoff and beer, and ready for sleep."

Queen belched. "Well, I'm a man for sleep myself, but not necessarily unbroken sleep." He jabbed with his cheroot. "How about that *meisie*, the umbrella maid if I'm not mistaken. That bushbaby's got haunches as tight as a drum."

"But unwilling, I think. She looks as if she had swallowed a sourgourd."

"Well, she's got tits big as sourgourds," the Afrikander said, "and that compensates. She's just nervous—that's all."

It was true that, in contrast to the other sportively smiling women, the tall girl had a kind of supercilious look about her, but in fact it was illusory, an impression deriving from her almost Oriental cast of features, and a slightly downturned set to her mouth that was the natural shape of it. Her brown almond eyes, too, were more elliptical than round, and, probably because of her close association with Malendela, she was more ornately decked than most of the women.

In her own way she stood out from the tribeswomen nearly as much as her mistress did, and her distinctive expression suggested depths.

Queen pretended censure. "No sense of duty in you, *Jong*—no gratitude."

"Gratitude?"

"I had that umbrella *meisie* all picked out for you."

"Good politics?"

"Good politics—because I've a strong notion we are going to end up hereabouts."

"I know," Joachim said with a smile. "I even thought of a name for where we'll be, Robert."

"Huh?"

"There's a place in Australia, isn't there, called Queensland?"

The bigger man laughed. "Not bad. But I already thought of a better one—R and J, *Arjayskeep!*"

Queen watched Joachim amble across the arena, conspicuously overtopping the Banyoro, moving with his easy gangling stride. Queen congratulated himself again. You could go a lifetime and not find yourself a complete partner like Jo, and it looked as if young van Zyl had made up his mind, without saying so in so many words. Yes, Queen thought, it looked like Jo was for it, all right! A few yards away, Atelo squatted, gnawing on a hunk of meat. Queen leaned sideways and beckoned him. When the elder came over, Queen held out his tin of cheroots, and the headman's grin widened as the hunter explained what was in his mind.

"*Umabope kabope*, Induna!" the big *ryder* exclaimed. "Let our strength be joined."

Atelo nodded approvingly. "Be it so, N'kosi—I for one am for alliance with *Dukusa*. Let there be sons born of Banyoro and *Dukusa* to strengthen it!"

Atelo turned, ranging his eye around the crowd—then he moved swiftly across the arena. In moments he was back, shepherding the tall umbrella girl of the austere bearing.

Queen reached out for her waist and gently drew her closer. "What are you called, maiden?"

She shot a quick glance at him, then turned her eyes away without replying. She tried to recover her aloof expression, but Queen could feel the telltale tremor in her wrist. Atelo gave a tongue click of impatience. "Foolish one, do you not understand that the N'kosi is a great chief who has raised you to his armpit?"

Queen stroked her back from the buttock as you would soothe an apprehensive filly. "Do not scold her, Induna, she is only a calf."

He smiled at her and repeated the question.

"Nquina, Lord," she said quietly.

"Who protects the Queen's beauty and is pretty herself?"

She hesitated, then darted a glance at Atelo as if expecting a prod. "Yes, Lord." There was obviously no conceit in it, merely a necessity of replying.

Atelo studied her impartially with the eye of a trader offering full and honest value. "She is well-fleshed, N'kosi, and her breasts will hold much milk," he said critically. "Will you take her now?"

Queen smiled. "Yes, but she is not for me." He jerked his head. "For my brother, the N'kosi van Zyl," he said.

"Take her to him, Atelo," Queen said. "And you, Nquina, tell my brother that I have sent you to bear him company and warm his mat. Say also that it is the order of *Dukusa*."

Tryst at the River

Robert Queen lay prone in the shadow of the butte at the summit that was like a blunt tooth. Lower down the slope from behind, his horse, untethered, browsed the small patches of young scrub from which, while it was daylight, he would not stray beyond whistle call. It was mid-morning, and still cool and pleasant here.

With the penetrating Barr and Stroud's twelve-by-fifty, he had picked up the quarry from his vantage point first, and then signaled the direction to the two Banyoro hunters. It would be ten minutes or more before they got within vital stalking range, he reckoned.

The grass tract they were moving through covered a broad area. It would take the hunters twenty minutes to cross the pan without spooking the bull, he guessed, and then they had a short rise of low scrub after that. He turned his head the other way, and raised the binoculars again.

Following the line toward the quarry bull, Queen picked up the tiny wind movement in the grass. Then, just for an instant, he saw the two little men, bent low, glide across a small plot of shorter grass—naked sepia-skinned figures, each with his short bow, quiver, and stabbing spear. Higher up

190

from the hollow, half-dozing, ear-flicking the flies, the bull now rested on his belly.

It was fascinating to watch, like looking down at an ambush from the high tiers of an amphitheatre. Queen reached beside him and took up the Männlicher. If the Banyoro spooked the bull, or missed, Queen might still save the hunt for them.

He figured the range, allowing for the drop, and took a practice sighting on the bull—then slid a round up the breech, clicked over to fire position, then laid the rifle beside his elbow to check on the bowmen again. They looked as if they ought to be within arrow range in about eight minutes. But it wouldn't be easy because the bongo's hearing was extraordinarily acute.

He made a mental note to check on the hunters again in five minutes or so, and then he let his thoughts wander to more significant matters. Everything seemed to be going well. Atelo had not exaggerated. There had been plenty of the big clumsy river horses in the river below the falls, and the *mvutshini*, the place of the big concentrations, at the Lake of Sebangwe, had been a revelation.

The lake stretched about twenty miles. The prodigious variety of bird life had surpassed anything the *ryders* had seen before, and the presence of the birds confirmed an abundance of fish—probably grunter, pike, bream, barbel, as well as tigers too big for any bird to handle. Nor were these all the lake had to offer. The crocs abounded.

Of course the big saurians would not be so easy to come by in daylight because of the birds—the plovers, who picked the evil bastards' teeth and gave screeching warning of any approach. But you could get the killer reptiles at night, all right, them and their valuable hides, with reed torches, trailing bloody hunks of meat from dugout canoes.

Two more minutes passed. Queen brought up the Männlicher again. He studied the area ahead from above the foresight. Suddenly the bongo reared to his feet, as if bee-stung. Almost immediately he winced again, sharply, stung for a second time.

Queen lowered the rifle and took up the binoculars. Now, for an instant, the antelope was fully revealed in the sunlight, very handsome in his russety brown coat and distinctive yellow stripes. He broke into a trot, heading for the dark avenues of the forested higher ground from which he had ventured this once too often. His flight was not headlong, more of an instinctive retirement, because he had still neither seen nor heard any danger threat.

Thinks he's been bitten, hit hard by hippo flies, Queen concluded. But they've got the darts into him, all right. At this distance, Queen could not see the arrows, but a moment later the bull confirmed his conclusion. The animal turned his head and strained round to bite at the sticks.

He reached one and broke it off. But the poison was already into his blood. It was potent, this paste of venomous beetles and root juice, far more lethal than the *curare* used by the Jívaros of South America. The antelope began to move up diagonally across the face of the slope again, but walking now and showing signs of growing palsy, as the stupefaction and nausea mounted in him. He halted, went on again, reached the top of the rise, stumbling, and stopped a second time, head low. He made the effort again, then faltered, swayed, and fell heavily on his side.

Now the two small figures in the scrub stood upright and began to trot toward the downed bull.

Queen got himself a cheroot. Well, it was one way of getting meat. Small meat. Christ, he had had a bellyful of *meat*! And the *smell* of it, great *mounds* of it! It would be good *not* to hunt for a day or two. As for the tribe, let their overtaxed bellies relapse back to normal. Make them more appreciative of all the tusker meat to come when Queen started in for the big ivory. The white gold.

White! His thoughts returned to Malendela again. How did you go about winning a woman like that?

An uncivilized woman should be easier to please, and was she not uncivilized? Malendela, after all, was a woman, reared to observe the unceremonious African way of it. Then why had he not had his way with her, by God? As for van Zyl, Queen was pleased that Jo was fitting into the pattern of things very well, shedding some of his inhibitions, *and* using his skull. He seemed to have well and truly screwed himself into the affections of Malendela's umbrella girl, Nquina, and now the *ryders* had another friend-at-court beside Atelo.

Queen got to his feet and stretched his arms, yawning. Get back and lie around! Have a swim, maybe, and a damn good sleep between now and sundown, he decided. Bust loose with a bit of real drinking tonight. Whiskey, by God! No more of this native crap! Get good and merry, yes, but not drunk. Oh no, not drunk. That would be about as intelligent as kidding yourself you had tamed a leopard, or a *ratel* . . . a honey badger!

He put two fingers in his mouth and whistled. Down the hill the stallion lifted his head and loped up to meet Queen as he strode down the slope. He started to head directly back toward the kraal, then he had a thought that made him feel a bit foolish but, all the same, induced him to veer away on a circuitous course that would take him to the edge of the timber belt.

When he reached the trees, he dismounted and threaded in and out for a little while until he found what he was looking for. He came out with a bouquet of white lilies in his hand. When he got back near the wagon, he would sling his rifle, put the flowers in the saddle bucket and hide them with his

193

bandana. It was one thing to feel foolish—quite another to appear to be so.

*   *   *

Across the river the drumming had begun some time ago, and there were silvery reflections of moonlight on the surface of the water.

Tonight the smell of fat hippo meat sizzling lay heavily over the kraal, a welcome relief from the elephant steak of the past few days. And there was another change. Queen saw it as soon as she was within sight. Malendela was wearing the yellow nightgown. Yet she gave only a brief nod and the flicker of a smile in acknowledgment of the hunters' greeting. Beside her, Nquina was more demonstrative. Her wide welcoming smile flashed from one to the other before lingering on Joachim van Zyl. Queen moved through the empress's squatting entourage and took his seat beside her. His earlier air of geniality had dissolved now into a mask of impassivity, and the woman's seeming coolness made him regret that he had committed himself to the foolishness of the flowers. Abruptly, awkwardly, he handed the lilies to her without remark.

Clearly astonished, the white woman looked up at him from the blooms in her lap with a confused inquiring glance.

Queen cleared his throat. He nodded to the bouquet. "It is a custom among white people—of rank," he said stiffly, emphasizing the qualification. Then, more boldly, he said, "The flowers have no value, of course, but a woman knows by them how a man thinks of her."

It was pretty prosaic, though it had taken some mental groping to frame in the dialect. He hoped it would prove worth it. Malendela sat back in her throne, a hunk of steaming meat between her white fingers, pretending interest in the dancers. The thin stuff of the nightgown was diaphanous, and

194

clung like damp gauze from the warmth of her body. It lofted at the tips of her big breasts and fell about her dazzling body in a way that maddened Queen. But he showed no sign of his emotion.

He signaled a khamba girl and got two fresh gourds from her. Then he held up the square bottle he had made sure to bring with him. He pointed to the emblem of the white horse on the bottle. "Regard, *Inkosazana!* The white *injomane.* Sign of *Dukusa*, of white emperors and empresses."

He filled a gourd, handing it to her with a smile, and sat back to watch. She sipped it cautiously, and for a moment pouted her lips appraisingly. A second sip resolved her hesitation. She gave a flash of white teeth, then drained the gourd without pausing. She put a hand to her throat and gave a little gasp, smilingly, as the smooth douche of warmth took her.

Queen laughed explosively. "Downed like a trooper, by Christ!" he said in English.

Malendela sat rigidly, then gradually she relaxed and her wet red lips spread slowly in a beatific smile. She gave the Banyoro exclamatory tongue click of approval. "There is fire in it, N'kosi. Fire!"

"Yes," Queen grinned. "It is the fire of the gods captured in a bottle."

She looked appreciatively at him, nodding slowly. Nearby, Atelo squatted beside the two other hunters. The little headman was smoking a cheroot that Joachim supplied. At Queen's congenial glance, Atelo rose and approached the big *ryder.*

"Lord, when will you go to the end of the world?"

Queen smiled. "In two days time—if there is no feasting tomorrow."

"You wish me to guide you?"

Queen shook his head. "No. But do not fear, we shall not

195

lose ourselves. We have decided not to take the moving hut," he explained. "Only the *injomanes*, for the N'kosi and myself. That way we shall travel much faster."

The Banyoro seemed crestfallen. "N'kosi, I have not the swiftness of the *injomanes*, but I can run all day, stopping only for one short time when the sun is highest. Also, I can guard the *injomanes* at night," the grizzled black man said hopefully.

The Afrikander shook his head again. "Not this time, Induna. But there is a task for you here. To teach the Induna, Matshongi, *your* way of hunting, with the arrows. For that task I would not ask any other."

A few yards off, Matshongi grimaced over the small man's shoulder, but Atelo's face spread slowly to a grin.

"N'kosi, I will teach the Induna well."

Malendela turned in her throne, frowning. "Why do you wish to make this journey, N'kosi? Are there not in our country enough *imvubu, indlovu* . . . ?"

Queen reached for her gourd. "More than enough. But listen, *Inkosazana*." He held out the gourd and she took it abstractedly. "We know what lies to the south, the east and the north of your country." He jabbed a finger to the three compass points, and then to the west. "But we do not know what is *there*."

"There are mountains, they say." She made a click of impatience and flipped a hand toward the Ridge. "Like those. But that is all."

"I am pleased to hear it," Queen answered. "However, I wish to see it for myself."

She put down her gourd half-emptied, and pouted her full lips. "Tchk! It is a foolishness. Why do you not stay, hunt *indlovu* here?"

"No, it is the way of *Dukusa*," Queen said firmly. He put a hand on her arm, and knew as he did this that it was the first time he had touched her. "And it is for *your* sake we go. I

196

would sooner stay here with you all the time," Queen added with unmistakable meaning, the heat in him flaming up at the touch of her.

Her speech had become a little thicker, Queen noticed. "How is it for me?" the empress said huskily.

As if absentmindedly, Queen began to stroke her bare arm with the back of his fingers. The strap of the nightgown had dropped to her elbow, and most of one breast was revealed.

"One defeats trouble by being prepared for it, *Inkosazana*," he said confidentially. "I want to *know* what is there in the west, not to *guess* what is there, but to *know*. For that is the way to safeguard your country. He moved his hand to her back and she responded by moving forward to make room for his hand between her skin and the pillows.

"When will you return?" she said.

She felt incredibly soft, sleek, and the look in her eyes filled Queen with tingling elation. Her movement had eased the nightgown further from her, and both breasts fell into view, drooping voluptuously as her body canted forward.

"Five days." He held up the fingers of his free hand. "Perhaps a little longer."

"That is a long time," the white woman said sulkily.

"Five days, then—no longer. Atelo tells me that the huts you have built for us are ready?"

"Yes." She nodded. "One is bigger than the others," she said.

"You have seen it yourself?" Queen said, pleased by the speed of his invention.

"No."

"Then let us inspect it together," Queen said. "To make certain it is big enough." He smiled. "After all, I am not a small man." He rose to his feet and reached down for her wrist.

"Come, *Inkosazana!*" It was not delivered as a command, of

197

course, but there was a note of control in it that strangely moved her. She rose to his side, adjusting the straps of her gown.

At once the retinue of "wives" and councillors began to rise also, but she stayed them sharply with imperious negative gestures of her wand, and spoke to Nquina over her shoulder. Then Queen took her arm and they began to move unhurriedly across the arena, only the umbrella girl accompanying them. Beyond the torchlight, in the moonlit shadows of the hut, Malendela half-stumbled and Queen put his arm around her.

The trio of new huts had been erected near the entrance of the kraal. Two of the beehives, of average size, had been completed, but the third, markedly larger, still lacked the final thatch of roofing mats.

The big *ryder* caught the umbrella girl's eye. "Go now, *meisie*. I will watch over her highness."

The girl glanced at her mistress inquiringly, and received in reply Malendela's nod of dismissal. When the girl had gone, Queen made a motion toward the entrance of the big hut, and Malendela compliantly preceded him in. Within the moonlit dimness of the hut a circlet of stars showed through the arced frame-poles, but it took a moment or two for eyes to adjust. The floor was smoothed and hard-polished to a dull sheen with dried cattle dung. To one side thick new plaited sleeping mats were piled, and the mingled odor of sun-dried grass and murram was powerfully aromatic. Malendela stood with her back against the central stanchion, lips parted. Queen moved toward her avid with desire. He grasped her arms, drew her close, and kissed her neck, then along her shoulders.

Now he pressed down increasingly, kissing her misted mouth, lingering there, one exquisite breast lifted in his hand. She stood submissively as he slid the straps of the gown down over her wrists, and then, urgently, she herself writhed the

198

yellow folds down over the white curves of her hips until the filmy thing fell to her feet. Queen stepped back a pace. In the wan light filtering down, she was rapturously beautiful in her ivory nakedness. His eyes moved over her superb breasts to her waist and thighs, and then to the long legs that tapered to silver anklets.

"Glory be!" The brief cry of tribute had no meaning for her, but when he raised his hands, she moved close, her roseate nipples rigid with new sensation.

Queen unhooked his belt. He stripped off his clothes with burning impatience. Together they sank to the hard surface at their feet.

Malendela lay with closed eyes and parted lips, drunk with sensation, her hips moving in an involuntary thrusting motion, her long white legs drawn up at the knee. Her breathing was husky now as she arched her back and held her hips aloft.

Abruptly she closed her legs and pulled herself up to a sitting position. "N'kosi . . . !" She turned onto her knees, breathing heavily, and leaned her head to the floor and raised her buttocks to receive him. He started to come into her, but then she scrambled away and flung herself, panting wildly, against the thatched wall, her long white body clumsily wedged there as she strained against the grass wall and the floor.

He followed her there, crawling on his hands and knees, and when he had reached her he took her ankles in his hands and held them firmly. He leaned forward and kissed her mouth. Then he bent his head and kissed the nipple of each gleaming breast, tonguing them lightly as he came away. At last he pushed against her ankles so that her knees were folded and her ankles went all the way back to her buttocks. On his knees, he moved close and moved apart her legs as he came. She leaned her head against the thatched wall behind her, her eyes wide as she watched his movements and saw the great

199

male iron that stood straight out from his loins. He moistened his fingers with his lips and then lowered his hand to the small soft place between her thighs. He touched her there, gently rubbing, and when she was ready he came on his knees still closer, and now held her ankles again to push them against her and away to either side of her, and it was then that he touched her with his iron until it was partly in her and then more in her and then almost all in her and then in her to the hilt. It was then, that fast, when the male iron was all the way in, that she gave a little cry, and then another—again and again she cried out until the cry in her mouth and in her body ceased and she just lay with her back to the wall of thatch, eyes wide and swimming as the big man lost himself inside her.

Later, as she lay exhausted, her breasts pressed against his chest, her body filmed with the sweat of their lust, Queen kissed her golden hair and the sober thought filled him.

"By God, I want her, I want her always," he murmured to himself.

She raised her head, her eyes moist, her lips parted in readiness to speak. "Give me sons," she said. "Many white sons, *Inkosi Umlungu*."

Queen smiled down at her. "Fine sons," he said, "and beautiful daughters too—in the image of you." He reached for his bandana from his shirt pocket and dabbed her forehead. And as he made this loving gesture, an act of caring and nothing less, it came to Queen that his feelings had overtaken him—and that, further, he was no longer sure where politics left off and the heart of a man started.

*   *   *

Joachim van Zyl sat on his folded blanket with his first smoke of the day. He turned his head and watched Queen for a moment, packing francolin drum sticks, boiled eggs, and biltonged bongo into a saddlebag.

"A good night, Robert? Political?"

"Very political," Queen said, not smiling, his manner not a little solemn. "You could say that it was the most political night of my life."

"The plan hasn't altered, Robert? Through your political progress, I mean."

"Not likely!" Queen said gruffly. He finished stowing the bag and came over to the fire for more tea. Queen seemed unusually pensive, Joachim thought. The big man sat staring at the burning wood. At length he looked up with a kind of wry grin. "You'll find it hard to credit this, Jo, but you know, maybe it's something with me like you and Poyana—not just rutting." He shook his head like a man who has inadvertently amazed himself.

"Do you think it is the same with her?" Joachim said simply.

"Well, I think she's been waiting on somebody her own size for a long time," Queen said, poking at the fire with a stick.

"And you are it?"

"No complaints so far," Queen said. "And my services come pretty reasonable."

Joachim laughed. "Just the price of a country?"

"The country's not hers to give," Queen said mildly. "But we'll need three or four hundred Banyoro." He poked at the fire again, his eyes squinted. "We're going to build a place like Piet's, boy—one that will *last*. We'll blast the rock we need out of the river beds, like Morgan's father did."

"That's a lot of little men, Robert . . . three or four hundred. You think she will agree?"

The Afrikander winked. "I got a notion, Jo," was all he said.

Joachim shook his head. "I wish I had your head for these things, Robert—your *savvy*, as *Dukusa* calls it."

Queen did not reply. He went to his horse and swung up on

201

the big stallion's back. "Time our Princess learns to ride!" he called to Joachim as he headed his horse away.

An hour later, everything had been arranged. When Queen reached the kraal a crowd of tribespeople had assembled, for word of the empress's intended encounter with an *injomane* of the white men had quickly gone around. Already waiting in her chair beneath the *mkhuze* tree, Malendela rose expectantly as soon as she saw him but he signaled her to remain seated. It had occurred to him that it might help her confidence to first show her how completely and easily the horse could be controlled.

He did not consider himself a great horseman, but he could hunt horseback, stalk buffalo, run down cats as well as any *ryder*, and you did not grow up with the descendants of Boer Kommando horsemen since the age of twelve without learning some skills.

He put the horse into a *piaffe*, trotting slowly around the arena to clear the circle, not using the reins but controlling the animal with his knees.

Many of the spectators smiled and cheered, and from the corner of his eye he saw Malendela leaning forward and watching attentively. Queen trotted to the side of the arena opposite her, then turned and wheeled again and reared the stallion up onto his hind legs. Pawing the air, snorting, the horse made across the baked red compound, planting each hoof deliberately like a staggering reveler, but maintaining his balance until Queen brought him back down onto all fours again at the edge of the shade cast by the *mkhuze* tree.

He dismounted and laid a hand on the animal's neck, talking to him quietly while he pressed on the crest of his mane. The stallion sank to his knees, and twice dipped his head as if making explicit obeisance to Malendela before, at a word from Queen, he rose to his feet again.

The Afrikander was pleased with his play; it was in fact an old Boer tactic, whereby a horseman caught on open ground reduced the target of horse and rider to a minimum and was able to return fire across the animal's back, but the feat had seemed as if the stallion himself had wished to pay tribute to the regal lady. His performance brought an ovation from the spectators.

Clearly captivated by the display, Malendela arose and stepped forward. "So. Your *injomane* is not always fierce then, N'kosi? Perhaps he became gentle in the night?"

Queen caught a trace of coquetry in her tone and acknowledged it with a smile. "As I promised, *Inoni*, I have spoken of you to him. Now he also is ready to serve you."

Malendela seemed pleased at the word Queen had used, *Inoni*, the most graceful and beautiful of the antelopes. Queen held out a hand. "Come closer. Let him know you, scent you well."

Malendela put a hand on the stallion's neck, a shade hesitantly at first, but then stroking his muzzle and patting him with more confidence until suddenly he whinnied, giving her a start.

"It is all right, he is only greeting you himself," Queen said. "*Sakubona Inkosazana!* is what he says." He moved closer to her and put an arm around her waist. "Well, then, let us begin." He reached down behind her knees, swept her up and lifted her into the saddle, then swung up behind her, and a cheer rose from the crowd.

For a few minutes it was like a children's game, jogging around the circle, turning and repeating it. Malendela seeming to revel in the horse's easy motion.

"You like him?" Queen said.

"Yes."

"Shall we ride further then?"

"Where?"

"Where there are no people, along the river, skirting the trees."

For a second she considered, then she nodded.

203

Queen touched the rein and turned them toward the central aisle of huts, nudging the stallion into an easy canter. The splashing across the drift, flecking small droplets of water onto her bare legs, enchanted her.

"Now," he said when they were out onto the far bank. "You shall get more of the feel of him." He put the reins into her hands, his own hands over hers, and urged the stallion to a slightly quicker pace.

Soon, off to the left, Queen could see the outline of a *spruit*, a brighter green scar that wound across the pastel veld toward the river. He pressed close around her. "Bend forward a little, *Inoni*, over his withers, his neck. Hold tighter, and we will go faster."

He tapped with his heels and quickened the stallion's pace, and Malendela called out excitedly with mingled exhilaration and apprehension as they drummed toward the stream and then sailed over it.

"Oh, be careful," she cried out, obviously as exhilarated as she was alarmed. Queen laughed and brought the horse down to a walking pace. "Now we'll head back to the river and ride along the bank for a while," he said.

Presently they came to a glade like a chevron strip that fringed a semicircular baylet of the bank. When Queen reined in and dismounted she looked down at him inquiringly. He made a gesture around the clearing. "We will hold an *Indaba* for two here; one each, Banyoro and *Dukusa* . . . take a rest, also cool ourselves in the water."

"How do you know that I like this place? How do you know that I do not wish to return to my kraal?" she said, feigning a note of the old authoritarian style that was belied by the laughter in her eyes.

"Because you know that it would be a great waste of time, since we must leave you tomorrow," Queen said. He reached up and lifted her out of the saddle.

As he was unsaddling the stallion he felt her hand on his arm and turned. Malendela moved close. He gripped her soft upper arms and she lifted her red mouth as she had learned to do.

*   *   *

It was dusk when Queen returned to the kraal with the empress seated in the saddle with him, her long white arms clasped around his middle. There had been something of a furor when they had not returned by midday, for Malendela had never been absent from the kraal without an escort. But Joachim and Atelo had quieted the elders, and Nquina had added her reassurances. The entourage of councillors and elders were already assembled beneath the *mkhuze* tree for Malendela's return, but she brushed aside their fussing impatiently, dismissing them all. When they had gone, protesting but relieved, the empress bade Joachim and Atelo to remain, and, with Nquina, they made up the small group that was served by the khamba girls and the cook women. Though the talk flowed fluently with the beer and wine without sign of flagging, it was still early when Queen got to his feet. "Well, me for the mat," he announced. "Crack of dawn tomorrow." He grinned down at Joachim. "Be quite a ride to the end of the world come morning."

Malendela rose beside him. "I am also tired . . . *Imvubu!*" She glanced at the umbrella girl. "Nquina, take the N'kosi to your hut. Spread sleeping mats for him."

The empress held out her hand to Queen. "Come, *Imvubu.*"

It was assertive, and Queen knew it, and she said it as though it was a declaration of their association that she wished all should unequivocally understand. Yet the peremptory note that entered it suddenly worried Queen. He was uncertain suddenly—even a trifle alarmed.

But the big man smiled with, it seemed to Joachim, a new

light in his eyes, a gentleness Joachim would not have thought possible in the big *ryder*.

That night both white hunters slept within the kraal, and even so Matshongi, across the river, was not lonely. And in the morning, early, Robert Queen and Joachim van Zyl were gone.

"The End
of the World"

It was the morning of the fourth day since they had left the kraal, and they were halted on the crest of a range of tree-dotted hills. There had been no real need to climb to the crest—save to satisfy the common urge of all prospectors and trekkers to know what is on the other side. Indeed, Queen and Joachim had already seen enough, more than enough to confirm their highest hopes.

It was not just the untrammeled virgin hugeness of the land that excited Robert Queen. More than that, it was this and Malendela together, for now the land and the woman seemed wedded in a way that was different from the way they were related, one to the other.

Queen lowered his glasses and pushed back his hat.

"Well, Jo, think we've seen enough, man?"

The younger man nodded emphatically. "*Morgens* and *morgens* of it! Rich country. The equal of the Banyoro—maybe better."

"As good as the Zyl country?"

"Well, perhaps I am biased, since that is home to me." He thought for a moment of the vast rolling downs of the big country, the belts of black-green big timber, the fertility of the soil, the perennial *spruits*. "But, yes, as fruitful, I think. Very similar in many ways."

"Men's country, two men's country!" Queen cried. "And we don't even need to build beacons. This shall be our western boundary. Agreed?"

"Oh, indeed, this is quite far enough—from Malendela too," he slyly added.

Queen grinned, "Not to mention Nquina?"

"Well . . . yes," Joachim conceded.

The older man unslung the leather flask at his knee. "What is it they say with ships?" He made a sweeping semicircular gesture. "I name you *Arjayskeep*—and Christ help any with other ideas, black or white!"

"Amen to that, as they also say," Joachim van Zyl smiled, knowing he had made a bargain, but not exactly certain at what point it had been struck.

*   *   *

They made near to half a day better time returning, and, following the river, they sighted the kraal soon after noon of the sixth day. They headed directly for camp, still begrimed and fatigued, sending on an outlying herdsman with the word of their arrival. The tribesman ran hard to a second herdsman, and then the second man to a third, so that, walking their horses in, the hunters had hardly shouted to Matshongi at the wagon before a group of Malendela's guard came poling across the river with a message that all three would take their sundown meal beneath the *mkhuze* tree.

Matshongi had beer cooling in the river, and while he was unsaddling the horses, Queen and Joachim pulled off their boots and shirts before riding the equally dusty and thirsty animals down the bank to dismount in the water.

Getting scoured clean again and into fresh clothing left them with a wondrous feeling. Once they were shaved and

combed, it was bliss to smoke and doze in the shade of the
wagon, especially when their thoughts were stolen by the
pleasures to come. They roused themselves at sundown, and
went down to the river, each man, had he cared to admit it,
feeling anticipation that curiously bordered on nostalgia—as
though the Banyoro kraal itself had become a familiar and
piquant place.

"Will you speak to her tonight?" Joachim asked as
Matshongi pushed off the raft.

"Yes," Queen answered. "Tonight or tomorrow—not later
than tomorrow, I promise you." He paused in the act of
striking a match. "But you also, Jo. You talk to Nquina, give
her the whole pitch, explain it. Won't do any harm at all, I
fancy."

The younger man pinched his chin reflectively. "No, I'm
sure she will be for us."

When they came to the center of the kraal, Malendela rose
from her chair, smiling and, brushing formality aside, came
forward to greet them. Her leopard cape was loosely draped
about her shoulders and in the torchlight her plumes looked as
contrastingly black as her breasts and legs gleamed moonlight
white.

"Well, N'kosis, have the *injomanes* lost their speed that you
have been so long returning?" she said huskily.

There was clearly a trace of rebuke in it.

"Do you think we wished it, Your Highness?" Queen
smiled. He took her outstretched hand. "We rode far beyond
the end of your country, almost to the end of the world."

"And found nothing that we have not here, as I have
already told you," the empress said, again striking a note that
troubled Queen.

"No, but there was good reason for it."

"What reason?"

"I will explain later, Your Highness. It is a long and private

209

matter," Queen said to her, trying for a countering note of authority.

She raised her eyebrows. Then she smiled as if the stipulation had a different meaning for her. Beside her, Nquina stood exchanging sidelong smiles with Joachim. They ate their meal in comparative silence, and when they had finished, Malendela rose abruptly. There must have been those among her tribesmen who had dreams of sharing her couch. But all by now were aware that a state of intimacy had developed between the Queen and the white N'kosi of *Dukusa*. And the great majority, the elders especially, had accepted the arrangement with approval. For was he not a hunter of extraordinary powers, this huge white man, who provided more choice meat for all in a single foray than could the aggregate of their own providers in half a moon? Further, was he not an arbiter of *Dukusa*, a guarantee that the great white king beyond the Ridge had become their ally? It was a natural and practical advancement of benefit to all, this relation between their empress and the white Induna.

"Come, then, N'kosi," Malendela spoke. "Now you shall tell me privately what lies beyond the end of my country, and why you traveled so far?"

There was an element of genuine amusement in her smile, as though it was droll that a stranger should profess to define the limit of *her* territory. Queen took her arm. No woman, he thought, not even this one, was going to stop him, defeat the dream of *Arjayskeep*. Queen nodded to Joachim and the younger man signified his understanding with a dip of the head.

Across the arena, the darkness was accentuated by the aureola of torchlight around the *mkhuze* tree, and Queen put an arm around Malendela's waist, then drew her close, and kissed her before they moved on. Following her into her hut, he slid his hands under her arms and held her breasts. She laid her head back against his shoulder and closed her eyes. "Why have you been away so long, Lord?"

She had never used the term before. It confused Queen to hear her utter it, for the term conflicted with the distance she still chose to insert between them.

"So that I shall be with you longer, and oftener," he answered softly.

For a second, possessed by the rising sensation in her breasts, she did not try to unravel the riddle of his reply. Then she made to turn. "Tell me of this," she said quickly.

But Queen restrained her. "Later, later." He continued to kiss and fondle her until he felt her nipples stiffen. His sex stiffened in response and she could feel the heat of his body against her hip. She reached behind her to clasp his hardness in her slender white hand. With her other hand she loosed the betshu from her wide sleek hips and cast it after her kaross. Still holding him, she turned and drew him down with her onto the piled sleeping mats. At last she let him go so that he might take the clothes from his body. He pulled off his shirt and trousers and turned to her, kissing her belly and thighs and rolling her over to run his tongue along the hollows of her snowy back. She went up onto her knees to receive him into her, and this time he slipped his arm about her waist and dropped his hand between her thighs to touch the softness of her loins. She moaned and stretched her neck with pleasure. He laid his weight against her back, easing her flat to the floor, his arm pinned under her belly. He spread her thighs with his knees and then, pressing his hand to her belly, he raised her haunches. Then he took his hand away from under her and placed both hands at her hips and drew her buttocks back against him. Holding her this way, he held his own torso erect and drove hard, in one steady motion, up and into her, until she fell forward in frenzied joy, her hips beating from side to side to shake and tame the wild rampant force inside her.

211

*   *   *

Later, in the quiet that covered them, Malendela listened in silence as Queen explained his plans. He had already mentally drafted what he was going to say, and he began by describing the nature of the terrain they had seen, stressing that he was speaking of country more than three days march beyond her own kraal. Then, with his arms around her, idly stroking her cheek with his fingers, he started to unfold his ambitions.

Casually but firmly, he laid out the overall strategic consideration of his concept. That to the east and south of the Ridge stood Igonyela, backed by *Dukusa*, a formidable guarantee of her own sovereignty and her people's integrity against any threat from black or white as he had previously explained. In the more distant north, there similarly stood the powerful *Umlungu*, Lord, Groot Piet van Zyl, friend of *Dukusa*, and the father of the N'kosi, Joachim. He gave the relationship full emphasis.

There remained, then, only the frontier to the west. He pointed to it with the tip of his knife on the rough plan he had earlier scraped on the floor as he had been talking. "And there in the west, *Inkosazana*, the N'kosi Joachim and I will be your western rampart!" He slapped his hand on his knee with a gesture of finality and looked at her expectantly.

The smile that played about Malendela's lips was inscrutable—and there was no telling what it suggested. It crossed Queen's mind that though he probably loved this woman and certainly desired her, he knew very little of her deepest thoughts. He realized, recalling their very first meeting, when she had received him from the regal stance of her throne, that she was infinitely more clever than she seemed, and it worried him to suddenly consider that this strange white goddess among a horde of blacks might in fact be merely toying with him.

He was on the point of saying something, edging toward

the question that plagued him, but she put her hand on his arm.

"N'kosi, how many people would you bring?" she asked.

"At first not many, a handful. Perhaps ten or twenty moving huts," he said, holding up both hands.

"Warriors?" she said.

"Yes, but not for fighting. To work in the fields, to hunt, to train as *ryders* of our *injomanes.* Men like the Induna Matshongi."

She fell silent for a moment.

"How many wives have you . . . *Imvubu?*"

"Many fewer than you, Your Highness," he parried. "Of less importance than my *injomanes*, and, " something made him add, "I have no chief wife."

Her lips widened as though the answer seemed to satisfy her, and indeed she would have been greatly surprised if he had professed celibacy. But her next question seemed out of sequence. "How far is the end of my country, *Imvubu?*" This, again, with the little smile that could have been mockery or solicitude. "How far from our kraal would you make yours?"

"Four or five days," Queen said. Then he saw the look in her face and added, "But it would be much less by *injomane.*"

Quite unexpectedly she leaned over against him and placed her mouth on his, very expertly.

"Why must you make your kraal so far away, Lord?"

His expression slowly relaxed, and in the dim yellow light his teeth showed white against the mahogany of his face. "It would not be so far, *Inoni,*" he said. "With a fast *injomane* I could be here by midday of the second day . . . in time to swim with you in the river." He drew her close and stroked the deeply etched line of her spine. "And when you have learned all the business of the *injomanes* I will send escorts of *ryders* to bring you to me. We will not be far apart, Your Highness, for I will come to you often."

"When you come to me, *Imvubu*—will you touch me here?"

213

Malendela said, her hand cupping the sparse golden down at her thighs.

Queen did not answer with words.

It was dawn when he left, and from the entrance of her palisade, she watched him cross the arena. And if you could have seen the face she turned into the moonlight to watch Queen go, you would not have known what thoughts were hidden behind it. Yes, she could well appreciate the advantage of a new country at the end of the world. Given the combined resources of *Dukusa* and Banyoro, it would surely not be difficult to establish such a country—a vast land to be ruled by the Inkosi Joachim van Zyl!

*   *   *

On such warm velvety nights as this, Joachim and Nquina preferred a blanket and saddle-pillow in the open. The young *ryder* was seated with his back against a wheel of the wagon, Nquina stretched face down beside him on the spread of blanket. Matshongi had not returned from the kraal—and save for the animals nearby, the two were alone. It was very quiet, with only an occasional wisp of breeze from the river that had just sufficient strength to waver the smoke from the fire, and out across the veld the grass was surfaced with a yellow overlay of moonlight.

Nquina was about to turn on her back to offer her breasts when they heard the barely audible splash of a raft being slid into the water and pushed out from the other side of the river. Several minutes later they were able to make out the dark shape of the raft slowly rippling over the silver and black glaze of the water, and Nquina reached for her betshu. She peered intently out into the night, then broke off abruptly and sat rigidly upright.

"It is he, Lord, my father—and the one with him will be Tsheke."

214

"The Induna?"

"Yes."

"Who wants you for wife?"

She nodded, nervously, and Joachim patted her soothingly. He started to rise—then a thought crossed his mind and he took his gunbelt from where it hung on a spoke of the wheel and buckled it on. The two Banyoro dragged the raft out of the water, but only one man came up the incline toward the wagon, the other remaining at the water's edge. The man who stood before them was short and sturdy, his hair white. His manner was diffident but grave, as though he were reluctant but resolved to carry out an onerous duty.

"*Sakubona*, father of Nquina," Joachim said easily, "I welcome you."

"I see you also, N'kosi," the Banyoro said. He fiddled with the band on his wrist.

"I would have come to your hut," Joachim said, "but it is better that one should always be here with his *isibamu* in case of *ingonyama* or *ingwe*." He nodded toward the tethered dogs and hobbled horses, and then made an easy motion to the stocky man to settle himself down on the grass—but the Banyoro remained standing, shifting his feet, blinking.

"Sit!" the hunter said, still pleasantly but more emphatically. "Have I not already bidden you welcome, Elder?" He turned his head to the girl, smiling reassuringly as the older man took his place at the edge of the firelight. "Give your father beer, Nquina, for I think both our mouths are dry."

The Banyoro tentatively accepted the beer passed to him. He gazed at the smoldering embers before looking up.

"I wish to take Nquina to wife," Joachim said plainly.

"Ah!" The gray-haired man gave a click that seemed to be approving, yet his air of harassment still remained. "You would take her away . . . over the mountains?"

"No. She would stay here until we return in two moons'

time, or perhaps even within one moon, then she would go with me."

"Lord, are there many wives in your isigodhlo?" It was put equably enough, and Nquina also watched the hunter's face with noticeable expectancy.

"No, only one," Joachim said.

Momentarily a look of gratification came over the Elder's face. "N'kosi, it is an honor. You raise me to your armpit."

Joachim dipped his head in acknowledgment—and relief.

"What lobola do you ask?"

"N'kosi," the old Banyoro spread his hands, "for myself I would ask no lobola—the honor is enough." He paused with a look of regret. "But one who also desires her has already made offer."

"Tsheke . . . for his third wife," Nquina said astringently.

Joachim ignored the interruption. "That is understand-able," he said reasonably. "What does Tsheke offer?"

"Ten cattle."

"I will pay twenty cattle." Joachim spread his fingers twice. "She is worth that, and it is right that the lobola should be fair," he added. "I will pay half the lobola when we bring our first herds through the pass."

The grizzled tribesman tongue-clicked his appreciation of such munificence, nodding vigorously.

"You will inform Tsheke, then?" Joachim continued.

The Banyoro's face fell. In his satisfaction with the prestige and profit that the bargain would bring him, he had forgotten the difficult, if not dangerous, task of advising the disappoint-ed suitor. The Banyoro rose to his feet with a trepid smile and turned on his heel.

"Why is your father in so great a hurry?" Joachim asked.

"Tsheke! Tsheke is waiting, and he has to face his curse," she said. The hunter began to get to his feet, but she put a hand on his arm. "No. It would be worse if you intervened— my father will calm his anger."

216

"Well, it is understandable," Joachim shrugged. "Thirty cattle would still be small lobola for you."

"Lord," her eyes shown with exaltation, "I have been blessed." She sought for words. "You are a great N'kosi, a great husband."

He laughed. "Not great—big. Big is what you mean, a big husband."

"I am big also—our sons will be big," she said assertively.

He reached out for her, but as he took her by the waist they heard the raised voices across the grass. The wrangling broke off, and one of the figures began to stride toward them.

"Go." Joachim made a gesture to Nquina. "Quickly. Behind the moving hut."

The figure coming across the grass was half-crouched like a stalking man. Joachim could not see the man's face, but the Induna was outlined by the moon behind him, like a black imprint stamped on a nimbus of yellow—and when Joachim saw the bow rise, he flung himself sideways, firing twice as he rolled, then a third time.

Nquina's cry merged with a howl of pain, then the dark stooped shape spun around, dropping the bow, and ran, arms bunched, not directly for the river, but downstream, in the direction of the drift below the kraal.

Joachim picked himself up and Nquina ran into his arms. She was very agitated, trembling. "It is nothing," Joachim said. "Finished. He will not come again."

"The empress will kill him, *execute him*," Nquina said passionately. "I will tell her what he tried to do."

"It will not be necessary," Joachim said. "I tell you it is finished. He has had his warning."

*   *   *

For many days the three *ryders* hunted elephant—taking the largest specimens among herds of sometimes a hundred and more.

217

Their labor had been great, and now, on the eve of their departure, the three hunters were gathered with Malendela, Nquina, and Atelo beneath the *mkhuze* tree. The moon was fully risen, its rays amplifying the fitful torchlight to whiten the splendid pair of tusks that stood implanted on either side of Malendela's throne.

But in the morning the hunters of *Dukusa* would be gone. For some of the company there was a tinge of melancholy in the air. Both Queen and Joachim had sensed it, and had sought to bridge the awkwardness with bright chatter of practical matters. Queen spoke first: "Is it a fact, Atelo, that the north pass is easier both to climb and descend than the other?"

"Yes, Lord," the Induna said, "though it is a *river-of-stone* even simpler to defend."

"I understand that. But would it not be much easier for the moving hut? We would carry more teeth over it, yes?" Queen persisted.

The Banyoro grimaced as he gathered the implication of it. "Yes, Lord, but," he shook his head in emphatic rejection, "that way leads . . ."

The Afrikander raised his hand. "Into the Milebi country, yes. Yes, I know that." Queen drew on his cheroot as the Induna frowned disapprovingly, then shrugged and glanced at Malendela for support.

"Well, I think we will go by the north *poort* just the same, eh, Jo?" Queen said abruptly as if he had not heard Atelo's vehement objection at all.

"Are you mad?" Malendela said. "*Imvubu*, the *Ingwenyas*, the Milebi, would take you."

At this, Nquina shot a glance of apprehension at Joachim, then turned to the older man entreatingly.

"Lord, what the Empress says is true."

Queen smiled. "No, I am not mad, *Inoni*, for even if the

hyenas did come upon us—which is unlikely since we will cross only the tip of their country—they would not dare harm *us*. They would bear *Dukusa's* revenge."

Malendela stiffened, and her voice took on a regal tone. "You shall not go that way, N'kosi! I forbid it."

Queen gave no sign of yielding, but only smiled at her effort to reassert her authority.

"You cannot forbid it," he said evenly. "It is not your country."

Malendela's eyes flashed, but she checked her reply.

Joachim put down his gourd. He wished to end the quarrel between them, to see them lovers again. Yet he too was alarmed at Queen's plan.

"You are really serious about this, Robert?" he asked.

"I am," Queen answered flatly.

"But," the younger man gestured inquiringly, "don't you think we can get the loaded wagon through the south *poort*?"

Queen nodded. "Yes, but we would need two more trek beasts. We'd have to dump a lot of good ivory, *Jong*, or take days unloading and manhandling it on the bad steep stretches. But that's not the only thing." He glanced around at the expressions of the others. Then he bent down and motioned them all to gather closer and look over his shoulders as he began to make a plan on the brick-hard ground.

"We can take all our ivory through the north pass without trouble because of the easier slopes, whereas the south pass would take three or four more days longer because there are many difficulties for the beasts and the moving hut. That is one thing. *Now*," he said, drawing parallel lines with his knife to represent the mountain barrier, "here is the Ridge. Here is the north pass. Here is the south one. And here is Igonyela." He drew the alternative courses in the earth. "Now, you, Jo, figure the trek in days by either way. You, Atelo, knowing the slow pace of the moving hut, think of the times it would take

219

us to reach the kraal of Igonyela by either course—and tell the Empress yourself."

The Induna pursed his lips, then nodded slowly. Queen's logic was unassailable.

Joachim squeezed his chin dubiously. He could see even more plainly than Atelo the apparent advantages of Queen's argument, but his deeper concerns persisted.

"Speed is of the essence," Queen said conclusively.

"That is true," the younger man said. "But sometimes more haste makes for less speed. Isn't that also true?"

"Aaah! There is a risk, a small one, I agree. But those bastards won't dare spear us, *Jong*."

"Even so, what of the ivory, the wagon, the beasts?" Joachim said soberly. "Are not the Milebi said to be the biggest thieves in Africa?"

Queen tapped the pistol on his thigh. "I gamble they'd think twice before robbing a company of *Dukusa*."

Joachim regarded his boots. "I would like to hear what 'Shongi thinks of this, Robert," the young *ryder* said unexpectedly.

"What for? He does not come into this," Queen said dismissively.

The younger man bridled slightly. "He takes the same risks. He is a man like us."

"Oh yes, he is a man, all right, but a man that is not afraid of anything," Queen said abrasively. Joachim's seeming dissension had already nettled the big *ryder*. But now he sought to mute the sarcasm. "Look, Jo," Queen said mildly, "you've got to chance your arm at times, boy!"

A flush of color rose in Joachim's cheeks.

"Very well, Robert, let us go by the north *poort*, then," the young *ryder* said, his lips tight.

But Malendela was less willing to make peace. Her mouth drawn with reproval and anger, she started across the circle

220

toward her own quarters without a backward glance. Queen went after her and overtook her. He snatched at her arm, but she did not turn her head or speak until they had entered her hut. Then she rounded on him passionately.

"Your talk is foolish, dangerous, N'kosi," she said, again formal in her address. "Have you no wish to return to us?"

The big *ryder* drew her close, but her body did not yield to him.

"You know better than that, *Inoni*. You must know why I want to take the swiftest route," he said feelingly.

She studied his handsome face, searching there for proof of his claim. Despite herself, she felt the stirrings of her body, the buzzing in her loins. She put a finger on his lips, and then, to show him what she wanted, she went slack in his arms.

Emperor Toad

It was close to sundown of the second day since they had left Malendela's kraal, heading northeast for the second *poort*, and they had made excellent progress. At first Queen had begun to wonder whether Atelo had been at fault. Not because of the extra day's trek to reach the more northerly foothills of the Ridge, which he had reckoned on, but because their first glimpses of the lower slopes had been anything but encouraging.

For as the blue of the Ridge had gradually assumed its true colors, the binoculars had revealed its lower jaw to be an apparent maze of formidable, if not impossible, going for the wagon. The whole terrain had seemed to be dotted with serried clusters of strangely contoured *kopjes*, like deracinated anthills.

But distance had exaggerated the apparent complexity of the route, and Atelo had taken them through well enough on a weaving course that had occasioned no problems of any consequence. Moving off at dawn, they had climbed steadily over long zigzag stretches free of obstacles, and now they were camped at the beginning of the crest of the second *poort*, the moorland tract surrounded by towering bluffs.

Queen's early doubts at the deceptively threatening aspect

222

of the foothills had given way to increasing good humor as the party neared the summit of the pass. Also, leaving the others to make camp, he had ridden on a spell before the light failed, and had seen nothing to suggest that there would be any difficulty in finding a course across the craggy tract that formed the shoulder of the range.

He had returned now, and when he had unsaddled he made across to the small cooking-fire adjacent to the wagon. Many figures, standing or squatting, were gathered around two of the fires nearby, for now the numbers of Banyoro had been swelled by others of Malendela's permanent guardians of the pass from the far side of the moor.

Joachim handed him up a mug of beer, which Queen drained without pausing, and handed back with a grin. "Well, warriors, we have done pretty well, eh?" He looked at Joachim first and could not quite disguise the note of self-justification in his voice. "And the passage across the rim will be easy enough." He reached down for the mug that Matshongi had refilled for him, and nodded to where Atelo squatted beside a strange Banyoro, who also wore the leather skullcap of a headman. "We are much pleased with you, Induna—this other sour-faced Induna also, eh, Boetie?" Queen nudged Matshongi with his knee. The big African nodded slightly.

Atelo grinned and Queen laughed.

"The toughest part is done, Jo—already," Queen said, sinking to his haunches. He tapped his knees with satisfaction.

"I hope so, too."

"*Hope so!*" Queen was plainly exasperated at the younger man's caution. "Goddamn, Jo, Atelo swears the descent will be simpler going yet. It will be a cinch, man."

"I didn't mean that," Joachim started, then he broke off, not wanting to seem more of what Morgan sometimes called a pessimist. He half-expected a sharp-edged reply, but it did not come. Queen put his hand on Joachim's shoulder.

"Aaah, forget the Milebi, boy. Ain't a chance in a hundred." He held out the flask with a grin. "Have a good dram, lad."

Queen lit up and drew on his cheroot, and Joachim did likewise. Across the way the figures of the squatting Banyoro bowmen were silhouetted around the fires.

Malendela was well safeguarded, Queen thought, and he was aware of a sensation of comradeship with the little men.

*   *   *

The blood-orange sun rose slowly, issuing thin shafts to behead and whittle away the mist drifting over the crags, and the oxen stood inspanned.

It was time to be moving, and Queen bent down from the saddle. "You have been a good friend, Atelo," he said, "and we shall not forget." Queen held out a tin of fifty cheroots. "Smoke one of these each night, and tell the *Inkosazana* that we shall return before they are finished . . . by the *south* pass, with men, *injomanes*, cattle, and moving huts."

Atelo showed his small teeth. "Lord, our sentinels will tell us when you come—and we will send warriors to help you."

*   *   *

The first long stretch from the eastern head of the *poort* wound down the face of the escarpment at a gradient that gave Matshongi difficulty in curbing the pace of the wagon, and several times Queen judged it prudent to drag-chain a wheel.

After one such interlude, he rode forward as the sweating, steaming beasts were halted for a rest on a flatter section of the way that ran like a roofless cavern between lofty near-vertical bluffs. He was a few hundred yards around a shoulder of the face when he came suddenly on his first unobstructed view of the full vista of the lower horizon. Fifteen hundred feet below, the empty yellow plain stretched out uninvitingly, shimmering in the heat haze. There was no sign of any living

224

presence, though Queen swept the land for several minutes with the glasses. Even the trees were few and far between, as though little but scrub, dwarf palm, and cacti could draw sufficient subsistence, and only the call of a cruising *korhaan* disturbed the hostile, brooding silence.

The contrast with the fair and fecund country of the Banyoro was remarkable and complete, like passing from a brightly decked room into the somber chambers of a morgue. Still, the disenchanting prospect did not affect Queen's humor, for the main thing was that they had made such good progress and the way ahead looked facile enough in terms of passage for the wagon.

When Queen got back to the others, Joachim looked up inquiringly. "Big country?"

"*Morgens* of it, bleak and dour," Queen said. "There may have been passable grazing once, but the game, the herds have gone long since."

"Water?"

"There's a *spruit*, starting from somewhere up here, I suppose. Grows into some kind of a river further out, I imagine. You can't see where the pass finishes down there yet, of course, but the water won't be far from it, I reckon. The water near the Ridge will be all right—but even a mile or two out through all that alkali, it'll be as *brak* as hell for sure."

"Give the beasts all they can hold when we get down, then?"

"Yes. Fill the cask and every skin we've got, too."

Queen saw the flicker of uncertainty cross the younger man's face again, and brushed it aside. "Oh, Christ, nothing to worry about, boys, the going's easy—we'll get 'em up to a tripple. Keep 'em at it till the heat's really up, too."

"Well, if that's how it is, flat and firm, I mean, we could keep on trekking when the moon comes up."

"Christ, that won't be necessary. We'll be across this corner of hyena-land before sundown tomorrow, *Jong*," Queen said easily.

They reached the river in the late afternoon—it was not far from the foot of the pass, as Queen had guessed—and they outspanned at a crook of its course by a cluster of cactus and stunted palm.

While they were watering the horses and oxen, Matshongi called from the wagon to say that soon they would need some kind of meat for the dogs. Queen made a grimace. "Baboon or dassy is about all they're likely to get for the next day or so. What's in the box, then?"

"Some biltong, *spek*—enough for ourselves," the African answered.

"The box is packed with horn and seacow teeth," Joachim reminded Queen.

It was true enough that they had used every available scrap of wagon space for the valuable stuff. But Queen had anticipated at least the normally ubiquitous veld fowl. He spat expressively. "I'll take a turn down the river in a little while."

Joachim looked up, about to dump his saddle. "It's not important, Robert—rest yourself."

Queen considered the river again. There was a certain amount of coarse green grazing that followed the banks. There had to be some fauna and it was near to the time when most creatures had to drink. He shook his head. "Might find something better than the salt tack—just maybe could do with it this time tomorrow, too." When he had fixed the tent, he got the Männlicher from his saddle bucket. Francolin or grouse were still the likeliest possibility, even though he had seen none flying in. But it was the sound-carry he was thinking about. With the twelve-bore, he would have to use both barrels, maybe more, to get enough birds to be any use, and the range might be too much for anything bigger and better. He climbed up onto the wagon and stood upright on the box, scanning the largely flat landscape with the glasses. He picked up a small parcel of zebra about a mile away, though he was not looking merely for game. But that was all.

He jumped down from the box and started off along the river, using the bends and the straggles of scrub and mopani. A pampero of wind had sprung up, and it was coming from the southwest. The wind made him curse because he had to wade the river, but more particularly because it would carry a gunshot a long way northward.

He had been walking about half an hour when he heard a snorting of wildebeest and knew that he was coming up on a watering place. He got down and edged forward on his elbows until he had got to where the bush petered out. After a while the wildebeest departed through the kweekgras. About a quarter-hour later, nearly a score of zebra came in. About an hour later a pair of warthogs came out of the bush across the open stretch. As Queen edged forward, his shirt sleeve caught on a thorn bush, then pulled free. Immediately the pigs wheeled at the sound, and Queen took a fast flyer at the larger one as they charged away from the water. The boar squealed as the pain creased his neck, but he kept moving. The Afrikander pulled back the bolt and fired again, bringing down the warthog just short of the bush. It had taken two shots, but that night they would eat.

Back at camp, they bedded down late, their bellies full of pork. Queen and Joachim went into the small tent, and Matshongi took his blanket and kaross under the wagon. For the time of a cheroot the young *ryder* watched Queen as the older man settled into sleep. Joachim himself could not sleep, so pervasive was his instinct to be gone from this place. Near to midnight, he took a turn around the camp before arousing Matshongi. His uneasy feeling seemed to have passed, and in just a short while after settling down he was sleeping soundly.

For fully an hour Matshongi sat cross-legged with scarcely a movement, gazing impassively into the firelight and only occasionally raising his head to the flutterings of a hawk-moth or the soft whirr of a goatsucker's wings. He was considering whether he should elect to remain at *Morganskeep* or, obliging himself to look ahead, offer his permanent services to the N'kosis, Queen and van Zyl. And he had almost, laboriously, reached a compromise solution when one of the dogs raised his head, mumbling in his throat, and began to test the air with his nose. The African moved the shotgun closer to hand and then he too sniffed the night.

He rose to his feet and began to make a slow circuit of the camp, skirting the recumbent beasts, the gun ready in his hands. There was no untoward sound or sign. But the hound nosed the air again, hackles risen, and this time was joined by another. Matshongi dropped to one knee, and just as he raised the shotgun to his shoulder, he heard the swoosh and thud as the warning spear landed quivering a yard from where he crouched. He rolled sideways against a wheel of the wagon, calling out, and in moments Queen and Joachim were on their knees beside him.

The first pink streaks were forming in the eastern sky now and they could make out the shadowy figures of spearmen all around the camp. With their Colts and the twelve-bore, they could maybe have gotten ten or a dozen, but there were nearer a hundred of them.

"Don't shoot unless they try to pin us," Queen said tersely.

When the spear volley did not come, Queen straightened up and shouted above the snarling and barking of the dogs.

"Who dares to challenge a camp of *Dukusa*?"

The reply came stridently, shrilly, in a dialect akin, though differently accented, to that of Igonyela's people.

228

"We are warriors of Bejane, *Umlungus!* Lay down your *isihamus.*"

"Who speaks for Bejane?" Queen shouted imperiously.

A figure moved forward, flanked on either side by three others with spears poised. The man halted ten yards from where the *ryders* stood. In the mingling of fire-light and filtering dawn, he showed as a heavy-hewed man, taller than the others, young, but bloated of face, with an arrogant expression, wearing the headband and plumes of an Induna.

"What is this talk of laying down *isihamus?*" The big *ryder* said harshly. "Do you think you face pygmies, unimportants?" Queen stood erect, five or more inches the bigger man.

"You are prisoners of the king, *Umlungu,* and we take you to him," the Milebi said. "I speak for him."

"And I speak for a greater king," Queen barked. "*Dukusa!* You have heard of him?"

"We know of him, *Umlungu,*" the Milebi said with a gesture of indifference. "A moselekatse of *Umlungus—*few *Umlungus,*" he said offensively.

"No, Milebi!" Queen snapped. "Not a moselekatse! A *Dunguzela* of the kings! Whose arm stretches far beyond his country, as the *Umlungu* Marao knows well."

The mention of Marao seemed to have some effect. Queen followed up his random thrust expansively. He gestured to Joachim and Matshongi. "My brother is also a N'kosi of *Dukusa,* this other man an Induna of our tribes. Remember it!"

"Aiw! You march with us now, or we kill you now," the African said shrilly, wildly. He shook his fist in emphasis, and the circle of spearmen stamped and shouted at the prospect. A warrior stepped forward, a fork-bearded man with one blank red socket from which the eyeball was gone. He reached for the gun at Queen's hip, but the Afrikander sent him reeling back with an angry cuff.

229

At once the spearmen yelled and surged forward, but the Induna halted them with a raised hand and shouted imprecations. Yet there was no sign of clemency in it.

Queen saw his opportunity and took a pace forward.

"Listen well, Milebi! We will go with you to your kraal. But you will tell these *umfaans*," he made a sweeping gesture, "these small *imfenes*, that any who lays hand upon a N'kosi of *Dukusa* will feel the wrath of Bejane, as he, Bejane, will feel the wrath of *Dukusa*. Be warned now, *Secocoeni!*"

It was a term that acknowledged a degree of authority, yet was subtly derogatory, implying more a leader of rabble than a captain of ordered warriors, and the distinction was understood well enough by the headman. For a moment they stood eye to eye, Queen stony-faced, the Milebi's features working with fury and frustration. Then the Milebi dropped his gaze. He turned and began to shout angry commands to the spearmen.

Queen took his hand from the butt of the Colt and brushed the sweat from his forehead. "Some bloody trekker, some bloody politician, I turned out to be, Jo," he said bitterly.

"Just bad luck, Robert," Joachim said evenly. "Perhaps we had too much good luck."

Matshongi shrugged his silent agreement with the younger man, but Queen shook his head again.

"You stayed them, Robert," Joachim said. "It might have gone badly if you had not," he added, but his face showed no pleasure in that comfort.

*   *   *

It was mean country, mean and unrelenting, and it had a savage affinity, Joachim thought, with the men who marched on either side of the wagon and horses. They were tallish for Africans, some as tall as Zulu, but lean, hawk-faced, lacking the substance of Matshongi, the forthright bearing of a Zulu.

230

It was late afternoon now, a day and a half deeper into Milebi country, and the trek had been a nightmare. They were halted now by a shriveled sixty-foot fig tree—itself gripped in the macabre embrace of a parasite of its own species. Queen glanced up through the gaunt arms of the doomed fig. Gray rain clouds, outlying harbingers of the big seasonal rains to come, were scudding across the sky, streaking long shadows toward the Ridge.

Queen glanced from side to side at the black faces. Then he raised the binoculars hanging from his neck. Out across the stony plain he could just make out a series of wispy streaks that were too closely grouped to be grass fires. He lowered the glasses and called roughly to the headman, pointing. "That is the kraal?"

The Milebi stared back inscrutably, then nodded shortly without answering.

"I think they were *waiting* for us," Joachim said when he had Queen's attention.

Queen frowned incredulously. "You mean you think we were bushwacked, *ambushed?*"

Joachim leaned toward him. "They are surely a fighting detachment, Robert, not a hunting party."

"By God, you're right, *Jong!*" Instinctively he turned and looked back toward the distant blue peaks of the Ridge. "A bloody great squad of the bastards like these . . . I'd have picked them up for sure if they hadn't been lying-up doggo." Queen began to nod, then suddenly ceased. "Wait though. How could they have *known?*"

Queen mulled on it. He had more than a little to occupy his thoughts as his party trekked toward the waiting Bejane under the escort of the Milebi.

*   *   *

In the sunlight of early forenoon the kraal looked substantially larger than those of Igonyela and the Banyoro. Perhaps two thousand huts, Queen guessed, filled the dwelling section of the settlement between the inner and outer bomas. From the main entrance an aisle ran straight to the central arena; beyond it stood the Great Hut of Bejane, flanked on either side by the palisaded enclosures of the King's isigodhlo, housing a hundred or so wives, and the *isibaya* of royal cattle, for which the penalty of unauthorized entry was summary execution.

Some time before they reached the kraal, a motley stream of tribespeople had begun to issue from it, silent, gaping, scowling figures with the cold blank eyes privation makes. They stared at Queen's party as the wagon and horsemen were ushered through the entrance of the kraal, the rank odor of dung fires, refuse, and human excrement strong in the village air. The adults, clearly apprehensive of the horses, drew back as Queen and Joachim passed, pressing back against the huts, before some of which stood poles hung with human skulls.

Flanked by the escort, the train of wagon and riders moved into the cattle corral where a handful of gaunt-ribbed nondescript creatures straggled about.

The *ryders* dismounted, and the headman signaled for them to follow him. But Queen shook his head emphatically. "Did not Bejane require time to prepare to receive the emissaries of *Dukusa?*" he snapped. "Are we not here to make palaver with him? Or is it intended that we should leave within an hour or so? For if we are to make palaver, our *inyathis* and *injomanes* must first be unyoked, pastured, watered!"

For a moment Queen stared challengingly, then he turned on his heel with a word to Joachim and Matshongi, and they began to outspan the oxen and unsaddle the horses. The furious headman stood in the corral in silent rage. Such an attitude from a prisoner was beyond imagining. In all his experience, victims cringed and begged, fearful of the agonizing fate they knew would follow any resistance. In admiration of Queen's dauntless browbeating, the way he turned the tables on his captors, Joachim tried to stiffen his own bearing. He fished for a cheroot, and from the wagon Matshongi cracked the long whip like a pistol. Ostensibly to stir the freed oxen, but the whip ripped the air, like a wordless warning, above the heads of those crowding too closely. Relieved of their yokes, the oxen moved ponderously across the corral toward the water they smelt, indifferent to their hosts, the Milebi cattle giving way before the bulk and stature of their strange kin.

Queen rose to his feet from where he had been sitting, back against a wheel of the wagon.

"All right, *Secocoeni*," he barked, "now lead us to your king."

Shrilling orders to the escorting spearmen, the Induna led the way through the entrance of the plaited enclosure fronting the royal hut. Queen could see him halt, raise an arm in salutation, then drop to his knees.

Bejane lay sprawling beneath an awning of yellow thatch. A massive monument of gleaming black fat, half-reclining, half-leaning upon a pudgy boneless elbow. Around his beaded forehead a headband of leopard skin held three scarlet crane feathers. Ornaments hung from his small thick ears, half-hidden by the swell of his jowls, and a necklace fell to breasts like those of a very old woman. White furry garters at his knees and elbows contrasted with the glistening oily jet of Bejane's skin.

On either side of him knelt girls young enough to have been his daughters. One dabbed at his sweating brow with a pad of crimson fungus, and caressed his breasts like a suitor. The other petted his vast gelatinous thighs beneath a betshu of wildcat tails that barely concealed his genitals.

233

His features were blurred by obesity, the eyes squeezed into slits by porcine raspberry-colored cheeks blotched with yaws. Himself swollen near to bursting by the constant craving for food, it was well known that Bejane ruthlessly wiped out obesity among his subjects. It was simple: if you were fat, you were put to death; if he was fat, he was king.

Scattered at respectful distance were the king's court, notably a jester dwarf and a snake-charmer. The dwarf possessed no arms, and his small hairy hands protruded directly from the sockets in his shoulders like questing tarantulas. The other grotesque, a vulpine figure with an atrophied leg, had been given a circular berth of several feet radius around him. A python was coiled about his neck and torso, and he was feeding live mice to a writhing mess of smaller snakes in a woven basket.

Flanking these councillors were grouped a representative score or so of the king's wives, entirely naked save for their ornaments and the single flamingo plumes of their rank. Adjacent to the women, also marked by the flamingo feather of patronage, watchful for any tell-tale constriction of the King's features, for the monarch possessed little control over his sphincter, stood the *Yenkosi*, wiper of the royal anus.

But the figure who riveted the hunters' attention was the man who stood to the rear of Bejane. He wore a wide-brimmed hat and the leggings of an Afrikander. Assuredly Marao! Strongly built, and sprouting a growth of stubble, the half-grin on his swarthy face was clearly a grimace of mockery and malice.

Queen steeled himself. He raised his hand and briefly spoke the customary greeting, studiously avoiding, however, the larding of deferential phrases such as might suggest his acknowledging some inferiority of rank.

"King, this *Secocoeni*, this little man who claims to speak for you," Queen gestured contemptuously toward the nearby headman, "seems not to have heard of *Dukusa*. I say he does not speak for Bejane, for Bejane surely knows of *Dukusa*, and we are N'kosis of *Dukusa* . . . *Dunguzela* of those kings south of the Milebi!" he rasped.

Bejane screwed up his eyes, squinting myopically at the three tall *ryders*. They were the biggest men he had ever seen.

Mechanically, he dipped his stubby fingers into a bowl beside him and plopped a handful of roasted termites into his mouth, leaving two or three of the grubs sticking to his upper lip like an awry moustache. One of the kneeling women leaned forward to brush away the white ants, but Bejane petulantly buffeted her aside, knocking over a second bowl from which aromatic wisps of smoldering hemp curled upward.

Now at last he spoke. His voice had the hoarse mumbling cadence of semi-intoxication, and Queen frowned with the effort of trying to make something of it. But it was unintelligible.

Queen glanced at Joachim. "We'll get no sense from this toad today—bastard's addled stupid from smoking *Dakha*." He spoke in English, but in any event the contempt on his face was plain enough.

Slowly, through his blurred senses, it occurred to Bejane that these prisoners, incredibly, were unaware of his magnificence, did not realize that he, Bejane, held their lives in the hollow of his sweating palm. For, far from cowering, they had an air of arrogance, insolence.

The ire rose in him chokingly. He struggled slowly to his feet, and stood swaying like a palsied hippo on his gouty swollen legs. He began to speak again, thrusting forward his bullet head, and this time some of the words were distinguishable.

Umlungus . . . creatures of the white moselekatse . . . *Dukusa* . . ."

He paused for breath and, in the moment of portentous silence, a woman broke into a fit of coughing. Inexplicably, the sound seemed to arrest him. He turned, lower lip drooping, toward where the luckless interrupter sat among the company of his wives. He would show these foreigners what disrespect of his greatness augured. Bejane pointed, squeaking an order to a headman who, in turn, shouted urgently to the harem guards attending the women. Immediately two of the guards rushed forward, jerked the ashen-faced woman to her feet, and dragged her out into the open.

The woman fell to her knees before Bejane. She raised her head, showing the whites of her eyes, inarticulate with terror.

"Greatness! Calf of the Great Elephant!" she screamed.

Indifferent, as if unaware, Bejane nodded swiftly to the spearmen and eagerly, as though to impress the ruler with his adroitness, a captain of the spearmen came forward, locked his arm around the girl's throat, and with a powerful practiced movement, broke her neck. The incident had been enacted in mere minutes with savage efficiency, and now other spearmen lifted the limp body and carried it from the enclosure through the silent crowd.

Benjane's bleary eyes followed the removal of the corpse for a moment, then gazed back at the big *ryder*. Queen felt the hairs rise on his neck, but he returned the crazed stare with granite impassivity.

Bejane began to rant again—spasmodically, incoherently, only a spattering of words or phrases uttered intelligibly. His intent was plain enough, and Queen's hand moved to his thigh, a riot of thoughts racing through his mind. If this was the end, if the madman was about to order their execution, then by God he was also ordering his own. Queen's fingers reached the butt of the Colt as the diatribe continued. He could get three into that great distended black belly before they could spear him.

But then, as Bejane's rambling invective seemed to be reaching its unpredictable climax, the man in the shadow of the awning came forward. He alone of the onlookers had noted the movement of Queen's hand and rightly read the quickening situation.

Marao placed a hand on Bejane's massive arm and began to talk to him in a low tone, stroking the heavy black flesh soothingly. Except for brief references, it was difficult to hear what he was saying, but to Queen the gist seemed to be that these men of *Dukusa* were not deliberately offering insult or provocation but, stupidly, simply did not understand the Milebi tongue.

He, *Alambanzi*, friend and well-wisher of the Milebi, who not only understood all white men tongues but their secrets too, would acquaint them with the King's greatness, the crime of unauthorized entry into Milebi country, the dire penalties for such, should he, the All-Powerful, so decree. Then, tomorrow, the King could pronounce judgment.

Bejane grew calmer by degrees. At last he slumped onto his couch.

Marao straightened up and turned. He moved to where the hunters stood. "The King will parley with you, tomorrow," he said in English. "There is no hurry, he is—tired."

"Bloody stewed, you mean," Queen said acridly. "Stewed to the bloody gills." But this time he did not mention the reed pipe.

The swarthy man shrugged. "You want me to tell him that? You want me to continue to act in your interest?"

"And yours," Queen said. "Don't forget that, *Smouse*. But your interests just might also include our ivory, mightn't they?"

The half-caste shrugged again. "You are not a greenhorn. This is Milebi country, no? Everything in it belongs to him." Marao got a tin of cigarettes from his pocket, but he did not offer them. "You have made an alliance with the Banyoro," he said, lighting a cigarette. "Bejane does not love the Banyoro. Any friend of the Banyoro is his enemy."

Queen hesitated. He could insist that the "alliance" was merely an agreement for them to hunt ivory, of no political significance. But he was shaken by the accuracy of Marao's information. Just on the point of replying, he felt Joachim's insistent hand on his arm.

"Behind the women, Robert—see him—Tsheke?"

There, just for a second, Queen glimpsed the malevolent grinning face of the fugitive Banyoro.

He turned back to Marao: "You are not a greenhorn either, friend—yet you think the fork-tongued tales of the Banyoro jackal, Tsheke, are reliable?"

"Not to me—of no importance to me," Marao said with seeming indifference, "but enough, more than enough, to the king." Marao pointed with his cigarette. "Listen, I remind you again—you can thank me that you are not riding the stake already—all of you."

"All right, we thank you. It's because you're a white man, isn't it?" Queen said with simulated artlessness.

The innuendo seemed to have penetrated the half-breed's veneer of imperviousness. He shot a pointed glance at Joachim. "Whiter than him, maybe."

The Afrikander ignored it. "And you are not interested in how the ivory is got, how to deal with the Banyoro for it, how to cross the Ridge without being pincushioned . . . ?" he said sardonically.

"No." Marao made a gesture of inconsequence. "I am interested in much bigger things than that, Englander. Later I will tell you—before they skewer you—and then, if you got sense, real sense, maybe I will save your hides." For the first time Marao showed his teeth in a grin. "You know how good they are at the skewering, Englander?"

"You know how good *Morgan* is with rifles?" Queen answered. He paused for effect, then pressed ahead. "One other thing you better get through his head, Senhor. If we don't return, Morgan will come—be sure of it." Queen put a hand on Joachim's shoulder demonstratively, "and van Zyl will come from the north, and they will wipe the Milebi from the face of the earth, and that will include you as well as him, *Senhor!*"

The half-caste stared back at Queen with frank loathing. It would give him great satisfaction to see this English Afrikander suffer the stake. But Marao's ambition was greater than his hatred, and this Queen might prove useful. One day, and soon, he, Marao, whom they called *Alambanzi*, the whip-snake, would rule a country more than twice the size of Morgan's. And Morgan would be glad to acknowledge it, and him.

Marao turned and walked back to where the sweating glutton slumped, gulping from a khamba of palm wine. Again, he spoke to him in the same conciliatory tone as before. Prudently, he made no mention of the Afrikander's blunt inflammatory warning, but emphasized that he now knew the prisoners *were* high-ranking N'kosis of *Dukusa*, not, as they might have been, mere hunters of the *Umlungu* chief. Thus, they were hostages of great value. Slowly, patiently, he expanded the theme of his argument, outlining again the plan which he had first laboriously expounded before the spearmen had been sent to intercept the hunters, and which now had the added force of their ranking.

The scowling despot listened in silence, sprawled in a sweltering heap. Marao's persuasive words were within his torpid understanding, but the pre-eminent thought in his mind was, still, that these inferiors did not understand his greatness. Of what consequence was the hostility or friendship of this far distant *Umlungu* upstart, *Dukusa?*—

ruler, so he had learned from time to time from captured itinerants, of a miserable handful of mongrel followers in a remote and negligible country. He, Bejane, ruled a kingdom so wide he had never even seen its furthest bounds himself.

Grudgingly, he decided to accede to Marao's plea for the hunters' temporary reprieve. But first, he would again remind them of his own omnipotence, and of their own lowly station. He nodded for them to be brought forward. "*Umlungu!* You speak of this *Dukusa* . . . an *impungushe* . . . a small jackal, who rules a small *isihaya* of small jackals. . . . Do you not know that I, Bejane, command ten times the numbers of this white sparrow?" He looked round wildly for some demonstrable token of his contempt and absolute supremacy, and his eye lighted on the scrawny figure of the snake-charmer. He growled an order, and the snake-charmer bent over a basket and, with a quick movement, drew out a yard-long snake. He held it up, allowing it to weave like a reed in wind eddies, still peering into the basket, then darted his hand in again and withdrew a second reptile. Those nearest to him fell back, and two spearmen moved closer to Bejane on either side, their long blades lowered protectively.

The lame man limped back a few yards from the bunched brown-mottled vipers. He began to croon a kind of moaning lullably and the coiling vipers began to glide forward toward him until, as he ceased abruptly, they also halted and reared like sticks. Twice the lame man made circuits of the cleared space, halting the snakes in the same fashion every few yards, returning them to his basket with a toothless grin.

Bejane made a gesture indicative of the mystical powers within his command which he had evidenced. He wobbled a step nearer the big Afrikander and gesticulated triumphantly.

"Can *Dukusa* speak thus to the *ibululus*? Even the snakes obey me, will attack only if I order it!"

Queen glared back into the puffy face. "*Dukusa* speaks with many snakes, King," he said incisively. "Snakes that spit faster and a thousand times farther. Send for our iron snakes, our *isibamus*, and I will show you."

The mouth of the black colossus fell open at the half-understood challenge. He turned with a look of puzzled inquiry, and Marao came forward to his side to translate. When he had finished, Bejane slowly nodded his comprehension. He barked an order to an Induna nearby and a runner was immediately dispatched to the cattle kraal. He returned carrying two of the guns, holding them warily, like objects of lethal unpredictability.

Queen took the rifle and shotgun from him. He handed the Belmont to Joachim and clicked a round into the barrel of the Männlicher. He had already decided on his target, but now he looked around as though seeking a suitable objective at random.

He called to Marao. "Tell them to clear a passage to the *isibaya*, man!"

He turned to Joachim. "Bust some horn if I can. You pick out a pair of vultures while I'm trying."

The younger man looked over the heads of the tribespeople along the tops of the serried rows of huts. Every here and there the inevitable resident vultures perched alone or in pairs. He checked the shells in the twelve-bore.

"All right, Robert. *Geluk.*"

"Yeah . . . you too, *Jong*," Queen said. "Make it good, boy." With the trace of a smile. "There's a lot of politics in it."

The spearman had cleared a wide aisle through the crowd now, right down to the royal cattle corral. Within it, a cluster of Bejane's beasts were gathered, their heads thrust over the wall, gazing at the packed ranks of tribesmen. Queen leaned his shoulder against the corner upright of the canopy, acting relaxed, easy, while in fact he was concentrating, figuring the likeliest proposition, figuring the snapshooting risk.

He made up his mind. In for a penny, in for a pound. Give them something to see, ponder on. There was always Jo, and Queen was very confident of Jo's skill with the shotgun. Queen made his choice and pressed the catch over to hairtrigger.

The boom of the Männlicher merged with the deadwood crack of splintering horn, and the bull bellowed, swinging away, one sickle-shaped tine jaggedly sundered at the base. As the beasts lumbered off in alarm, the invariable reaction of their kind that Queen had counted on, he snatched back the bolt and swung onto another head. Again, he shattered the horn, this time a little above the base.

Beside him Joachim, tight-lipped, had brought up the long-barreled Belmont almost to the vertical, for he, too, had decided it was worth attempting the most spectacular form of politics. The bird he had noted, separated from its flock and directly above the kraal, was gliding at a height of about a hundred and fifty feet, and Joachim had estimated the bird's arc and pace. As the vulture made a new approach, the hunter rode the bead with him, then, he drew ahead and, as the black shape swept into the perpendicular, the young *ryder* fired with the full-choke barrel. The big bird faltered, then fell like a stone.

The speculators whispered and murmured among themselves, obviously impressed with the hunters' display of their lethal efficiency.

Bejane glowered sullenly. He called out to the *ryders*. "Killers of birds and cattle! Of what use are your iron snakes against a great army of warriors?" He summoned a look of scorn and turned to glare around him, his voice rising to a choleric bellow. "Do not heed the tricks of the *Umlungus*, Milebis." He waited for the dutiful chorus of acclaim, then continued the fulmination. "Have I not told you how our forebears dealt with the white men and their iron snakes at

242

Isandhlwana?" The recollection of the name seemed to stimu-
late him like a draft of liquor, and Bejane swung back to the
hunters with a leer of triumph.

"*Isandhlwana!—Umlungus!*"

"*Nkambule! Mosega! Blood River!*" Queen snapped. "Did
your forebears also hand down the stories of *those* battles,
King? Did they tell you of what the handful of *isibamus* did to
the massed spearmen at *Blood River?*" he said, raising his
voice. And then he shouted, "*And there were no Milebi at
Isandhlwana, King!*"

Bejane stared fixedly into the stony hard-set face of the big
ryder. It was true—that there were no Milebi there—and the
grotesque monarch knew it. He raised a stumpy shaking
finger. "*Umlungus*, know this . . ." He broke off, fumbling for
words. "If the *impungushes* of your king should ever set foot
across my borders, it would be *Isandhlwana* . . . your miserable few iron snakes against the forest of my spears." Again, he
cast wildly about for a means of demonstrating his unpitying
ruthlessness and unrelenting purpose, his terrible invincibili-
ty. Intuitively, the smoldering headman of the escort spearmen pushed forward.

"Greatness!" he screamed. He gabbled urgently into
Bejane's ear and then, receiving assent, he rushed away,
signaling two of his spearmen to accompany him. They
returned, dragging a man, bound at the wrists and ankles, and
dropped him in a heap at the king's feet.

At a nod from Bejane the tribesman was jerked to his knees,
his wrists arm-locked behind his head. Slowly, gradually, the
headman pushed the blade of his stabbing spear into the
victim's armpit. The suffering man writhed against his cap-
tor's grip, but he made no sound. The headman paused, then
pushed the blade in farther another inch. But still no scream
came from the agonized man, no sound from his contorted
face. Again the headman pushed the blade deeper, still

drawing no scream of agony. Knowing that just a fraction more would pierce the heart, the headman glanced inquiringly at Bejane.

Bejane raised a hand and the headman withdrew the spear. Blood spouted from the wound. The swooning tribesman fell forward on his face. He had known that his only hope of earning reprieve lay in silence throughout the ordeal. He also knew that should he besmirch his king's honor by uttering a sound, he would suffer the greater and more prolonged agony of the anus stake. It was a remarkable show of stoicism, and it clearly improved Bejane's mood to have a record of his powers put before the *ryders*. Vindicated, he rounded triumphantly on the hunters.

"You see, *Umlungus*, bird-killers! What are bird-killers to the silent warriors of Bejane? Enough of birds and cattle! Can you kill swift *warriors* with your iron snakes? Even women?" At this, the fat man scanned the cowering women, then pointed, "Take that one . . . and that one . . . her too!" Bejane waved away their pleadings. "Put them into the *isibaya*. Let them run back and forth like goats to avoid the stings of the iron snakes." He turned to the hunters. "Now, N'kosis of *Dukusa*—let us see you kill running *people*. I order it!"

Joachim turned to face the big *ryder*. "No, Robert, I won't do it. We cannot . . ." He felt the pressure of Queen's hand on his arm and broke off.

"We of *Dukusa* do not kill women or children, King," the Afrikander said, as if amused at the notion. His lip curled expressively. "That is for apes and hyenas, not warriors."

Now the snake-charmer sidled close and whispered in Bejane's ear, and the ruler's scowl slowly changed to a smirk. "Then you shall prove the worth of your iron snake against men, cattle-killer! Against the Milebi warriors! In the Valley."

Queen glanced at Marao. The half-caste absolved himself with a shrug. "It is where the king tests picked spearmen against each other. Bush-fighting, warrior-training . . .

244

except that the fighting is *positivo*, real." Marao grinned sourly. "A place of scrub and bush, and they know it well," he added meaningfully.

"The *Umlungu* made much of the fewness of the white men who fought at the river. Let him, then, fight two Milebi warriors in the Valley." Bejane uttered the challenge derisively, holding up two fingers.

The hunter ignored the taunt and turned to Marao. "How big a ground area is it?"

"About five, six hundred yards . . . half as wide," the half-breed said.

Queen turned back to Bejane with a look of disdain. "Four men, King," he called out for all to hear, "and I will use only the small *isibamu*. But grown men." He jerked his head to where the vicious young headman was standing. "Not boys who play at warriors like him."

Bejane stared stupidly.

"Three warriors . . . and *him!*" Queen said acridly. He stabbed his finger at the ghoulish figure of the snake-charmer.

For long seconds there were only the small sounds of shifting feet, the croak of a raven high overhead, the droning of insects. . . . Then, as those who had heard it conveyed the white man's staggering proposal to those beyond the inner enclosure, the rising chatter of excitement ran through the crowd.

As the enormity of the big *ryder's* demand dawned upon him, the witch-doctor's expression changed from amazement to outright alarm. He ran forward and dropped to his knees before Bejane's couch.

"Greatness! Lion of Lions! Do not heed the *Umlungu*, beware his cunning. He seeks only to deprive you, Heir of Chaka, of the power of my medicine. The snake-charmer's voice rose shrilly. "The medicine that will protect your warriors from the *isibamus* of all white men!"

"Silence!" Bejane placed the broad pan of his pudgy foot on

the lame man's face and thrust him away. Still pondering the hunter's startling suggestion, Bejane pointed to the huddled figure with his foot. "He, Amblongo, is not a warrior," he said fatuously, as though he found the request intriguing but impractical.

"He is a grown man," Queen said incontrovertibly, "and there is a strong reason. Is he not the maker of the medicine he tells you will shield your warriors, your spearmen, King? *Who better to prove the truth or falsehood of this medicine?*"

Bejane knitted his brows in muddled contemplation. The crouching man crept nearer and began to lovingly caress the swollen bloated feet of his monarch, but the fat man kicked him away with a curse.

Queen called out again. "Why do you hesitate, King?" Queen hawked and spat toward the groveling figure. "And why does he fear so if his medicine is strong, stronger than the medicine of my small snake. Will he not make the strongest medicine for himself?"

"He is not a warrior." The obese man could only repeat sullenly. "I will send another."

The Afrikander shrugged indifferently. "Send another, then—making four," Queen held up four fingers. "If you too are afraid of my medicine? But send the *mundumugu* also!"

Bejane opened his mouth, but the hunter ran on quickly, forestalling him, pressing his advantage. "*Are* you also afraid, King . . . of the medicine of *Dukusa?*" It was like a whipcrack, deliberately provocative, stinging the gross man's ego. Bejane's face twisted in confusion, his monstrous soft body quivering with anger. It was incontestable that Amblongo's medicine was worthless, as the whole tribe would recognize, if it could not protect the witch-doctor himself. Bejane flung out an arm. "He goes to the Valley!"

The prostrate snake-charmer reared to his knees with a wail of dismay. He flung his arms around the king's knees, but again Bejane kicked him aside, snarling an order to the headmen.

From the shade of the awning, Marao had watched the byplay, amused at its outcome. It suited him to have the witch-doctor out of the way. This Queen was indeed proving useful.

He did not give a damn for the hunters' lives, although it would be desirable to have Morgan in his debt.

As for the snake-charmer, good riddance, for it was he who had been the chief barrier to the plan toward which Marao had been gradually shifting Bejane. He had seen a number of Bejane's gladiatorial engagements to-the-death between spear-men, and knowing the added hazard to any man unfamiliar with the terrain of the Valley, Marao would not bet on Queen's chances of survival. But if, in the process of the pending mortal combat, the hunter could at least kill the stinking hindrance there would be some gain from the business.

Marao moved forward to the king's side. "Great one, you have acted with much wisdom, as always. It is shrewd to test the strength of Amblongo's medicine—and if it is stronger than the *Umlungu's*, we will still have the others with whom to remind their king of your generosity."

Bejane growled petulantly. He spoke, "The Valley . . . tomorrow . . . now take them away."

Marao straightened up and moved across to the hunters. "Tomorrow, *manha*, then, when the light is good," he said to Queen. He lit a fresh cigarette. "Listen, forget the pistol *absurdo*, I'll see you get the rifle—with it you might have a chance. But don't try to use it on anybody else," he gave his humorless grin, "because I'll be above you, and because these two would be cut up alive. It's like a theatre, you see. They call it the Valley-of-True-Warriors, but it's more of a ravine than a valley. Steep sides, you can see over most of it from either. Mostly patches of thick bush in the bottom, but the stuff is only chest high, like the height of furze, maize . . ."

"Forget the rifle," the big *ryder* said. "Just the Colt and the knife."

"Yes, but . . ." Marao shrugged. "With the rifle . . ."

"I believe I said just the pistol?" Queen said. "And make sure you remind the toad I don't need but the wee snake for boys and *mundumugus*. Be sure you get that through his skull."

Marao made a sign to the headman in the background and the escort of spearmen closed in around the hunters.

The Valley

It was sweltering in the semi-darkness of the prison hut. When you first entered it was like plunging into a cavern after the yellow brilliance outside. But when your eyes had grown accustomed to the darkness, you could make out objects, a water pot, sleeping mats.

Their pockets had not been emptied, and Queen lay smoking with his head near the door. There was nothing to do but wait. Joachim pulled himself over to where Queen lay prone. "This hellish business of tomorrow, Robert . . . it's not right that you should fight alone," he said urgently.

Matshongi voiced his agreement.

"Yes, tell them we will fight together," Joachim said. "This Marao can arrange it with the fat pig."

Queen said nothing.

"But one against four, Robert!" the younger man said. "You haven't got eyes in the back of your head."

"Three, not four," Queen said laconically. "I don't count the lame one."

Joachim brushed the comment aside. "And another thing. Why in God's name did you refuse the rifle?"

"Speed," the older man said. "Could make all the difference."

"But you might get chances, at a distance . . . before they can close up . . ."

"Against *bosjesmen* stalkers? In heavy cover?"

"Still, the range, Robert . . ."

"That cuts two ways, lad. They can't risk a miss any more than I can. To be sure of me they've got to come within range of the Colt."

Joachim fell silent. In the momentary quiet, they could hear Marao's voice nearby. He seemed to be giving an order to the spearmen, and a moment later, he called through the entrance for the *ryders* to come outside.

The guard, a dozen or so spearmen, stood in a wide circle around a cooking-fire.

"You want beer?" Marao motioned them to seat themselves within the circle.

Queen nodded.

Marao turned to Queen. "If you live, your stay need not be long, a week, even less—unless you are fools."

Joachim spoke up. "Man, do not fool with us! What is *your* interest?" he hissed with uncharacteristic vehemence.

The swarthy man showed his irritation. "Are you the leader, then, *umfaan?*" Marao glowered at Joachim. "After tomorrow? Because tomorrow concerns *him?*" He nodded toward Queen. "And after tomorrow, he may no longer be with us?"

"I'll be here, all right," Queen said. "Don't you worry about that, Senhor."

Two women arrived with earthen pots and gourds. Marao gestured them to serve the hunters. "You have much confidence, maybe too much, my friend," he said. "The pig will send his best killers, and they are very practiced."

"I have been practicing quite some time myself," Queen said.

"I hope so," Marao said, taking a gourd. "The thing with

250

the birds and cattle was good for the pig to see, but tomorrow it will be much harder than that." Marao shrugged. "You see, sometimes I trade—like you—a few guns here and there, skins, gums, rhino horn, ivory. Where is there any difference from you?" His mouth shaped to a sneer.

"Gaspipes and muzzle-loaders from the scrap yards?" Queen raised his eyebrows. "You make a good profit, but the only thing they ever hit is themselves. Two or three rounds, and the gaspipes blow up in their faces," Queen said.

Marao grinned. "Some I have taught to use them safely— fasten the gun to a tree with a string to the trigger. But how do you know what I do—what I sell?"

"Every trader on the coast knows your game."

The half-breed's eyes narrowed. But the big *ryder* went on before he could make any reply. "Some even call you king already," Queen lied. "But you're only a crown prince so far—or maybe a treasurer, eh, Senhor?" Queen took a pull of the lukewarm beer. "But I've nothing against that, either. Nor would Morgan have—so long as you got the geography right!"

"*Cigarro?*" For the first time Marao offered from his pack. He took a long speculative draw of his own cigarette. The implied tribute, backhanded though it might be, was not disagreeable to him: This Englander, this Queen, was he not an adventurer with whom one could come to a practical understanding? Was he not after kingship lately?

Marao dragged on his cigarette. "The big pig is hard to reason with," he said, smiling his thin grimace. "The *imbecil's* answer to guns is that spearmen have only to attack in the night."

"You do not seem to admire your lord and master," Joachim said. "Why don't you speak out plainly?"

"Lord and master?" Marao spat contemptuously. He tapped his boot. "The boot will be on the other foot soon, *umfaan*. They war all pigs, ignorant pigs, Igonyela, the

251

Banyoro, these." He gestured with his hand. "Bejane is merely the biggest pig, the most valuable, although the stupidest." Marao got to his feet and wiped the sweat from his neck with a ragged bandana. "You want to sleep outside . . . here?" A thought occurred to him and he grinned crookedly. "Or do you want some women in there?"

"None like those crows we've seen," Queen said. "But we might have a bottle left in the wagon—if there's anything left in the wagon?"

"Come and look for yourself if you want." Marao spoke to the guard and two of the spearmen moved up behind them.

Four other spearmen were posted around the wagon when they got to it. The ivory looked intact, and more surprisingly, the rifles were also there. Queen reached behind the driver's seat and began to rout around until he found the last square bottle where he had hidden it.

"How about our pistols?" Queen said over his shoulder.

"I've got them," Marao said. "You'll get yours in the morning."

* * *

Queen lay on his back, head pillowed on one of the blanket rolls he had brought with the whiskey from the wagon. The night was sultry, oppressive. Joachim and Matshongi were already sleeping, though sometimes the younger man moved restlessly. It was past midnight now, and Queen could not sleep.

He was afraid, of course—as every hunter is afraid beforehand. He thought of Malendela, of Morgan, of his dead father, of Joachim and Matshongi; he thought of his dream, of *Arjayskeep*, and then of Bejane and the test that morning would bring.

Queen had killed men before, white as well as black. Marauders. For there were always some ready to relieve a hunter, a trader, of his hard-earned gains, and they came in both colors. And over the years he had learned things about the anatomy of fear.

He permitted himself only one brief deliberation on the impending encounter in the Valley. These Milebi were as deadly as a mamba. But they were still only two-legged beasts—of less formidable striking power than an elephant, a lion, and with no more intelligence, if as much, as a wounded buff. He took a last good slug of Logan's and let himself go dreamlessly into sleep.

*　　　*　　　*

The detail of men had been walking for the best part of an hour since leaving the kraal. An Induna led, then Queen and Marao, flanked and followed by an escorting score of warriors. The Induna was not the one who had ambushed the hunters at the Ridge, but was an older man. The younger captain, one of the participants delegated by Bejane, had already preceded them with another group of spearmen. He was, by record and repute, the most redoubtable of their younger killers, Marao had said. For though there had been others with more triumphs to their names, none had possessed the same fanatical zeal to achieve the rank of Induna, nor so far accomplished his tallied six victories with comparable swiftness.

From the kraal they had taken a winding course over ground which, though not steeply inclined, rose continuously, and now they had reached the near end of the Valley. It was longer than Marao had guessed, more than six hundred yards, Queen judged, and was shaped like an elongated pan or basin. Both sides were precipitous, allowing a view from either that would range over almost the whole extent of the ground. The pan was predominantly carpeted with bush and secondary growth, the only profuse vegetation the gray soil

253

would support, but between the thickets of brush there were glades of rank waist-high *kweekgras*. It was a place where the successful survival of any man, or beast, committed to kill or be killed by a dangerous enemy, would depend on two things—consummate stalking skill and speed.

For several minutes Queen surveyed the general aspects of the terrain. At the far end of the Valley, on the high bluffs that terminated the pan, he could just make out, he thought, several black specks—men. He stretched out a hand for the glasses, his own binoculars, which Marao was carrying, and confirmed his impression. Then he began to quarter the ground systematically.

He lowered the glasses and drew on the cigarette that Marao had given him. "How much longer do I wait here?"

"Not long. The pig has arrived now. Any time they'll send up some smoke, then you start in." The renegade pointed. "Take a look, along there to the right, where the cliff juts out—that's the King's *balcao*, his theatre box."

Queen raised the binoculars again. He picked up the projecting abutment about halfway along the arroyo. Bejane himself was temporarily obscured by the sweating litter-bearers who had borne him from the kraal and by the spearmen of his guard. But now he saw that larger groups of watchers were gathering at various vantage points along the opposing cliffs.

There was a bizarre, unreal atmosphere about this whole macabre contest. It had all the qualities of a dream and seemed now less like an uncomplicated duel than a grandiosely staged drama.

He took another look at the place he had particularly noted. It was a *bult*, an outcropping of gray-white rock about two-thirds the way along toward the eminence where the King's party were gathered, and near to the center of the pan. The cairn consisted of three large boulders piled against each other like an island rearing out of a glade of brown *kweekgras*. He marked an ilala palm that stood roughly opposite the *bult*, at the top of the valley wall, and near enough to the edge to be visible from the bottom of the pan. Then he stubbed out his cigarette and took another from the pack that Marao held out to him.

"How do I know they haven't already started in down the other end?"

"You don't," Marao said. "But you needn't worry—they won't. They're watched, same as you, and the pig would have them castrated if they disobeyed his orders."

Queen pushed the brim of his hat a little higher on his brow. He pulled the Buntline from his holster and spun the chamber. It clicked neatly and the bullets shone like gold in the sun. So did each of those in his pocket, placed there for quicker reloading than you could manage from the belt.

"That's it." Marao nudged Queen and pointed. "There's his signal now."

From somewhere adjacent to the jutting butte along the edge of the face a white puffball had risen. Queen got to his feet and stared at it for a moment, then looked out over the heat haze dancing over the surface of the brush thickets below.

"Watch yourself," Marao said.

"You too," Queen said harshly. "If the others don't get back to Morgan, that will be the biggest mistake of your life, and you bloody well better remember that, friend—because Morgan and Papa van Zyl would find you no matter where you went."

Queen began the descent into the sweltering bowl, slithering a little at times on the steeper screes. Before he had reached the foot of the slope, his tension had changed to alertness, and there were no knots in his stomach now, because now he was committed, and his brain was wholly occupied with the mechanics of it.

255

He headed for where the *bult* was located in his mind's eye, skirting the big islands of brush and loping across the patches of *kweekgras*, not running, but moving fast. He worked steadily to the right until he could see the topmost fronds of the landmark palm on the cliff silhouetted against the sky. About five minutes later, threading inwards from the direction of the monitor tree, he found the outcrop. One rugged boulder, about the height of a man, rose vertically from the hard scorched earth, and two other rocks, chest high, lay just in front of it, jumbled together like the two halves of a crag sundered by lightning. It was better than he had gambled on, because it eliminated the biggest risk, surprise from behind, and any attacker was going to have to come at him from either side or in front.

He stuck the pistol in his waistband and moved swiftly across the grass. At the edge of the glade he forced a yard or so into the scrub and fixed his hat so that just a little of the crown showed above the top of the bush. It occurred to him that he didn't know whether the Milebi would fight singly, each on his own initiative, or by a concerted action. Either way any distraction, however momentary, would provide a considerable advantage; the vital seconds' difference between snap-shooting and studied accuracy.

He moved back along the oval glade, paying out the fishing line he had taken from the wagon before leaving the kraal on a pretext of requiring a rod for the Colt. When he had got over behind the horizontal rocks, passing the line through the gap between them, he tried the rig-up. A slight tug moved the clump of brush near to his hat sufficiently to make just a faint rustle of foliage and enough movement to catch a sharp eye. Now Queen squatted, his back against the tall rock, settling in to wait.

The young Milebi Induna had not struck Queen as a man much able to temporize. He was too governed by rankling anger, and he lacked the patience to hunt inch-by-inch, like a stalking chameleon, no matter how long it took. On the other hand, he might order the others to precede him, to decoy Queen into exposing himself. But, assuming that they *had* made a plan between them, it would likeliest be, Queen reckoned, to quarter the ground in pincer style, perhaps in converging stalks, so that if he, the quarry, spotted one of them first and opened up he would thereby announce himself to the others.

Half an hour passed and there was only the drone of the flies to hear. Up there on the bluff, Queen imagined, the fat toad would be champing and swilling under his awning at the lack of activity, if he had not already sunk into a stupor.

Queen lifted the Buntline from the bandana he had laid it on and wiped the sweat from his brow, neck and hands, then put the gun down beside him again and pressed his palms against the coolness of the rock behind him. When he heard the *korhaan* call, he stiffened abruptly, less because it was magnified by the silence than because there was no planing bird overhead. The call came again, but the sound was slightly different from the first, higher pitched, and still no sign of a cruising bird, much less a pair.

The minutes dragged by. Queen waited, resisting the impulse to rise, breathing through his mouth, straining his hearing. Then he heard a tiny sound, no more than a faint whisper, like a murmur of corn stalks barely disturbed by the slightest breeze. But there was no drift in the air, not enough even to waver the smoke of a cigarette, and he knew that someone, something, was moving along the glade to his right.

Again he rejected the impulse to rise. He waited long enough for a stalking man, or a browsing buck, to draw level with the cairn and move ahead. Then, silently, on his toes, he inched up until his eyes rose above the tabletop of the rock. The crouching figure just a few yards ahead was turned away, peering intently along the straggly wall of brush. An easy shot, but the spearman was the only living thing to be seen, and he seemed to be rooted. Either he had spotted the telltale scrap of brown felt further along in the scrub, or he was waiting for somebody, or both.

The Afrikander sank down behind the rock again. He found the line with his free hand and worked it gently, then again a few seconds later. If the Milebi had not already seen the blob of color in the foliage, he would have done so now, and it would keep him riveted for at least another minute or two.

The sweat was beginning to run down into Queen's eyes, and he brushed it away with his sleeve. He waited. Nothing showed or stirred, and it seemed as if whoever had given the second birdcall did not exist, or was lying doggo himself. It would be asinine to let the first enemy move beyond sure-fire range, to pass up the one certainty. Queen started to rise again, then caught a fleeting reflected glint from the far end of the glade, of something mirrored in the sun for a fraction of a second, like a sliver of glass, or a burnished spear point. He stayed down, watching the place, and a moment later the head of a stooping man showed partially above the grasses.

Now the first spearman had come into Queen's line of vision. The lean African pressed close against the edge of the scrub and straightened up sufficiently for the other Milebi to see him. Twice he made a sign indicating where their quarry was supposedly placed. Then, when he was sure that the other spearman understood, the first man bent low and began to inch forward.

In the same instant Queen rose to his feet. Both Milebi were concentrating on the place where he was presumed to be, working to converge until they were sure of pincushioning the spot, each carrying three javelins.

He laid the long barrel across his forearm, following the

slight intermittent rippling in the grass and ignoring the figure just a dozen strides away to his right.

He fired on the instant that he next glimpsed the tenuous outline of the crawling man and the African reared upright in the grass with a cry that could have been shock or could have been pain. Queen fired again, and this time there was no question about the source of the scream.

Before the second shot rang out, the first Milebi had whirled, but in the instant that he hesitated, unsure of his target, Queen laid a round into the man's chest. The African staggered and reeled backwards, the spears dropping from his hands.

Queen reloaded, his back against the big rock, listening hard for sounds other than the receding gurgles of the dying men. Then he ran along the glade, pausing only to recover his hat and shove it into his shirt and seeing as he went the frothy cake of lung blood that foamed from the nearer spearman's mouth.

Queen worked his way in the direction of Bejane's position on the cliff, stalking the brush islands, running bent low when he had to cross an open strip; he left a trail through the *kweekgras* that a blindworm could have followed, even sometimes deliberately traversing a bare patch where the gray dust retained the imprint of a boot. For ten or fifteen minutes he kept this up, gun in hand, through the eerie brooding stillness of the maze, but always heading toward the north wall of the pan. It was pure guesswork, but it seemed to Queen likeliest that the Induna would expect him to head the other way, as far as possible from the main body of spectators on the bluff. Queen *wanted* now to be spotted from the cliff. For it was a dead certainty they would signal the Induna the way he had gone, and that was what he wanted, but not too soon. Minutes later, loping across an open court, he heard distant shouts and knew that they had seen him. He quickened his pace, heading

259

straight up the Valley, only slackening to snake through the
bends, uncaring of any further glimpses he gave of himself,
concerned instead with making a distance from the *bult* that
would take a pursuer, moving cautiously, long enough to
allow Queen the brief respite he needed to do what he had to.
He had made a hundred yards or so when he heard the shouts
from the cliff top again, and knew that this time he had not
inspired them himself. One of them, almost certainly the
Induna, must already have been near to the outcrop at the time
of the shooting, and must have begun to follow up his trail.
Queen was moving along an unusually narrow avenue of
rising ground, not much wider than a game trail now, and as
he ran, he saw again what a totally malevolent place this was.
Neither forest nor veld, but silent, hostile, cramped, like a
graveyard in a nightmare.

The rib of the rise was a flat arid strip of shaly intersection
that ran on down the incline. Queen paused for half a second,
then abandoned caution and ran, sometimes slithering, down
the scree, each scuffling footfall raising puffs of dust. Fifty
yards or so through the bend at the foot of the grade, he
stopped and snatched a backward glance. Here on the flat he
could pick out his own track stretching through the grass for
twenty yards or more, and it would be the same in reverse for
the Induna.

Now he had to backtrack.

He forced into the scrub and began to work his way back on
a course roughly parallel to his trail from the scree. It was
plaguey chest-high going, sometimes nearly impenetrable,
and it would have been easier to crawl through the labyrinth
of tunnels beneath the underwood, but it would have taken
longer and there was no way of knowing how much time he
had left.

When he had thrashed back as far as the bend, Queen
halted against a stunted palmetto. Standing upright, his head

just brushing the fan of the dwarf tree, he could see the stretch from the bend to the crest of the scree. He leaned back against the palm and settled to wait, shaded from the burning yellow eye overhead. Fifteen or twenty minutes later he saw the small puffball of drifting dust, and it brought him up sharply. Someone, remarkably, had crossed the rib and made down the incline like a ghost.

Scouring the brown sea, Queen located the slight movement in the grass-heads. He watched the soft ripple until it was nearly level with him across the glade, then he sank down onto his toes. He allowed the other man time enough to move farther on. Then Queen began to worm through the cover— on his belly, inch by inch. A yard or two from the verge, he rose on the balls of his feet until he could see over the scrub. The Induna was yards ahead, along the glade, and now standing, slightly crouched, staring at the place where the hunter's trail seemed to cease.

In another second or two, he would probably drop down and move on again. Queen burst through the fringe of the scrub—but he tripped and stumbled heavily. As he fell, he saw the Induna whirl, his arm go back, and in the same breath of time Queen felt the stab of pain and yelled—then again— with the shuddering anguish of a mortally stricken man, as he pitched full length.

The Milebi came bounding through the high grass, his face lit with savage triumph, stabbing spear jubilantly upraised to pig-stick the dead or dying *Umlungu* again and again, and at five yards Queen came to life and shot him through the stomach three times.

Queen reloaded and ended the black man's agony with a bullet slammed into the back of his head.

The javelin spear had gashed his left arm above the elbow, but it was only a flesh wound, and the honed edges of the spearhead were so sharp that the cut was finely drawn. It

261

would knit up well enough. He bound it as best he could with his bandana.

Queen began to work his way up the Valley, systematically quartering the ground, pausing to listen for minutes at a time, watching for any outcrop from which his last quarry could skewer him before he knew it. Two or three times during the next hour he knew that he had been observed from the cliffs, yet there were no shouts. Likely the significance of his reappearance had given them something to ponder on, plus the fact that they had heard no paeans of victory, no shrill yells of *Bayede!*—only the sound of gunfire. Certainly they had had none of the entertainment they were accustomed to, none of the sudden electrifying mortal duels in the sun that delighted them. Queen visualized the glowering pig under the awning on the bluff, baffled, fuming, ranting.

It took another dragging, broiling hour without sign or incident to reach the head of the Valley, and it began to look as if the lame witch-doctor must have gone to earth in the scrub. Queen glanced up at the angle of the sun. There was not much time left now. As Marao had said, the deadline hour was sundown. Then they came in to recover the losers' bodies, and if he was still missing, Bejane's wolf-packs would root out the unloved betrayer of their champion for themselves.

For just a moment he considered reverting to his earlier strategy, choosing a cache and letting the desperate fox seek *him*, as he could afford to do. But it would probably only result in a further wearisome period of stalemate, and the idea went against the grain. He moved on again, threading toward the southwestern corner of the Valley. Here the ground was even more arid and open, with just a few vagabond dwarf palms, threadbare patches of *kweekgras*, and a scattering of boulders from the cliffs. None of the boulders would have hidden a goat, and the terrain did not seem to hold any kind of prospect, yet, as he emerged from the last of the thickets, he heard excited shouts from the terminal bluffs. The figures silhouetted against the sky seemed to be very much agitated at Queen's appearance, two of the tribesmen setting off at a run as though to carry information. Possibly they were flabbergasted, or chagrined. Or possibly it was something else.

He moved into the shade of an undernourished palmetto and straightened his aching back against the bole, studying the converging walls. A man could only cast a spear from the top, he thought, and thus he would have to expose himself on the brink. Opposite to where he stood a scant trickle of water issued from the lower face and maintained a small pool, hollowed out from the shaly sub-soil. The water looked crystal clear, its surface shining like glass in the blazing sun, and although it was likely lukewarm, so near to its source it was probably good. Queen licked his dry lips. There was no cover within two spears' casts of the *washout*, and though he saw that the spectators on the cliff were now grouped at a point on the crest that jutted out like a promontory, they were curiously silent.

Only the slight crunching of his boots on the gritty ground disturbed the yellow stillness as Queen moved across to the hollow. He took a quick look around, then dropped down onto his stomach at the water's edge. He drank quickly, a gulp or two, then raised himself on his elbows, listening, but nothing stirred. He looked down and was just on the point of lowering his head again when something moved, in the mirrored reflection of the rock face in the water. He snatched up the pistol lying beside him and flung himself, rolling, to one side as the javelin spear plunged into the ground a foot away from his back and rebounded from the stone underlay with a metallic clang.

He began to fire from where he lay supine. His first shot whined and ricocheted away, leaving a puff of gray dust beside the figure on the ledge thirty feet above him. But the second took the witch-doctor squarely in the act of hurling his second javelin, and the spear clattered from his hand. Amblongo stood rooted on the shelf, mouthing soundlessly, a ragged hole torn through his throat, unable to move toward the fissure which had been his refuge before the third shot bludgeoned him flat against the wall. Now, at last, he pitched headlong from the spur to the stones below.

Queen refilled the chambers of the Buntline and returned the gun to his holster for the first time in the several hours that he had stalked the Valley. Over his shoulder he heard random shouts from the buttress farther along, and saw that the spectators were moving up closer. He got to his feet, walked the few paces to the sprawled body and turned it over with his boot, so that those on the cliff-edge could see the contorted face and the welling blood.

Queen grinned with triumphal fury, the violent animal in him stirred to raving. He roared up at them: *Bayede! Bayede Dukusa!*

Umabope Kabope!

Marao's shack stood at the far end of the kraal from the king's enclosure. It was made of the same grass thatch as all the huts, but square, with a full-size doorway, a window over which hung a roll of hide that could be fastened down, and a portico of plaited-reed that made an oblong of shade. Along with the adjacent cluster of conventional beehives that were the nucleus of Marao's isigodhlo, the shack was set well apart from the main body of huts.

As the escort squad approached with Queen between them, the half-caste rose and gestured to the two spearmen on either side of Queen to stay where they were. He jerked his head to the big Afrikander, and when the hunter had sat down, Marao reseated himself on the other upturned cask under the awning and tossed over a cigarette.

"Well, you did pretty good in the Valley. Very *competente*." It sounded as though he saw practical value in it as well as achievement.

"Good for the gaspipe business you mean," Queen said. "You ought to pay me a commission."

"Good for both of us maybe." The swarthier man leaned back against the thatch, thumbs hooked in his belt. "You are like me, eh? Killing *swarts* never troubles your *estomago*, never gives you the *depressao*? They are *all* trash, cattle for milking. You know that." He waited, but Queen only shrugged.

Marao turned away to call to the watching women over by the huts.

Among the girls who came across carrying beer and fruit, one was by contrast plump and lighter-skinned, with the apprehensive air of a captive, her firm breasts and buttocks jouncing attractively as she walked. Queen guessed her to be a kaffir of the coast.

Marao followed the bigger man's passing glance. "You like the *meisies*? You want to borrow one like that one, with the big *tetas*, the big *ancas*?"

Queen ignored the renegade's leer. "You bring them *up* country too, then? I thought all that kind of merchandise went the other way?"

Marao jerked his head. "The pig thirsts for Igonyela's women, and the choice Banyoro virgins, as he believes they are. Sometimes I oblige him with a fat kaffir calf . . . for four Milebi," he explained.

Queen felt the bile rise in him, but he stifled it. "Aaah! Let's forget all this shit about women. Get to the bones of it, the business you spoke about, man."

"Women are a part of the business," Marao said. "Given the right connections, chosen women have more value than cattle." He took a long draw of his cigarette and watched the smoke drift away. "The point is whether *you* have the brains as well as the stomach, *amigo*?" he said finally. "The *vigor* to be as big as Morgan, as Juwawa . . . ? Perhaps bigger."

"I can count, all right," Queen said laconically. He pulled his nose between finger and thumb as if weighing his words. "The trouble with some, not Morgan or Albassini, was that they didn't know how to count, how to hold onto what they got."

"Correct."

"And you reckon you do?"

"I shall be bigger than Morgan, *amigo. But,* it would be easier for two of a mind, and more, more *prontamente* for each. The one would follow the other, yes?"

"What other?"

"The Banyoro. You would get the Banyoro. I would guarantee it, it would be in my interest."

"You better begin at the beginning," Queen said. "I'm listening."

"Bejane and the Milebi are going to swallow Igonyela, take his country."

Queen laughed. "In his *dakha* dreams."

"That's true enough—he's dreamed of it for years," Marao said. "But, make no mistake, they are going to do it, I promise you."

"You mean he's really got the tribe worked up to it, ready for a full-scale war?" Queen said.

"Ready and boiling eager." The swarthy man nodded emphatically. "Igonyela is land and cattle and women for the taking. And the people are lean, envious, desperate as hungry wolves. They didn't need much working up—they've got nothing to lose."

"Except their skins," the Afrikander said.

"Pah! You think that counts, a few *lancas* . . . fifty, a hundred . . . for the women and cattle they get for it? Slaves too. For years Bejane has told them of the slaves who worked for Chaka's people. And there is another thing that appeals to them mightily, the easiness of it. Igonyela's people are sheep, not fighters."

"But Morgan's are, and a bloody sight more effective fighters than any Milebi rabble," Queen said pungently. "Don't the toad and his baboons understand *that?*"

Marao shrugged. "It does not worry them because they have the numbers, and what you are overlooking is that it will be over, before Morgan ever hears of it. . . . *Do you not understand that?* Overnight Morgan will have a new neighbor. Why should he care? Why should he want to throw away men of his own because of a tribal adjustment beyond his boundaries?"

Queen laughed. "They think that, eh?"

"Well, *would* Morgan want war?" Marao challenged.

Queen shrugged noncommittally. "How would anybody know that? He might."

"To what end? The mouse is his brother, his *amado?*" Marao said scornfully. He waited, and the hunter's silence only confirmed his belief, was clearly a reluctant admission of it. "No, in that, I would agree with them—and I am doubly sure Morgan would not fight if *you* explained the way of it to him!"

"Morgan is his own man," Queen said after a pause. "I couldn't guarantee anything."

"But you will be able to, I think, when I explain that what is going to happen will suit him well, even increase his own security in the end." The half-breed leaned closer. "Listen. After they have taken Igonyela's country, when Bejane sits in the mouse's chair, sooner or later, when they have prepared, it is their plan to attack Morgan. It will be a surprise attack, without warning, and the pig is convinced that it cannot fail. I tell you solemnly, this is his great and glorious ambition. To destroy the white king, *Dukusa.*"

Queen stared incredulously. "Christ, the Zulu dream . . . Chaka resurrected!" Queen laughed derisively. "Morgan will make chopped meat of his rabble."

"Don't be too sure. The rabble might surprise you, and in a little while I will show you why," Marao said cryptically. "Not that Morgan need worry, because it will never be put to

the test . . . and you will be able to explain to him that he will
have me to thank for that."

"You mean you think you can talk Bejane out of it?"

"Talk, stay Chaka the Great with talk? No, but I will stop
him all right." The shark-grin spread expressively. "The way
they stopped Chaka. *Permanentemente!*" He drew a finger
across his throat. "When they have dealt with the mouse, I
will deal with the pig. Rid us all of him."

"Well, that would make a good talking point right enough,"
Queen said. "If you could really do it—and survive to talk
about it?"

"Survive? Listen, the Indunas and the *conselheiros* are mine
already, all of them. They will get many cattle, women, and
guns—and they know it. I could give the word now. Have
them make a porcupine of him with spears, split his fat *ancas*
on the stake, *now*! But you couldn't believe that, I suppose?"

"Why not?" Queen said. "I just didn't realize you had got
that far yet."

"All right!" Marao seemed satisfied with the concession.
"Now I show you something, *associado*, and then, I think, you
will see what I mean about Igonyela, and, after him, the
Banyoro."

*   *   *

When they had saddled the horses, Marao led the way to
the kraal entrance. He had a gun in his saddle-bucket and a
pistol in his belt, but all the same an escort of six spearmen
walked three-a-side abreast of them, as Bejane had ordered.
Presently the half-breed turned toward a ridge of high ground
about a mile distant from the kraal. It rose from the plain like
an elongated ramp and hid the view beyond it. Soon afterwards a curious sound of chorusing voices began to reach
them over the grass, and, as they drew closer, the murmuring
became punctuated with strident yells that seemed to be

shouted orders. From the crest of the slope the ground fell away in a wide park, a great dry stretch devoid of vegetation. There, in that place, a host of milling spearmen filled the sprawling forum. They were a wild mass, an orchestral nightmare of human abandon.

"Behold the wolf packs of Bejane—the 'rabble,'" Marao said with sarcastic emphasis. "More *formidavel* than you thought, eh?"

It was undeniable. The stamping, chanting mass of tribesmen was distinctly menacing.

Before each close-mustered group of warriors stood a plumed Induna, and each group in turn was formed into three regiments. The whole phalanx of warriors was shaped like a buffalo's head, and though Queen had never dreamed to see the phenomenon in living reality, he recognized it immediately. The battlepiece of Chaka! The spectacle was like a vision from the famous tactical formation of the Zulu and the Matabele. But Queen did not laugh at the archaic aspect of it. These hawk-faced killers *could* annihilate Igonyela's untutored innocents beyond any doubt. They seemed to have arrived at the conclusion of some kind of martial ceremony.

"Watch," Marao said. "For the *rite* of the-potion-which-gives-valor-and-deflects-enemy-spears. If they were really going to fight, they'd get *dakha* to help, as well. Just enough. So that they want to kill for the pleasure of it."

An incantator and his red-and-white-daubed auxiliaries moved between the rows of spearmen with vessels of bull blood.

Marao took a drink from the flask at his knee and held out the skin. "You want to see more?"

"Know your enemy, they say," Queen said sententiously. "I've got the time."

"They won't be your enemy if you convince Morgan. They'd be allies who could win you a country."

"You being their sovereign Lord?" Queen said.

"You still not sure about that, eh? Watch, then, who gives the orders already." Marao stood in his stirrups and hailed the Induna standing before the massed warriors below them. When the man turned, Marao shouted again, giving his voice an authoritative rasp of command and emphasizing the order with a gesture. "*Maihlone, Maihlone*—arm and attack!"

The Induna grinned, signifying his understanding with a shake of his tufted spear, then he turned back, raising his arms above his head, and roared at the ranks of spearmen. "*Umabope kabope! Umabope kabope!* Let all our strength be joined!" The other Indunas took up the cry, completing the chain of command.

Queen was incredulous. Marao had inculcated them with Zulu martial tradition, even down to the penultimate order that preceded an attack. Except that they lacked the physique and the bearing of Zulu, the delusion was complete.

No whisper of sound came back now, and after the earlier hubbub of chanting and shouting the silence was impressive. The army of warriors began to move forward on their bellies like a noiseless migration of land crabs that had the overall outline of a single giant crustacean with claws extended. For two hundred yards or more the stealthy advance went on, then suddenly the Indunas rose to a crouch in concert, and the warriors sprinted forward before dropping down again.

Queen watched the tide of bodies flow forward with a growing feeling of foreboding. This was only a sham of course, an attack on a kraal; the stalking crawl exemplifying how they would cross open terrain as they eventually came within visual distance, and the running where there was natural cover. And Milebi were not Zulu, however much they thought they were. But Igonyela's pacific people were even further removed from the fighting capacity of those supreme warriors of decades before.

Continuing the pattern of crawling and running alternately, the warriors had now bellied forward to a point some three

271

quarters down the training ground. Smoke began to rise from the ground at a dozen equidistant places around the wide crescent of prone spearmen, and with the first billows, the Indunas sprang to their feet. "*Usuuthu, Usuuthu! Bayede, Bayede Milebi!*"

Even from a distance the massed chorus had a curdling maniacal quality, and in those instants of the feigned final charge, Queen was convinced: he saw in his mind's eye the burning boma, the avalanche of avid killers, the slaughter of the confused and terrified tribespeople.

For a while, as they turned their horses back toward the kraal, accompanied by the marching escort, Queen and the renegade rode in silence. Finally, Marao edged his horse nearer. "Well, you convinced now, *amigo?*"

"Of what?"

"Of everything I tell you." He jerked his head back toward the tribesmen. "First, that they *will* overrun Igonyela's kittens like a plague of cheetah."

"Taking is one thing, keeping's another."

"Aaah, Morgan again." Marao made a gesture of impatience. "Morgan is not a harebrain—he will not fight."

"He will if I tell him of the toad's big dream and say nothing of the rest of it," the English Afrikander said. "How do you know I won't do that?"

The half-breed grinned scornfully. "Why do you try to keep up the bluff? Morgan has only a handful of men."

Suddenly Queen realized that Marao knew nothing about the guns, the Lewises. Aloud he said, "All right! Let's say it goes with Igonyela according to the plan. Then what about our friends beyond the Ridge?" He tapped his chest. "How would we take the Banyoro, tell me that?"

The half-breed squinted obliquely. "You ask *me* that . . . knowing well how? Easy! You know the *poorts*, you are their friend. You take enough picked warriors with you, say enough to fill three or four wagons, then you free the pass, and we come through with the main force. *Facilimente!*" Marao wagged a stubby finger. "And to make it more easier, are they not *expecting* you to return with wagons?"

For a second Queen was stunned. Then he remembered Tsheke. He brushed a fly from his neck. "Yes. But I doubt it would be that easy."

Marao smiled. "It is only a matter of timing."

"You mean attack at night?"

"Of course. Once we have wiped out the sentinel guards at the head of the pass, there will be no problem. We follow the river on their side and take them at night . . . like you saw back there in the training ground, like that." He smirked. "I know a lot more about the *territorio* than you think—eh, *amigo?*"

Tsheke again! Queen pursed his lips reflectively. "Sounds all right—might work."

"Without doubt."

"And then you would take over me along with the Ban-yoro?" Queen said with simulated disenchantment. "They don't call you *Inyala* for nothing—eh, Senhor?"

Marao seemed to enjoy the joke. "Don't lose no sleep over that—you got nothing to worry about there."

"Why not?"

"Wouldn't make any sense. Listen, I get this country and Igonyela, making one very big country. That is more than enough for my plan." He leaned sideways confidingly. "I will be a *millionario*, much more a *millionario*, than Morgan, *amigo*. *But*, if I tried to rule more than that, overreach myself, I defeat myself, cut my own throat. Too much is no good. *Impractivel!*"

"What's the big consideration, then? What do *you* get out of this Banyoro business?"

Marao cupped his hands. "The same as we all get, the same

as we all *got* to have." Marao hesitated. "Security! The security to run our own countries how we want. I get Morgan at my front door, you at my back, and the same works for both of you."

"What they call a tripartite alliance?" Queen said. "Storm-proof."

"With each minding their own business and no interferences, black or white." He took a fresh cigarette and held out the tin. "You said it yourself, and you were right. They lost countries in the old days because they didn't know how to hold onto them—they didn't put their security first."

"True, that's the practical politics of it. But it takes money, guns, trained *ryders*—to look out for yourself and your neighbor."

"Correct, and you got it in the right order too. I get the first two in just the time it takes to send two trains to the coast," Marao said with convincing assurance. "Then. . . ."

"Trains of what?"

The half-breed ignored the interruption. "Then I bring in *ryders, sistematico*, until I got all I want. After that, I get more money whenever I want it," he said as an afterthought.

"I'll bet the *ryders* will speak Portuguese?"

"Most will. But *Griquas* also—they are good with the *swarts. Firme.*"

Queen tried again. "Get back to the trains, the money part . . . I'll need it just the same as you, won't I?"

Marao grinned appreciatively as if the question posed no real problem and showed the kind of venial realism he understood.

"*Naturalmente!* Once you, once *we* have crushed the Ban-yoro, made them *domesticado*, like they all did," he pointed a finger, "your Morgans and van Zyls also—you take out all you want . . . ivory, horn, hides, gums . . . and you send your own wagon trains to the coast, the shortest way, half the distance. Not the long way south and east, as you would have had to do without me."

"For you to hijack?" Queen said sourly. "There's one wagon lying there already, if you remember."

"Don't worry, you'll even get that one back. I even give your wagons escort to the Coast if you want." Marao paused as if considering whether to explain why his assurance was cast-iron. "Listen, like I been telling you, we live and let live. It wouldn't do me no good to rob you, would it? Besides, I shall have all the merchandise I can handle."

"Igonyela's herds?"

"They're good herds. I shall sell cattle," Marao said.

"Uh huh!" Queen lit a cheroot and puffed deeply. "Of course there's a trade, or was. Pays a lot higher than cattle or ivory, they say . . ." Queen rolled his cigar between his fingers and smiled broadly at Marao.

"Gold . . . stones? Aaah, pie in the sky! You could spend a lifetime for nothing—most of them do."

"Not that, the other kind of ivory . . . black ivory," Queen said phlegmatically.

Marao stared closely. "You know about that trade?"

"Not much . . . never ran into it . . . expect that some made a lot more a lot faster than the horn and ivory men—I know that. But I guess it's played out."

"What you mean, played out?" Marao said curiously.

"The law got on top of it."

"Your information is not quite correct," Marao said guardedly. "Some police made the trade difficult, but that only made it worth more, much more, to those unaffected."

"You mean it can still run to money, real money?"

The renegade grinned at the magnitude of the understatement. He nodded. "Very substantial."

"Black ivory, huh?" Queen mused. He cocked his head and spoke as though thinking aloud. "The Banyoro are runts, but their women. . . ."

"Would be worth a lot more than your tusks and horn, *amigo*."

Marao had made up his mind now about this Englander. He put a hand on the hunter's shoulder. "Listen, I can take a train through any time. This is how it works. I send a message. I got good friends on the Coast. They know the business . . . *eficientes* . . . they hide them up, the dhows come in at night. Easier than loading cargo," he grinned. "The merchandise loads itself. No trouble." Marao laughed.

They were nearing the kraal entrance now, the spearmen on either side of them beginning to dawdle, and Marao held out his flask. "Here, *amigo*, have another drink, I think we got something special to celebrate, eh?"

Queen stared back without answering.

"Well, you got till tomorrow to make up your mind, but I think you made it up already, eh, *amigo*?" the renegade said expansively. "If so you can travel with the warriors tomorrow."

It was at this point that the big *ryder* suddenly understood. "What? You mean they're going south for Igonyela *tomorrow*?"

"That surprises you?" Marao said. "They'd have gone long before this if the Banyoro hadn't happened in with his information; they've been preparing for long enough. I had much difficulty getting the pig to hold off till they brought you in, but eventually I got through his head the great opportunity that it was."

"Opportunity? You mean having us for hostages?"

"Exactly!" the renegade said. "To make sure that Morgan understood, that he make no trouble afterwards. And then, also, I begin to think that just maybe I can kill the two birds

276

with this, even three, depending on whether you proved a man of business, a man who knows what it's all about."

Queen forced a grin. "Quite so, my friend," he said. "I know what it's all about." And again the big *ryder* grinned.

Marao led the way through the kraal to the cattle corral, and in the short time that Queen followed in file he got the handcuffs from his saddle pouch and into his pocket before they drew up by the wagon. He unsaddled quickly and began to look around, examining the axles and undercarriage, as if busy checking the fittings. Marao had dismounted and was striding toward him. As he came, he tossed Queen a new tin of cigarettes. "There will be much reveling in the *aboura* tonight to celebrate the dispatch of the impis. You will still be under guard, of course, but I send you a couple of bottles if you like."

"Drinkable stuff?"

"*Aguardiente*, brandy, *Portugues*," Marao said.

The renegade started away, but then turned with a leery grin. "You sure you don't like me to also send you a woman?"

"Funny, I was just thinking about that," the big *ryder* said. "Could you make it the light-skinned one—the one who brought the fruit?"

The renegade nodded. "She is for the pig. A new one. But he has not seen her yet—so he won't be any the wiser. How about the other two?"

"In one hut? Queen said heavily. "The hell with them— they can sit outside with the watch dogs. Just the kaffir will do."

At a signal from Marao, the spearmen closed up on either side of Queen as he moved away from the wagon.

Look Back
and Remember!

There was much to tell, and Joachim and Matshongi—jubilant at Queen's return—listened avidly as the big Afrikander recounted his duel in the Valley.

But now what Queen had to tell them about the mass demonstration of warriors on the training ground and his devious discussion with Marao filled Joachim with dismay.

As soon as Queen had finished speaking, Joachim bent forward and gripped the older man's arm. "We must prepare Igonyela and the N'kosi, Robert. We must make the breakout now! At once!"

"We must wait," Queen said impassively.

The younger man seemed shocked. "No! Right now! Let one of us make an excuse to fetch something from the wagon. Two of the guards would go with him. Then we jump the other two and run for the horses!"

"No!" Queen shook his head.

"But *time* is the important thing, Robert! We gain nothing by waiting," Joachim said passionately.

The older man shook his head even more vehemently. "How far you think we'd get? Use your head, Jo. We'd be stuck pigs before we got halfway across the kraal, before we

278

reached the squad at the entrance, *and* riding bareback at that. We've got to have guns and our saddles, *Jong*—that's for sure."

Joachim glanced distraughtly at Matshongi, but the African *ryder* only nodded his agreement with the English Afrikander's verdict, and Joachim turned back to Queen again. "Have you *any* plan—*any* idea, then, Robert?"

A shadow fell across the doorway and a woman came through the entrance of the hut. Diffidently, she set down a khamba of beer and two bottles, then moved shyly to the big hunter's side.

Submissively, as though she had been well instructed in her role, she dropped to her knees beside him. "Not now, my *umfaan*—later," Queen said. "When the moon is risen." He touched her arm and motioned her to leave. When she had gone, Queen lifted the edge of the sleeping mat where he had put the handcuffs. He gestured to the two sets of irons.

He began to outline his idea. When he had finished he sat back and glanced inquiringly at each.

"It is a good plan, N'kosi," Matshongi said. "Given the stupidity of the pig."

"Which we may be able to thicken further—thanks to our benefactor, *Inyala* the king-maker." The Afrikander nodded toward the bottles the woman had brought.

"Yes, yes, Robert." Joachim nodded enthusiastically. "A good plan!" The prospect of positive action had lightened the burning frustration that had possessed the young *ryder*.

"All right now—we had better decide if we are going to try it, then?" Queen said surprisingly. He offered Marao's tin of cigarettes and took one himself.

"You mean *when* . . . when tonight?" Joachim frowned.

"No—I mean *if*." Queen blew out the match and exhaled. "If it is *worth* it . . . if it makes horse sense in the long run?"

"Worth it?" the younger man stared, incredulous.

"We are none of us old men yet, Jo . . . you least of all,"

Queen said evenly. "We've all got a lot of living in us yet, there's a big future ahead of us, across the Ridge. For Boetie also if he chooses. What we have to decide is whether we should take this chance."

"*What!*" The young man's voice rose in vehement disbelief. "You mean we should not risk our skins here, now?" the younger man said, and now the disbelief in his voice had given way to scorn and rage.

"Skins?" Queen laughed shortly. "*Skins!* I mean that the risk we shall take will not be bullet or spear. *The anus stake, man!* And it will not be a risk, it will be a certainty. Of course there is still one alternative . . . for just one of us to try it! There's a good chance Marao would save the other two, at least till he found out whether they counted for any negotiating value with Morgan."

Queen leaned back against the thatch, and in the silence that followed, he said: "I am laying it on the line. That is all I can do." He dragged on his cigarette, and blew out the smoke slowly.

Characteristically, Matshongi's face gave no indication of his inner thoughts. What the elder N'kosi had said was clearsighted and true. Not coward's talk nor evasion. Knowing this I will join with him in whichever way he himself is for, the African thought. He is not a fool, and he does not fear death, and I am the son of a moselekatse of Zulu, and I do not fear death, and this we have in common, as certain other things.

As for Joachim, he did not know what to think except that his friend was either betraying them or betraying his own courage. Yet Queen had always proved steadfast. What was it, then? That the big *ryder* knew something more, something he chose not to reveal?

"That other way, Robert . . . of one man going," Joachim said earnestly, "do you truly believe that Marao would, could save the others?"

280

Queen eyed him narrowly, suspecting what was coming. He nodded. "I'm pretty sure. But," he shook his head, "I've got to be frank, Jo. It, well, it might not work if it was *me* that went." Queen cast about for words to validate his integrity. "If it weren't for that, if I thought it *was* the best thing, *I* would go." It sounded unconvincing, even suspect, to himself.

But Joachim said simply: "I know that, Robert." He glanced at Matshongi. "We both know that."

*   *   *

It was evident that Marao had convinced Bejane that Queen now counted as an ally who would lull *Dukusa* until he, Bejane, was ready to order the assault on the *Umlungu* Chief. For when the renegade's messengers came, it was with a request to attend the ceremonial carousing presaging the dispatch of the Milebi warriors to the invasion of Igonyela. But the two spearmen remained to augment the four still maintaining guard on the three *ryders*.

Bejane, sprawled on his couch like a gross black sea lion, seemed largely insensible to the militant tributes, to the chorusings which, save for the substitution of his name, faithfully echoed the paeans of Chaka's warriors of long before his time.

By now he had already dispensed the first of the divertisements periodically introduced to lend variety to the ritualistic proceedings of singing and dancing, and was looking for something more to entertain himself. Hungrily, the pig eyes searched the teetering mass of tribespeople before him, cowed to silence now by a look they knew well enough. Suddenly, triumphantly, Bejane pointed and croaked an order. At once warriors of his bodyguard moved into the throng and returned dragging the unfortunate tribesman whom the King had indicated.

Bejane glanced down malevolently at the gleaming bald

281

pate of the man held prostrate before him, pleased with the proof of his own vigilance. He crooked a stubby finger, and when the summoned elder bent over him, Bejane muttered briefly. There was no doubt that, whether through ignorance or defiance, the transgressor had not been overtaken by natural baldness, and had manifestly shaved his head deliberately—a major offense, because only a subordinate chief, and then only with royal assent, might emulate the royal prerogative of a shaven pate. The transgression was, therefore, unpardonable, and the punishment would correctly fit the crime.

Bejane nodded to the captain of the guard. The pinioned man was jerked to his knees and then, with a single massive blow of his *knobkerrie*, the captain crushed in the offender's skull.

Bejane bent forward to examine the efficacy of the execution, peering critically at the dead man's mashed cranium, the mingled blood and gray viscous substance dribbling from the brow, coursing down the ears and neck.

Amused, but not adequately, Bejane contemplated the seven palm stumps set in the center of the arena. All still remained untenanted, an unusual and tedious circumstance. The despot glanced querulously around his immediate circle of attendants. Surely there were, must be, other malefactors held for later justice? At last bodyguards were dispatched to bring forth a sufficiently serious offender from amongst those still awaiting sentence behind the royal hut.

The failed rainmaker was thrust forward through the throng around the awning and hurled on his face before the king. His calling, a profession ironically forced upon unfortunate incumbents by heredity, was beyond doubt the most intensely harrowing office within the tribe. And currently, such miserable crops as the women and child workers had induced from their debilitated soil drooped flagging and withered in the scorched ground, for there had been no trace of rain for many moons. A man who had lived for a decade in almost perpetual fear, the rainmaker had so far survived from one hair's-breadth escape to the next, often by purchasing intercessions with the witch-doctors. He was thirty years old now, nearing the stage of a veteran practitioner by Milebi standards, but the lines and furrows in his gaunt face were those of a man twice his age.

With an effort, for they had bound his hands behind his head—and he knew the likely portent of that, too—he got to his knees and began to entreat Bejane for mercy, his eyes on the ground, speaking in a low voice that was barely audible above the slobbering cloaked breathing of the obese monarch. Humbly, penitently, he ventured to recall past successful appeasements of N'gai, and specifically he begged for two more days, even one, in which to repeat the most powerful inducement of the *izinyanga zemvula* rite.

In pleading for a repetition of his supreme rain-making ordinance, however, he had only increased Bejane's animosity, for the ceremony irrevocably prescribed the sacrifices of a prime black ox and a ram from the royal stock, that the king had greatly begrudged in the first instance. When he realized this, saw with hopeless finality the added resentment in the king's adamant face, the rainmaker's pleading became much more animated. Now, despairingly, he implored only a swifter, more merciful end than the manner of binding his hands had augured.

Bejane cut through the luckless plaintiff's final appeals with a growled order to the expectant Induna. Warriors seized the kneeling man and carried him, reduced now to the writhing and sobbing of dreadful anticipation, to the three specialist executioners waiting in the center of the arena.

Supervised by Indunas and spearmen of the king's body-guard, the crowd began to divide into two separate segments

283

of men and women, each semicircle facing the other and leaving a central aisle between them, so that Bejane could clearly observe the central proceedings without moving from his couch.

Warriors swung the body of the rainmaker into a head-down position, and the chief executioner went over to the seven sacrificial stumps. From the center of each palm bole, set in the ground like the piles of a marsh hut, a sharp-pointed stake projected vertically like the lead of a pencil. With the discriminating air of a fencing master considering a choice of foils, the chief executioner withdrew a stake from its socket in one of the logs and returned to the quaking prisoner.

The rainmaker was held fast, legs forced apart. Another of the executioners placed the point of the stake between the pinioned man's buttocks and held it in position with out-stretched arm. Then the principal slaughterman stepped back a pace, eyed the shaft for a second, and swung his club two-handed.

The rainmaker's first scream pierced the crowd noises like a blazing bolt of molten iron. But the blows were not delivered with the frequency or the force that would have brought the victim's excruciating agony to an early conclusion. The art of the executioner, and the reward he could expect from Bejane, depended on the maximum prolonging of the impalement.

When the shrieks of the spitted man changed to the hoarse gabbling note that was, to his accustomed ear, the crucial point of prolongation, the mace-bearer threw down his club with an air of artistic achievement. The stake was now driven sufficiently deep. The body of the rainmaker would hold erect. Resuscitated with pails of water which the executioners spilled over him, the man was still capable of voicing his agony a while longer.

Promptly now he was turned upright and carried to the stanchions. There he would remain, his moans merging with the rising din as his fellow tribespeople capered and recommenced the dancing and singing.

Queen shot a glance at Joachim's face, and was about to say something, when Marao suddenly appeared, accompanied by two women—one of them the girl with lemon-pale skin and bovine expression. He had a bottle in his hand, and jerked his head toward the palm stumps. "The pig has an eye for discipline, no?" Marao laughed, and raised the brandy bottle in his hand.

"I'll drink to that!" Queen said. "In fact, we'll *all* drink to it," he said pointedly, for the whiskey seemed to have been offered only to him, as if the others were not present. "We are all the same here, *camarada*, all men of sense and reality." Queen nodded at Joachim and Matshongi.

"You mean you have explained to them? They understand?" Marao asked with quickened interest.

Queen uncorked the bottle, took a pull, and handed the bottle off to Joachim. "Here, Jo, it's the right kind of stuff to go with this kind of entertainment—give Boetie some too." He turned back to Marao. "Oh, yes, *amigo*, they understand, all right. You don't think they came with me to the Banyoro for their health, do you?" He jabbed an emphatic finger. "I'll tell you something else, *amigo*. They're bloody good *ryders*, not greenhorns. They're the kind we'll need."

Marao screwed up his eyes. "That is good. *Sensato*," he grinned. "And when we take the Banyoro, they will get a better deal from you than from Morgan, eh, *amigo*?"

"They know it," Queen said crisply.

The half-breed nodded toward the two women. "Well, I bring you the *palido* one, like I said." He looked at Joachim and added expansively, "And you, young one, you can have the other one."

"Not for me," Joachim said dully. Marao made a face of disgust, and turned his attention back to Queen. "Take the

285

kaffir with you when you have seen enough of the pig's fooleries" he said. The renegade turned to the semicircle of guards squatted around the hunters and addressed them in a rapid flow of dialect, with gestures to the kaffir girl.

*   *   *

Impelled by the rising wind advancing from the east, the storm reached the precincts of the kraal much sooner than Queen had expected. It broke very suddenly, with a big flash that bathed the arena in milky light, filling the heavens with a booming crash like the onset of a barrage; minutes later the *ryders* felt the first spattering of heavy drops.

Further across the compound Bejane struggled upright from his couch. The gross ruler shot anxious cowering glances at the sky, his great shoulders hunched in dread. He shambled back through his awning into the presumed greater security of his hut, howling for more torches and his entourage of women. Within his hut, he would lie sweating and trembling, beneath a living blanket of girls, protectively draped across the mound of his body from head to toe, and remain there until the artillery of the heavens had moved on.

The mob of braver tribespeople, most of them drunk with beer and wine, and some staggering, were now leaving the arena to continue their reveling under cover—and as the rain began to pelt down, the *ryders* and their escort followed the migration toward the aisles of the huts, the kaffir girl following at their heels.

Skirting across the arena, they passed the grotesque, crumpled figure of the rainmaker, the tide he had so frantically invoked now mizzling down his tortured body and widening the dark puddle around his tree of purgatory.

*   *   *

The air in the prison hut was abominable. Each of the three

men and the woman in the hut, in their differing ways, listened to the rain and waited.

Joachim sat hunched and chafing, staring somberly at the slanting rain pattern which curtained the entrance. Queen was stretched out, resting on his elbow, smoking. Across from him, Matshongi lay curled on his mat, his eyes closed. Beside Queen the kaffir girl knelt passively, scarcely moving, wondering about the white man's way of doing it.

At last the big *ryder* regarded her: "Sing, *unkonka*, shy one," Queen demanded. "Sing us the songs of your tribe and as loudly as you can!" He grinned at her bemused expression and called across to Matshongi. "Rouse yourself, Boetie! You follow when she has done. Give us the songs of *Nkosinkulu, N'kosini, The Valley of the Kings . . .*" He looked at Joachim. "You also, Jo—after Boetie, or . . . better . . . with him."

The younger hunter stared back, disbelieving, earnestly resentful now.

"Sing any bloody thing you want, Jo—sing *The Great Sky and the Silence*, the old Boer one," Queen commanded.

The girl began, a lilting chant of the coast tribes that told, untruthfully, of the beauty of their women and the vigor of their lion-hearted swains. When she had drawn to a faltering close, smiling uncertainly, Queen patted her thigh. "Now, *unkonka*, take these to the warriors outside." He poured hefty slugs of brandy into the four extra gourds they had brought from the *aboura*. "Tell them a gift from the N'kosis of *Dukusa*, their new allies, which will warm them much more than their beer. Say also that they can have more of it when they want it."

The girl crawled through the entrance holding two of the gourds, and when Queen had handed the others out to her he nodded to Joachim, and himself began to launch roundly into song.

The girl returned. And together they all sang in full force,

287

only pausing sometime for one or the other to break wildly into a new melody, as though each had reached the point where song overcame them. Then at last Queen raised a hand. "All right, time to give our pals another drink." As Queen went through the entrance, the sound of Matshongi's bass rolled after him.

Outside in the rain the four spearmen, huddled in their blankets and karosses, shields tilted against the streaming downpour, rose unsteadily to their feet.

"*Sakubuna*, warriors! You need warmth and rest," Queen said expansively. He flung out a hand in emphasis and held up the bottle with the other. "*All* need warmth and rest, for tomorrow we march together against the cowards of Igonyela!" Queen staggered from one to another pouring brandy into each man's gourd.

The spearmen exchanged frowns and glances of perplexity, then one of them spoke.

"*Umlungu . . . N'kosi Umlungu*." He grudged the correction, but there was no doubt of what the hunter had done in the Valley. "You mean you are going to fight *with us*, with our impis?"

"Of course," the Afrikander said even more emphatically. "Have we not made alliance with your king? Has not *Ipyala*, our friend, yet told you of it?"

But was this not the gesture of a friend? Of allies, not captives? Even more convincing was the incontestable fact that the three hunters would have been long since executed had they been anything less than friends!

Queen took another swig from the bottle. As though suddenly taken by a generous thought, he said "Listen to me, warriors, there is room enough for two to share the dryness and warmth of the hut. Let two drink in warmth with us," holding up two fingers, "dividing the time left until sunrise. Then the other two?"

288

He waited for a moment, then turned with a shrug as if he did not intend to spend further time in the rain with stupid men too obtuse to throw off their own miserable lot. But as Queen turned to reenter the hut, two of the spearmen moved after him.

Inside the hut, Joachim took the Milebi's gourds and refilled them, smiling in comradeship.

"Warriors, tomorrow and after that there will be long days of marching." Queen made a grimace of resignation.

"That is true," the first spearman said morosely.

"However, there will be a great *aboura* when we take the kraal of the cowards. Plump women, fat beef, servants, much wine . . ." The second Milebi's eyes gleamed wolfishly.

"Yes, but before that the days will be long and the nights will be very cold, and we shall sleep uncovered," the Afrikander said. "The rains have come."

"True also," the first spearman said. "And I do not like that cold." He was older and thinner than the other guard, and he clearly disliked the prospect intensely.

"Be warm while you can then," Queen said. He drained his own gourd and handed it to the girl. "Drink, my friend, and when it is finished I will send the girl for more." He watched them closely as they emptied their gourds. And then Queen rose and went closer to the central pillar of the hut, the heavy palm bole to which prisoners were commonly bound back to back. He nodded to Joachim. The young man tossed both pair of handcuffs and Queen caught them, then held them up to catch the bright gleam of the plating in the light of the padella.

"Warriors, friends!" he called out. "See the bracelets of *Dukusa*, not common ornaments! Armillas of magical properties, for men of valor. Watch!" Queen stretched out his arms on either side of the log and Joachim closed the cuffs over his wrists, but did not snap them, and then Joachim removed them. "See!" Queen called. He motioned the spearmen to

289

draw closer. "Put out your hands and learn the strength and magic of these bracelets."

In seconds both spearmen were manacled to the pillar, agog at the fascinating ornaments linked around their wrists. Matshongi and Queen seized their throats, singing as they choked the Milebi to death, the gasps of the dying men overwhelmed by song.

Across the floor Joachim held the girl pinioned, his hand clamped over her mouth. Eyes wide with fear, she watched as Queen tore the *simi* from one of the dead Milebi and crawled toward her on his hands and knees. "Make no sound, my sweet, and you will come to no harm. But if you call out . . ." Queen held the long knife before her face, then gave it to Joachim. "Keep her quiet, Jo . . . and don't hesitate." He stared stonily for a second.

Joachim felt the tremors run through her as he repeated Queen's warning. And then he broke into song again.

Queen, this time joined by Matshongi, slipped outside again. The Afrikander called through the driving rain to the two huddled spearmen, who struggled to their feet. Queen held up a bottle for them to see.

"More, warriors?" He grinned. "Better than rainwater, eh?" Matshongi also held up a bottle, the club he had taken from one of the dead guards concealed behind his back as he moved forward.

One of the spearmen stepped forward, teetering as he came, his gourd held out in anticipation. Queen smashed the bottle over the man's head and caught him by the throat as he slumped. In the same instant, Matshongi rose on his toes and one could hear the bones shatter from the force of the murderous blow.

Queen dropped the man, utterly brained. The second guard lay sprawled on the ground, his head bashed in by the crushing blow from Matshongi's club.

290

As if it all had been carefully rehearsed, Queen kept watch while Matshongi dragged the corpses into the hut and Joachim handed out the terrified girl to the older man.

"Listen, *listen*," he said to the girl, his hand tight on her arm. "You go with us to the *isibaya* now. If any person calls out to you, you say that *Inyala* has sent for us. When we reach the cattle kraal, you will be free—but if you cry out or try to run," he touched the Milebi knife thrust in his belt, "I will slit your throat and belly. Do you understand?"

She stared anxiously, speechlessly—but when he shook her again, she nodded.

The prison hut stood twenty or thirty yards from the north boma of the village. Gripping her elbow, Queen ran across the open gap to the wall with the girl, and they waited as Joachim and Matshongi came on the run to join them. Here and there chinks of oil-wick light showed at intervals along the rows of huts.

They made another long stretch of the wall fronting the deserted aisles of huts, the woman panting from fear and exertion. Queen checked the way ahead, judging the distance that remained to the *isibaya*. When at last they reached the palisade of the corral, they strained to see over the fencing without being seen. The driving force of the rain had slackened now to a steady drizzle, and through it the *ryders* could just make out the blurred tableau of the wagon and the hobbled horses gathered near it.

Queen hunkered down and the others crouched beside him.

"Two of them, I think," he said, "guarding the wagon. What do you think, Boetie?"

The African nodded. "Yes, two, N'kosi. Sheltering beneath it."

"We'll have to take them from either side," Joachim whispered. He tapped the knife in his belt. "Try and hit them simultaneously and stop their mouths . . ."

291

"Who stays with the girl?"

"Nobody."

"You don't mean . . ." Joachim glanced down at Queen's knife.

"No," Queen said shortly. "Just lay her out. I'll do it. But not yet—when I come back."

"*Back?*"

"The *guns*," Queen said tersely. "Marao's hut." He turned to Matshongi. "Be sure there is no sound from the woman, Boetie, *no murmur.*" He rose to a crouch and began to lope along in the shadow of the palisade. He knew exactly where he was now, and just where the shack lay, about a hundred yards ahead.

When Queen saw the square shape of the hut showing just ahead, he halted. No chink of light came from under the door. Queen crouched and edged along the side of the shack until he reached the window. The hide drape was only pegged at the corners and he raised it slightly with the tip of his finger, listening hard. There was no sound from within, only the soft ploppeting of the rain on the roof and the awning. He moved further along and rose upright with the knife in his hand. There did not seem to be any fastening to the door, but he put his shoulder to it, threw his weight against it. It gave easily.

The place was empty.

Behind him a puff of wind flapped the curtain with the sound of a gentle slap and rustled the thatch of the awning where the layered grass had loosened from the canes. He found the packing case table. A Männlicher, his own or Joachim's, lay on another case with an opened box of ammunition and one of their bandoliers hung on the wall, but there was no sign of the other guns anywhere in the hut.

He opened both cases, but there were only tin dishes, tools, and liquor, and nothing was under the pallet.

He filled the magazine of the rifle and pocketed more ammunition. Light chinks showed from two of the women's huts, but the court was still deserted and he ran across it for the darker shadow of the wall. The others were still crouched against the palisade, the girl between them, silent and staring. Queen thrust the rifle into Joachim's hand. "All there was, but still worth it." He jerked his head. "All quiet?"

The younger man nodded.

"All right! Boetie and me, then—over the fence. You give us time enough to reach the wagon, then you come after us, fast, but don't, for Christ's sake, don't fire unless we're in real trouble." Queen turned to Matshongi and whispered rapidly for a moment or two—then the African began to move further back along the palisade. As he went, Joachim's attention went with him, and Queen dropped a short swift chop against the kaffir woman's jaw. She dropped like an unstrung puppet.

Now Queen began to belly-crawl toward the dark shape of the wagon. Thirty yards on the silence was broken by voices. He lay motionless, head down, until the brief exchange had ceased. A cow lowed from somewhere at the other end of the corral, and then, much nearer at hand, a horse whinnied nervously. Queen turned, feeling stones dig into his groin, and headed at a right-angle for the rear of the wagon. Ten yards from it he halted, bunched himself, and gave the signal, the hiss of the cobra.

At the answering hiss, a blanketed figure tumbled out from beneath the wagon with a cry of alarm. Queen sprang forward. He hit the startled spearman a tremendous blow in the stomach, and had the retching man on the ground; twice the big knife rose and fell. Queen heard the cry over his shoulder, and was rising as the second man appeared, slower than the first guard to grasp the significance of the cobra's hiss. His spear arm flew back to hurl, but the blade that came from behind and went flat to his neck was faster, and so powerfully yanked back against flesh and cartilage and bone that the head almost fell away from the body.

Matshongi swung the virtually headless Milebi around like

a top until the body spiraled down into a lifeless heap. Queen and the big African were staring wordlessly at each other as Joachim came on the run, the rifle clutched in his hands.

"The saddles, Jo! The horses, Boetie!" Queen whispered, and ran for his own horse and began to unhobble him.

It was then that they heard shouting from the far end of the kraal.

"For Christ's sake, Jo! The saddles!"

"There's only one, Robert!" Joachim threw it down.

Queen swung up and joined the younger man rooting around in the wagon. But there was only the saddle he had used when he had ridden out with Marao.

"I will ride bareback, N'kosi." Matshongi had the saddle across the stallion.

"No, let me—I'm well used to it." Joachim strode toward the other horse, but Queen cut in urgently. "No, *no!* Run for the gate—then get up behind me. You're much lighter than Boetie."

They trippled across Marao's open court for the south boma. There were still no signs of activity. But as they turned into the wide aisle between the front line of huts and the wall, men were running toward the main entrance of the kraal with torches spluttering in the rain. Queen snatched the rifle from Joachim's hands, dug in his heels and charged, with Matshongi's horse at a gallop alongside him. About a dozen spearmen were forming up to block the way. The big *ryder* fired as the horses cantered ahead. He had just time to work the bolt again as the horses reached full gallop. He fired one-handed—then swung the rifle by the barrel like a club.

Before the roar and flame of the shots and the thundering of the hooves, the Milebi wavered, and then broke as the howling horsemen smashed into them. Queen reeled in the saddle from the blow of a flung *knobkerrie*, recovered, and clove through the throng, savagely flailing around him. Beside him, almost abreast, Matshongi beat about him with his whirling club.

Joachim felt a hot stinging pain in his arm, but he clung on grimly with his knees and other arm, and then they were through the melee and out onto the open veld.

"Matty! Matty is down!" Joachim screamed.

For a second, in the aberration of his fury, Queen seemed not to have heard. Then he brought the horse round in a swirling wheel. Fifty yards back, halfway between themselves and the wavering torches at the gate, Matshongi's horse was on its side, thrashing and shrieking, spear hafts projecting from its flank and belly. Matshongi had just got to his feet. He plucked the long blade from his thigh, blood streaming from the severed artery and from a second wound in his shoulder, and braced himself.

Queen fired into the knot of spearmen advancing from the kraal. He dropped one man, then another, and then the magazine clicked empty.

Matshongi turned. He made a sweeping gesture and shouted. "Go, N'kosi! Go!" Then he turned again, pulled himself erect, and began to move toward the advancing pack of Milebi, his club held across his broad chest.

Joachim made an effort to dismount, but the big *ryder* held him in the saddle. "No!" he shouted, and then he whispered, "No." Queen wheeled the stallion away and they rode hard across the open ground. At the top of a rise he reined in and turned once more. The yelling mob of Milebi near the gate were just discernible, clustered around something on the ground, their spears and clubs rising and falling.

Again the younger man struggled to dismount, but Queen locked him in his arm. "Just look back, Jo, and remember," he said, his face hardened like stone. Then his heels dug in, and he kept the horse to a run until the night closed in black all around them.

295

Message
to Morgan

They had pressed on steadily for the best part of an hour before Queen became aware of the young *ryder's* wound. It was when Queen felt Joachim slump and then shift position to grip Queen's belt that Queen understood. He reined in and dismounted near a gully that held water.

"Jesus Christ!" the big man swore when he saw the wound. Even in the dim light Joachim's face showed drawn and pallid.

Queen got the wad of gun-cloth from his saddlebag. The spear had grazed Joachim's ribs and then gone all the way through his upper arm. The bone did not seem to be broken, but the gash was wide and the blood ran as if there was no stopping it.

Queen made a pad of the mutton-cloth and sponged at the blood until he could see the ragged edges of the thing more clearly. Then he spread the wad lengthwise and folded it, binding it tightly around while Joachim pinched the gaping lips of the wound together. With brushwood and his bandana Queen fashioned a tourniquet, and adjusted the length of his bandolier to make a sling.

He sat back on his heels. "Should hold it still and that's the main thing," Queen said, knowing otherwise, knowing the

296

curse of a climate where infection spread with lethal rapidity, and thinking of the long, long trek ahead.

Joachim tried to smile and Queen tried to smile back. But both men knew what was ahead. "You ride," Queen said. "I'll walk a while."

"Too slow," Joachim said. "I'm all right now."

"Keep that arm steady as you can, that's the main thing, boyo. We'll walk till sun-up," Queen said flatly.

The rain had begun to slacken, driven by a gathering wind. Queen helped the injured man up into the saddle, slung the rifle on his shoulder and took the bridle in his other hand and began to head south. They marched this way until the first streaks of the false dawn had come and gone. Then Joachim slid from the saddle and begged Queen to ride for a while, but the big *ryder* still refused. So they kept on marching together, through the true dawn and until the sun was fully risen before dropping down beside a *spruit* that was no longer dry, its choked tangle of myrrh and sanseveria scrub glinting wet in the hard sunlight.

The stream seemed to come from a ridge of higher ground far to their right and then skirted a hill a little way ahead. But the plain it traversed was arid undulating veld land, and you could not see far in any direction because of the rolling folds and the scattered islands of acacia.

The bandage looked like strawberry mush now, but the fly pests had not yet arrived and the blood drippings did not seem unduly fast.

"Throbbing like hell, eh boy? Pretty sore? But it looks as if the damn thing's drying up all the same," Queen said, still knowing otherwise. "Must have the knack of good healing, you must. Me, I bleed like a stuck pig for nothing at all." Queen kept up this sort of patter from time to time, and from time to time he studied the young *ryder's* face, the haggard skin grayer and grayer each time Queen looked. "Now you rest

297

that arm another few minutes while I take a look from the *kopje* up yonder," Queen said.

He called to the stallion browsing the scrub of the *spruit*, swung into the saddle when he came, and began to lope easily across the flat. From the crest of the ridge, the land ahead stretched away in a limitless sameness, but far, far away to the west, Queen could see through the freshly clarified air a straggling outline that rose from the horizon and was a deeper blue. It would be all of fifty miles off, maybe a good deal more, but it had to be the great Ridge, and Queen felt a stab of elation because now, with that distant landmark on their right, there would be no difficulty in setting the fastest, most direct course for Igonyela.

But as the good feeling rose in him, the prospect of hope, he heard a shout and wheeled. *Joachim was running!* And running toward *him*, moving to cut him off, spearmen were racing down the talus of the ridge from which the *spruit* had seemed to emanate. There were about a dozen of them, and with them a single horseman rode; now he began to forge ahead of the tribesmen toward the wounded man.

Queen spurred the stallion hard and pounded back down the hill onto the flat at full gallop. Teeth gritted, heart hammering, Joachim was running for his life, summoning all the strength his legs had to give. He was losing nothing to the Milebi, but in minutes he would be overtaken by the rider coming at a tangent, and the man had already drawn his pistol. The aspect of the two horsemen charging was like a combat of knights, but without chivalry, in deadly earnest, and in which the prize was no accolade of prowess but the life of the injured running man. Bent low, calling to the stallion, Queen's mind raced. Marao had too much start, too much ground advantage on him. Only the range of the Männlicher might cancel it and he dared not waste another second.

298

He brought the stallion to a rearing standstill and slid from the saddle in one movement, shouting the firing order to the horse. The exhausted stallion froze as commanded, his flanks heaving a little but his back steady enough as Queen laid the long black barrel across it.

Marao was nearing the point when he must veer to come up behind the running man. Queen followed the horse with the foresight, drew fractionally ahead, and fired. The brown mare reared with shock, almost unseating her rider, and Queen returned the bolt as she came down squarely again. This time he raised the bead a shade, and the horseman jerked erect in the saddle as though he had touched an electric current. He fell forward, then pitched out of the saddle, and was dragged along before his foot dropped out of the stirrup and the mare raced away on a fresh course, panicked and stung by the bullet that had furrowed her mane.

Now Queen was in the saddle again and blasting toward the runner, more than a spear's throw ahead of his pursuers, and even gaining now, for the destruction of their *Umlungu* commander and the spectacle of the charging fury of the Afrikander had clearly daunted the spearmen—except for the rabid yelling Induna who raced at the lead of the pack.

The hunter leaped from the saddle again as he reached Joachim. "Up, Jo!" He turned as Joachim struggled up into the saddle, then Queen stood, the rifle across his thighs, teeth bared in a murderous grimace. He let the Induna come on to almost the distance of a spear's cast before he brought up the gun, and then, as the throwing arm went back, Queen shot him full in the face. Before the empty shell had hit the ground, Queen dropped to one knee and laid a heavy load into the next spearman's belly. As the man faltered to a halt, Queen swung to a third Milebi and took him between the shoulder blades. This was proof enough. The spearmen left standing turned

299

and sprinted away, the hysteria in them so great some flinging away their weapons as they sprinted for distance and cover.

Joachim's face was drained with stress. The blood dripped freely from the crook of his arm now, and he seemed incapable of speech.

Queen studied the sodden blotch that was the young *ryder's* arm. "Set us back with that arm, did they?" Again, he tried to smile at Joachim, but couldn't. "Let's see if the *smouse* can provide anything useful," Queen said, and trotted to where Marao lay prone, face in profile, bloody lips drawn back from bloody teeth in a contorted grin.

Queen stripped him and checked his gear. There was a tin of cigarettes and some matches, a roll of whipcord, and the man's bandana. The pistol lying nearby was one of their Buntline Colts, and Joachim's Männlicher had been slung across the half-breed's shoulder, the magazine full, but no ammo other than what Queen found in Marao's chest pouches, and there was no bandolier.

Queen rebound the wound with strips of Marao's shirt and covered it with more shirting to keep out the flies. As he worked, he checked the lacerated flesh for hints of bad color.

When both men were mounted, Queen behind now, so that he could check Joachim from slipping from the saddle, they headed to the hilltop. Before and behind them, bounded only by the horizon and the vague distant blur of the escarpment, the yellow-brown plain stretched endlessly, and the overhanging pall of silence seemed matchlessly immense.

It was Joachim who saw the smoke.

"Jesus, Robert . . . *there!*"

Queen followed the direction of the other man's gaze, shading his eyes, then nodded. "Right!" Queen frowned. "Can't be a cooking fire, not this time of day, and it's no grass fire. Signal fire. Hundred to one on it. Pursuit party, for sure!

And for sure there must be more coming after them. A lot more."

"They'll never catch us now—this far ahead," Joachim said, his voice very weak now.

"Don't worry," Queen said. "We'll keep ahead of them, lad."

*   *   *

It was mid-morning of the second day now. Sharing the rest in two watches, they had been traveling steadily since the skirmish at the donga. They had stuck to a pattern, marching most of the night and moving in relays of walking and riding. Their progress was frighteningly slow. But each time they had ridden they had, without taxing the stallion, set a pace appreciably faster than that at which a man could trot. By Queen's reckoning, they should have maintained their lead.

Since dawn they had crossed two rivers and there would be a score or more ahead. But despite the storm that had rolled ahead of them, the fordings had been easy enough, little more than fetlock deep, no need to hunt for drifts. Direct crossings without delays had seemed like a good omen. But presently they were traversing a fold of rising ground, and when they had crested the rise Queen's hope fled. The river below them coursed powerfully, and it was very wild!

He swore vehemently. "Must have been a freak cloudburst here—either that or the storm hit the Ridge up near the source."

"We'll find a drift," the young *ryder* said.

From the rise they could see a fair distance up and down the river, but there were no obvious shallows.

Queen spat. "*That* could take half an hour—if we were really in luck—or it could take hours!"

"Or twice as much still if we weren't lucky," Joachim said.

301

Queen nodded and moved the horse slowly down to the water. He watched a swath of dead osier brush swim by. From here, the surface flow did not seem impossibly swift, but boulder tips here and there were lapped with frothy spume, and there would be a strong and treacherous undertow beyond any doubt.

"We'll give it a try," he said, "taking it slow and steady, me leading."

"I can wade, Robert, and if we each take a rein . . ."

The older man broke in explosively. "You'll ride him! I'm free to swim if I have to! You just watch that arm. Besides, it will steady him with you up." Queen wrapped the pistol belt around his neck, cross-slung his rifle, and took the stallion's bridle.

The water rose slowly at first, wavelets lapping against the horse's legs and his own, then rising to Queen's knees, then to his thighs. Slowly, feeling with his feet, sometimes half-stumbling, threading between the scatterings of visible and submerged boulders, he forced on a further hundred yards toward a heap of big rocks. In the lee of the pile, he rested for a while, breathing deeply, and raised his voice above the roar of the water. "The next stretch will be the tough one. If I have to let go—swim for it—give him his head and hang on! He'll swim it, all right!

Queen launched out again. For seventy yards further the water still drove around his waist, then it began to deepen, and the pull of the current grew increasingly stronger. They were into the central channel now, and the water rose to Queen's chest, the unrelenting pressure of the flow was almost irresistible, so that his foothold was repeatedly swept away in mid-stride. Queen leaned against the current like a man in a hurricane, laboring from one outcrop to another, pitting his strength and weight against the force of the thundering torrent. The water was almost to his armpits now, and their progress across the open strips was broken as they were thrown back downstream. They would flounder forward a few yards, and then be swept in a curve like careening fish dragged off course, so that now they were a hundred yards downriver from where they had entered the wide water.

Now they were stationary, horse and man bearing against the hillock of a submerged islet as Queen braced himself for the next gasping effort. He stared at the expanse of riffled brown flow still ahead of them and saw that, miraculous as it seemed, they were halfway across. More than halfway. He gave a forward jerk of his head, sucked in air, and plunged forward. For a few yards he made his way ahead, then suddenly the bed beneath his feet was gone and he went under. He felt himself being swept downstream, but held onto the bridle; seconds later his head broke water, and his toes bottomed on bedrock.

They were over the fistula they had blundered into, but he had no thought of respite. The momentary sensation of drowning had driven everything from his mind except the determination to get through this last sector before he weakened and they were swept back again into the millrace of the main channel. Plodding, stumbling, Queen ploughed on, twenty yards, thirty. Then the water level began to descend to his waist and the jag of the current eased. He slogged toward a heap of jetsam piled against a rock, dropped the bridle and steadied himself against the boulder, breathing in gulps. Jesus God, Robert Queen thought, as he slumped against the rock trying to quiet his heart, oh Jesus God!

*   *   *

For a while Queen lay flat on his back, hat shading his eyes from the torrid noonday sun. Nearby, spread on porous bank boulders already hot enough to cook an egg, his clothes were laid to dry. A few yards away Joachim sat with his back

303

against a rock watching the stallion nuzzling the sparse bank vegetation. Overhead the sky was clear cobalt, but further back the way they had come a scattering of dark clouds showed against the white and blue feathers of the cirrus.

"More rain coming, Robert," Joachim said.

Queen turned his head and looked for a moment. "Might be a bloody good thing at that."

"How so?"

"*We've* crossed this one direct. Any more rain, and I'm bloody sure *they* won't, not direct anyhow."

The pain in Joachim's arm had been bad for hours now, and it seemed a different kind of pain, deeper-seated, a kind of rumbling. But he had said nothing about it and now he gave the trace of a smile because the Afrikander's note of hope had buoyed his own failing heart for it all.

"Do you feel ready to move yet, Robert?" the young *ryder* asked tentatively, half apologetically. "You riding, of course—I've had it easy."

Queen returned the younger man's flicker of a smile. "You're a hard bloody *voorloper*, all right, *Jong*. We could lay right here and laugh at 'em if they came up the other side back there right this minute. They haven't got a one could throw a spear a quarter the way over, and I'd just love 'em to show long enough to try it. But, yes, all right, man—we'll go now."

He got into his clothes and whistled to the stallion. When the big horse came trotting back, Queen pushed Joachim up, the young *ryder* too weak to argue, too dazed to frame a protest. But just as he was himself about to mount, a small patch of color along the riverbank caught his eye. Queen stroked his horse in that direction. It was the nepenthe plant, all right, leaves shaped like miniature pitchers. The big *ryder* gathered nearly all of them, sticking the bundle into his shirtfront. Joachim watched inquiringly. "Pitcher plant," Queen said, and winked. "Old Doc Queen can still teach you something yet, eh, *Jong*? Juice is a pain killer . . . really works . . . will come in handy for that arm next time we dress it."

All through the long grueling heat of afternoon they slogged steadily ahead. Since the breakout the only food they had shared had been a nest of guinea fowl's eggs and some wild figs. Now, both men were ravenously hungry, and it was the sight of partridges planing down to a gully that reminded them of it. But there was no risking the rifle, the report would carry miles over such flat unbroken country. It would be no use, anyway. They had no shotgun, and without the advantage of spreadshot, it would be nearly impossible to get more than one of the birds. Besides, the heavy softnose bullet would pulverize a partridge's small body. It was useless.

Even so, they had no other prospect of food, and Queen had almost decided to stalk the partridges when, with a sudden uproar of grunting and squealing, two creatures burst from the mopanis up ahead. Cut out and headed off from its family root-hunting along the donga, the young wart-hog ran with frantic desperation. A stone's throw behind the pig, following its weaving course as though invisibly attached to its victim, the cheetah gained on its quarry with every lightning bound. In a matter of seconds the small drama reached its climax, and the death screams of the pig ended as the cat's incisors sank into the pig's throat.

Queen fairly leaped with excitement. "Eh, Jo, eh?" he cried. "Never thought I'd be grateful to a bloody cat. Walk on up to the trees, see if you can get some wood together, while I collect our supper." Queen slid from the horse, then remounted when he had helped the younger man down.

"Try and finish him with just one, Robert. Wait till he's set right," Joachim said. "The noise, I mean . . ."

"You must be joking, *boyo*," Queen said, and cantered toward the crouching tableau on the veld some two hundred

305

yards ahead. The big slim cat stood ready for Queen, saw the horse and man coming, stood away from the wart-hog, ears flattened, tail twitching with anger. It spat with malignant emphasis, but when the horseman still came on steadily, the cat seized the piglet by the neck and started to lope away. Queen dug in his heels, and as the cheetah heard the galloping hooves behind, it began to streak in earnest. Unhampered, it could have made twice the pace of the horse, though not for long. But burdened as it was, the cat dropped the pig and turned at bay in less than a hundred yards, panting, mouthing its rage.

Queen came to a standstill twenty yards away. He reared the stallion, let it paw the air, a display of the size and shape of the horse-and-man aggressor. Then he vaulted down and began to walk toward the bunched fury, rifle on hair-trigger and a round in the chamber. But he brandished the gun like a club and now he began to shout as he walked.

The cat stood his ground, poised to charge, but the human voice was too much for it, and the cheetah wheeled and ran. Queen swung the dead wart-hog over his shoulder and strolled back to the horse. The pig was a half-grown sow and so fresh her pork would be tough, but the thought of the liver and kidneys made his mouth water.

*   *   *

The grass here was sour but green. To the south, occasional clumps of palm and banana had begun to dot the savannah. The mopanis would give screening and there was sufficient water in the donga for their needs. They went through the trees and down the gully a little way, where the cooking fire would be hidden, and began to search for wood. But the young man's face was very drawn, and Queen made him quit the search for wood.

"Use your head, *Jong!*" He pointed to the bank of the rill.

"Get yourself settled. You've lost a peck of blood, boy, and you're still losing some. What you need is sleep, and pig's blood. After we've eaten, we'll take a look at that arm, make a *lappie* poultice with the leaves, and then you'll sleep."

Joachim closed his eyes and waited for a moment until the floating specks had cleared away. The new deep pain was louder now, brasses joined the woodwinds, and sometimes now Joachim had spasms of near-swooning and clouded vision.

Queen began to move off up the gully, figuring to risk making camp and letting Joachim sleep until midnight. When he had the dry grass and wood set up, he made fire a way he had learned from his father, using the powder of a bullet wrapped in rag and pounded with a stone to set the cloth smoldering. He cut the pig's offal into strips, pierced the slivers with a green wand, and hung them over the fire. By the time he had knee-halted the stallion and found more wood, the meat was ready enough and they ate it half-raw, savoring the heavy sustaining blood content.

It was nearing dusk by the time they had finished eating and Queen turned to the task of peeling away the sodden bandages. They had moved across the donga into the open to get the best light and, kneeling, Queen bent closely to examine the angry-red oozing gashes on either side of the young *ryder's* arm. For a long time he studied the torn flesh—and when he straightened up, he could not disguise his eyes.

"It is not good—eh, Robert?"

"I don't know, Jo—not really, you know."

"It is *vrot?*"

Queen said nothing, trying to look away as if he had something more important on his mind. "Tell me the truth, Robert!"

Queen lowered his glance again to the ugly lacerations. The lips of the wound were blue-green, and the blood issued easily with any small movement. But there was also the thing that he had dreaded, the faint odor he thought he detected. He looked up again, this time hard into Joachim's half-open eyes.

"I don't know, *Jong* . . . I don't know enough. But we may have been unlucky."

"If it is *vrot*, the leaves will be of no use, the poultice?" the younger man asked quietly.

"They may help the pain. They cannot kill infection."

"How long will it take before it is certain, Robert?"

"Hell, I don't know, *boyo.*"

Joachim looked away. He drew in a breath. "Then should we not take the arm off soon? Now?" he said levelly.

"I couldn't do that, Jo—I just don't know enough." Queen stared across at the fire. He turned his head again and saw the look in the young man's face that was not fear, not bitterness, but a terrible abiding disappointment. "Wait, boy—wait." He gripped Joachim's good arm. "That isn't the only way— there's another if you catch it soon enough, and we're soon enough." Queen didn't know if this was true, only that he had once seen it done to a running gangrenous wound in the thigh, had helped hold the man down, and the man had survived and recovered, with a scar in his leg that you could have laid a cigar in. But the man had his leg.

"Yes?" Joachim's face had lighted up with expectancy, an artless look of belief that made Queen's heart wince.

"It's a bloody tough thing," Queen said slowly. "There will be more pain than you have ever imagined, but it kills the infection and seals the bleeding."

Joachim was silent. He stared at the fire, his lids drooping, his face blanched.

"All right?" Queen said.

"All right," Joachim said.

The big man nodded. He began to move along the bottom of the donga hunting the stones in the edge of the rill. When he had three that were long enough and smooth enough to satisfy him, he returned to the fire and made a criss-crossed pattern of wood over it, placing the stones on the raft of branches so that they would also subside onto the heart of it and lie on the coals.

Joachim sat with his back against a rock. He was very tired now, and the pain gnawed incessantly. But he felt the strange calm of a man whose spirit has been abased and then restored.

Queen watched the stones and the fire. The wood was nearly consumed now and the stones lay in the bed of embers that glowed red whenever the night breeze touched them.

"One thing first," Queen said with measured emphasis. "When I do it, you have got to hold on, like you never held onto anything before."

"I understand," the younger man said quietly. Queen took a forked stick and raked the stones to the edge of the fire. "Now give me your arm."

He took the young man's wrist tightly, then took up the first stone with the pad of wet rag he had made from the discarded bandaging and brought the flat surface of it down onto the wound, pressing hard into the lips of the gash. Above his own concentration, he heard the frightful indrawn gasp, the hiss of tortured tissue that was like the sound of meat plunged into boiling fat; the smell of scorching flesh filled his nostrils. But he held Joachim's wrist like a vice, exerting all his strength, bracing his weight against the other man's writhings, pinioning him against the boulder at his back until Queen himself could no longer bear the heat of the stone through the steaming rags and let it fall.

When Queen turned, Joachim was on his knees, head thrown back, body tautened like a bow, swaying back and forth from the hips and moaning, eyes squeezed shut, mouth twisted into a grimace of purest agony.

Queen hit him hard, below the ear, with the edge of his

hand—and caught him in his arm. Swiftly, he doused the rags in the water and snatched up the second stone. This time he seared the underside of the wound. The senseless man stiffened as if a bolt had been hammered through him, mouthing inarticulately, mind beyond the evidence of pain.

When it was done, Queen made a poultice from the juice of nepenthe leaves and bound the wad in place with shirting. He lifted Joachim and laid him so that his head was pillowed on the saddle. And then Robert Queen sat back to watch his friend. From time to time the man moaned and stirred. But, mercifully, he slept.

*   *   *

Several times during the night Joachim rose to silently pace back and forth, the motion seeming to give him some kind of solace. But when dawn broke, he was sleeping again, and Queen had moved a little way along the gully to wash himself without waking Joachim.

When he returned the young *ryder* was on his feet, eyes drawn and ringed with the exhaustion of unremitting stress. But his resolution, and the dominating urge to push on had not weakened.

Ahead of them an isolated *kopje* rose from the flatness of the plain. It was the first hill of any account that they had encountered since full daylight and Queen nodded toward it. "Baked some strips before I doused the fire last night, Jo, we'll take a good look from the *kopje* and eat some pork while we're doing it."

They kept walking until they had led the horse to the top of the hill. In the foreground, a herd of migrant wildebeest were heading toward the eastern horizon, but, save for the straggling gnus, there was no other sign of animation. Behind, the yellow sea offered even less evidence of life, yet Queen could

310

not rid himself of a feeling that it was not empty. It was several minutes before he noticed the far-off speck on the great tan carpet.

It took a further moment of concentration to determine that the black speck was not some stationary feature, a patch of *vlei*, say. Queen waited until he was quite sure, because it could still have been a small parcel of animals—buffalo or kudu—but then he knew for certain that it was not.

He had to tell Joachim.

"It'll be another pursuit group, all right, knowing you're wounded and counting on us resting up."

"How far back you reckon, then?"

"Hour. Not much more." Queen shook his head. "Listen," he said slowly. "They've been following our spoor, it's plain enough . . . so they'll know we're walking and riding, not making the pace of a horse, and likely they'll believe you're in bad trouble by now. Pretty soon they'll come up on the remains of the fire, and they'll know from it that we're not far up ahead. That will bring them on, hard as they can go. Likely by sundown. We've got a bloody long way to go, a bloody lot more rivers to cross yet, and we might have to make detours, hunt drifts—we don't *know*. That's the danger . . . and if they jumped us in the night . . ." Queen stared around him, as if looking for something. Joachim tried to follow him with his eyes, but the effort made him dizzy and he gave it up. He looked blankly ahead.

"What do you want to do, Robert?" he said tonelessly.

"Blast 'em!" the big *ryder* said shortly. "Stay and blast 'em—in daylight—just as soon as we find a place suits us. Ambush the bastards."

Queen touched the sling of his rifle. "Six in here, counting the spout, and not forgetting the hair-trigger."

The hour was nearly gone before Queen found a position

311

that looked tenable. What he had been looking for was a place to hide the wounded man, and the horse, a place that was within easy distance of some feature, a *bult* outcrop, a donga, that would give him separate cover. The island of trees was as good a redoubt as they were likely to find, with a wide open view of the plain behind them.

"We stand here, then, Robert? Keeping within the trees?" Joachim said, near to fainting; working to hold himself in the saddle.

"You will, *boyo*," Queen said. "Except you'll sit, stay mounted."

"Oh, no, Robert, not on your own—I can use the pistol well enough."

"I know you can, and you would, Jo, but the pistol is one reason why I want you to stay here." He saw Joachim's puzzled expression and continued, "I want to get two or three fast, on the hair-trigger. I do that and the others may run, like the first lot. If not I'll stalk the bastards up through the *djik*." He shrugged. "Trouble is though, I'm going to need the pistol in case it comes to that . . . there wouldn't be time to work the bolt."

Joachim looked helplessly at the ground, nodding.

"Don't worry, it will work," Queen said brusquely.

*   *   *

Left alone, Joachim tethered the stallion and began to search the copse until he found a seedling tree that was not too firmly set in the leaf mould of its progenitors. Working with one arm, it had taken all his strength, but finally he had managed to uproot the seedling and drag it along to the fringe of the trees.

He saw the first wisps of smoke curling up from the donga—Queen's diversionary fire. That would be the focal point of the attack, assuming that it followed Queen's plan.

Joachim laid the sapling against the bole of one of the outermost trees. Sitting behind his improvised screen, he found a position where he could fork-rest the rifle through the branches with a clear view down along the donga and over the forefront of open ground. His good right arm was free to work the bolt. Now he settled in to wait and watch, his back rested against the other side of the tree from where the rifle was propped.

Queen positioned himself in an elbow of the donga. Lying against an incline, he could see the expanse of grassland before him through a gap in the sansevieria straggling over the parapet. Standing upright, he could overlook the brush in the watercourse on either side of him.

It was Joachim who saw the phalanx of Milebi first, from his higher elevation. He gave the signal birdcall. The Milebi came over a rise, and then were lost in the fold for a moment or two before Joachim could count them with certainty. When they came out onto the flat again, there were seven of them, counting the Induna who led, moving uniformly at their steady martial trot.

They had seen Queen's smoke some time ago, and now already, far out still, they began to move warily, coming forward at the crouch. At five hundred yards they dropped to their bellies, and though there was little real cover an enemy would have been lucky to descry any of them as they came on unless he had already known what was happening. For there was only the fleeting glimpse, sometimes, of a black back crossing an arid patch where the grass grew thinly, or not at all.

Queen concentrated on a strip of ground two hundred yards out where the alkaline dust showed through and that was in line with the smoldering fire he'd made. Minutes passed. He saw a body snake over the tract. He lowered his head to the stock and transferred his attention to an area just beyond the distance of a maximum spear throw from the donga, waiting for the silent rush—and when they rose from the grass he was ready.

He dropped the Induna, a few yards ahead of the others, before the man was fully upright, and an instant later he thumped a second spearman, firing as the Milebi ran forward into his foresight. Now they were running hard for the donga, fanning out, each holding the first of his javelins poised for the throw. A spear arced just over his head and another plunged into the sansevieria beside him. There were two warriors coming right at him now, several yards apart, their faces charged with hate and the insensate disregard of danger. They were high on *dakha*, and there was no fear in them as they came. He had just time to fire once more, dropping the spearman to his right and grabbing for the pistol at his hip when he heard another rifle report and the oncoming Milebi screamed and fell. Queen grabbed up the rifle from where he had dropped it, rammed back the bolt, and got the spearman through the head as he lay moaning and clutching at his smashed hip.

Christ! There were only three now! And Joachim was, by Christ, shooting! Queen felt a surge of savage elation at the success of his tactics, and for the luck of the shot from the trees. Now he could make a wide detour to the trees, keeping beyond spear range, and since Jo had somehow found a way of using his gun, with every confidence of crossfire support. Queen crouched down, refilled the magazine of the Männlicher, and waited several minutes. Nothing stirred. It seemed clear the Milebi had abandoned the initiative. He slung the rifle on his left shoulder, taking the Colt, and began to move out very slowly.

At a bend in the donga he halted, brushed the sweat from his eyes, and had just edged around the elbow when he saw the tip of a spear and fired into the brush below it. He knew that he had missed, and before he could fire again, the spearman rose, but there was another shot, and the Milebi shrieked and pitched forward across the brush that had hidden him. He hung draped over a yellow ramal like a sack, and Queen could see the red stain between his shoulder blades, but just the same he shot him through the ear as he drew close.

He heard Joachim's shout, followed by another shot. He scrambled up the bank of the donga.

The two spearmen, unnerved by the death scream of their comrade and the firing from both sides, had now broken from the donga and were running hell-for-leather back the way they had come. The foremost runner had already made a hundred yards and, with instinctive canniness, was weaving like a buck pursued by a cheetah. But the second man, slower to jump cover and less clever, had not gone far and was running straight. Queen's first shot missed narrowly, but his second took the fleeing Milebi in the small of his back.

The Afrikander let the rifle slump in his hands. It had not been the total destruction he had wanted, but it had been good. Queen started for the trees, then broke into a run, shouting as he went. "Bring the horse! Jo! Bring him!"

The younger man came from the trees, leading the horse, just before Queen reached the copse. Queen sprang into the saddle, dropping the rifle and pistol at Joachim's feet, then reaching back to check for the other rifle in the saddle-bucket.

Out across the plain, well away, the Milebi was still running, slackening pace now, feeling safe. But when he saw the horseman starting after him, he ran full speed again. Bent low in the saddle, urging the stallion to full gallop, Queen began to cut the quarry's lead. The Milebi veered toward an islet of scrub, the only achievable refuge within his vision. Queen reined in, drawing Joachim's rifle from the saddle-bucket.

He fired from the saddle and his first shot whined past the

runner's head. The Milebi was less than a spear throw from the scrub now. When the rifle crashed again, he crumpled.

Joachim had seen no real purpose in the pursuit and slaughter of the last Milebi. What he *had* seen was the look of obsession on Queen's face, a kind of fierceness that transcended revenge. It was something else. It was killing.

*   *   *

The light was beginning to fade. It was important to push on, find drinkable water for the horse, for themselves. But they had only gone a few yards from the trees, when Queen pointed.

"What about him?"

Joachim followed the big *ryder's* outstretched arm. In his absorption with what had occurred, and his desire to be gone from the place, he had forgotten. "Yes," he nodded, turning the horse's head, and they rode back across the donga.

The Milebi had been mortally hit, but he was alive. It was the spearman who had burst from the donga, and he seemed to have been trying to reach the gully ever since he had been shot, for a wavering blood trail marked his excruciating progress.

When they drew up beside the senseless figure, Queen reached for the pistol and slid to the ground. Then, abruptly, inexplicably, he turned, thrust the gun into Joachim's good hand and walked away.

Joachim took the pistol. It was right that they should share it. He aimed carefully and fired.

*   *   *

It was noon of the third day now, and since the critical fight at the donga they had crossed a dozen more rivers. There had recently been substantial rainfall, and the rivers had been running toward full capacity. But none of the crossings had been as arduous as the first major test far back in the Milebi country.

They had reached another river now, a sullen treacly expanse as brown as peat, from which, here and there, in the fierce heat, thin vapory wisps like airborne cobweb strands rose from the shallows. From the saddle Joachim peered down at the murky barrier. It was impossible to judge the likely depth of the water, the strength of the underset flow.

"A bad one, Robert?"

Queen did not reply.

They were hours finding a drift and a long time crossing, and when they'd made it to the other bank, the immense fatigue was visible in both men, the test of these fugitive days telling on them powerfully. They sat on the opposite bank, trying to restore themselves, but the weariness was too deep now for the little respite Queen could dare. Joachim's face was deep-laid with the lines and shadings of pain and fatigue, but when he saw Queen's face, saw the ruin of their flight reflected there, he said: "You ride him for a spell after this. I'll walk for a while." His voice was barely audible.

Queen leaned back on his elbows, surveying his out-stretched legs as the tension drained from them. "No, we'll rest here a while longer, and then we'll both walk, but taking it easier." He nodded toward the stallion. "He can't take much more of this."

"All right." The younger man looked at the horse, and then out at the veld that lay ahead of them, then back the way they had come. For a long moment he studied the panorama around him, oblivious to everything save the grinding effort of the long trek and the nagging throb of his wound.

In the mid-afternoon, leaving dead flat country, they approached a gradual incline that stretched for two or three miles to either side of them, like a ramp thrown up by gargantuan ploughshares. Nearer to the summit of the slope

317

they became aware of a curious murmuring sound that was like the muffled rumble of far distant thunder. Involuntarily, they quickened pace and then, at the brink of the incline, stood thunderstruck.

Before them, all along the foot of the screes of the ridge thirty feet below, a vast multitude of beasts were moving in such close-packed proximity that a man could have walked across their backs. The unending cavalcade was made up of thousands of buck, but here and there large pockets of taller beasts, zebra and wildebeest, were mingled with the living tide. Over all hung a strange air of uncaring listlessness, as though the animals had lost all normal apprehensions.

Joachim shook his head, amazed. "I've seen migrations, of course, but not like this—not like a *sea* . . ."

Queen nodded. "I've heard of them—not ordinary seasonal migrations—happens very rarely, but it happens. Drought. Bad drought where they come from, months without any let-up."

"But . . ." It came to the younger man now that the curious sound they had heard was the noise of countless hooves that only scuffed and did not pound the ground. "They're *walking*."

For an hour they watched the broad tide of lyre-shaped horns and plodding dust-caked bodies roll by before they were able to move on again, marching and riding, until, as the sun began its descent in the western sky, they saw at last the smudge of Igonyela's fires and, soon after, heard the faint lowing of cattle. If there had been strength in them left to do it, they would have cheered with triumph and with joy. But there was no strength left in them for that—not even to consider their great fortune, the great fortune of their escape—and their salvation. There was nothing left in these *ryders* now save an abiding quiet and the dream of the hell they had left behind them. They had come through something huge and impossible and horrible. It was a tale their bodies told but which their hearts could never narrate. Whatever it was, it was over. It had changed them in ways that would never be changed back again, and it was over.

They slept.

And as they slept that long and delirious night, Igonyela's drums carried the message to *Dukusa*.

Leproso
de Nambana

Santoro detached one heel from the rail of the *stoep* and reached down for the bottle on the boards beside him. The gentle coastal breeze felt good, and his new shantung silk shirt and white Lisboan terai filled him with a sense of well-being. But then he always felt good in Nambana.

For one thing, there was his friendship with the trader, the man Sancho Baro. And there was the food, the liquor, and the women.

He finished off the wine and dragged himself to his feet. At the door of the saloon, he shouted across the half-filled room for another bottle, and then returned to his chair on the low balcony outside. The street leading up from the waterfront was crowded with strollers. Yellow, brown, Asiatic and coal-black faces, workers and riff-raff intermingled with a sprinkling of Afrikanders, farmers, and planters. A grizzled African tribesman clad simply in an old black bowler hat and a reed skirt came by Santoro's balcony seat, and was followed by a slim hawk-faced Arab in flowing white burnous, attended by a bodyguard of two burly Nubian slave-mariners. It was a dazzling display, this motley throng.

Along past the walls of the old slave compounds, that now

held only·the likes of sheep and goats for purchase, yet still sometimes witnessed the passing of long columns of shackled humans in the dead of the moon, on the far side from the harbor, stood the Glee Hall. It was a rickety iron-roofed barn where the native brews of beer and wine came dirt cheap, and nightly there was shuffling dancing to the beat of drums and tambourines.

Abruptly, down by the stockades, the flow of people began to break away to either side and Santoro bent forward over the rail to see what had altered the stream of traffic into two eddies. He peered uncertainly, then he saw what had parted the crowd, and slumped back into his chair again.

The leper plodded slowly up the incline toward the docks and the harbor, his head lowered and his tattered Panama pulled down to hood his eyes. But when he had labored on fifty yards or so and saw the white of Santoro's hat above the rail, the leper came toward the *stoep.*

He halted in front of Santoro as if wondering whether it would be worthwhile to speak, and instinctively Santoro drew back with repugnance.

"A fine evening, Senhor . . . *resplendescente?*" the leper said at last.

His voice was sepulchral and what he said was an entreaty. He could have been a mulatto, or pure Portuguese. It was hard for Santoro to tell, because the man's lips had already atrophied, leaving an enlarged mouth portcullised by dead interspaced teeth, and the cast of his features was blurred, had washed away as the flesh had melted away. What was left was a skull over which parchment had been tightly drawn.

Santoro thought to ignore the man, but at length he nodded. "*Si, resplendescente!*" He sought urgently in his pocket, then leaned over the rail and held out a piece of silver, beckoning with it.

"*Nao, nao,* I do not seek alms, Senhor," the leper said

hollowly.

"Take it . . . *take it*," Santoro said sharply. He made a gesture that was part insistence and part dismissal.

The man hesitated, then he shrugged weakly as if he realized that to protest further would be futile as well as ungracious. "*Obrigadò, Senhor . . . !*" He started off again, made a few steps, then halted and returned. He pushed the coin through the rails at Santoro's feet and looked up with what was meant to be a smile.

"*Nao*, I do not need it . . . I am not a beggar, Senhor . . ." Again he made to move along, then another thought occurred to him, and he pointed to the coin. "Do not fear to take it up; it is only *contagioso* at certain times."

The man shuffled away, and when he was out of view, Santoro wiped his hands with his bandana and took a quick sip of the wine.

He turned his mind to the serious business he had still to conclude with the trader, stretched himself, rose, and went along the *stoep*. Sancho Baro had just disposed of the last of his business engagements and was seated by himself at a table near the door of the *salao* from which he could see all who entered and left the bar. The trader was a short, thick-set man in his middle fifties, with a walnut complexion and excellent teeth, and he was dressed in the same suit of crumpled white duck Santoro had always seen him in.

The trader smiled a greeting and nodded to the other chair, pouring out a fresh drink. "Well, *camarada*, what do you think of the new girls, then? Passable, perhaps?"

The *ryder* raised his thumb. "Fresh as the dew, real *flamas*."

"Good, the *flama* will compensate for when the freshness passes, for the freshness always passes."

"*Verdad!*" Santoro nodded pointedly. "But for the little *bobbejaan*, Igonyela, one who does *not* have to have the *flama*, yes?"

322

"But is merely pure white," the trader said. "That is all—eh, Manoel?"

Santoro shrugged. "The whiter, the better . . . and the bigger, the better." The *ryder* put a finger to his temple and twisted it graphically.

"It will not be easy," Sancho Baro said, taking up his drink. "Very difficult, in fact."

"Aaah! What is difficult? You told me yourself before this, Indian women can be had in Mogadiscio for two English pounds, Javanese, Greek. . . ."

"You said *really* white," the other man said, "and that is what is difficult. Those ones are yellow. Is your *bobbejaan* a color-blind man, then?"

"All right! The white ones cost more." Santoro shrugged again. "We pay more, we pay what it costs. That is understood. I am authorized to settle price."

"As I said, you do not understand, brother," the trader said. He finished the boiled prawn he had been eating and wagged his fork assertively. "It is not just a matter of price!"

"Oh, no?" Santoro interrupted, with a touch of sarcasm.

The trader smiled. "Price is not the difficulty, *camarada.*" He motioned with his fork in explanation. "Time, amigo, time. It will take several months, my friend."

"That is no good, brother," Santoro said sharply. "It is also ridiculous," he added on a note of finality.

Again the older man smiled tolerantly. "It takes time because it has to be *arranged*, man! Through several, through a chain of *associars*, like myself. Such women have to be brought from Marsala or Brindisi or Messina, and it is complicated and costly."

"I have already said that we can pay it," Santoro said flatly, stubbornly.

"Yes, but even so, it may still take several months unless we are lucky," Baro persisted.

The *ryder* tapped the table with his fingertips. "Little brother, this business is very serious, like all *Dukusa* business." Santoro glanced up meaningfully. "You got *bigger* business suppliers? Bigger buyers of *all* you sell?" he said pointedly.

"All right then." The sturdy man smiled resignedly. "I take a trip north, the next boat. I see what I can do with it."

The sounds of some kind of altercation, catcalls and a woman's voice raised in distress, came from across the *salao*. Santoro turned his head. The big chestnut-red complexioned man with the black beard who had the girl by the wrist looked like a prospector down from the veld. They were over against the wall, and he was dragging the woman with him, a young *negro* whore.

Santoro slid the big knife from his hip. He brought it up and, without seeming to aim at all, he threw it with vicious force. The blade stuck quivering venomously in the wooden wall not more than a foot away from the bearded man's face. The florid-faced Afrikander froze, startled, then he rounded, and the buzz of conversation suddenly stilled. Santoro lacked the solid bulk of Morgan, Queen, Kolenbrander, and his appearance was deceptively mild. The big bearded man's expression changed from surprise to rage, and he started forward, a spectacle of fury. A man beside him caught at his sleeve and said something, but the livid Afrikander wrenched his arm away and continued.

Then, at ten feet, he saw the long revolver in Santoro's hand and checked abruptly.

"The girl is already spoken for," the *ryder* said. "By me!"

"Christ!" the Afrikander began to rant, his big hirsute hands opening and closing. "You might have stuck me . . . for that *swart* cow . . . I'll tear you to pieces. . . ."

Santoro's voice cut through the blustering tirade like the

crack of van Rieberk's horsewhip. "You want the holes in the belly, *rooinek?* You want that right now? Go back to your sow-fucking friends, *rooinek*," Santoro snarled.

"No," Sancho Baro said evenly over the hunter's shoulder. "He does not want to go back to his friends, Manoel. He has remembered urgent business at the Glee Hall, where the sows are free. He is leaving us, *imediatamente*, and his friends are leaving us *imediatamente*, too." The trader nodded to the taller of two mulattoes standing at the bar. The mulatto came forward with a club that he had slipped from the belt at his back. He prodded the bearded man with his club, jerking his head in the direction of the door.

It was oppressively hot in the saloon now and the creaking fan in the ceiling simply pushed the smoke from one pocket to another. The trader nodded, following the departure of the Afrikander and his two companions, and the two Portuguese went out after them onto the *stoep* again.

The trader filled two glasses from the fresh bottle that, with grateful glances at Santoro, the young black woman had hastened to bring them.

"I had not realized that you were so skilled, so *exacto*, with the knife, Manoel," he said musingly.

Santoro shook his head. "Merely a correction, a small misunderstanding," he said.

"No, I mean accidentally—just a few inches—it might have stuck in his neck."

Again Santoro shook his head. "No. Only if I had intended it."

"Do your friends also use the knife well?" Baro asked thoughtfully.

"All *Dukusa's ryders* are *competente* with their tools," Santoro said with frank pride.

A shadow crossed the patch of yellow illumination from the

saloon. Santoro turned his head and saw the drooping figure in an old white hat pull himself up the steps and shuffle along the *stoep* toward them. The man halted where they sat. In the shadowy light, his face seemed to have only one orifice, for his nostrils and upper lip were gone, leaving a hole like a figure eight. His ears, too, were merely jagged holes in the sides of his head, and he had only one eye, the other having been eaten down to the bone.

He took a step nearer to the table and Santoro recoiled, dragging back his chair. "Stay where you are, keep your distance," the *ryder* said harshly. "You should know that, *leproso*."

"No, it is all right," the trader said surprisingly, kindly. Baro looked up at the frightful death-mask of the man and smiled broadly. "You will find your basket behind the door of the stable tonight, Emilio."

"*Obrigado*, Sancho. . . ." The leper started away, then turned his head. "I hope I did not startle your guest," he said listlessly. "*Adeus, cavalheiros*. . . ."

Santoro looked away without replying, but as the living cadaver slowly descended the steps he saw with a grimace of abhorrence that the hand on the rail had only a thumb and four stumps. Instinctively he spat. "Cristo! Those ones should have the bells they used to make them wear. They should not be allowed to creep about like that, spreading the curse."

"Some say they do not spread it," Baro said equably.

"Aaah!" Santoro made no attempt to keep the loathing out of his voice. "They should be shot and their remains *queimado*, burnt, *camarada*."

"Not so," the merchant said, though his tone seemed to lack conviction. "It is their pain—their right to live, after all, is it not?"

"No!" Santoro shook his head emphatically. "Of what use to themselves or anyone to live like that?" He brandished his cigar assertively. "I tell you I would never let myself get like him," he tapped the gun on his hip, "and no priest would stop me."

The trader stared out at the sheen of moonlight on the water, weighing the contrasting logistics of it as he had done many times before. "That is easy to say."

"I mean it!" Santoro said with heat. "To live in that hell of pain and degradation? Unthinkable. Even the animals know better."

"That is true," the trader said slowly. He pulled his lip reflectively.

"Of course." The hunter jerked his thumb. "How long has that one to go?"

"*Que saber?* Two, three years—it has been very slow with him."

"*Three years!* The *ryder* put down his glass, shaking his head.

Sancho Baro examined his broad fingernails. His expression was unusually serious, troubled, and it was clear that he was having some difficulty in finding words that properly suited. Finally he looked up and exhaled a stream of smoke as though he were tired of pondering an unpalatable but inescapable subject.

He said, "Listen, Manoel, it may after all be possible to settle this business of the woman without any delay. Promptly. Right here."

Santoro smiled. "Well, that is the right kind of talk at last. You have been holding back on me, eh, *astuto?* Withholding the goods to increase the price?"

The trader shook his head, his manner indicating any levity was undesirable. "It will be entirely your decision . . . if the woman suits, that is . . . and I warn you, it may be beyond you."

The *ryder* raised his eyebrows. "I have already told you I have full authority—within reason." Santoro wagged a finger reprovingly. "And I cannot think you would want to go beyond reason with us, eh, *amigo?*"

The trader brushed this remark aside. "It is not a matter of money."

Santoro frowned. "What, then?"

"I will show you," Sancho Baro said. "Come—follow me!"

The trader led the way to a thatched lean-to building that jutted from the back of the warehouse. It was sparsely furnished, a table and stools and three palleted bunks on either side. But it looked almost clinically clean. There were three women in the kitchen. Two were nondescript near-naked black Africans and their gleaming ebony bodies starkly contrasted with the fairness of the third woman, even though only her head and neck were exposed above a shapeless *kanzu* that trailed to her feet.

Santoro's eyebrows rose. He clicked his tongue and a grin spread on his face. "A recent windfall . . . unusual, eh?"

The trader gave a trace of a smile, though his manner was still solemn. "We call her Brancura," he said.

The *ryder* nodded appreciatively. "And aptly. She is *cremoso*, all right, milky."

Sancho Baro gestured the girl to precede them into the dormitory room, and when he had closed the door behind them he sat down on one of the beds and spoke slowly to her, as though addressing a child or a foreigner. "Brancura, this is Senhor Santoro, a man of much importance, who may become your *Baas.*"

"*Saudacaos*, Brancura," Santoro said. "What is your age?"

She smiled but shook her head negatively and glanced toward the trader for support.

"She would not know," Baro said. "A kind of foundling. Perhaps eighteen, twenty, no more. She is not really a *bobo*, merely slow of understanding, and she rarely talks," he added, speaking as if the girl were not present.

328

Santoro laughed. "In itself a virtue—I wish more had it."

"Yes, she has others, too, which should suit you well. She is completely *contente*, docile—and she is more used to black than white. Her mother was black, a coast woman, but her father was white, a seaman. From scraps I gathered, I would think he was a Swede," the trader said. "Clearly she follows him almost entirely. An exceptional case, but not unique. I have seen several in my time."

"Certainly paler than any I have seen from such a combination, as white as a *merino* lamb," Santoro said. "But what of the rest of her? Is she *consistente*?"

"Of course! That is why she covers herself, to preserve her color," the trader said. He studied the cigar that he held between his finger and thumb. "The Arabs would pay a great price for her, but . . . judge for yourself." He waves a hand to the girl. "*Embula*, Brancura."

Dutifully, without sign of embarrassment, she slipped the billowy Mother Hubbard over her head with an air, it struck the hunter, that suggests this was not the first time she had been called upon to display herself. But now, as she stood fully revealed, Santoro's mind emptied of all else save the creamy body she displayed, the soft warm color of rich milk rather than cold marble.

"Cristo!" Santoro grinned. "She could have albino in her, except that her eyes are black."

The trader nodded. He made a back and forth gesture to the naked girl. "Walk!"

Obediently, she started to pace back and forth between the bunks, her walk a kind of waddle so that each massive thigh could circumnavigate the other, yet her queer motion seemed graceful. At each short step of her heavy well-shaped legs, all the swelling roundnesses of her body moved distinctly, and yet in a kind of rhythmical unison, breasts shuggling, thighs and haunches swaying, belly gently trembling.

As she neared him, Santoro reached out for her arm. She halted compliantly while he ran his hand down the furrow of her wide back and over her enormous buttocks. "*Maravilhoso,* Sancho!" He laughed. "A dish fit for an emperor, amigo!"

The trader smiled matter-of-factly. "She is fond of her food, and we feed her five times a day. Plenty of fat *porco* and *batatas,* with confections between." He made a sign to the girl, and she wriggled back into her shift.

"You think she would suit?"

Santoro snapped his fingers. "Consider her sold to us, *amigo.*"

"Oh, no, not so fast as that," Sancho Baro said sharply. "As I told you, she has a value other than money—but we will go and discuss it."

Santoro frowned. "*Pronto,* then." He extended a hand.

When they were seated on the *stoep* again, the trader poured fresh drinks.

"Why did you play the fox, why did you not show her to me in the first place?" Santoro asked curiously as he watched the filling of the glasses.

The trader hunched his shoulders and let them fall. "Various reasons. There is an Arab, very rich, whose agent, his dhow captain, has already inspected her, but he, the agent, has had to return to his Emir for authority to pay a higher price than he was permitted to offer."

"Aaah!" Santoro spat over the rail. "You would have let her go to those ragbags?"

"Not necessarily—in fact, probably not. After the Arab had gone, I had almost decided to keep her here . . ." The trader paused for a moment, then peered over the rim of his glass. "You really want her, then—Brancura?"

"Heaven sent!" the *ryder* said.

"It will be a matter of how *gravemente,* then."

"Get to the meat of it," Santoro said, a touch irritably.

"All right, I get to it . . . and then you will see why it is not an easy thing for me," the trader said soberly. He studied the end of his cigar, and then he pointed with it. "You have killed men in your time, eh, Manoel?" He made a quick gesture to dismiss any implication of rebuke. "In your situation . . . the *primitivos* . . . I would expect it."

Santoro stared back with surprise.

"Several," he said at length. "Primitives, and white men—cases of no choice."

"And they are not things . . . when it happens . . . that affect you. Linger in your mind?"

"Of course not—do I have the look of a *penitente*? What is this all about?"

"Brancura, it is about Brancura," the trader said slowly. "You see, the price of the girl is a service, a very personal service. To kill a man for me."

Santoro felt a sudden prickling of his neck hairs, though his expression told nothing. "Jesu Cristo, Sancho, you think I am a common *assassino*? That I murder for money?"

"No, no, no—it is not like that at all." The trader shook his head vehemently. "Not murder . . . the opposite."

Santoro had a sudden presentiment which repelled him. "*Who is the man?*" he said stonily.

"Emilio."

"The *leproso*?"

The trader nodded.

The hunter recoiled with revulsion and amazement. "*That* wretched *ofensivo*, that creeping agony?"

The older man's expression changed slowly to a look of tragedy. "The *ofensivo* is my half-brother," the trader said simply. "We are of the same father. Once we were really like brothers. Partners. *Here*," he concluded, his eyes saddened.

"*Deus!* I never knew that!"

"No, it was before your time, before we met."

331

Santoro took a long smoldering draw of his cigar. There was no need to inquire the reason for the proposition. His own words had epitomized it . . . the *creeping agony.* "Why *me?* Why do you ask this of *me?* There must be others," he said finally.

"No." The trader shook his head. "Blunderers, *crassarios,* who would make a shambles of it. *Indigno de confianca,* untrustworthy, also. With you it would be swift and sure and silent, perhaps, too, *com solidariedade . . . a countryman. . . ."*

Santoro drank off some whiskey. "You mean with the knife, of course?"

"Yes," the Trader said, his eyes turned to the street. "And there need be no corpse for anyone to find."

"So?"

"The sea! A cleaner burial place than any leper's tomb, and when the tide comes in, the sharks come with it."

"You are quite certain you want this, Sancho? *Positivo"?* Santoro said searchingly. "It will not linger intolerably in *your* mind?"

"Yes to the first. As to the second . . ." The trader made a gesture of resignation. At length, he smiled briefly. "Naturally, you will need time to consider."

He started to rise, but the *ryder* motioned him to stay. "No, wait, let us come right to the bone of this. You will not sell the girl to the Arab, but equally you will not part with her to us unless I do this thing for you?"

Sancho Baro nodded. "Do you blame me? Would you not do the same?" The sincerity in the man's face and voice was undeniable.

"All right . . . admitted."

"You will consider it, then?"

Santoro bit off the end of a fresh cigar and spat it over the rail. "I already have."

"And?"

"I will do it, amigo."

The merchant nodded.

Sancho Baro rose. "Come with me," he said.

*   *   *

Brancura sat, a great white hat on her head, a bag of ripe figs in her lap, enshrouded in her shift and an air of docility. She scarcely spoke, and when she did it was chiefly to offer a simple yes or no. She was a most incurious creature, Santoro thought, but presently her taciturnity suited him well enough, this white Negress, which was how the *ryder* thought of this woman.

It was getting toward the full heat of midday now, and they were still passing through the Settlerised country of the Coastal Belt. Once or twice in the early forenoon they had passed within sight of Plattland farms—thatched *rondavels* that presided over clustered barns and reed or turf-walled huts for housing the field-workers. Brancura had perked up then and pointed, wanting to observe the homesteads more closely, but Santoro had shaken his head and kept the oxen plodding ahead.

Thus far he had been greatly occupied with his thoughts because the incident of Emilio had given him much to ponder about.

They were rolling directly into the sun now, and the heat had mounted considerably. Even with the shade of her bonnet, Brancura's cheeks were moist with perspiration. Santoro tilted the brow of his own hat against the rays and squinted ahead. It was still well-watered country that they were passing through, with plenty of *spruits*, and when he made out the stream, he edged the team toward a stand of fig trees nearby that looked down onto it.

"We will stay here a while, *isinkwe*—cool some wine in the *spruit* and eat some eggs." The *ryder* touched her arm and jumped down from the box of the wagon and went to the head

333

of the oxen. When he turned from tethering the leaders, the woman had climbed down. She stood watching him, her face impassive. Santoro wiped the sweat from his face and neck, then gestured with his bandana. "*Embula!* Take off your *kanzu* and go cool yourself in the *spruit*, take two bottles of wine with you also, and cool them for me."

She stood still, not unwilling, but crinkling her brows a little until she fully understood. Then she pulled the shift over her head and let it fall to the grass. The sunlight filtering through the umbrella of the trees dappled her strange flesh with shadings and rosettes that somehow emphasized her creamy fairness.

Santoro took the cigarette from his mouth and watched her for a moment, feeling the mounting desire in his groin.

"There, there, pigeon, go take your bath! He gave her buttocks a pat of dismissal and, smiling dutifully, she made her way down the grassy slope to the stream, her stately waddle bringing a smile to the *ryder's* lip.

Near to sunset Santoro outspanned near the edge of a *spruit* where a pool made a place convenient for watering the oxen. By the time he had gathered enough wood to last through the night and finished the other sundown chores, the first stars had begun to wink. He had just started a couple of the trader's big steaks to fry, and settled for a cigarette, when he heard Brancura approaching and turned his head. She was naked. Her breasts jiggled gently, catching the firelight with their motion. Her manner was unmistakable: It was clear what she wanted, what she expected to follow. She plopped down beside him, pressing close with her breasts and belly to be petted and stroked, and he pushed her down onto her back.

Cristo!

It was not easy for a man of his appetites to be faced with such temptation and to tear himself away from it—but the *ryder* did. He had bought her for Morgan, for Morgan—to bestow as an unblemished gift, and like any merchandise, its integrity must be honored. And his master must be honored too. It was not without pride in his station as a *Morganskeep ryder* that Santoro reflected upon those principles. "It is time you made your bed in the wagon," he said. She got up and he patted her big behind fondly. "Go, *namorada*, sweetness," the *ryder* said, willing to applaud himself for the character he had proved, a strength he saw arising not so much from his own virtues as a man, as from his prestige as a senior *ryder* of *Dukusa*.

The moon had risen now. It shone on the backs of the oxen, and laid over the savannah a patina of mother-of-pearl. It was a time of night that Santoro always enjoyed, the time when the world was calm and ethereal. A wave of peace entered him and penetrated to all his extremities. He thought of the trader, the leper, of his colleagues at *Morganskeep* and of Morgan and of this strange woman that he conveyed to a destiny no less strange. But mostly he thought of the trader and the leper— brothers. There was mystery in it, what passed between these brothers and what passed between all men who forged a bond between them. It was wondrous, the *ryder* thought, this feeling that sometimes moved in people; and the feeling was here, this night and all the nights that followed, abiding with the thing that he had done. Emilio, abiding with *that*.

"*Embula*, Brancura!" the *ryder* whispered in his dreams, and the strange obesity mutely discarded her pillowy shift.

"*Vaya con dios*, Emilio," the *ryder* had said when that agonized creature had stood mutely before him, its appalling skull straining to convey a smile of gratitude. The leper then discarded his life as willingly, had shed it like a shift whose fabric was no longer bearable.

"*I am not a beggar*," the leper had said when he saw the knife. And the *ryder* had understood.

335

Bulalane Impisi!

Within the outer circle of a dozen or so of the more senior *ryders*, there were ten other men who made up the concentric eye of the *Indaba* behind the hill. Four of them were Africans. They were the Induna of *Dukusa* . . . Senzana, Umbaca, L'Guna and Inungu-the-porcupine, whose four warrior detachments lay sleeping on their shields. They had jogtrotted all day, as they had the previous two days, halting only for brief meals of biltong and cobs.

They had reached almost this far by near to sundown, and when the mounted scout had returned, Morgan himself had gone forward to verify that the Igonyela kraal had not yet been taken. Then he had moved them up to the hill. Now the inmost company, the cabal of *Dukusa*, were gathered around him. These men were Manoel Santoro, who had returned with the fat white woman Brancura two days before the message had come over the drums—the taciturn leathered Hans van Rieberk; the husky blond Andries Kolenbrander; Martinus van Zyl, brother of Joachim; and Robert Queen.

Morgan seated himself on the boulder they had left for him and turned the point of his cheroot toward where Queen was squatted. "The pig still dreams, eh?"

Queen passed a hand over his face. He had had little sleep for the past two days. The message of Igonyela's drums had gone out unceasingly, but you could never be dead certain that a message had gotten through without error or misinterpretation and he had ridden very hard from the kraal, taking no chances and leaving Joachim behind. He nodded shortly. "Yes, the same—the battle formation, the Buffalo Horns, everything—I saw it myself!"

The big man glanced at his men and smiled. "Well, so be it." He turned back to Queen. "How would you rate their numbers?"

"Forty- or fifty-to-one against us," Queen said. He glanced at Senzana and Umbaca. "Say a score of Indunas, twenty detachments, against ours."

Kolenbrander threw in his comment. "And what is that when we have the chatterboxes? We have only to keep beyond spear range. Even with rifles only . . . five hyena every minute! I soon cut my forty down to nothing."

Morgan turned back to Queen. "Refresh my memory, Robert. The gully on the west side of the kraal. A hundred yards or so across the bottom? Less?"

The younger man closed his eyes, furrowing his forehead. "Less, I would guess."

Morgan clapped both hands on his knees. "That is it, then."

Morgan called over his shoulder to the nearest *ryder.* "Find me a *lappie,* a mug of *spek,* fat, and some sticks."

When they had made a lampwick with the cloth, fat, and cord, he gestured them to gather around and began to draw his plan on the ground, using the sticks to show the disposition of the four Lewis guns, the warrior detachments of L'Guna and Inungu, and those of Senzana and Umbaca farther back. Twice he went carefully over it, until each man nodded his understanding. Then Morgan doused the makeshift lamp and got to his feet.

337

"Understood then?" He glanced around. "Satisfactory?"

Senzana cocked his head. "Providing these new *isibamus* can really speak with the speed of a thousand spears?"

"You will see," Morgan said.

"But at what range do we set them, Piet?" Queen raised an arresting finger. "The range is important. It wants to be near enough to waste nothing, but far enough not to be overrun."

"Yes. We will back up the slopes just enough to give us the elevation, with Senzana and Umbaca's detachments back of us."

"And the time, N'kosi?" Martinus interposed quickly. "That is important, too. We cannot wait for them to attack the kraal. If they broke through the boma before we struck them there would be much killing of our . . . friends . . ."

Morgan recognized the underlying concern in his voice and understood: In one sense Martinus had a greater personal involvement than any of them. Certainly Joachim would be among the first the Milebi Indunas would seek out for butchery.

"Don't worry about the young one," he said. "Joachim has come through much. He will come through this too."

Morgan turned to the others of the *Indaba* with a sweep of his hand. "We'll move up, then! *Maak los!*"

With himself at the head, the long silent wedge-shaped column began to string out westward, toward the crest of the ridge ahead of them that was flung up against the night sky. The first dozen *ryders* led their mounts side by side in pairs, four of the horses carrying the machine guns. They preceded the detachments of Senzana and Umbaca, and were followed in turn by the complements of L'Guna and Inungu moving ahead of the remaining *ryders*.

At the end of the levee they would make a wide semi-circular detour to the head of the gully, and reach their positions there in about an hour or so. Morgan led them, and that was good, and you followed where he led. The oiled skins of the warriors glistened in the starlight, and only the soft wash of a foot or a hoof against a tussock betrayed their ghostly march.

*   *   *

Queen lay back against the slope, behind the boulder outcrop that he and Santoro had selected. Sometimes the night breeze from the plain brought the faint odor of meat turning over fire.

Morgan and Martinus had made an emplacement along to the left of him, and Kolenbrander and van Rieberk were somewhere across the gorge, each with a *ryder* to feed in the cartridge belt. Over to the east the morning star had begun to blink through the first lids of dawn. Thin wisps of whitish mist hung knee-high over the veld, and drifted like a straggled carpet of smoke trials toward the higher elevation of the gully.

Presently Santoro polished the lenses of his glasses and leaned forward into position, elbows on the rock. He swept the foreground, then focused on the kraal and began to count, ending at twelve.

"Twelve what?" Queen reached out a hand for the binoculars.

"Stakes, Roberto," the olive-skinned man said, tight-lipped. "Stakes before the kraal."

When Queen had adjusted the focus to his own vision, he swept over the islands of Milebi squatted around their dwindling fires. Then he moved the picture closer to the boma. There were six figures mounted on anus stakes to one side. He moved the knurled screw a shade to sharpen the image and saw that the other six mounted objects were heads, children's heads.

339

Santoro took a bite of tobacco from his plug and spat the first bitter lick aside. "They must have caught the poor little devils in the open. Drovers and herd boys likely. *Diabolico!*"

"Perhaps it is a good thing that the pot has boiled over," he continued. "Obliging the extermination of the pigs."

"Too bloody right," Queen said shortly, savagely. He stared out across the plain. The sun was half-risen now, bisected by the horizon, and he could make out the Milebi Indunas beginning to marshal their groups of spearmen. "For Christ's sake, what is Piet waiting for?" He spoke more to himself, impatiently, than to the other men.

"Perhaps for them to take up their battle order, basket the eggs all together," Santoro correctly guessed. "Don't worry, the N'kosi will choose the right moment."

From his slightly high position on the slope, Queen could see the heads of Morgan and his gun-layer, Martinus, further down the gorge, and he wanted to shout to them to give the signal, for now he could faintly hear the ritual chanting of the Milebi goading themselves, supplementing the potent *dakha* they had smoked, preparatory to the berserk attack on the silent defenders behind the boma.

But then, at last, he saw Morgan lower his binoculars, cup his hands to his mouth, and heard the korhaan call. It floated clearly on the limpid air, and as it died away, the detachments of L'Guna and Inungu rose from the grass and waited. From the lee of a butte, six *ryders* rode out to join them. As prearranged, one of the *ryders* fired a single shot toward the kraal, an announcement.

Down on the flatness of the plain before the kraal the plumed spearmen shouted and the chanting fell away to a murmur barely audible to the men in the gorge. The twin phalanxes of L'Guna's and Inungu's detachments began to march, a silent oblong wall of spears and shields across the

340

ravine. They did not lope, as they would normally have done, because the Milebi were to be given ample time to make their dispositions, nor did any man speak.

The Milebi had seen them now, and through his glasses Morgan watched the shouting, gesticulating Indunas with a thin smile of satisfaction, one hand resting on the thick barrel of the Lewis gun lying, padded, as he preferred it in preference to the tripod, across the top of the rock. Not many men had the strength to take up a Lewis like a rifle, but Morgan could even fire it from the saddle. Still grinning, Morgan spoke to Martinus without turning. "Look at that, then, Mart—you will never see that again, man. They are making the Zulu Horns, the battlepiece of your grandfathers!" He lowered the glasses and handed them to Martinus.

Now the calm grim-faced companies of the two Indunas of *Dukusa* and the six mounted African riflemen had passed out of Morgan's view, Martinus studied the faces of the Milebi Indunas, moving the lenses from man to man within the animated concavity of the Horns. Some still stared incredulously toward the mute warriors moving down the arroyo, but most were grinning and laughing hysterically, shaking their javelins as they exhorted their spearmen.

They were out onto the flat now, a hundred yards short of the poised Horn tips. L'Guna and Inungu raised their arms and halted. On their flanks the six *ryders* brought up their guns and fired in a volley, deliberately over the Milebi's heads.

As the echo of the fusillade died away, the Milebi mass surged forward, shrieking insanely. "*Usuuthu! Usuuthu Bejane!*" The detachments of L'Guna and Inungu answered by turning away in flight, as though suddenly demoralized, the six *ryders* heading them back toward the gorge.

Screaming with mindless expectation, the main body of Milebi pounded after them, and on the flanks the twin prongs

341

of their battle-piece strove to overtake and encompass the runaways. But the retreating warriors, the fleetest of Morgan's warriors, maintained their lead, and the first discharge of Milebi spears fell short of them.

Now they were into the arroyo and behind them the Horns of their pursuers converged and compressed in the mouth of the canyon. The two bodies of L'Guna's and Ingunu's warriors sped on past the snouts of the first and second pairs of Lewis guns peering down across the pan, the horde of screaming spearmen in full cry at their rear. Then as the forefront of the hysterical Milebi mob moved into Santoro's sights, the thundering staccato roar of the *ryder's* Lewis spoke, and was joined by the stuttering chorus of the other three.

On both sides the deadly crossfire tore great swatches from the packed black frieze of bodies, crumpling its vanguard, ripping out big lateral chunks from its core with mechanical precision. Engrossed with the pursuit, utterly surprised, the Milebi surge was amputated at the torso.

Terror and confusion turned into panic as the frontal rank of spearmen, confronted with an invisible wall of death, wheeled, milling into those behind in their effort to retreat from disaster. And all the time the lethal hail continued to pour down into them, overwhelming the cries of the wounded and the dying.

Of the Milebi Indunas still on their feet, three or four strove frantically to lead forays against the spewing racketing Lewis guns. But behind each emplacement now stood two riflemen, *ryders* charged specifically to bear down on the Indunas. Unceasingly the crossfire bit more savagely into the crowded ranks, and the body began to disintegrate, the lightly wounded in wild retreat, running the murderous gauntlet of Morgan's and Kolenbrander's guns.

Higher up the gorge now, L'Guna's and Inungu's detachments had turned. As the guns of Santoro and van Rieberk tailed off, these warriors charged the Milebi. They were bigger and broader men than the Milebi, born of Zulu and Matabele warrior forebears, and this time they came neither slowly nor silently, their resonant chorus rolling and echoing along the steep sides of the valley wall, the more impressive, more chilling answer to the earlier Milebi battle cry.

"*Bayede! Bayede Dukusa!*"

And further down the arroyo, as the rearmost cadre of the Milebi remnants drew level below them, Senzana's and Umbaca's detachments rose from the rocks and tamboekie grass, avalanching down the slopes from either side, and another great shout smote the frantic spearmen.

"*Bulalane! Bulalane Impisi!*" Kill the hyenas!

The impact of their charge, and their flying spears, cut deeper chunks out of the flanks and hindquarters of the body of fugitives racing from the valley. The rest turned at the mouth of the gully and ran frantically, blindly following their leaders toward the last refuge of the river.

Now Morgan, on horseback, signaled the final sequence of his plan for total death, and the cortege of *ryders* thundered from the gorge at full gallop and began to thread their way through their own warriors. Here and there up ahead a Milebi, crazed with fear and desperation, the pounding hoofbeats in his ears, wheeled and cast a spear. None of these escaped.

Those of the Milebi still out in front had now begun to fan out into two ragged groups, most streaming after the fleetest of their leaders, and with these it had become a terrible race for the river near to the kraal. The horsemen were almost alongside the slower body now and as they drew ahead Morgan led them in a swerving wheel, driving between the two groups like a wedge.

The horsemen swung again after the foremost spearmen, the sobbing Milebi now leaping, falling, plunging into the river. But Morgan and the other *ryders* were out of their saddles, running along the bank as the L'Guna detachment came up, and the execution was complete.

Spears and bullets tore gaps from the figures in the river, and the water was streaked with blood that shone like oil in the sun.

*   *   *

Morgan stood, legs astride, staring across the river. He had laid down the Lewis now, and the black Männlicher hung in his hands.

Kolenbrander came up beside him, but Morgan pushed away from him and mounted his big white horse. He cantered toward the kraal, halting briefly to put a hand on Joachim van Zyl's shoulder, where the young *ryder* stood just outside the kraal gate.

Within the kraal the tribespeople pressed around Morgan's horse. *Dukusa! Dukusa!* they chanted, and he raised his hand in greeting, and the people fell to their knees as if before a god.

*   *   *

They started to tripple back across the savannah near midday—far sooner than Morgan had anticipated, for the destruction of the invading Milebi had been astonishingly swift.

Queen rode alongside Morgan now, and they rode in silence. At length, Queen spoke: "I would like to ride for the Ridge."

Morgan did not answer at once. He got a cheroot from his breast pocket and Queen waited while the big man bit off the end and lit it.

"Found the prospects there good—did you, Robbie?" he said finally.

Queen nodded.

"Listen, Piet," Queen said. "It is not the prospects, not entirely. It is also what is mine—to have what is mine."

"And Joachim?" Morgan asked.

"I think him too," Queen answered.

"Later," Morgan said. "We will talk later, all right, Englander?"

*   *   *

He had been riding for an hour now, and for that time the veld had been gradually growing more fresh and beautiful as the sun transformed the overlay of dewy grass into a vast, sparkling, *diamanté* carpet.

It would have been grand if Jo could have ridden with him, Queen thought, but soon they would ride together again. Soon they would ride ahead of a long wagon train, cross the big Ridge and establish their country—together.

It would take from here to the summit of the pass to figure out all the ways of it, from here to the summit of the pass to form up in his mind the vision of Malendela.

Epilogue: Bastions in the West

He came here every morning, to the railing of the watch-tower of *Morganskeep*. It was his custom to come here at this hour—and nothing kept him from it. The same could be said of his goals and ambitions. A large share of the continent knew that; an even larger share, now, knew that this man lay claim to a vast domain. Nothing short of killing would stop him, and no one had done that—thus far. And as for him, he would stop at nothing—and surely not at killing if that was called for. But of course he preferred politics.

The massive Afrikander stood there in the early morning light, his tall, broad form perfectly erect before the railing, and now, as he lighted his first cheroot of the day, his belly tight with eggs and sausage and the good black coffee brewed special for *Dukusa's* taste, Piet Haydn de Morgan swept his eyes across the vast expanse that fronted the keep. It was a ritual of sorts, raising his telescope and sweeping his vision left to right, as far as the lens could reach, the grassland stretched golden in the morning rays, the outcrops blue, the smell of warming grass he knew so well. It was all his, more so now than ever—because of politics and, yes, because of killing. The Milebi surrender had been swift and ignominious, the swollen bullfrog Bejane captured and hung, his land a vassal settlement. But the killing was over now, over and done with these five, six months. People had called it a massacre, which did not displease him. The word was good for politics. Let them remember it that way, a massacre, and be afraid. There was only one *Dukusa*, and his name was Piet de Morgan, and he was *Dukusa* as was his father before him. Such fear was good for politics—fear and friends.

But who exactly were your friends? And did any last forever? Robert Queen. Joachim van Zyl. He could count on them. Good men, reliable men—they knew the way of it. But what of their strengths against the tests pressed on them by others? For these tests would come, he had no doubt of it. Could his friends hold what they had against all who came to take it from *them*? If your friends gave way, you stood alone. Or your sons stood alone—or their sons—and in time, the generation that succeeded you or the one that came after, in time *they* lost what you had taken for them.

The big man pushed away from the railing of the square turret and drew deeply on his cheroot. What was this foolishness that made him think this way? Why waste thought on preposterous forebodings when his domain had never been more secure. *Dukusa's* shield spread well to the west and north now, for the interests of Queen and Joachim were like farflung bastions of the interests of *Morganskeep*. Credit the killings and credit the politics and credit the widening prospects of his men, the *ryders* he had shaped and then freed to earn their fortune.

Sweet Joachim. Not so sweet anymore, although the gentleness would never leave him. But it was overlaid with bark now, the hard substance of a man whose work had put a hide on him you'd never get off without a chisel. Let his scar tissue remind him what men can do—and endure. And let his marriage to Nquina yield alliances that issue ever more of

347

their kind. For marriage was the politics of it too—and if Malendela should wed the Englander, so much the better also.

Queen. The man was a mystery still, and yet Morgan saw much in Robert Queen that he recognized in himself—a man of immense appetite and boundless desire. Queen had *Aryays-skeep* now—and if he were wed to the Empress Malendela, what would he have then? Yes, Morgan knew this man, the deep, wide place his hunger would seek to fill. It was good to have a man like that standing vigil in the west. "Political confederates," a fancy phrase. Sentinels, that's what they were, Robbie and Joachim—their own men first but also sentries, tireless guards walking your outermost life of defense.

It comforted the big Afrikander to end his morning reverie with this affirmation. It had been like this for weeks now. And each morning he would conclude his wandering thoughts this way, seizing the one sensible straw from the many that the hand of chance held out. All was very, very well—with Robbie and Joachim in the west and north, with *Arjayskeep* founded and expanding, all was very, very well.

Morgan took one last glance at what was out there, letting his wide gaze linger for an instant longer. He did not smile at what he saw. But it was there, at the pit of what was in him, that fierce pride in having what he had and in knowing that few had anything its measure, out there under the great sky and the silence.

He touched the railing once more before turning from his solitude to the duties of the day. He reached his hand out and placed it lightly on that wood, and then let it rest against the smooth hard grain—solid evidence of what had sprung from his forging. *This is mine*, he might have said if he were a man given to ceremonial speech. But he said nothing.

This huge, grave man, his russet hair flashing silver and bright in the early morning sun, said nothing as he turned away and climbed down the stairs from the tower onto the *stoep* to meet the newcomers, the young *ryder* candidates who had arrived that morning. But as he came toward them, striding across the veranda and down the five worn steps onto the ground where they waited, he looked into each man's eyes. What could they know of what it all had cost? And of the payment, in blood, that one distant day might howl to be made?

But he said nothing of this, either.